# MASTER
## OF THE GAME

DEMONS
OF ELYSIUM

# JANE KINDRED

RIPTIDE
PUBLISHING

Riptide Publishing
PO Box 1537
Burnsville, NC 28714
www.riptidepublishing.com

Master of the Game
Copyright © 2014, 2023 by Jane Kindred

Cover art: L.C. Chase, lcchase.com
Editors: Grace Stack, Carole-ann Galloway
Layout: L.C. Chase, lcchase.com

ISBN: 978-1-62649-992-8

Second edition
November, 2023

Also available in ebook:
ISBN: 978-1-62649-991-1

# MASTER
# OF THE GAME

DEMONS
OF ELYSIUM

## JANE KINDRED

**RIPTIDE**
PUBLISHING

*For Randy J., who crafted love, strength, and beauty with his arcane arts.*

# TABLE OF CONTENTS

# CHAPTER ONE

I n the low glint of autumn light stealing in at the curtain's edge, sweat painted his boy like a pale stroke of elemental radiance. *His boy.* Standing in their rented room, Belphagor savored the words in his head. Though they weren't quite true. He and Vasily were being punished—which meant *Vasily* was being punished— for the mutual mistrust they'd nearly allowed to tear them apart. Vasily had to earn back the right to officially be Belphagor's boy, and Belphagor had to earn back the right to own him. Vasily was clearly infuriated that this was taking weeks rather than days— and now into months.

And Belphagor loved nothing better than infuriating his almost-but-not-quite-yet *mal'chik*.

Vasily jerked against his bonds, his mouth full of pillow, having bitten it in frustration as Belphagor took his time with the discipline. Belphagor stroked the leather tails of the tawse against Vasily's sideburn-scruffy cheek, soft and sensuous, a hint of forgiveness. As Vasily breathed out a sigh of release, Belphagor withdrew the forked strap and whacked his ass. He could tell it smarted by how deeply the flesh dimpled upon impact and by the angry red stripe it left instantly. Vasily roared into the pillow and gave it a violent shake like a hound with its prey. Feathers burst into the air with the sudden fervor of a pent-up ejaculation.

Belphagor couldn't maintain his serious demeanor surrounded by floating white bits of down reminiscent of the fluffy seedpods of poplar trees so ubiquitous in Russian summertime. He climbed onto the cot and straddled Vasily's hips, rocking forward to make sure Vasily could feel his erection through his pants.

"I think your pillow got a little overexcited." Leaning down, Belphagor tongued the spiked caps of Vasily's piercing at the side of his neck until the frustrated demon made a reluctant moan into the wreckage. "Still mad at me?"

"*Da, ser.*"

The sensuous growl said it was precisely the kind of mad Belphagor liked: riled and tingling with elemental fire that couldn't be seen in the celestial sphere. But Belphagor could sense it like an aura—feral, sexual, firespirit energy almost pulsing against his skin. Slowly, he unlaced the black elkskin pants he wore for the express purpose of driving Vasily wild.

"But you want me to fuck you." It wasn't a question.

"*Da, ser.*"

Belphagor would have described the words as *grudging* if not for the generous handful he'd closed his fist around after sliding his palm between Vasily and the bed. He took a bottle of oil from the table beside them. "Do you want me to untie your hands?" The long hesitation made his cock bob in his lap.

"*Nyet, ser.*"

Belphagor bit his lip in anticipation as he lubed up with a dollop of almond oil. He loved bringing Vasily to this state—incensed and so aroused that he was ready to concede any point to be fucked.

Belphagor threaded his fingers through Vasily's locks. "That's a good boy."

"But not *your* good boy." This last was a helpless groan as Belphagor opened him with an insistent thrust.

His hand now freed, he slipped it underneath Vasily once more, oil-slick palm sliding over the ample erection. He rocked into Vasily slowly, eliciting an equally slow and rather melodious moan for a firespirit. Vasily had been aching to be fucked for days, and Belphagor had been enjoying prolonging that ache until he was feverish with desire.

Heat engulfed Belphagor's flesh, just enough to drive him mad with arousal as he knotted his fingers into Vasily's locks—a handful of vivid red snakes—and fucked him hard. Watching the muscular ass ripple and bounce while he pounded it made him even harder, skin slapping against skin like experienced hands against a tight-stretched drum, the tempo wild and frenzied.

Vasily whimpered while Belphagor stroked him in time with his rapid thrusts, two fingers and a thumb driving Vasily ever closer to a thunderous climax. Vasily's ass tightened, and he let out a guttural roar, his whole body jerking out the load that had been building for a week.

As the tension in his muscles rushed out, Vasily melted into the cot, taking what Belphagor gave him without resistance, all soft whimpers and sighs, until Belphagor let go at last and shot deep inside him. Collapsing on top of him with a satisfied groan, Belphagor wrapped Vasily in his arms and breathed in his steamy scent—and nearly inhaled a feather. He blew out to dislodge it from Vasily's skin. They were both covered in down, sticking to their sweat as if they'd been tarred and feathered.

"What's the matter, boy?" The low murmur accompanied a kiss on Vasily's shoulder.

Vasily turned his head, lips plastered with feathers. "What do you mean?"

Belphagor grinned. "You look a little down in the mouth."

Vasily stared at him for a confused beat and then burst out laughing, making Belphagor's cock twitch inside him. Belphagor squeezed him contentedly. He loved the sound of the gruff firespirit laugh.

"I think I've got feathers up my ass," said Vasily ruefully. "We'll be picking them out of body parts for days."

Belphagor kissed his cheek and sat up, gently pulling out, and untied Vasily's wrists. "So what do you say? Have you taken sufficient punishment for me yet? Am I forgiven for neglecting you at the wingcasting table?"

Vasily rubbed his wrists, propping himself on his crossed arms. "I suppose."

"Or was that not really what you were angry about?" Belphagor dragged his nails across the reddened stripes on Vasily's skin, eliciting a soft hiss. "Are you still pouting over having to earn your place at my feet?"

Vasily sighed. "It's not the earning; it's the waiting. It feels like you're punishing me for—" he paused and picked a feather off his tongue "—for something else."

"What else would I be punishing you for?"

"Playing with Silk, for one."

Belphagor raised an eyebrow, tugging at the piercing in it. It would never have occurred to him to punish Vasily for enjoying another demon's attentions—an angel's, yes, but never a demon's. And he could hardly blame Vasily for being a bit enamored of the aptly named Silk. The young, dark-haired demon was not only a sleek, lovely twink piece of ass, he had his own dominant tendencies that would have sweetened the pot for Vasily. Heaven knew Belphagor himself had rarely resisted a succulent bit of tail when it was dangled in front of him, though he was trying to break that habit. Vasily didn't quite see casual sex the way he did.

He opened his mouth to say as much, that it had never crossed his mind to be jealous, but then it dawned on him: Vasily *wanted* Belphagor to care, wanted to know Belphagor was jealous, because to him that was a sign of real love.

"I gave you my blessing to play with Silk." He hardened his voice a bit. "But if you want me to punish you for enjoying it so thoroughly, I'd be happy to oblige."

Vasily tensed beneath him. "How would you know how thoroughly I enjoyed it?"

"I'm merely taking Silk's word for it."

"*Silk's* word? When did Silk talk to you about my . . .?" Vasily's voice trailed off with a hint of embarrassment.

"Your enthusiasm? I believe it was one evening while we were watching your Geyser Special." Vasily had become somewhat of a celebrity of late for the jack-off performance he put on at the Stone Horse by popular demand. He didn't seem to mind the attention he received at the male-only brothel for demonstrating his unique skill and his impressive endowment, but he hated the name Silk had given the act.

Which made Belphagor want to say it all the more. "I don't recall his exact words, so I suppose I'll have to judge for myself. We'll visit the Horse this evening, and you can suck Silk's cock while I watch." He punctuated the pronouncement with a firm smack on Vasily's feather-plastered ass. Glancing around at the mess, he shook his head. "*Bozhe moi.* It looks like we fucked an angel until it burst."

Vasily tried to convince himself Belphagor wasn't serious, but they'd only been at the Stone Horse a few minutes when Belphagor took Silk aside, negotiating with him privately. Silk returned with him, looking smug.

Although Belphagor owned the brothel, Silk was the public face of the Stone Horse—the *madam*, for lack of a better word. He looked quite sharp this evening in a charcoal suit with a silvery sheen, a striking contrast to his fair skin and a perfect complement to his dark, slicked-back hair and smoke-colored eyes.

"Well, hello, sweetie." Silk almost purred as he kissed Vasily on each cheek. "I understand I'm in for a treat." He smiled at Belphagor. "Shall we take him downstairs to the dungeon, or should I whip it out right here and have him give it a go in front of everyone?"

Vasily blanched as Belphagor considered. It seemed an eternity before he answered.

"I think a private show will do fine. But let's use a regular room. We can save the dungeon for another night." His gaze washed over Vasily as if he were an inanimate object. "Tonight I want to determine how much punishment he deserves."

"Excellent." Silk took Vasily's arm, leading him to one of the larger rooms.

Once they were inside, Belphagor closed the door and took off his coat to hang it on the back, revealing a prominent bulge beneath his leather pants. He snapped his fingers at Vasily. "Yours too. Unless you want Silk to come on your fancy velvet."

Silk smirked while Vasily removed the frock coat. "If everything goes as I intend, it's all going down his throat."

"Nevertheless." Belphagor hung the coat on the peg with a shrug. "Doesn't hurt to be cautious. Sometimes he's messy."

"Stop talking about me like I'm not even here." Vasily tried not to let it show how hot this was making him.

Belphagor folded his arms and frowned. "You get to say one thing in this scenario, boy, and one thing only. Your safeword. If you have a problem with this, I suggest you say it now, because your mouth is about to be full."

Vasily swallowed, lips tight with resentment, and shook his head.

"How do you want him?" Belphagor addressed Silk, no longer paying Vasily any attention. "Do you prefer to sit or stand while you fuck his hole?"

Silk unfastened his trousers and took out his cock, stroking it thoughtfully. "Standing is always good for leverage."

Distracted by Silk's slow stroking, Vasily yelped in surprise as Belphagor shoved him to his knees.

"Crawl to him."

Vasily obeyed, his whole body tingling. He stopped in front of Silk, and Belphagor stepped up beside him.

With his fist in Vasily's hair, Belphagor leaned close. "Should you regret not having offered your safeword when you had the chance, remember our signal." Their silent safeword was three taps on Belphagor's wrist. Vasily had never had occasion to use it, and he didn't intend to now. Belphagor yanked his handful backward. "Now open."

As Vasily complied, Silk moved in close and held his cock for Vasily to take, but Belphagor shoved him onto it before Vasily could do it himself.

Silk let out a long, low groan as he slid over Vasily's tongue and went in deep. "Damn, you forget how warm he is."

Belphagor chuckled. "I *never* forget."

As Silk rocked, the soft curls at the base of his cock tickled Vasily's lips while Belphagor drew Vasily back and forth in a steady, complementary rhythm.

"So how's business at the Horse lately?" Belphagor spoke as if he and Silk were engaged in casual conversation at the bar.

Silk gasped as Vasily concentrated the heat in his saliva and slicked it around Silk's engorged flesh. He was damned well going to make sure Silk couldn't carry on in the same tone.

"Never better," Silk managed.

Vasily swirled his tongue up the shaft as Belphagor pulled him back, and Silk grabbed him by the shoulder as if he'd become unsteady on his feet. Planting his legs farther apart, Silk picked up speed, and Belphagor reciprocated with the fist in Vasily's hair.

Vasily hardly needed to do anything the way the two of them were making efficient use of him, but he did anyway, pursing his lips and letting his heat play there as well. Eyes closed as he abandoned himself to the experience, Vasily groaned in surprise at the touch of Belphagor's hand at his fly, releasing him.

"There's a good boy." Belphagor nibbled at his ear, stroking him slowly. "You're going to come for Silk and show him how much you appreciate having that sweet dick in your mouth." He yanked on Vasily's hair. "Aren't you?" The soft murmur had become a sharp command.

Vasily hummed in the affirmative, trying to nod, though Belphagor was doing his best to make it difficult for him.

"Move those knees apart." Belphagor jabbed him with the tip of his boot.

It forced Vasily into an awkward position to move them any farther apart and maintain the height of his head at an accessible level, but it pushed his pelvis forward, giving Belphagor a perfect angle. Despite the left-handed grip, Belphagor brought Vasily swiftly to the edge. But before he could come, Silk exploded inside him with a delightful moan, his hips within the expensive suit rocking and swaying against Vasily's eager mouth.

Before Silk finished, Belphagor pulled Vasily off, and jism spurted onto Vasily's cheek. "Told you he was messy." He pushed Vasily back onto his heels and stood, unlacing his pants. "Selfish boy. Now you'll wait until I've had my turn. Then we'll see whether you'll be allowed to come at all."

While Belphagor massaged himself, looking down at Vasily with dark eyes dancing with anticipation, Silk put himself back together and leaned over to whisper in Belphagor's ear.

One corner of Belphagor's mouth turned up in a way that promised trouble. "Undress him."

Silk pulled the shirt over Vasily's head and started working his pants down, sending a shiver along Vasily's spine. At a stern frown from Belphagor, Vasily stood to give Silk better access, stumbling back against the bed behind him while Silk tugged the pants over his boots.

"On your back." Belphagor jerked his head toward the mattress. "Head over the side."

Vasily balked. "Over the side?"

"Do you want this in your mouth or not?" Belphagor stroked his inflamed erection, his fist choking it beneath the head.

Hell yes, he wanted it. But that didn't mean he had to like the way Belphagor was ordering him around like meat in front of Silk.

"You have five seconds to get in position before I change my mind and let Silk take you to the dungeon while I find someone else to pleasure me."

The idea briefly tempted him, but he wasn't going to let Belphagor out of his sight with that raging hard-on. Vasily climbed onto the bed and stretched out on his back perpendicular to the wall, dropping his head over the side as he'd been ordered—but he glared fire upside down as Belphagor stepped close.

"Oh, my Heavens." Silk fanned himself. "If I hadn't just come, those eyes would make me absolutely ruin this suit."

Belphagor pushed his cock between Vasily's lips, and all Vasily could see were the dark, downy balls in his face as Belphagor began to fuck him. "Look at the mast on him." It was the same conversational tone he'd been using before. "Stick a sail on that thing and you could power a small ship. You've swallowed it before, though."

Silk hummed his ascent, taking Vasily's cock in hand. "Oh, yes."

Vasily jumped and groaned at the slippery stroke of Silk's tongue against the head. Belphagor didn't let up as Silk wrapped his lips around it and began to work himself down. Helpless beneath the two demons, Vasily braced his boots against the opposite wall, grabbed the bedspread, and held on for the ride. With Silk's smooth mouth around him, he almost came immediately, until

Belphagor reminded him with a twist of his nipples that he was supposed to wait. He held back, squirming beneath Silk, while Belphagor seemed to be taking his sweet time.

Silk sucked him noisily as Belphagor slapped into Vasily with low animal growls, and Vasily thought he might lose his mind trying not to come, until Belphagor at last let go inside him with a shout. Swallowing hard, Vasily gave up and burst into Silk's mouth, struggling to keep the heat to a tolerable level and moaning with relief.

Both demons let up on him at the same moment as if they were sharing silent communications over him while he lay shuddering at their mercy. Before he could do more than take a ragged breath, Belphagor knelt, his mouth descending. Vasily stretched his arms back and wrapped them around Belphagor's neck, limp and happy under his kiss.

When Belphagor pulled away at last to let him breathe, he and Silk helped Vasily collapse more comfortably in the center of the bed, curling up on either side of him to siphon off his firespirit warmth, the bastards. Not that he was really complaining.

Silk perched his chin on Vasily's chest. "You're such a damned liar."

"Liar? What'd I lie about?"

"Said you weren't a submissive."

Belphagor let out a sharp laugh and wrapped his arms tighter around Vasily. "He's submissive when he wants his mouth full of cock." He nipped Vasily's neck about the spiked jewelry. "But now I know how much punishment you're in for, boy. And I'm going to enjoy planning it almost as much as I enjoyed watching Silk stuff your gob."

Vasily tried not to let Belphagor see him smile, turning toward Silk to gather him closer. His eyes drifted shut. He was fading fast, exhausted and spent in every possible way. "You do that."

The room began to fall away into a blissful, postcoital nap when an uproar from the parlor made them all sit bolt upright.

# CHAPTER TWO

"Get his clothes." Belphagor dove for Vasily's pants, swearing as he struggled to get them on over the boots he'd stupidly left on him. Looking bemused, Vasily took over and pulled his pants up while Silk found his shirt.

Silk nodded sharply at Belphagor. "Your laces."

Belphagor laced up his breeches just in time, the three of them standing awkwardly in the center of the room as the heavy boot of a Power kicked open the door. A glance at Vasily revealed a glistening streak of spunk in his sideburns, but there was nothing to be done about it now.

"What's the meaning of this?" Silk charged forward with an authority and fierceness Belphagor wouldn't have expected. "This is a lawful assembly—and you're in Raqia, not the fancy parlors of Elysium."

The stout angel looked Silk over with obvious disdain. "You're the proprietor?"

Silk put his hands on his hips. "I'm the manager. What's this about?"

"The Supernal Army has received information that your establishment is engaged in the sale of minors."

"That's absolute slander." Silk's eyes blazed to rival a firespirit's. "I employ only consenting adults."

"And yet it's well known that you were lately a resident at the infamous Fletchery," the angel snarled. "Just how old are *you*?"

Belphagor stepped in with air of authoritative calm. "Silk is twenty-one years of age. And I'm *his* employer. I own the Stone Horse, so whoever is making such accusations will answer to me."

"You." The Power came into the room and stood in front of Belphagor, presumably to intimidate him with his height. "And you might be?"

"My name is Belphagor. I'm a resident of The Brimstone."

The angel's eyes narrowed. "I've heard about you. Not surprised to find you in the thick of this. You'll come with me."

"Just a damned minute." Vasily moved toward them, and the angel flinched.

"It's all right, Vasya." Belphagor put a hand on his arm, silently willing him not to show the fire in his eyes. While such elemental demonstrations weren't exactly against celestial law, most angels, if they believed in it, considered it a kind of sorcery, and it would only make things worse. "If the officer has questions, I'm happy to answer them." He let the angel escort him through the door.

In the parlor, soldiers were roughing up the rent boys, demanding proof of age from those who looked younger, and most of the patrons had scattered. Those who remained and those who couldn't convince the officers of their professed ages were hustled outside, persuaded by fists and clubs to the head and chest.

Silk was visibly seething as he watched them go, though he was smart enough not to try to interfere. "Where are you taking them? They've broken no laws."

The angel who'd finished binding Belphagor's wrists behind his back swung about toward the younger demon and cuffed him on the temple. "Unless you want to join them, you little ponce, I suggest you back off."

Behind them, Vasily stood in the doorway, fists at his sides, and Belphagor shook his head in warning, but Vasily wasn't in submissive mode anymore. He barreled toward the angel, but before he could land a blow, a trio of Powers descended on him and tackled him to the ground.

Bound and held firmly by the arresting officer, Belphagor could do nothing but watch as their blows rained down. *Stop, sweet boy. Don't resist.* He wanted to say it aloud, but experience had taught him it would only make matters worse.

As the angel yanked Belphagor toward the exit, Silk's curses rose over the din. Knowing Vasily was in Silk's hands would have to suffice until Belphagor could get back to him.

Explanations and answers weren't forthcoming. The arrested demons were herded through Raqia and across the Acheron River that separated the lively squalor of the Demon District from the stately, pristine streets of Elysium. Angelic mothers watched wide-eyed and gathered their golden-haired children to their skirts. Apparently, a handful of bound rent boys, despite being surrounded by a small army of imposing angels, presented an imminent danger.

They were led up Palace Avenue to the gray stone Conciliary west of the Winter Palace. At least there was no Kresty Prison here in Heaven as there was in St. Petersburg, Elysium's earthly counterpart. No prisons at all, in fact—only the gallows for those found guilty of violating celestial law.

Belphagor sat on the stone floor beside the others, waiting to be interrogated. One by one, they were taken into an adjoining room from which none of the demons returned. When it was Belphagor's turn, he went without protest, letting the angels shove him onto a hard wooden stool before a table. On the other side sat Captain Poiel, the officer who'd arrested him.

"So." Poiel looked him up and down. "You're the infamous Prince of Tricks."

Belphagor raised an eyebrow. "I had no idea my reputation had made it past the Acheron."

"Don't be modest. Every angel with a fondness for gambling knows of your reputation."

Belphagor shrugged. "I thought I was here to refute your charge of trafficking in underage sex."

Poiel clasped his fingers together on the tabletop. "You own an interest in the Stone Horse."

"I do."

"And you own the demon they call Silk."

"I don't own him. He's a free demon. He works for me. And that's his name."

"You deny that you purchased him from his former owner at the Immacularium?"

Belphagor's gaze hardened. The Immacularium, more commonly known by its cruder moniker, "the Fletchery," had been an *actual* underage brothel. The authorities had turned a blind eye to it until angels had been implicated in its dirty business.

"I ransomed Silk from the peddler he was sold to after I exposed that vile den and had it shut down. But I did not *purchase* him."

"What about the twelve boys who live with this 'Silk'? Right next door to your perverse house of ill repute."

The Lost Boys were another matter. They'd been the last of the Fletchery's "unsullied merchandise." Belphagor had tracked them down—sold to a gangster in the world of Man to be offloaded to clients who relished not only molesting children but violating what they believed to be angels—and had brought them back to Raqia where they belonged. That they were under his guardianship was certainly true, but by celestial law, a male demon couldn't foster demonic children. It was considered unsavory. Yet owning them outright was an unquestionable privilege of any demon who could afford to buy them.

Captain Poiel was still waiting. "Do you deny that you own these youths?"

Belphagor gritted his teeth. "Legally."

"Legally, what?"

"I am their owner, according to angelic law. But they have nothing to do with the Stone Horse or any other trade." This wasn't entirely true. But the trade he was training them in involved more pedestrian crime—such as any respectable demon might deal in. He was teaching them the fine art of picking pockets, cutting purses, and gathering useful information.

Poiel lifted his hands from the stack of papers on the table and picked up one of the vellum sheets. "These boys arrested with you. None of them are your underage slaves, then? You aren't pimping them out to the perverted lot who frequent your establishment?"

Skin prickling with anger, Belphagor shot to his feet but was swiftly pushed back down by the guard who'd brought him in. "My boys are not slaves." It was all he could do not to spit the words. "And they are not employed at the Horse or in any other aspect of the trade."

"Your 'boys.'" His lip curled with distaste. "Then you merely partake of them yourself. Not a crime, of course, so you needn't prevaricate."

"I do nothing of the kind. I am their patron. In the strict financial sense of the term. And I don't appreciate your vile accusations." Beside him, the guard cuffed him without warning, and Belphagor nearly tumbled from the stool without his arms free for balance.

Poiel's demeanor remained icily cool. "You are here because you are suspected of illicit dealings. You will suffer any and all accusations I put forth, and you will answer my questions without elaboration unless I ask for it." He stacked the papers in front of him once more. "To reiterate, you assert that you own an interest in the establishment known as the Stone Horse. You employ as its manager the demon known as Silk—for whom you paid a 'ransom.' You own twelve underage demons who reside next door to your brothel with its manager, yet you claim none of the demons you employ are under the age of consent."

Put together, it certainly sounded suspicious. But he'd merely enumerated the facts Belphagor had confirmed.

"That's correct."

"How many of these have ties to the Union of Liberation?"

"I beg your pardon?" He'd missed a sharp turn of the captain's mental carriage.

"Don't pretend not to understand me. You were acquainted with several members of that treasonous society before Duke Elyon of the House of Arcadia met his untimely end at the gallows—and his fellow Unionists along with him. I have it on good authority from an officer who recanted his membership before the society was exposed. An officer who, if I am not mistaken, stood for you as your second in a recent unlawfully conducted duel."

Belphagor remained silent.

His interrogator didn't wait for him to confirm the statement. "Among those detained with you this evening was a small faction of Unionist sympathizers. Liberationists, to be more precise, as that unlawful association is no more. These angels have confessed to using your establishment as cover for their meetings with Fallen agitators posing as whores."

"What?" Belphagor leaned forward, feet planted on the ground, making the guard behind him drop a firm grip on his shoulder.

"Interesting." Poiel observed him. "You seem surprised. Your boy Silk is rumored to be arranging these liaisons." He lifted his brows. "And that surprises you as well."

Could Silk actually . . .? "That's preposterous. Silk is no revolutionary."

"More than one brought in this evening attested to it."

Belphagor dismissed the idea with a snort of derision. "If this is about Unionists and agitators, why all the insinuations about underage pandering?"

Poiel smiled. "Merely to remind you that you are in a precarious position, and that it would behoove you to cooperate with the newly established Elysian Office of the Peace in our investigation, lest that position tip in a direction you will not like."

Blackmail. Again. Fabulous.

Vasily twitched as Silk dabbed at his cuts and scrapes with a wet towel. "I'm fine. Quit poking at me."

"Those bastards." Silk's gentle prodding had become rather more forceful, and Vasily hissed and grabbed the cloth away from him. Silk sat back on his heels. "It's outrageous that they can get away with this."

"What the hell did they want with Bel, anyway? We have to do something." He got to his feet, trying not to let on to Silk that he might have a broken rib.

Silk stood with him. "There's nothing we can do, Ruby. They're the Host. We're the Fallen. We have absolutely no rights."

"But they can't hold him without cause."

"They can do whatever they damned well please. Did you miss the part where they're Host and we're Fallen?" Silk folded his arms, a stance that had significantly less gravitas than when Belphagor assumed a similar pose. Silk was far too slender and graceful to fit Vasily's image of a dominant. His cheeks warmed as he recalled exactly how dominant Silk had been this evening, and he glanced away before Silk spoke again. "You can't go charging into Elysium to liberate him, so don't even think about leaving here right now."

Vasily turned back and glared. "Am I supposed to just let them hang Belphagor for whatever trumped-up charge they're holding him on?"

"If he isn't released by morning, I'll . . . send word to Phaleg."

"*Phaleg*?"

Silk and the angelic officer had seemed to hit it off when Belphagor introduced them a few months ago, but they'd had some kind of falling-out that Silk refused to talk about. He hadn't so much as uttered Phaleg's name since the night the angel had left the Stone Horse and never returned.

"He's loyal to Belphagor." There was something in the short, clipped way Silk said this that made Vasily suspect Phaleg's unrequited feelings for Belphagor had caused the rift. "And he has pull with the principality. He won't let Belphagor be hanged." Silk relaxed his stance as if it took conscious effort and tucked his arm through Vasily's. "Come on. You can't go back to The Brimstone like this alone. You're sleeping at The Boudoir tonight." It was Silk's name for the apartment Belphagor had purchased above the bakery next door. Silk and the the Lost Boys shared it with their friend Anzhela.

Upstairs, Anzhela fussed over him like a fond auntie—though she was four years his junior—insisting on bandaging the worst of his cuts. "We heard the commotion, and we could see the officers in the street from the front window. The boys wanted to rush downstairs and take on the angels themselves, but I made them stay put."

"Good." Silk leaned against the wall. "We don't need them to be involved in this—whatever it is."

"Since when do they arrest whores in Raqia?" As Silk had, Anzhela poked Vasily aggressively, irrepressible anger making her ministrations rougher than she'd no doubt intended.

Ducking away before she could wind more gauze around him, Vasily went to the fireplace to stoke the flames with an irritated exhalation. "They've arrested whores before. One of them, anyway. Tabris."

Anzhela was subdued. "That was different. She wasn't arrested for whoring, and no one raided the brothel. It was because they found her with—"

"Her sister's body," Vasily cut in. "You don't think I know? Believe me, I've been kicking myself for getting involved with that fool Elyon in the first place. If I hadn't put myself in a position to be framed for the attempt on the principality's life, Sefi wouldn't have been arrested, and that damned Cherub wouldn't have snapped her neck."

"You couldn't have stopped him. It wasn't your fault."

"But getting involved with angels was. That's all they care about, after all—other angels. That's the only reason they'd raid a whorehouse, like when they raided The Cat as part of Belphagor's trap for the fletchers. They didn't care about underage demon whores then, and they don't care about them now. It was the angelic patrons they were after." Vasily turned his back to the comforting flame. "That's what this has to be about. It's something to do with the patrons they arrested."

Silk made a dismissive sound. "Who cares why they're harassing us? It's harassment, pure and simple. And standing here fretting about it is getting us nowhere." He put his hand out to Vasily. "Come on. Let's get some sleep. They're not going to hang him tonight. They'd want an audience."

"Very comforting."

Rising, Anzhela gathered her first aid kit. "But true. Don't worry, Vasily. We'll figure out what's going on in the morning.

He'll be fine. Whenever the girls at The Cat got picked up for soliciting on the other side of the river, they were only held overnight."

He supposed Anzhela knew what she was talking about. She'd grown up at The Cat, groomed to be the brothel's next procuress by her grandmother, Masha—who'd died under mysterious circumstances, while Anzhela was sold off to the Fletchery. But if this was political and not merely harassment . . .

He sighed and took Silk's offered hand. It didn't bear mentioning that when Tabris had been taken, the Ophanim Guard had tortured her for days for the sheer pleasure of it and wouldn't have released her at all if it hadn't been for Belphagor manipulating Duke Elyon into letting her go. Who was supposed to do the manipulating now that Belphagor himself was the prisoner?

After closing the bedroom door, Silk slipped his arms around Vasily's neck. "Stop worrying, my ruby plum. Or do I have to get *firm* with you and make you take your mind off it?" He pressed his slender body against Vasily's to emphasize the word.

Although it elicited a similar response, Vasily shook his head and extracted himself from Silk's arms. "I can't. Not while he's in angelic custody."

Silk bit his lip with chagrin. "Sorry. I lose my mind a little around you. Especially after being reminded tonight of all the fun we had last summer." He climbed into bed fully clothed and extinguished the oil lamp on the nightstand, patting the mattress beside him. "Come on. I promise not to molest you."

Vasily took off his shirt—otherwise, he'd be sweating all night—and climbed in beside him.

Silk slipped under his arm and curled against his chest. "*Bozhe moi.* You're just cruel, putting this here when I'm not supposed to be molesting you." He sounded far from bothered by the circumstance. They'd always slept well together.

"Silk?"

"Mm?"

"What happened with you and Phaleg?"

Silk stiffened beside him—and not with arousal. "He was too uptight. *Angels*."

After sleeping on the stone floor of the Conciliary with his arms still bound behind him, Belphagor was glad to be dragged awake before dawn and unbound so he could eat the cold gruel they shoved at him. But before he'd finished, he was back in front of the captain who'd questioned him the previous night. Poiel stood as he entered, which seemed an odd way to begin an interrogation.

Belphagor sighed. "So, what is it you intend to extort from me?" He was tired of the game.

Poiel's smile was unfriendly. "You've proved to be of little use to me in the business with which I've been charged. But no matter. As I mentioned last night, I've gotten all the information I need from your fellow whores. But someone higher up seems to think you'll be useful." The hard set to his jaw said this "higher-up" was someone whose position he resented—perhaps envied for himself. He turned to the guard at the door. "Let the major know the demon is ready to talk to him."

The door opened before the guard touched the latch, admitting a young officer with the gilded locks of the aristocratic order and stern ice-blue eyes. "Leave us." He spoke without looking at the others. "I'll take it from here." As they went out, he sat behind the table and narrowed his gaze. "Sit down, Belphagor."

Belphagor sat and folded his arms. "Phaleg. I suppose you're going to tell me what the hell's going on."

"I don't believe I asked you to speak." How quickly the tables had turned. Whatever had happened between Silk and him, Phaleg clearly blamed Belphagor for having brought them together.

Belphagor waited respectfully. It had been a mistake to presume a right to familiarity, using Phaleg's name in this setting as though they were friends or even peers. Belphagor was merely a demon gambler, thief, and whoremonger, while Phaleg was the Chief of Security to the principality of the Princedom of the Firmament of Shehaqim. Never mind that he was also the principal shareholder of The Cat and the Stone Horse. The fact that Belphagor had been the first to bring him to his knees and make him grovel and plead to swallow demon cock was immaterial.

Phaleg regarded him, unblinking. "What do you know about the Union of Liberation?"

The words gave Belphagor a frisson of déjà vu. It was the question he'd once asked Phaleg in the darkness of a dusty Raqia room while his uniform lay crumpled at his ankles, hand furiously pounding his own desperate erection and Belphagor's spunk drying on his lip. It was the moment the heightened color had gone out of Phaleg's cheeks as he realized he'd been played. Deceived and humiliated, he would still do anything Belphagor bid him—even if it meant betraying princedom and principality—just to feel for the first time in his young angelic life authentic and whole.

Belphagor's mouth turned up at the corner. "I know the sound of it on your lips still instills me with inappropriate desire."

Phaleg placed both hands on the edge of the table and shoved it in Belphagor's direction, looking a bit surprised as it scraped a few inches across the stone floor. "I'm not here to play games with you."

"What *are* you here to do with me?"

"Your establishment is a known haven of Unionist sympathizers."

"*My* establishment?"

Phaleg still gripped the edge of the table. "My financial interest in the Stone Horse was contingent upon the condition that no illegal activity be conducted within its confines."

"I wasn't aware any had been."

"Then you're not paying attention. Perhaps you ought to take an interest in the affairs of the demon you've given full control over our investment."

Now they were finally getting to the point. "This is about Silk, then."

An involuntary flinch at the name gave away that there was more to this than Silk's alleged anti-supernalist activities.

"Did he hurt you, Phaleg?"

Phaleg's expression hardened. "Wasn't that the point?" He shook his head, dismissing further discussion on the topic. "The reason I had you brought in—"

"*You* had me brought in?"

"The reason I had you brought in instead of meeting with you in Raqia is that the current political atmosphere in Elysium is extremely tense. I can't afford to be seen to be in collusion with anyone at the Horse. I'm selling my interest—"

"Selling? To whom?"

"Not to angels, don't worry. To you. I know you don't want to be the public face of either of the brothels I agreed to put my name to, but it's too dangerous for me to continue. Not only for political reasons, but because of the assumption that I sympathize with the kind of business being done there."

For the first time in this conversation, Phaleg's telltale blush rose in his cheeks. He was painfully beautiful in the pristine way of his kind, all the more for the desires he couldn't suppress yet remained ashamed of. Not the sort of beauty Belphagor generally preferred, but with their history, he couldn't deny it had an effect on him to see the color rise in Phaleg's translucent cheeks. It made him think of the pink he'd brought to Phaleg's nether cheeks on more than one occasion.

"Have you been accused . . .?"

"No." Phaleg avoided his eyes. "Only a few drunkards mouthing off while in their cups and making insinuations. No formal accusations."

"I'm sorry. I never meant to put you in such a position." It was dangerous for any angel to be perceived as having a genuine interest in his own sex. Male prostitutes might be used on a lark, so long as the activity was part of a bonding experience between fellow angels putting demons in their place—and so long as the angel took the dominant role. But actual preference for the intimate company of one's own sex was considered deviant and suspect.

For an officer of the Supernal Army, it could mean immediate dishonorable discharge and the potential to be stripped of noble rank as well. And in a worst-case scenario wherein the angel's involvement might be deemed to have compromised the security of the princedom, it meant treason—and hanging. Exactly what Phaleg now risked if seditionists were truly using the Horse as a meeting place.

Phaleg's eyes darted to Belphagor's for a moment. "I'm well aware of what position you meant to put me in." His color deepened. "*Ser.*" The whisper was barely audible.

Belphagor leaned closer. "I don't own you, dear boy. I can't. You know that."

"Of course I know it." Phaleg closed his eyes briefly as he spoke, as if he wasn't quite aware he was doing it, before he fixed his gaze on Belphagor beseechingly. "But you'll help me, won't you?"

"If I can. What do you need me to do?"

"The principality means to sign the Liberation Decree." The document had long been the Fallen's Holy Grail. It promised, in theory, to give demons and angels equal status under the law and to free the Fallen from the yoke of celestial serfdom. It would also give those whose families had labored for the houses of the Host for generations the autonomy to earn facets in their own right. They could choose to stay on as freely employed individuals or earn their living elsewhere, as they pleased. Principalities had promised to sign it before. It had formed the basis of the movement behind the Union of Liberation, which Phaleg himself had once professed to support.

"And this is a bad thing?"

"Queen Sefira is with child again." It was an odd change of subject. "There are those less sympathetic to the plight of the Fallen who feel Helison should never have taken the throne. They've been content to wait for his brother, the Grand Duke Lebes, to challenge him. They believe he'll try to reason with the principality and ask him to abdicate in favor of Lebes's rule since Lebes has a son.

"But now that Sefira is once again with child, there is hope—and fear—she will finally give Helison a son of his own. The anti-liberation faction can't take the chance that if some tragedy were to befall the principality, he might yet leave behind an heir. If Helison doesn't recant his promise to sign the decree, they intend to assassinate him before the heir can be born, placing Lebes on the throne. By celestial law, the line of succession will pass over any as-yet-undelivered offspring if another Arkhangel'sk takes the throne first. Sefira hails from the House of Arcadia, and with her husband's death, she would once again be considered to belong to that house, which is facing its own succession issues."

Belphagor sat back on his stool. "The principality told you all this?"

Phaleg shook his head, running his fingers through his close-cropped curls. "The threats came to me anonymously. I learned what else I could about Lebes's backers—they call themselves 'Traditionalists'—through my old Union contacts. Helison is aware of his brother's loyalists and has spoken to the grand duke about the rumors. Lebes claims he has no plans to challenge Helison, and Helison believes him. He thinks it's all talk on the part of malcontents—just as he once believed about the Union of Liberation—and he will not give in to intimidation."

"So what does this have to do with me?"

"The principality wants your cooperation in monitoring the activities of anyone fostering dissent in your establishment."

"You mean he wants me to spy." As he spoke the words, Belphagor suffered a less pleasant instance of déjà vu. *To spy.* It wasn't the first time someone had asked this of him.

Phaleg nodded with a shrug—a tell belying his actual concern. "More specifically, to spy on Silk."

"I see."

As on that long ago occasion, an angel wanted him to spy on someone close to him. Though in that other time, it had been one of the Malakim—a sect of self-righteous pricks from the order of archangels who made it their mission to convince Men of the virtues of Heaven. And the object of his espial had been someone far more important to him.

Belphagor observed Phaleg. His stern demeanor at this meeting masked inner turmoil. It was Phaleg, in fact, who seemed to be in the position Belphagor had occupied those many years ago. Between a rock and a hard place because of the whims of nobility. "And is that what you want?"

"It's my duty to protect the principality and the supernal family. But he won't heed my warnings or advice in this matter. What I'm asking you to do—what I'm presuming upon our prior bond to ask you to do—is to use the information you glean to find a way to persuade the principality not to sign the Liberation Decree."

The greater significance of this request eluded him for the moment. Perhaps he wanted it to elude him. But what stood out starkly was the word *prior*. "Do we no longer have a bond, Phaleg?"

Phaleg had been avoiding Belphagor's eyes, but he met them now, and his blue ones—the color of the supernal celestine stone in the signet rings the nobles wore etched with the symbols of their houses—were full of heartache. "You said we were not to see one another again after. And I accepted that. I understood your reasons. It was wise counsel. But then you summoned me and brought me back into your world, and I came. For you. You must have known I could never refuse you."

"Phaleg—"

"I don't regret it. It may not have been wise, my agreeing to be the front man in your enterprises, but I accepted with full knowledge of the risk. The Celestial Silk Road had to be closed. The drovers needed to be stopped and brought to justice. But it was very difficult seeing you again."

Belphagor rose and came close to the table. "I'm sorry. I'm a selfish demon. I thought perhaps I could keep you near without doing you harm so long as there was no intimacy between us. But I saw how cut off you were from what you needed and desired, and I thought perhaps Silk could give that to you. I made a mistake."

"No." Phaleg smiled sadly. "*Nyet, ser.* It wasn't a mistake. It's not your fault things didn't work out between us. But I thought it meant . . ." The charming blush had risen once more in his cheeks. "I thought you wanted him to use me."

"You went to him to please me?" He'd never wanted that. Damn, he'd screwed this up.

"No. No, not that exactly." His color deepened, and Phaleg looked down at the table with the bashfulness of a young ingénue. "Though I would. If you told me to let anyone use me, demon or angel, because it pleased you, I would. But I desired Silk. He's—he's beautiful and complicated. And a bit cruel. Like you. I couldn't help but desire him. But I thought it was your way of telling me you released me."

Belphagor reached his hand across the table, and Phaleg took it, his own trembling. "It was, sweet boy. I had to release you. You deserve to be free. To love and be loved by someone who desires to make you suffer because you desire to be made to suffer by him. Someone who will cherish that suffering and that hunger for it. Someone who needs to use you as desperately as you need to be used by him. You deserve what Vasily and I have, and I can't give it to you."

"And yet you speak of a bond."

"Of course there's a bond." He closed his fingers around Phaleg's hand until he elicited a soft, involuntary sound of pain. "My cock was the first in your mouth. My jism the first you tasted. Your first penetration was at my command as you drove yourself onto a phallus made of stone while you whimpered and pleaded for more."

"Heaven help me." They were the same words he'd uttered in his desperation while Belphagor had sundered him. There was no question that if Belphagor ordered him to, right here and now, Phaleg would strip and climb onto the table to be used and degraded in whatever fashion Belphagor took a fancy to, regardless of the fear of discovery. He was sorely tempted. But even he wasn't that much of a bastard.

"There will always be a bond," he said in a gentler tone. "But I will do my best never to abuse it."

As Belphagor released his hand, Phaleg nodded, his throat working as if he couldn't get air through it. "Then you'll help me?"

"Of course I'll help. All you had to do was ask." He tried to remember exactly what Phaleg had asked him. Imagining Phaleg's violation had given him a rather distracting erection. "You want me to stop the principality from signing the Liberation Decree," Belphagor recalled with a frown. "Against my own best interests and the interests of those I love."

"It's not what I want, but he must be stopped, or this next attempt upon his life will succeed. Heaven isn't ready for liberation, as much as it pains me to admit. It's not the right time."

"There will never be a 'right time' for angels to see the Fallen as individuals worthy of self-determination." Belphagor couldn't keep the bitterness out of his voice.

The color in Phaleg's cheeks now was less charming. "Perhaps not. But there will be a *better* time. If Helison is killed, it will set back the cause for decades. With Lebes and his faction in power, any hope of liberation will be lost for a generation. And the only way Helison will see that the timing isn't right is if he understands the extent of demonic sedition in play—whether from those seeking to force his hand or from the faction backing the angels bent on deposing him."

"And if it implicates Silk?"

Phaleg paled. "That isn't what I want. But if he's plotting against my principality—Belphagor, I cannot ignore it."

And there was the difference between them. Belphagor hadn't given a fig whether the beautiful Russian prince he'd spied upon had been plotting against the tsar.

"If I do this, there must be some concessions. I will not take part in any activity that will result in any arrests or executions—or further battery—of anyone but those I can confirm have serious intent to harm the principality. And I must have assurances that conditions for the Fallen will improve in the absence of the decree."

Phaleg's expression was difficult to read. "The first condition is without question. On the second, I can only give him my counsel. I cannot guarantee that he will take it."

Belphagor nodded. It would have to do.

Talking to Belphagor had stirred everything up again. Phaleg had tried to put Silk out of his mind. He'd spent the past weeks putting it all out of his mind—his desires and the pleasures he'd taken in the company of demons. He was a nobleman and a soldier and ought to apply himself to higher pursuits.

Ah, but those low pursuits. He'd never imagined how right it could feel to grovel at the feet of a demon, what ecstasy could be reached in the unrelenting blows of a crop or a cane delivered with the cruelty of one who enjoyed his torment. And being penetrated—Phaleg dropped the ledger he was reading and gripped the arms of his chair at the fierce and sudden urges that seized him at the memory of Belphagor directing him to spread himself open on the head of the greased stone cock, driving himself down onto it again and again. It had been his introduction to anal pleasure, a secret desire he'd harbored since his early youth.

He'd played at penetrating himself with his fingers, though he'd never dared to use anything else, but virtually every orgasm he'd ever had during self-pleasure had been the culmination of a wild, wicked fantasy: being kidnapped by a band of Fallen brigands, taken by each in turn as they humiliated him, defiling him thoroughly by spilling their seed into his mouth. In his fantasies, they'd forced him to come, making him admit he wanted to be used and to beg for more. Every hot and frantic release had him whimpering, *Please don't stop. Please, I want more.*

He'd carried it with him every day of his life and never told a soul, fearing exposure and ridicule or worse—yet not fearing it enough to stop. The day Belphagor had turned the tables on him after soliciting him, Phaleg had surrendered with indescribable relief. The shame had been greater for actually carrying out what had hitherto existed only in the darkest recesses of his mind, but Belphagor had held him and cherished him afterward. As if Phaleg were precious and divine, not in spite of the things he'd done, but because of them.

He hadn't believed anyone else could ever make him feel as whole and genuine as Belphagor had. He also half-suspected Belphagor had beguiled him with his airspirit influence. Like the brigands in his dream, making him desire what ought to go against a decent angel's nature. If trickery had been instrumental in that pleasure, though, Phaleg wasn't sure he cared. After all, he'd conjured the beguiler himself in the darkness of his room with his whispered pleas.

But then Belphagor had introduced him to Silk—given him to Silk, it felt like—and Phaleg had discovered it hadn't been an isolated beguilement. Silk's brand of sadism was more playful than Belphagor's but no less physically intense. As with Belphagor, Phaleg had wanted to please Silk, wanted to endure whatever he wished.

Silk had added verbal abuse to their "play," something Belphagor had never done. In truth, Phaleg wasn't sure how he'd have taken it from Belphagor. Though he looked little older than any of them, Belphagor was like a father figure in some ways.

But Silk was a peer. He teased with a gleam in his eye, calling Phaleg a worthless slut as he knelt naked on the floor licking his own jism from Silk's boots. He said the things Phaleg had imagined: *"You like that dick in your mouth, don't you, sniveling pup? Suck it harder. Show me how much you want to swallow my load, and prove what a pathetic little pervert you are."*

Like Belphagor, Silk controlled his right to come, which made the eventual orgasms so intense he sometimes thought he might pass out. Silk always ran his tongue through it and kissed Phaleg sloppily to make him taste it, saying, *"That's the taste of a dirty angel whore who comes when he's defiled because he knows he deserves it."*

But he was thinking in the present tense, and there was no present with Silk—nor could there be any future. Whether or not Silk was implicated in a plot to overthrow the principality, he'd made his true feelings about Phaleg perfectly clear. Phaleg disgusted him, and the intense play they'd engaged in had been nothing but a joke.

# CHAPTER THREE

$S$ ilk watched Vasily sleep, soft snores sending warm breath into the air. He wanted to wake him by sucking his cock. He wanted to lose himself in the smoky taste of Vasily's hot come and forget what he'd done to Phaleg. But just because he wanted it didn't mean he should have it.

Vasily and Belphagor were finally patching things up, and he didn't want to come between them. Though he certainly hadn't minded the opportunity to *come* between them, and he was glad Belphagor had finally brought Vasily around to be played with. He envied them more than he cared to admit, and his envy made him angry because it meant he wanted what they had. And what they had was love.

And love was bollocks.

He rolled onto his back. He had to send a message to Phaleg this morning. He'd promised Vasily. Would the angel read it? He had a feeling Phaleg would, if only for the privilege of being abused. He'd never met anyone who craved it more or took it with such—

He had to stop thinking about Phaleg naked and at his mercy. Silk had crossed a line, and what he'd done seeped into every moment of pleasure they'd shared and sullied it, like rot taking hold.

The session had begun like any other, with Phaleg tied spread-eagle on the bed while Silk rigged up Phaleg's cock and balls in a bit of fine silk rope to torment him. He was breathtaking, fear and longing in his eyes and his cock so hard it might have cut glass.

"You like being on display." Silk took the crop from its case and drew it over the bare skin. "Being helpless." He swatted Phaleg's nipples several times in succession, watching his water-color eyes brighten with unshed tears and his chest turn pink. "Having that pretty cock bound and thrust forward." The next strike was lower. "The center of attention." This time, Silk struck the trussed-up cock, and Phaleg's cry of pain ended on a wistful moan of pleasure. A bead of pre-come glistened on the tip.

"Liked that, did you?" Silk smiled with menace. "Bet I can make you come without touching you. Only my crop beating you off."

Ever since he'd learned how Belphagor had trained Phaleg not to come without permission, Silk had demanded the same. He took it as a challenge, a competition in which Phaleg's orgasm could be both a reward and another transgression to be punished.

Silk alternated his strokes, both nipples and cock an angry red and erect. "You want to come, don't you?" He pressed the leather against the incensed flesh, and Phaleg made an incoherent noise, the struggle to maintain control contorting his features. Silk increased the intensity, restricting his attention to the strangled cock. Surely, Phaleg couldn't hold out much longer. But he hadn't counted on Phaleg's almost obsessive need to obey.

One of the angry red marks split open and began to bleed.

Silk stared at the trickle of red, his own flesh going hot and cold in successive waves. An irrational urge to flee—from the room, or perhaps from the house entirely, to be elsewhere, anywhere but here—seized him, followed by an overwhelming surge of rage. He had to work hard not to beat Phaleg in earnest, and the urge horrified him.

Instead, Silk slapped the crop against the bed frame with all his force, making Phaleg flinch. "Look at yourself! Look what you've allowed me to do! Is this what you want? You want blood, you little bitch? That's what it takes to get you off?"

This wasn't the verbal abuse Silk used in play. He'd never spoken to Phaleg with deliberate cruelty. Phaleg merely stared at him, aghast.

Silk tossed the crop down and left him tied and gagged in the back room. He tried to cool his temper, tried to understand what was happening inside his head. Wheedling and whimpering echoed down long-unused corridors in his mind.

After leaving Phaleg alone for almost an hour, he returned, feeling like shit. But when Silk removed the gag from his mouth, Phaleg didn't rage. He begged for forgiveness. Silk despised him a little for that—which made him despise himself more. He tried to ignore the unkind thoughts as he worked roughly through the knots, but when Phaleg fell weeping into his arms, he couldn't control himself any longer.

Silk held still, providing no comfort. "Get up and get dressed."

Phaleg recoiled and got to his feet unsteadily, his eyes downcast as he pulled on his clothes. The defeated look only incensed Silk more. He clenched his fists at his sides, resisting the urge to scream and strike him.

His parting words were pure spite. "Don't forget to leave your crystal on the bureau. This isn't charity work."

Phaleg straightened, no longer the trembling submissive but an angelic officer in uniform. Without expression, he dropped his entire purse on the bureau and walked out.

Silk's face burned as he thought of it now. He hadn't been charging Phaleg when they were together. It had been mutual desire between them. He still didn't understand why he'd reacted so strongly. Phaleg had groveled at his feet and begged to be used. He'd submitted to every sort of torment Silk had chosen to mete out, let himself be thoroughly debased and humiliated, and all of it had made Silk want him more. Why had this one moment so enraged him?

A hazy memory tugged at him. Something he'd done. Or let be done to him. Something pathetic. The demon Kezef, who'd broken him in during his early years at the Fletchery, had reduced him at times to little more than an animal. The brothel management had allowed Kezef to do what he liked so long as he caused no permanent damage to the unfortunate boy who'd earned his attentions—and so long as he left the boy technically a virgin so they could offer that prize to the right buyer when Kezef tired of him.

But it wasn't that. He hated *Kezef* for those moments, not himself. Trying to pinpoint what bothered him made his heart beat too fast and tightened a sick knot in his stomach. So he was going to stop that. Right now.

"Ruby." It was the alias Vasily had been assigned at the Fletchery as part of Belphagor's scheme to entrap its patrons. Silk thought the name suited him. He murmured it again in Vasily's ear and nipped his earlobe.

Vasily stirred. He almost always woke with an erection, and this morning was no exception. Silk slipped his hand into Vasily's unbuttoned pants. "Would you like some help with that?"

Vasily breathed deeply, a smile curving his lips between his ruddy sideburns. His eyes weren't yet open, like a newborn kitten or pup. Silk wanted to eat him up.

Vasily's hips tilted, his cock gliding through Silk's purposefully loose grip, and he moaned appreciatively before his eyes flew open and his sleepy, content expression changed to one of worry. "Belphagor."

Silk's hand slipped away. *Belphagor.* Of course.

The last Belphagor had seen of Vasily had been beneath the boots of the gendarmes. After being released from the Conciliary and not finding him at home, Belphagor began to worry. He didn't bother to check the game room or the bar; Vasily rarely patronized the rest of The Brimstone on his own. At any rate, their bed hadn't been slept in.

He hurried through the early-morning bustle of Raqia merchants and shopkeepers setting up for the day, wishing the flat he'd purchased for the others wasn't so far from The Brimstone. But he'd wanted to keep the boys away from the less savory aspects of Raqia life—the Stone Horse notwithstanding.

The atmosphere there was more like a private gentleman's club, and he'd deliberately set it up that way. It didn't attract the sort of drunken, rowdy revelers and ne'er-do-wells common in the busy streets closer to the bank of the Acheron.

His wingcasting face was firmly in place by the time he arrived at the flat. He'd hoped to have a longer interlude to ponder Phaleg's request before facing Silk, but it couldn't be helped. Whether the principality ought to be persuaded not to sign the Liberation Decree was immaterial; if Silk was bringing unwanted attention to his club, Belphagor needed to know. He'd made a career of avoiding attention, his skill at influence perfected after his first fall to the world of Man. Personal loyalties aside, his first duty was to protect what was his—and in particular, his boy. Even if Vasily wasn't technically his at the moment.

Vasily's popularity was no small component of the Stone Horse's allure. For Vasily's safety, if for no other reason, Belphagor had to be certain the Horse remained untainted by angelic politics. As with the imperial intrigue Belphagor had become embroiled in when he'd fallen years ago, its supernal counterpart was dangerous to demons. Regardless of what had become of his long-dead Russian prince.

The delicious scents of warm sugar and yeast from the bakery on the ground floor followed him up the stairs. If Vasily was safe and sound, he'd head back down and get some breakfast for the boys.

When he knocked, Anzhela greeted him.

"Is that him?" The gravelly rumble carried from the kitchen, cheering Belphagor immensely. Vasily popped his head out, looking only a bit worse for wear. Judging from the bandages tied around his arm and on his forehead, Anzhela had been tending to him.

Before Belphagor could enter, she insisted he remove his shoes as if they were in a Russian household in the world of Man, presenting him with a pair of hand-knitted *tapochki*. He couldn't help but be touched by the gesture. Sold out of Heaven along with the Lost Boys, Anzhela had made it her purpose to ensure their safety since. That she was the only girl from the Fletchery he'd been able to find after the proprietors had unloaded their "merchandise" weighed on him.

At nearly sixteen, Anzhela had been considered less valuable. Which showed what cretins and fools the traffickers had been. In any context, Anzhela was priceless. She'd been the one to help him understand at least a semblance of what it meant to be a woman when he'd been glamoured as "Beatrix" during a past scheme.

Once Belphagor had the slippers on, Vasily practically bowled him over. As Belphagor kissed him, he had to cover his compromised dignity by pulling Vasily's hair hard enough to elicit the firespirit equivalent of an undignified squeak.

Belphagor let him go with a smirk. "Missed me, I see. But not too much. You slept with Silk, I take it."

Vasily blanched. "I didn't *sleep* with him, I—"

"Relax, dear boy. It's all right if you did."

"But I didn't—"

"Though I'd have to punish you, of course. If you had."

Vasily closed his mouth, delightfully confounded.

Silk paused on the stairs from the attic with a look of relief. "Belphagor! Thank Heaven. I was about to call in a favor from .. . But they let you go?"

"Just kept us overnight to 'teach us a lesson.' Trumped-up charges. Somebody must be jealous of our success."

Silk searched his eyes but seemed to take this at face value. "Well, I'm sure the boys would love it if you'd come upstairs and let them know you're okay. They're doing their lessons, and Anzhela insists they treat it like a real angel school and stay in their seats until they've finished their assignments."

"I've finished *mine*," Ruslan called down with a tone of frustration. The youngest of them, he was also the brightest student and easily bored.

Belphagor laughed. "I have a quick errand to run first." It was definitely pastry time. "Vasya, you'll have to help me. It may require extra hands."

As they headed downstairs, Vasily cleared his throat behind him. "I really didn't do anything with Silk. After the three of us, I mean."

Belphagor smiled. "I know, dear boy. You're the worst liar I've ever met. Which is why I don't let you join me at the wingcasting table very often or agree to play doubles with you. You'd drive me to penury in a single evening. Plus, I'd have tasted him on your tongue. You never pass up an opportunity for a mouthful of come."

He'd reached the bottom, and Vasily nearly stumbled down the last few steps. Belphagor had to steady him. Unnerving Vasily was his favorite game.

"Are you calling me . . .?" Vasily's voice ground to a gruff, airless halt in his throat, as though outrage had rendered him mute.

"A whore?" Belphagor offered. He slid his hand between Vasily's legs and cupped him. "You're *my* whore. My sweet come-whore. I'm thinking of taking you back to the Horse tonight after I have Anzhela paint up your eyes in that seductive kohl and selling you to the highest bidder." He ran his hand up over the curve of the inevitable erection as Vasily sucked in his breath, eyes blazing. "And we'll deal with this—" Belphagor squeezed his fingers around the heat in his hand "—when we get home." He released his grip and opened the door to the bakery. "But right now, it's a tad inappropriate."

"You're unbelievable."

"I know."

After arming themselves with enough baked goods to feed the Supernal Army, they headed back, but Belphagor had brought Vasily with him for more than an extra pair of hands. He paused at the foot of the stairs. "Something else happened this morning that I wanted to talk to you about privately."

Vasily turned, juggling a paper-and-twine-wrapped packet of pastries, two pies, and a loaf of warm bread. "Something happened?"

"The arrests weren't merely for harassment." He juggled his own packets with a sigh. "There have been accusations that anti-supernal activities are being conducted at the Stone Horse under the cover of solicitation. And that Silk is facilitating them."

Vasily scowled. "That's ridiculous. Silk doesn't give a rat's ass about celestial politics."

"Which is why he would have no problem taking money from subversives."

Vasily's silence said he couldn't refute this logic.

"There were also confessions from the angelic patrons they arrested."

"*Confessions.* We all know how they get those, Belphagor. They use the Ophanim Guard to—" He broke off abruptly, the slight kindling of heat in his eyes immediately dissipating. "Beli . . . Did they . . .?"

"No, I'm fine. There were no Ophanim, and I was only questioned by an officer. No one tortured me. But this morning, they brought me before Major Phaleg. It was apparently at his behest that I was arrested."

Vasily's expression gave away the jealousy he'd never quite gotten over when it came to Phaleg. And Belphagor had certainly given him good reason in the past. His relationship with Phaleg had commenced right after he and Vasily had fallen in love. It had been conducted in the process of trying to rescue Vasily— and later to clear Vasily's name of treason—but it had happened nonetheless.

"Why? What did he want?"

Belphagor lowered his voice, though there was no way they could be heard from down here. The stairwell had given him another flash of déjà vu. He hadn't realized until now how similar the flat was to a certain Petrograd apartment. "He wants me to spy on Silk."

"He *what*? What the hell happened between them?"

"Phaleg wouldn't tell me, but I don't think it had anything to do with this. He's as loyal as they come."

"Yes, I've noticed."

"Vasya. His feelings for me are entirely one-sided."

"Horseshit."

Belphagor reddened slightly. "I'm not saying I don't care for him at all, but I have no desire to be intimate with him."

"Oh, for fuck's sake, Bel. You have a desire to be intimate with anyone with a penis who shows the slightest submissive tendencies."

He glared at Vasily for a long moment before conceding the point. "Yes, all right. He's lovely and deeply masochistic. But there's desire and then there's yearning. I have no yearning for anyone but you. You should know that by now."

Vasily shrugged his shoulders in a gesture that said he should but nevertheless didn't.

"At any rate, how I feel about him has nothing to do with this. His loyalty in this case is to his principality. There's more to it than that, of course, but I don't have time to go into it now. I just wanted you to be aware. I might need you to help."

"To help do what, exactly?"

"Gather information. I thought you might have more rapport with some of the talent."

"*I* have more rapport? You hired most of them—and *hired* most of them, if you recall. Those first few weeks after the opening when you were trying to establish your reputation as a rake."

Belphagor had been trying to establish that he'd broken up with Vasily and had moved on. It was part of the trap he'd concocted for the fletchers. But he knew it still stung. It was why he was atoning by not claiming Vasily yet as his boy.

"They believe they were hired on Silk's behalf. As far as they know, I'm only a patron, one who paid them well to do nothing. They're far more likely to open up to you as a fellow working boy than to me."

Vasily nearly dropped one of his pies. "You paid them to do nothing?"

"I've told you this before. It was all for appearances. You know that. Why are we rehashing this conversation?"

"You told me you didn't sleep with Khai while he pretended to be your—" Vasily stumbled on the word "—boy. And you told me everything you did was for appearances, but I thought you must have at least ... Nothing?"

Belphagor set his packets on the step, took Vasily's from him, and placed them beside the others before sliding his arms around Vasily's waist. "Nothing, sweet boy. Nothing with anyone but you since we returned from the world of Man. You've enslaved me. Do you not know that?"

Vasily's arms encircled his shoulders, and Belphagor laid his head against the warm, hard chest. It was an odd stance for the two of them, a reversal of what some might see as their obvious roles. But there was only so much symbolic—and literal—dragging down to his level that Belphagor could manage. Sometimes being encircled in his boy's arms was perfect.

"Don't take this the wrong way." The rumble and crackle of Vasily's breath in his chest as he spoke reminded Belphagor of the sound of firedust smoke after a deep hit on a pipe. "But the reason you're a master at the gaming table is because no one can ever tell when you're lying. I'm not accusing you of anything, but how can you expect me to know you've told me the truth when you're so adept at bending it?"

That smarted a bit. "Because, love. You're the one demon in all the spheres I will never lie to. Not unless I have a good reason." He pulled away and gathered their purchases once more. "But I see we still have trust issues to work through, which confirms it's not yet time for you to be my boy again."

Vasily snatched up his pies. "So you're going to punish me because I doubted you."

"No, love. I'm going to punish you because I've *made* you doubt me and haven't earned back your full trust. You've agreed all my punishments are to be yours. Perhaps you didn't understand that I am always hardest on myself."

Vasily tried not to think about the implications of their discussion while Belphagor disrupted lessons to share their bounty. Anzhela disapproved of indulging the boys, but Belphagor insisted that since he was old enough to be their grandfather, his role was to spoil them.

Vasily doubted Belphagor was quite that old, but he'd always evaded the question of age. He'd spent enough time in the world of Man to get a multitude of tattoos, but he couldn't have had more than a decade in which to do it. The aetherless air there caused rapid aging, and Belphagor looked only a few years older than the average celestial. There were no telltale lines on his face or white hairs on his head.

Though age was a difficult thing to gauge in celestials. Angels remained in the State of Grace from early adulthood until their lives began to wind down some two centuries later, with aging only visible in the last few decades. But in Raqia, so many demons fell and returned from the world of Man over differing spans of time that a great deal of variety existed.

As Anzhela headed downstairs, Belphagor called after her. "Take Vasya with you. I want him painted up for tonight."

Vasily gaped at him. He'd assumed the talk about selling him to the highest bidder at the Horse had merely been meant to get him hot.

Belphagor smiled, unwrapping a bun. "Well? Go on. Give the girl something to do while she's mad at me."

"The girl can still hear you," Anzhela called from the parlor, which set the boys laughing.

Belphagor made a halfhearted effort to look stern. "Tut-tut, boys. You don't want to end up with extra schoolwork. Anzhela's only looking out for your welfare."

Shaking his head, Vasily followed her. Belphagor really did seem to play everyone. Maybe it was instinct. Or habit. He wondered if Belphagor was even aware of it.

Silk beamed at him, tagging along as Anzhela led him to the dressing room. "Painted up, is it?" He perched on his hip on the fainting couch with his knees drawn up beside him. "He's bringing you out to the Horse again tonight?"

"Seems that way," Vasily grunted. He sat at the dressing table while Anzhela took out the cosmetics box.

"And why are we grumpy about this?"

"Because he says he's going to sell me to the highest bidder."

"He's going to *sell* you?" Anzhela's exclamation coincided with a squeal of delight from Silk.

"You don't understand the way they are." Silk planted his elbows on the arm of the couch and rested his chin in his hands. "Ruby likes it when Belphagor treats him like a piece of meat. Don't you, my succulent plum?"

Vasily didn't answer as Anzhela tilted his head up to start on his left eye.

"Anyway, they have some kind of magic word Ruby's supposed to say if he doesn't."

Vasily huffed. "It's not a magic word."

"Stop moving." Anzhela placed his head firmly back into the position she required. It seemed everyone wanted to top him these days.

"It's a *safe*word." He was careful this time not to turn his head.

"Sounds like magic."

"It means that if I don't feel safe, I'm supposed to say it so he knows I'm not just—"

"Being a petulant firespirit." Silk laughed and sat back out of range of any potential retribution. "So what's the word?"

"Seraphim." His cheeks warmed as he wondered whether he should have told anyone else. Was that supposed to be kept private between the two of them?

Anzhela grimaced. "Seraphim? That's a horrible word. One of them came to The Cat when I was little. A member of the supernal family visited one of the girls, and they have Seraphim guards who follow them everywhere. The Seraphim are supposed to be celibate. They don't reproduce sexually. But, apparently, they can still have sex."

She shuddered and set down her brush. "They have the most awful voices. Like someone's banging around in your brain with a hammer. The Seraph wanted to entertain himself while his ward was occupied, but Masha told him no. He roared at her in that voice, but she stood her ground. It seems one of them had set upon some poor girl a few years earlier and burned her pretty badly. They're extremely warm."

"Ruby can—"

"Don't." Vasily didn't want to think about what the Seraph had done, and he didn't want to believe he had a Seraph in his ancestry. Though of course it had to have been one of the three firespirits of the Second Choir—Seraph, Ophan, or Cherub. It was why the Fallen all had different dominant elements. They were the products of illicit unions between the various choirs.

Silk drew his knees up to his chest and wrapped his arms around them. "So if you say the word, Belphagor stops whatever he's doing?"

Vasily started to nod, but Anzhela had taken up her brush again. "That's the idea. I've really only used it once."

"What was he doing?"

"Silk!" Anzhela glared at him. "You don't ask that. It's none of our business."

"Sorry." Silk watched her thoughtfully as she painted a corner flourish. "I wonder if I should have . . ." He pressed his lips together as if he hadn't meant to speak, but what he'd left unsaid became obvious when he spoke again. "Did Belphagor say whether he saw Phaleg?"

Vasily tried to pretend to be keeping still for Anzhela, but Silk met his eyes in the mirror. *Damn it.* Belphagor was right. He was a terrible liar, even when he didn't open his mouth.

"What do you know?" Silk demanded.

He wasn't about to betray Belphagor's confidence, but there was no point in lying, since he'd already given himself away. He let Anzhela turn him about to paint the other eye. "I can't tell you."

"Did he tell Belphagor something about me?" Silk seemed to take Vasily's silence as confirmation. "If he thinks he can defame me after he consented to everything we did—"

"No one defamed anyone." Belphagor spoke from the door. "We had a little talk. He never said exactly what happened between you, but if you'd care to tell me yourself, I'd be happy to give you my ear in private."

"There's nothing to tell." Silk folded his arms. "He got squeamish like a little angel bitch. Probably ran home to Mama."

Vasily was glad the look on Belphagor's face wasn't directed at him.

"All finished." Anzhela broke the tension, turning Vasily toward Belphagor. "What do you think?"

Belphagor's dark eyes glinted with erotic menace. "Perfect."

The Stone Horse wouldn't be hopping for hours. Vasily reluctantly accompanied Belphagor back to The Brimstone. It was one thing to walk around Raqia like this at night, but parading about in broad daylight in eye paint wasn't his idea of fun. Luckily, all it took was a spark of flame in his pupils to convince any demon who considered ridiculing him to hold his tongue.

Belphagor clearly had plans for him. As soon as the door to their room closed, he pressed Vasily back against it and began unbuckling Vasily's belt.

"Is my punishment starting already?" He managed to deliver the words with a normal level of gruffness.

Belphagor kissed his throat as he released the buckle and worked rapidly through the buttons. "No, sweet boy." He freed Vasily's swelling cock, wrapping it in his fist, and Vasily groaned. "Unless you consider having your cock swallowed a punishment." Belphagor dropped to his knees before Vasily could react, and his own knees nearly buckled as Belphagor's mouth closed over the head. It was rare for him to be on the receiving end of this pleasure.

The Brimstone was quiet in the early afternoon, and Vasily bit his lip to keep from making noise. He savored the sound of Belphagor's mouth on him—the light *pop* as Belphagor pulled himself back and the slick *slap* as he brought Vasily's groin to his face. Just a hint of vocalization gave away the size of what he was taking in.

Vasily realized he was holding his breath. As soon as he exhaled, a loud groan escaped him, and he couldn't keep quiet any longer. He pressed his shoulders to the door, hips loose in Belphagor's grip, and made all the noise he wanted.

Belphagor got louder too and more vigorous with his motions, until Vasily couldn't take another second. With a low growl that morphed into a drawn-out "*Da!*" he spilled into him, making sure he tempered his element. Belphagor swallowed with an appreciative moan, and Vasily watched while the spunk pulsed into him.

When Vasily was spent, Belphagor drew himself slowly off, as if he didn't want to let go. He sucked the head once more for good measure before finally releasing him. Vasily thought he might faint.

"Damn, you taste good." Belphagor stood and took Vasily's head between his hands to draw him down for a kiss. He nipped lightly at Vasily's bottom lip while Vasily tried to catch his breath and ran his tongue over the swell. "Taste that. It's like a smoky scotch." Belphagor rubbed his thumbs over the piercings on either side of Vasily's neck, making him shiver. "Come to bed. I had to sleep on stone last night. I want to take a nap with you."

This sounded like an excellent idea to Vasily, who felt like he'd been sucked within an inch of his life. Not bothering with his clothes, they curled up on the cot, Belphagor spooning Vasily with his arms wrapped around him, his untended erection pressing against the small of Vasily's back.

"Don't you want to fuck me?" he asked sleepily.

Belphagor responded with a playful thrust of his hips. "I always want to fuck you. I'm pretty sure you'll let me do it later."

# CHAPTER FOUR

Belphagor had to feel for his pocket watch in the nightstand drawer to find out how long they'd slept. A pale, charmed filament of aether inside the glass illuminated the face. It was past dinnertime. He'd really wanted to fuck Vasily, but that would have to wait. Belphagor had other plans for him tonight.

He kissed Vasily's temple, making him stir. "Time to get moving, love."

"Moving?" The word was a charming growl. The coal-fire rumble in his voice was most prominent upon waking.

"You're on auction tonight, remember?"

Vasily sat up as Belphagor rose to dress. "You're really going to sell me."

"Your ass, to be precise, but yes." Belphagor slid aside the little curtain to the recess in the wall that served as their wardrobe and rummaged for a shirt. "You can, of course, invoke your right to tell me if you aren't comfortable with the idea. And I will take your level of comfort under advisement." He felt the warmth of irritation coming off Vasily from three feet away.

"My level of comfort."

Having found the item he wanted, Belphagor leaned back out of the wardrobe, unbuttoning. "I do take your comfort into consideration, you know. Most of the time, I consider how best to impinge upon it."

Vasily's eyes had a lovely spark to them. "You—" He went red in the face, whatever expletive he'd been about to utter strangled in the heat of his throat.

Belphagor shrugged his sleeves off his shoulders, revealing the tattooed cross that marked him in the world of Man as a king of thieves. Vasily's eyes were always drawn to it. Anyone's were, really. It was impressive. "I, what?"

"You just love playing games, don't you? It doesn't matter what I think, so why should I tell you?"

Belphagor licked the corner of his mouth. "I can still taste your come. Are you really going to get into a snit about the games I play after the head I gave you?"

Vasily rose, looking like he might punch him. Belphagor loved that look. "Is that why you did it? So you could throw it back in my face and manipulate me later?"

"My dear boy, if I had thrown it back in your face, you'd be positively sticky with it. It would have ruined your eye paint. You're quite prolific." He smiled at Vasily's look of outrage as he buttoned up. "If you don't want to admit to enjoying my games, you should probably put your dick away. It seems very interested in this conversation."

Vasily's cheeks flamed to rival his eyes as he tucked his erection into his pants. "Fuck." He wrestled with his belt. "Sometimes I want to knock you on your ass."

Belphagor perched his boot on the vanity chair and laced up. "I know you do." When finished, he started on the other. "And it makes me want to hogtie you and fuck you until you lose your mind."

He crossed to where Vasily stood, letting him see that regardless of the fact that he towered over Belphagor and outweighed him by a good forty pounds, Belphagor still had the upper hand. "Kneel, sweet boy. You need to calm down."

Twin fires of fury and desire warred inside the burly frame. Vasily knelt, his eyes practically dripping magma.

Belphagor cupped his cheek. "Do you have any idea how beautiful you are when you're like this? I swear, one of these days I'm going to burn up in your radiance." He stepped closer, his crotch at Vasily's level. "I'm half-tempted to make you suck me, but with the way you go at it, your eyes will water, and Anzhela did such a lovely job. The heat of your arousal is already melting the paint a bit."

Vasily's breathing deepened, but he didn't respond.

"Your comfort and my enjoyment of compromising it aside, if the idea of my selling you is too upsetting because of any past experiences—"

"No," Vasily cut in. "*Nyet, ser.*"

The reason things had gotten so messed up between them in the first place was because Belphagor had failed to see he'd pushed Vasily too far, and Vasily had failed to tell him. He'd been afraid the tone of things tonight might be too much like that other occasion.

Belphagor rubbed his thumb over Vasily's bottom lip, trying to rein in his desire to forget the whole thing so he could have him now and for the rest of the night, until they were both aching. "But you promise you'd say the word if it was."

"I promise. *Ya obeshchayu.*"

"Sweet boy. I think we may be getting the hang of this thing."

Now to pull Silk into the game without letting on that he was a pawn in it.

As they crossed the streets of Raqia, Vasily turned up the collar of his velvet frock coat to hide the fact that Belphagor had looped a light chain around his neck. Belphagor had permitted him the high collar while they were out on the street.

He'd dismissed Vasily's protests against the chain. "How else am I to pass you off to the highest bidder if I don't have you on a lead? With your size compared to mine, no one would believe I owned you outright. Unless, perhaps, I had you service me on command. Would you prefer that?"

After a moment of hesitation that was an instant too long, Vasily had sullenly growled that he would not.

"What I'd like you to do tonight," said Belphagor as they walked through the chill autumn air, "is to maintain the level of resentment that leash is currently engendering. The appearance of resentment, I mean. I would never ask you to have a particular feeling. Your feelings are your own. If you do indeed continue in this level of quiet seething against me all night, I'll be extremely gratified. But even if you're heartily enjoying yourself, I must insist you behave as if you are not. Can you manage that?"

Vasily glared at him in the dark, knowing his pupils were glowing. "Can I manage to act as if you're treating me with utter contempt because it makes your cock stiff? I think I can."

Belphagor briefly pressed his arm. "Good boy." They walked on, and after a moment, he spoke again. "Do you want me to tell you the game?"

"Sorry?"

"After the Fletchery, you said you would have gladly done as I asked if I'd told you what I was doing, that it was my arrogant secrecy that hurt you. I thought perhaps I should tell you the details of my plan tonight."

Vasily moved closer to him. "That's all right, Beli. I trust you."

"Careful." Belphagor's voice was low with affection. "You keep being wonderful and I may have to take you straight back home and fuck you senseless."

Once inside the Stone Horse, however, Belphagor's demeanor changed.

Silk, in a tailored cream suit in his namesake fabric, approached and admired Vasily's coat. "My, isn't he delicious?" He ran his hands over the lapels with a little shiver.

Belphagor shrugged. "Take the coat. He won't be needing it."

Vasily tensed as Silk slipped it off him. Belphagor liked to fuck with him over the coat because he'd earned it whoring for Duke Elyon. Despite how he'd gotten it, it was the only nice thing Vasily had ever owned, and it meant something to him.

Underneath, Belphagor had dressed him in a high-necked sweater in deep maroon and a pair of steel-gray cargo pants, both of which he'd bought for Vasily in Moscow. The sweater fit him snugly; he'd filled out more since that first trip to the world of Man. Around the high collar, the chain hugged his throat, the loose end hanging to his waist.

Belphagor hooked his thumb through the loop at the bottom and yanked. "Come."

Instinctively, Vasily balked, yelping as the metal links tightened against his throat.

"It's called a 'choke chain.'" Belphagor let out the slack with a flick of his wrist. "Designed for dogs in the world of Man. If you obey, you'll experience no discomfort. If you resist, you'll gag yourself repeatedly. Frankly, I can think of better things to gag you with." He tugged on the end to remind Vasily of the swift action. "And if you don't get your hands away from it this instant, I'll make you come to heel for the rest of the evening on your hands and knees."

Everyone was watching them now. Couples engaged in negotiation on the couches turned to ogle him. There were more angels in the crowd this evening, Vasily noted, as though the arrests had actually given the place added cachet.

Silk, with the velvet coat over his arm, adjusted an obvious erection. "You have my utmost admiration, Belphagor. I cannot *wait* to see how this is going to play out."

"Come," Belphagor repeated. Vasily dropped his hands and fell into step, almost blinded by the heat in his eyes, as Belphagor led him to the center of the room. "I'm sure you're all familiar with my firespirit."

One of the rent boys piped up from the sidelines. "I thought he was Silk's firespirit."

"I lent him to Silk for a bit after I'd tired of his attitude. But he belongs to me. And tonight he needs to be reminded of that. What am I bid for his favors?"

"His favors?" The rent boy's angelic patron looked dubious. "He looks like he's ready to burn off any appendage that comes near him."

Nervous laughter rounded the room.

"He'll do as I say." Belphagor yanked on the chain. "Won't you, boy?"

Vasily's teeth ground together as he bit back the answer he wanted to give. As usual, Belphagor was taking this too damned far. But he'd agreed. He could either say *Seraphim* or suck it up. "Yes, sir," he managed to growl.

"Oh my Heavens, Belphagor." Silk lifted the back of his hand to his forehead with a dramatic sigh. "Put me down for ten carats."

"Ten carats?" The doubtful angel scoffed.

"Fifteen," said a patron to his right. This one had the look of nobility from the Order of Principalities. But not military.

"Twenty," Silk countered.

"Twenty-two." This from a demon merchant Vasily had given a hand job before. It was quite an offer coming from one of the Fallen.

"Forty carats."

The voice behind him made the back of his neck prickle. Vasily turned his head to see a tall, devilishly handsome demon with ash-colored hair and amber eyes standing in the entrance, dressed to the nines. *Kezef.* No way in hell was Vasily going to bend over for that psychopath. What was he even doing here?

Belphagor regarded Kezef coolly. "I believe you've wandered into the wrong establishment. And believe me, you couldn't handle him."

"I handled him fine the last time I bought him."

Belphagor pulled on the chain before Vasily could make a move. He must have telegraphed that he was going to go for Kezef's throat. "You've never bought *him*, you pompous bore. You paid to humiliate a boy half your size."

"And you do it for free. It's marvelous. Forty carats."

"Do I hear twenty-three?" Belphagor turned away from Kezef as if he weren't there.

"I've bid forty." Kezef cast an amused smile toward Vasily that made his stomach sour.

"The bid is twenty-two. Do I hear twenty-three?"

The angel raised a finger. "Twenty-three."

"Twenty-five." Silk's counter came almost before the words had left the angel's mouth.

"Twenty-six." The demon merchant gave Vasily a friendly nod.

Kezef folded his arms. "He was happy to take my money when I paid him here at the Stone Horse."

Belphagor went dangerously still. Vasily hadn't told him about the night Kezef had come to the Horse while he was performing what Belphagor and Silk insisted on calling his "Geyser Special." Kezef had egged on the crowd to make Vasily strip while he jerked off, a subtle way to lessen the power Vasily wielded with his confidence in that particular skill. He'd tossed a bag of facets at Vasily's feet with the rest of the donations so Vasily couldn't refuse to deliver what he'd already been paid for.

"Thirty carats." Silk's bid broke the tension. The bidding continued, and any attempt Kezef made to increase it was ignored.

When it reached fifty, an absurd amount Vasily couldn't possibly live up to, Belphagor put up his hand. "I'll take the rest as silent bids while I relax with a drink. I didn't anticipate such enthusiasm. Silk, have one of your boys keep a tally, if you would."

Kezef still stood in the doorway as Belphagor led Vasily to a seat in the corner. He thought Belphagor wouldn't humiliate him any further with Kezef looking on, but Belphagor jerked the chain when Vasily tried to sit next to him.

"Kneel," he snapped, his pupils swallowed up into the darkness of his eyes. *Shit*. He was angry about Kezef's claim, which Vasily hadn't refuted.

He knelt, furious that Belphagor would let Kezef see him this way. Belphagor was punishing him for something he didn't even have the details about. Not that it wasn't Vasily's fault he didn't have them, but, *damn it*, Kezef was gloating, and Belphagor was rewarding him.

When Vasily darted a glance in his direction, Kezef raked him with a knowing gaze that made him feel naked. "So, Prince of Tricks. Too afraid to go toe to toe with me, are you? Can't take the gamble?"

"Try me any time at the wingcasting table," Belphagor replied. "But unless I'm mistaken, Silk's boys are all booked for the evening. And any other evening you may venture in. Silk?"

"Indeed." Silk gestured toward the door with a flourish as if to usher Kezef out. "I'm afraid you'll have to find your pleasure elsewhere."

Kezef bowed and nodded to Belphagor. "I'll take you up on that offer. Count on it."

When he'd gone, Vasily opened his mouth to explain, but Belphagor twisted one of the links around his finger and pulled him back. "Don't speak. I don't want to hear it."

While Belphagor drank his absinthe, Silk's boy made the rounds taking bids before Silk collected them at last and approached Belphagor. "The high bid is eighty carats."

Vasily's stomach dropped. He would have gaped if Belphagor hadn't been holding the chain so taut.

Silk glanced at the list. "Gaspard—the merchant. I have to tell you, Belphagor, I don't think he can afford it. I suspect he felt pressured and let things get out of hand."

Belphagor twirled a link around his finger. "And what was *your* bid?"

Silk grinned. "Seventy-nine. I figured it was coming out of your pocket."

"But you didn't want to go over eighty." Belphagor sounded amused. He stroked Vasily's throat absently. "Tell him he's been outbid, but I'm gifting him twenty minutes. And if Vasily doesn't do a good job, you have my permission to take him down to the dungeon for a caning and send him back upstairs naked on all fours. But if the merchant leaves satisfied, the boy's yours for the rest of the evening to do with as you like. Though, in that case, no marks. I plan to give him some myself when we get home, and I prefer a fresh canvas."

"Very good." Silk bowed.

Belphagor handed the chain to him. "Stand, boy."

Prickling with humiliation and arousal, Vasily stood, refusing to look at Belphagor.

"Unless you want him to crawl," Belphagor suggested.

Silk seemed to ponder it, reeling Vasily in link by link. "Ruby looks angry enough to torch the room if I push him any further. I'll keep him on his feet. He's more impressive that way."

Gaspard seemed a bit put out that he'd been outbid, but he agreed to the gift graciously and took Vasily into a private room, where he asked for nothing more than what Vasily had given him before, though he wanted to hold the chain while Vasily did it.

"If this was all you were going to ask for, you offered far too much," Vasily advised him as he stroked Gaspard vigorously.

"I got carried away," Gaspard admitted with a groan as he came.

"Easy to do with Belphagor involved."

Gaspard leaned back on the bed, catching his breath. "Does he always treat you like that?"

"Not in public."

"You shouldn't be his slave."

"I'm not his slave, I'm—" He couldn't say *his boy*, because he wasn't. Not yet.

"Demons owning demons. It's not bad enough the angels think they can treat us like chattel. We have to sell our own." Gaspard sighed and put himself back together. "If you ever want to get away from that master of yours—"

"He's *not* my master."

Gaspard shrugged and handed him a twenty-carat pouch.

"You don't have to pay."

"It's what I originally offered. And he shouldn't have the right to sell you. This is yours."

When Gaspard had gone, Silk came in, his eyes sparkling wickedly. "I thought about telling Belphagor you'd been a very bad boy for the merchant so I could redden your ass, but I can't resist showing off my prize for a bit. Perhaps I'll take you to the dungeon later." He waved his hand, snapping his fingers in an idle gesture that epitomized his style of dominance. "Well, come on. Get up and hand me your leash."

Vasily stood and approached him but folded his arms.

Silk laughed low in his throat. "Oh, is that how we're going to be? I thought I'd never get to play with *this* Ruby. I can already tell this is going to be the best seventy-nine carats of Belphagor's I've ever spent." He hooked his finger through the loop and gestured as if directing a horse, clucking his tongue. "Come on, boy."

Seething, Vasily let Silk lead him out into the parlor, every eye on him but Belphagor's. The rent boy Belphagor was shamelessly flirting with winked at Vasily. *Damn it. Khai.*

The bronze skin, contrasted with angelic golden curls and jade-green eyes, made him stand out in a crowd. Khai, short for Mikhail, was an angel's bastard. Being a single generation from the Host made him highly sought after among Fallen and Host alike—the latter because he was a novelty who looked something like them, and the former because despite their status, many of the Fallen accepted the prevailing wisdom that the Host were superior. Which was bullshit.

Regardless, Khai was stunning.

Silk dragged Vasily over to the bar and murmured something to the bartender. With a grin in Vasily's direction, the bartender cleared the counter.

"Take off your shirt." Silk dropped the leash, delivering the order with an air of annoyance. "You look like you're sweltering. What is with that high collar?"

"It's from the world of Man." Though he'd thought the garment foolish the first time he'd put it on, he felt a bit defensive. Reluctantly, he tucked the chain inside the collar and pulled the shirt over his head.

Silk slapped the polished wood countertop. "Hop up."

"Hop up?"

"Which word did you not understand?"

Silk was enjoying this too damned much. Vasily hoisted himself onto the bar.

"On your back."

He blinked at Silk to give him a glimpse of the building flame in his pupils before he obeyed. Lying flat with his arms at his sides, he jumped when the bartender poured a shot of spirits into his navel, his lower abs hollowing automatically to form a well.

"Drinks are on Ruby," Silk called out and then sucked the liquor from Vasily's skin. When Vasily moved his hand to his abdomen involuntarily, Silk grabbed both his wrists and stretched Vasily's arms above his head. "Don't make me tie you down, my lovely plum. I'll be tempted to start tying other parts."

The chill of spirits struck his navel once more.

Silk turned to the crowd. "Don't be shy. He doesn't bite without my say-so."

After a moment, the first taker approached—angel or demon, it was hard for Vasily to tell without lifting his head off the bar, which Silk prevented by pulling the chain taut in the other direction. Vasily held his breath while the patron sucked from his hollowed abs, and Silk led the room in a cheer as the bartender poured again.

"Hold the leash." Silk pulled the collar tighter beneath Vasily's jaw and put it into his hands. While another patron drank, Silk kissed him playfully. "You can say that word to me if you need to. Your magic word with Belphagor." He paused as Vasily glanced up at him. "Or is that personal? Do we need a different one for us?"

Vasily wasn't sure, but the effect of the liquid pouring onto him made it difficult to concentrate. And Silk noticed.

"Well, well." Silk projected the words with enough volume for everyone around to hear. "Ruby seems to be enjoying his role. We should give that thing some air."

Vasily gasped as Silk undid his belt and pants and dipped a hand into his shorts. This wasn't the same as his "Geyser Special." He had no control, and he felt exposed. He wanted to tell Silk to stop, but his tongue didn't seem to be working, and he hadn't told Silk about the three taps.

Silk had Vasily's cock in his fist, and he yanked down the shorts with the other. "Couldn't you just eat him up?" His tongue strafed the head, and Vasily jolted and moaned. "I think we'll leave that right there." He rolled the pants down below Vasily's balls and moved away from the bar. Patrons were now jostling to drink the shots from his belly, their heads brushing his erection as they bent over him. Vasily closed his eyes, frozen between the thrilling sensations and utter mortification.

One of the patrons took his time, licking at the little well of alcohol and making Vasily squirm, finally running his tongue up Vasily's abs in a line toward his chest until he was close to his face. "Do you want me to stop him?" *Belphagor.*

Vasily opened his eyes in surprise.

"I was going to let him have free rein with you for the evening, but I think he's getting carried away."

Vasily swallowed. "Maybe a bit."

"I'll speak to him." As Belphagor straightened, Vasily saw Khai behind him. Yet another patron drank a shot from Vasily's navel while Belphagor slung an arm around Khai and kissed him on the neck, apparently in no hurry to talk to Silk after all. Vasily knew the flirtation with Khai was part of Belphagor's act. But it seemed he was going for being a complete dick this evening. Vasily looked up at the ceiling, trying to ignore the sounds of them making out with each other. Out of the corner of his eye, he saw Belphagor's hand slip down Khai's pants.

"I see you two are enjoying yourselves." Silk had returned from wherever he'd been wandering, his tone amused.

"Indeed." Belphagor let the word hang in the air for a few beats. "Are you?"

Silk seemed to recognize the challenge in it. "Why wouldn't I be?"

"I sold you the boy's ass for the evening, but you're not using it."

"I think I'm putting him to good use."

"If I wanted everyone in the Stone Horse to have a turn, I'd have simply bent him over a chair and invited them to line up."

Vasily started as Belphagor tugged the chain out of his hands and prompted him to a sitting position. A trickle of spirits dripped into his groin.

Belphagor's expression as he stared at Silk held trouble. "Why don't you just fuck him?" The color that rose in Silk's cheeks seemed to amuse him. "Don't tell me you're shy after everything else we did to him last night. Believe me, the boy will take it happily. He'll do what I tell him and like it."

Silk was quiet, and Vasily was getting a bad feeling. He started to say something, but Belphagor tugged the leash again, forcing him to jump off the bar to avoid being choked.

He pushed Vasily toward Silk. "Let's go. I want to see you fuck him."

"Why don't *you* fuck him?" Silk shoved Vasily back, making him stumble into Belphagor, nearly toppling him. "Or sell him to someone else if that's all you want."

Belphagor dropped the leash. "Look, Silk, I didn't—"

"Better yet, go fuck *yourself*." Silk turned on his heel, and Belphagor gaped after him while Vasily buttoned his pants and fastened his belt.

After a moment of inaction, Belphagor turned to Vasily, his expression scornful. "I'm disappointed in you, boy." He grabbed the chain once more and jerked it hard. "Get your coat."

Vasily forgot Silk's odd behavior, livid that Belphagor would play at pinning the evening's failure on him. When he came back from the coatroom, Belphagor and Khai were lip-locked by the door. He pulled on the coat and went out past them. Fuck Belphagor. Vasily wasn't going to be the butt of his scheme this evening any longer.

Belphagor followed and fell into step beside him. "You're angry with me."

Vasily glared at him. "Angry? Why would I be angry? You've only been a complete ass all night. And what the hell was all that with Khai?"

"I'm a little confused, Vasya. You agreed to trust me on this. You didn't use your safeword. Yet now we're back where we were before."

"No, we aren't back anywhere. I didn't say I didn't trust you. I said you were an ass."

Belphagor looked thoughtful. "I see. Well, it's true this evening didn't go precisely as planned. And for that I'm sorry. I'll have to consider what the penalty will be." That sounded promising. "But is there something you wanted to tell me?"

"Tell you?"

"About Kezef."

Vasily blanched. He'd almost forgotten. "It's not what you think."

"Never mind what I think or don't think. Trust requires communication, and it seems you've withheld something from me. Again. So out with it."

Vasily sighed. Belphagor had a point.

They'd reached the alley behind The Brimstone, and Vasily paused. "I didn't tell you because it was just Kezef trying to make himself more important than he is. He came to the Horse the night you set up the raid at The Cat. I was entertaining a crowd, and he threw in his facets and told me to strip. I couldn't very well say no with everyone cheering, so I acted like it was no big deal. He came up to me after and said he knew he could get me to do anything, and I told him to go fuck himself. That's it."

Belphagor's eyes were menacing in the flicker of the lanterns hanging from the awning. "I don't like him messing with you. If he so much as utters another word to you, I want to hear about it, no matter how insignificant you think it is. Do you understand me?"

Vasily debated being offended only for an instant. That Belphagor wanted to treat him like property when it came to this actually made him a bit tingly. "*Da, ser.*"

Belphagor brushed his fingers over the back of Vasily's hand. "You've been an exceptionally good boy this evening."

Vasily snorted. "Don't get carried away, Beli. Wouldn't want to accidentally call me *your* boy."

Belphagor laughed. "I was going to say you might have finally earned that right." He took one of Vasily's hands and kissed his wrist. "What I can't decide—" he paused to push up the velvet sleeve and placed a kiss higher up, below the crook of Vasily's elbow "—is whether your petulance works against you or clinches the deal."

Whatever misdirection this arm-kissing was, it was working.

"I think," Belphagor mused as he walked toward the alley door, "that you have."

Vasily watched him hopefully.

Belphagor executed the play he'd been building toward. "But I haven't."

The hopeful feeling dissipated, and Vasily crossed his arms. "What is that supposed to mean?"

Belphagor worked his airspirit magic on the locked door. "It means more punishment for you, naturally. I have a rather thick skull. It's going to take some doing to hammer my own lesson home." His deep-ink eyes sparkled with delicious menace as he opened the door. "But I promise to hammer you mercilessly until I get it."

# CHAPTER FIVE

After the previous evening's adventure, Belphagor's reputation had taken another hit. But Vasily had come out of it with exactly what Belphagor had hoped to secure: the indignation—on Vasily's behalf—of both fellow workers and patrons of the Stone Horse. While Vasily gained the ears of sympathetic rent boys, Belphagor took Silk aside on the pretext of discussing business.

Silk ushered him into his private parlor and closed the sliding doors, turning about with a look of professional interest. "What can I do for you, Belphagor?" It was as polite and cool a reception as Silk had ever given him.

Agreeing to monitor Silk's activities for Phaleg notwithstanding, Belphagor had overstepped his bounds last night. "I came to apologize."

Silk's hands dropped from the door handles behind him.

"I put you on the spot, and it wasn't fair. I didn't really care for the spectacle you were making of Vasily, but I did say you could do as you pleased with him. It was up to him to use his safeword if he wasn't comfortable—although I ought to have established that between the three of us as well. So for my awkward handling of the situation and my inappropriate reaction, I apologize."

Silk slipped his hands into the pockets of his tailored suit. "Thank you." The velvety gray eyes that Belphagor could never quite read observed him. Silk could make a killing at the wingcasting table. "Can I ask you something?"

Belphagor inclined his head.

"About Phaleg. Did he tell you what I did?"

Belphagor took a seat on Silk's fainting couch and set his legs apart with his hands on his knees—a habit from the world of Man meant to display the threatening tattoos on his hands, though they had little meaning in Heaven. "Major Phaleg is an angel of the utmost discretion. He told me only that things hadn't worked out between the two of you. But it seems fairly clear that you hurt him in some way, and I warned you that you'd answer to me if any harm came to him as a result of your association."

"I drew blood." Silk wrapped his arms around himself as he blurted the words. "On his prick. He never told me to stop, just let me beat on him until I drew blood. And it made me angry."

"Injuring Phaleg made you angry at *him*?"

"He was going to lie there and take it like I was some kind of monster, like I wanted that!"

"And did you?"

Silk stepped forward in challenge but stopped, his face pale. "For a moment, I wanted to keep going. Heaven help me." The murmured plea was reminiscent of Phaleg. "Why would I want to hurt him?"

Belphagor considered the question, drawing on memories he hadn't touched in decades. They weren't ones he was proud of. "Revenge?"

"Revenge?" Silk looked ill.

"Against someone other than Phaleg. Someone he reminds you of, perhaps. When I was a young demon in the world of Man, I had some experiences I don't like to think about. I've never told Vasily, nor will I tell him, so you'll keep this between us." His tone allowed for no disagreement.

"When I had the opportunity to turn the tables, I lashed out, trying to take revenge on men who were no longer there. Where I was—the Russian gulag, they called it, the *Zona*—brutality was the only language anyone understood. It took me a long time to unlearn that. And longer—much longer—to learn that my desire to cause a demon pain in the act of mutual pleasure didn't make me like the ones who'd hurt me. It didn't make me the boy who'd suffered without consent at the hands of others taking their own misplaced revenge."

While Belphagor spoke, Silk sank onto the chair perpendicular to the couch. He hung his head, carefully oiled hair falling over his face. "I didn't want to do that to Phaleg. I didn't want him to make me that demon. That's why I sent him away."

"So he doesn't know what he's done to anger you."

Silk shook his head, appearing defeated. "I mocked him and treated him scornfully. If you wish to thrash me for it, you're well within your rights."

"Silk." Belphagor laid a hand on Silk's knee. "I have no desire to punish you for making a mistake. You're doing that quite well on your own. I think Phaleg is confused, though, and he ought to hear from you that he did nothing wrong."

"But if I say *he* did nothing wrong, then I have to say that I *did*."

"Shouldn't you?"

Silk looked up, his eyes bitter. "He'll hate me. Probably hates me already."

"I doubt that. But even if he does, he deserves to know he wasn't to blame. Give him the opportunity to forgive you. And in the future, you might try negotiating in advance and using a safeword when you find someone who takes such total pleasure in sexual torment. They are rare individuals, to be treasured."

"You seem to know a great deal about sexual torment."

Belphagor grinned from one side of his mouth. "Practice makes perfect."

While Belphagor headed back to The Brimstone, Vasily stayed at the Horse to cultivate his role as misused slave. He had to admit, the attention Belphagor's stunt had brought him wasn't unpleasant. That Silk had unwittingly aided Belphagor's efforts to spy on him made Vasily slightly uncomfortable, but Silk seemed pleased to have his company.

Though he kept his distance at first after Belphagor's departure—during which Belphagor behaved as though the Stone Horse had bored him and declared that Vasily could do as he liked—Silk was quickly put at ease by Vasily's casual air of business as usual.

He made no attempt to apologize for how things had ended the night before, but that suited Vasily. Whatever Silk and Belphagor had talked about after they'd disappeared together, Belphagor would tell him later.

Though Vasily hadn't noticed any talk of sedition before, now that he was listening for it, he recognized definite overtones in some of the interactions between the patrons and their hires. If he hadn't spent the afternoon with the working boys, he might not have noticed the coded banter. From some of the angels, it seemed nothing more than a means of ingratiating themselves. Sympathetic talk about demons' rights designed to lubricate further intercourse in much the same way as the liberal application of libations.

The more subtle indicators, however, were in the conversations between them and the demon patrons who strove to appear as their equals. A great deal of praise for the principality's brother, the Grand Duke Lebes, was bandied about. Helison was depicted as an oppressor, even though it was talk of signing the Liberation Decree that had turned angelic public opinion against him. It was enough to drive a demon to drink.

The arrival of Vasily's patron saved him from listening to any more bullshit. Gaspard wanted his usual and displayed his usual gratitude. Afterward, it was clear he was becoming at ease in Vasily's company. Vasily was happy to spend time in casual conversation for a few extra facets, and Gaspard seemed genuinely appreciative of the companionship.

Gaspard regarded him while they reclined among the cushions in the parlor. "Have you given any thought to emancipating yourself from that petty demon thug of yours?" Clearly, his orgasm and drink had combined to put him in a relaxed state.

"I don't need 'emancipating.'" Vasily downed his ale.

"We all need emancipating. Some more than others." Gaspard tilted his whiskey glass, staring at the line of gold liquid at the bottom.

"You suppose the principality will ever sign that decree? Liberate the Fallen?"

Gaspard threw back the last of his drink. "Not bloody likely. To be honest, I think it would do more harm than good if he did."

Vasily propped his head on his hand. "How so?"

"Plenty of demons depend on the system. Families have positions they count on with upstanding angelic households. They know their children will be taken care of, with a place in the house they serve, instead of having to sell them into . . ." He glanced at Vasily, cheeks reddening. "Not that there's anything wrong with your profession, of course."

Vasily shrugged. "No, but there *is* something wrong with families having to sell their children. It's a profession one should be able to choose if they please. I thought that was what the Liberation Decree was supposed to do. Give the Fallen the freedom to determine their own lot in life."

Gaspard laughed harshly. "That's not how it would unfold. I guarantee it. We'd all be free to go straight to hell as far as the majority of the Host is concerned. They'd damned well make us pay for our 'freedom.'"

"Yet you were the one saying I ought to be free. Seems a double standard if you don't think the same should be true for demonkind as a whole."

The pink in Gaspard's cheeks now held a touch of bashfulness. "I was rather hoping to lure you into my own service."

Vasily smiled amiably. "I'm already at your service. Anytime you like, whenever I'm here."

"That's the rub, isn't it? Your Prince of Tricks gets to decide when that is. Perhaps I should play a round of cards with him and challenge him to put you up as the prize." Gaspard winked, but Vasily had the distinct impression it wasn't entirely in jest.

Just after midnight, Phaleg showed up at The Brimstone, according to plan. To avoid bringing attention to his association with Belphagor, he'd come with a group of supernal officers.

Belphagor made a point of ignoring the party, but he'd taught Phaleg enough tricks of the game that he soon made his way to the master table.

"Any progress?" Phaleg asked as Belphagor dealt the cards.

Belphagor didn't bother to look up. "Nothing concrete. This sort of business takes time and cultivation."

"I'm not sure we have a great deal of time."

"Oh? Why's that?"

"The queen's cousin, Grand Duchess Tsirya, is also with child and close to her time, and they say it's making the queen anxious."

Belphagor flicked his eyebrow up as he perused his hand. "Competition?"

"You might say that. The grand duchess is her sister-in-law, Lebes's wife."

As Belphagor cast the die, Phaleg called it correctly without missing a beat. He was getting quite good. Belphagor surrendered a card. "So Queen Sefira is worried that if her cousin produces another son before she's able to . . ."

"She'll be branded as a liability to the Crown."

"*Salamander.* And you think this faction supporting Lebes will act as soon as Tsirya's child is born if it's another boy."

Phaleg's cast tumbled the die to Salamander, and he relinquished a card to the pile. "I believe they'll see it as a sign of the grand duke's superior genes, and whether or not the queen can deliver an heir will be immaterial."

Belphagor completed his latest hand with Phaleg's discard. "Full choir."

Sighing, Phaleg laid three Virtues and a pair of Cherubim on the table.

"So what would you suggest to speed things up?"

Phaleg gathered the deck and shuffled methodically. "Perhaps if we had evidence of a growing rebellion. Demonstrations, not uprisings; demons chanting slogans and marching about Palace Square. It's certainly happened before."

"You expect me to help you foster this rebellion, knowing decent demons might get beaten or hanged for it? All because the principality refuses to accept the truth of his own brother's campaign against him?"

"The Supernal Army has methods of dispersing a crowd without any arrests. I can ensure they'll use them, so long as everything remains peaceful."

Belphagor perused his new hand. "There's the difficulty, isn't it? Demonstrations are unpredictable. They can get out of control. What else have you got?"

Bouncing the die on his palm, Phaleg pondered. "Perhaps if we had someone in the grand duke's household to keep an ear to the wall there. It might reassure the queen that her fears are being taken seriously."

"Someone to occupy the little grand duke."

Phaleg paused in his cast and glanced at him. "The little grand duke?"

"He's, what, nine years old?"

"Seven."

"Must be getting in his mother's hair. I know very little about childbirth, but I understand the final few months of pregnancy are rather trying. Perhaps I might know of an angelic tutor willing to take the boy in hand." While Belphagor spoke, Phaleg had tossed the die. "*Bat.*"

Phaleg watched it land on Bat. "You're good."

Belphagor smiled. "Of course I am."

He beat Phaleg soundly—regretfully, only in the figurative sense—and collected his facets.

As Phaleg rose to make way for the next player, Belphagor gathered the cards. "I had a word with our mutual friend this evening."

Phaleg buttoned his coat, saying nothing and giving away nothing with his expression. He'd have done well to apply such self-discipline to the last round.

"I believe he regrets what happened. Should he make an overture to you, an attempt at amends, I think you should consider what he has to say. I can't recommend for or against accepting such an overture, but I vouch for his genuine contrition."

"I'll take that under advisement." Phaleg donned his cap. "Good evening to you, Belphagor. I hope to challenge you again soon."

Another player was already stepping up, and Belphagor had to be content with that. He hoped what little he'd managed to convey had been of some comfort. Unresolved suspicions aside, there was a connection between the two Belphagor couldn't help trying to foster. In a way, it felt like atonement for his own past, atonement to the young demon he'd been.

Of course, if Silk turned out to be in collusion with the seditionists, his matchmaking would be moot.

Phaleg dismissed the carriage as soon as they'd crossed into Elysium, preferring to walk the rest of the way. He needed to mull over Belphagor's unexpected words. Perhaps if Silk was truly sorry . . .

*No.* Phaleg shook his head. As Silk was fond of boasting, he took pride in never regretting anything. He was a hedonist in the truest sense of the word, and Phaleg couldn't imagine him admitting wrongdoing, let alone feeling contrite. But regardless of whether Silk claimed to regret what had happened, Phaleg wasn't sure it mattered.

He'd gone too far, making Phaleg feel like a dirty angel whore when they weren't playing, mocking him for his vulnerability. Belphagor had called Phaleg's obedience a gift. Silk had treated it like a joke.

Phaleg turned up his collar against the chilly wind from the Gulf of the Firmament as he rounded the corner to his street. He might not be able to forgive Silk, but it didn't stop him from longing. It didn't stop him from lying in bed at night and remembering Silk's lithe body slinking around him, teasing with its softness before a hard blow fell without warning. It didn't stop him from wanting Silk's cock up his ass, pounding him, filling him, making him ache, making him come.

It was the one thing Silk had never done, and Phaleg had worried it was a level of intimacy Silk simply didn't want to share with him. Perhaps it was where he drew the line between patron and lover.

Silk's parting words had confirmed Phaleg's suspicion. He'd been no more than a patron to Silk the entire time, a fool for his amusement. There could be no reconciliation because, in that moment, Silk had revealed his true feelings for him, and they were nothing less than utter contempt.

# CHAPTER SIX

Vasily was relieved to be back home at The Brimstone. He undressed in the dark and slipped under the covers, happy to find Belphagor awake and waiting for him.

Sinewy arms snaked around his waist, and Belphagor kissed his bare shoulder. "How did things go at the Horse?"

"Everyone thinks you're a bastard, and Gaspard thinks I need emancipation."

"Does he, now?"

"He wants to play you for me at the wingcasting table."

Belphagor laughed. "And here I thought he liked you. Surely he knows he'd never have a chance."

Vasily bristled. "Are you saying you'd bet me?"

Belphagor's arms tightened around him. "Are you presuming you'd have any say in the matter if I did?"

"I'd have my word, wouldn't I?"

"Ah, the boy's learning." Belphagor's breath tickled his neck. "Would you use it?" His hand stole downward and slid beneath the head of Vasily's thickening cock and cupped it. He knew exactly what effect his taunting was having.

Vasily breathed in, defenseless against his desire. "No."

Belphagor closed his hand around the shaft with the two-finger-and-thumb grip that promised Vasily a swift and merciless release. "Why not?" He started slowly, and Vasily tried in vain to stifle a groan. "Vasya. Why not?"

Vasily buried his face in Belphagor's side, digging his fists into the sheet. "Because," he moaned against the hard, unyielding muscle, "it makes me hot when you're a bastard."

Belphagor kissed his forehead, fingers thrumming rapidly over his flesh. "That's my sweet boy."

"*Your* sweet boy?"

"Be quiet and come for me."

The second part of the command Vasily couldn't help but obey, but the first was impossible. As heat burst out of him, Vasily arched beneath Belphagor's hand with a helpless roar.

"So close." Belphagor shook his head.

"What do you mean?"

"I'd nearly earned the right to have you, but if you can't be quiet when I tell you to, I can see I have a bit more work to do."

Vasily sat up. "Damn it, Beli—"

"Oh my. Now that's just sheer insubordination." He grabbed Vasily's locks and shoved his head down into his lap. "Let's see if this will keep you quiet."

Vasily tried to pretend he wasn't loving it, but it was no use.

Phaleg found himself at Silk's flat the following week. He wasn't sure why he'd allowed Belphagor to persuade him to meet the new tutor there. Belphagor had convinced the tutor to assist Phaleg in his investigation while Silk apparently remained unaware that he was the subject of it.

Playing the part of the tutor's illegitimate son, young Ruslan would accompany them to Grand Duke Lebes's residence in Iriy as a companion for the little grand duke. Even Anzhela had a role, posing as the daughter of one of the staff from the tutor's household. Her services as a maid would be offered to assist Grand Duchess Tsirya during her final trimester. Phaleg's influence with the principality had afforded him the leeway to take whatever measures he deemed fit to ensure Elysium's security.

When they'd finished working out the details, Belphagor not-so-subtly left Phaleg alone in the room with Silk. Phaleg glared at Belphagor's back as it disappeared through the door. Silk had placed himself directly between Phaleg and the exit route. The only way he could leave was to physically move him out of the way. His skin flushed with anger. Belphagor had manipulated him.

Again.

Silk put his hands into the pockets of his stylish pants—not as formal as the suit pants he wore at the Stone Horse but a similar, distinctly un-celestial cut with narrow calves and pleated fronts. A white silk shirt was tucked loosely into them, sleeves rolled up to the elbows. No cravat or collar, and open at the neck in a way that made Silk seem almost provocatively feminine.

Dark brows narrowed over the stormy gray of Silk's eyes. "I realize you'd rather be with Belphagor than with me, but I have something to say."

"'Rather be with Belphagor'? What's that supposed to mean?"

"Whatever you take it to mean, Major."

Phaleg didn't know how to respond. Silk had certainly never addressed him by his title before.

"I wanted to apologize for my joke about the facets. I didn't intend for you to take me seriously." He held out a pouch that looked like the one Phaleg had left.

Phaleg didn't reach for it. "Your joke?"

"Yes. It was in poor taste. I should have realized you wouldn't get it, being from your world."

"You're going to stand there and tell me to my face that I misunderstood you. That it wasn't your intent to demean me."

Silk pressed his garnet lips together.

"Go to hell, Silk." Phaleg moved to push past him, but Silk stepped with him, blocking his way.

"Oh, is that *your* attempt at a joke, Major? Or at demeaning me?"

"*Silk*—"

"You let me abuse you."

The flash of anger in Silk's eyes took Phaleg aback. "Wasn't that rather the point?"

"No, it wasn't the point! If you wanted someone to abuse you, I'm sure any of your angelic comrades would be happy to do it for free. As I understand it, all you'd have to do is tell them you have a taste for cock, and they'd gladly beat the shit out of you. What I *thought* you wanted was consensual submission."

Now Phaleg was genuinely confused. "I consented."

"Well, you shouldn't have. Not to that." Silk clutched at his carefully coiffed hair. "But that wasn't your fault, it was mine. We should have set ground rules. We should have had a word to say between us that meant we'd gone too far. Because I would have said it then, Phaleg. I would have told you it scared me." Silk looked young and vulnerable, all his artifice and sophistication gone.

Nothing could have shocked Phaleg more. He took a step closer. "Scared you?" Without intending to, he drew Silk's fingers away from his hair. "I didn't mean to. I didn't know I *could*."

"Well, *I* scared me." Silk laughed nervously, the uncharacteristic uncertainty still on his face. "And then I was petty and mean. Which isn't sexy at all."

It wasn't a word angels used, but the meaning was clear. Phaleg was sure he'd never seen anyone quite as "sexy" in his life. There was something about this unexpected side to Silk that made him even more alluring than he'd been before. Phaleg hadn't intended to forgive him—or give him the time of day. Now all he could think about was touching more of his skin.

"I thought I'd displeased you." He hadn't intended to say that either. He'd gone this far, he supposed he might as well go on. "In point of fact, I thought I disgusted you."

Silk looked down at their entwined fingers. "I'm the one who's disgusting. To treat you like that. There was no excuse."

"You're *not*. Don't say that." Phaleg dared to bring his other hand to Silk's cheek, and Silk's head snapped up in surprise.

"You don't know me at all." Silk's voice was a bare whisper.

"I want to know you."

"Why?" Silk's eyes narrowed. "I'm a demon. What value could there possibly be in getting to know me other than the thrill of perversion? Am I not your dirty little secret?"

"I thought I was yours."

Silk laughed harshly. "I have no secrets. Everyone knows about me."

"Everyone except me, apparently. So let me. Let me understand what I don't, what I can't on my own, by nature of being from another world."

Silk stared at him and then seemed to realize they were still holding hands. He withdrew his, and Phaleg's felt empty. "Are you forgiving me?"

"Do you want me to?"

Silk shifted his feet, storm-gray eyes for once looking into Phaleg's with naked honesty. "Yes." The delivery of that single word contained more genuine contrition than anything else Silk had said.

"Then I guess I am." His own words shocked him. He'd spent so many hours convincing himself that forgiveness was impossible. Phaleg offered a hesitant smile. "Can we start again? That is, if you want to."

"Yes." Silk echoed the expression, and the diffident young demon was gone, replaced once more by the sophisticated demimonde. "Only, not at the Horse."

Phaleg bristled. "Why? Are you ashamed to be seen with me?"

"Don't be absurd. You, on the other hand, ought to be more careful about where and with whom *you're* seen. People might begin to suspect you of consorting with the wrong sort."

In the flood of irrepressible desire and a host of complicated feelings, Phaleg had almost forgotten he was having Silk spied upon.

"Besides, the Horse is where I do business," Silk continued. "I don't want you to be business."

The warmth that spread through him at this unexpected statement warred confusingly with the knot in his stomach over Silk's possible connections with seditionists.

"I'll send word to you," said Silk with the sort of amused authority he exuded. "And you'll come to me here."

"Oh, will I?"

"Yes. You will. Then we'll talk about what you want done to you and don't want done to you. And we'll come up with a word to make sure there's no confusion between either of us about what you want. And then I'll give it to you."

Phaleg's cheeks blazed, and his elkskin breeches grew tight and uncomfortable.

Silk's gaze traveled over him, and his lips curved wickedly. "I think I'll keep these." He tossed the pouch of facets in the air and caught it. "Not as payment, but as collateral. Each time I have you, you can earn one back."

"I take it he accepted your apology," Belphagor remarked to Silk after Phaleg had gone. Phaleg's flushed skin as they'd come down the steps had revealed far more than his reticent tongue.

Silk smirked. "I'm not sure if it was my apology or my metaphorical hand in his pants, but I do believe he has a thing for me."

Vasily snorted from the kitchen where he was sneaking a bit of leftover pie. "Would that be a metaphorical thing or the thing in his pants?"

"Both, my succulent plum." Silk looked pleased. "Both."

Belphagor cleared his throat before Silk and Vasily got any more carried away. "I thought I'd take the boys out to the market for the afternoon. You two can stay here and discuss metaphor all you like."

Vasily growled at him over a bite of pie. "You're leaving me here?"

"I thought you'd want to make some facets again this evening. Or play with Silk. I have a title to defend at the tables. No offense, love, but it's easier to do without your sulking presence."

"My sulking presence." The fiery glower in his hazel eyes gave a perfect demonstration and made Belphagor wish he could spend the evening punishing Vasily instead of trouncing demons at the wingcasting table. Another sign of how far gone he was, but he realized he didn't care. Or, more to the point, *did* care and was actually pleased at the notion.

He leaned toward Anzhela beside him. "Paint him up again." As he rose and stepped toward Vasily, he drew him forward by the back of his neck until they were eye to eye, dropping his voice into a sensual purr. "It will look so lovely dripping from the corners of your eyes when I make you weep." He kissed Vasily briefly, holding him tight at the nape to keep him from jerking back the way he clearly wanted to. "You're delicious when you're pissed. See you tonight."

Belphagor let him go and turned to the boys who'd gathered eagerly behind him at the mention of an outing. They were grinning up at Vasily, whose face blazed. Belphagor supposed he might have been a tiny bit more discreet.

"He's insufferable." Vasily pouted. "I'm not going to the Horse tonight, and I'm not wearing the paint."

Silk reclined on the settee across from him. "Well, he did say I could play with you. I could take you to the dungeon and spare you the tedium of your merchant friend. I had Khai lined up for tonight, but I'm sure he'd be up for a bit of fun with you as well."

"I thought you'd made up with that *angel*. Don't you want to take him to the dungeon?"

Silk stretched his arms over his head, looking like a satisfied cat. "Why, my ruby plum, do I detect a note of jealousy?"

"Of course not. What do I care what you get up to with that angel?"

"Ah, there it is again: *that angel*. You *are* jealous."

"I'm not. He . . . bothers me." Vasily had to bite his tongue to keep from telling Silk about the order to have him watched. "Angels aren't exactly friends to us."

"Parts of him are friends to me." Silk winked. "But I told him I didn't want to see him at the Horse. I don't really care for the public nature of play with him. Patrons are intimidated when he comes in wearing that uniform, and while it's divine to strip it off him and spank him silly, it takes my attention from managing the house."

Vasily exchanged a look with Anzhela, who sat reading in the oversized armchair. "You're going to play with him privately? Here?"

"In my room, of course." Silk looked perturbed. "It's not as if I plan to string him up naked from the crossbeams right here in the parlor." He glanced at Anzhela. "Will it be a problem?"

Anzhela shrugged and went back to her book. "It's nothing to me. String him up wherever you like, so long as you keep him quiet." Her eyes darted up once more to Vasily's. "Quieter than him, preferably."

Vasily's face heated.

Silk grinned. "I'll stuff his elkskins in his mouth, and he can go home with a wet crotch and decide how he wants to explain it."

"Silk! That's hardly appropriate in front of Anzhi."

She glanced up again. "Have you forgotten I apprenticed at The Cat?"

He'd thought he couldn't be any more mortified. Anzhela had been present as the apprentice-madam at her grandmother's brothel the night Vasily had discovered his tastes ran to more than one variety of pleasure.

"Nothing could shock me." Anzhela turned a page. "It's the boys I'm concerned about."

Silk shrugged. "Nothing could shock them either."

"Well, it should. It's not their fault they were groomed at that awful Fletchery. They deserve to be innocent awhile longer."

Silk reddened. "Of course. You're right. I'll keep him quiet and send him home before morning. The boys will never know he's here. As for you—" Silk smirked at Vasily "—come with me to the Horse tonight, and I'll let you make all the noise you like."

Midday at the market was magical this time of year. The perfume of late-autumn fruits, blending with the smell of pies and mulling spices and sprigs of Aravothan pine, instantly transported Belphagor to the carefree pickpocketing days of his youth. The sensory feast was a prelude to a sort of annual defiance against nature as Heaven's capital began its customary season of merriment in the weeks following the equinox. At the start of the rivers' freeze, a wild, six-week-long party overtook Elysium, culminating in the return of the supernal family to the Winter Palace after the solstice. Despite the celebration's origins in the veneration of the Host, the excitement of the festivities spilled across the Acheron into Raqia.

The boys had been cooped up too long. An afternoon among the intrepid angelic shoppers seeking unusual gifts and treats was the ideal training ground for future thieves.

Belphagor sent them out in pairs and made a game of it—a sort of scavenger hunt—with each team assigned to return at the end of the afternoon with a particular prize. The chaos and excitement in the market meant there was little chance of getting caught. Should one of the boys be detected nicking a trinket or picking a pocket, he'd instructed them to toss the bounty back and scatter. As he circled the market, he kept tabs on the boys in case any of them managed to run into trouble.

To Ruslan, who'd be going to the duchy of Iriy in the morning with Anzhela and the tutor, Soluzen, he set the task of finding a rare trinket to present to the little grand duke as a gift. Soluzen would claim parentage of the boy, his bastard by a house servant, which Phaleg was certain would make him acceptable in Lebes's eyes.

Angels liked to flaunt the bastard sons born in their households, though they went officially unacknowledged since mixing angelic and demonic blood was a crime. But Ruslan had to appear savvy. He had the smarts for it in spades; the pretty novelty Belphagor had sent him after would seal the deal.

While magical objects wouldn't go over well at the palace, the hand-carved jade box was a talisman with the power to bring the little grand duke harmless treats—whatever he imagined that would fit within the box—without his guardians knowing. Its handsomeness and quaintness would appeal to the elder grand duke, while the secret purpose ought to win the younger over.

The first pairs back were the oldest boys. Bored with their studies, they were already champing at the bit to join the crew at the Stone Horse. Belphagor hoped the opportunity to prove they could excel at something else might keep them from straying toward their inevitable calling a bit longer. They met him at the appointed spot south of the gaming pavilions with smug expressions, each presenting him discreetly with their catches: a pair of hunting knives taken off a page's belt and a set of steward's keys to an angelic house.

"Well done." Belphagor was careful not to give too much praise. Pride in their accomplishment would be worth more than indulgent pats on the back. They were old enough that being treated like children didn't sit well with them.

The next few pairs trickled in with their prizes over a quarter hour, until all but two teams had returned. Ruslan and his partner were among the tardy. Belphagor had paired him with an older boy to be safe, but as the second-to-last pair arrived at a run from opposite ends, a prickle of unease set in.

"Anyone after you?" He glanced about them, pushing the other boys back toward the crowd watching the sidewalk games.

"Don't think so. We scattered like you said and tossed back the loot." Danila looked over his shoulder with a grin. "And the loot kind of scattered." Their assignment had been to acquire a string of Vilonese pearls Belphagor had planned to give to Anzhela for her part in the upcoming endeavor.

He scanned the aisles and alleyways. Charmed lights and hanging lanterns were winking into the fast-settling darkness. "Have you seen Ruslan and Olivier?"

The boys shook their heads.

"Stay here and watch the games. I'll be back."

He slipped through the shoppers that were quickly becoming the sort the market specialized in at night—significantly more inebriated than the daytime variety—and made another sweep of the area. Ruslan was likely to find what he'd been tasked with in the narrow row of kiosks dedicated to baubles and potions. This section, at least, was less populated with night business—but it also meant the boys would be more exposed.

As Belphagor threaded his way toward the end of the row, Olivier appeared, looking ashen.

Belphagor pulled him aside. "Where's Ruslan?"

"She caught him. The old crone caught him. I ran to get you. I wasn't abandoning him, I swear."

"It's all right. You did the right thing. Which kiosk?" His gaze followed where Olivier pointed. "You head back to the meeting spot. The others are there. If I'm not back in five minutes, you all hightail it for the flat, understand?"

Olivier nodded, looking miserable, and ran for the pavilions.

Belphagor stepped through the tented opening at a casual stroll, as if browsing the items in the front. He'd expected to find Ruslan trapped and possibly taking a switching from the old demoness, but a quick glance about the kiosk revealed Ruslan sitting on a stool weeping, while a woman who looked to be in her mid-fifties by the aging of the world of Man plied him with sweets.

"So there you are!" Belphagor's angry bark startled them both. "What has he done now?" He marched toward them, noting his act seemed to have Ruslan genuinely alarmed. "You can't get good help anymore." He lifted Ruslan from the stool by the arm and shook him. "Paid dear for this one, and he repays me in sloth and trickery. Was he stealing again?"

"Stealing?" The woman looked surprised. "Why, no, he wanted to buy a trinket for his mother. She's ailing, poor thing—overworked in some brothel—but when I told him how much it cost, he broke down crying because he didn't have enough. I gave it to him anyway. Couldn't say no to those sad little eyes. He was so touched he started bawling. I was trying to calm him down." The demoness paused and looked disapprovingly at Belphagor's grip on Ruslan's arm. "Bought him, did you, and now you think you can treat him like a work animal. He's a *boy*, and he deserves some kindness." She folded the waxed-paper-wrapped candies into Ruslan's other hand and patted it. "You give your mum the bracelet. I know it'll make her smile."

Ruslan nodded, sniffling, the candies clutched in his hand, as Belphagor turned him about.

"Can't be soft on 'em," Belphagor groused over his shoulder. "They'll steal you blind."

Once outside, Belphagor looked at Ruslan, amused. "Crying and candy and a sick whore mum, eh?"

Ruslan grinned. "Well, it worked, didn't it?"

"I sent you for the box. All you left with is candy and a cheap glass bracelet."

Ruslan reached into his coat and presented another item with a flourish: the jade box.

Belphagor was impressed. "Influence?"

Ruslan nodded, beaming. Another airspirit thief-in-the-making in Raqia. Belphagor might have to watch out for him in a few years' time.

# CHAPTER
# SEVEN

The trip to the Duchy of Iriy would take the better part of a week. As the principality's representative, Phaleg would make the introductions to Grand Duke Lebes. After his return, there would be no opportunity to learn what their spies had gathered until the grand duke came to Elysium to welcome the supernal family home for the season a month hence. Phaleg could only hope that those who wished to supplant Helison with Lebes wouldn't make their move before then.

The arrival of the coach to pick up Ruslan and Soluzen was a hit with the boys. While they were downstairs admiring it, Silk pulled Phaleg into the bedroom.

Silk's fingers lingered on the lapel of Phaleg's dress coat. "It's a shame you'll be away for such a stretch. I didn't realize you'd be going with."

"Only to deliver them. I'll be turning straight around and coming back on my own."

"But that's still, what, a week?"

"A week and a half, most likely."

Silk clucked his tongue. "Here I was looking forward to having a go at you as soon as possible."

Phaleg stiffened, adjusting his coat. "Having a go?"

"Yes, my dirty angelwhore. A go."

And just like that, Phaleg was under his spell, transformed from an officer taking umbrage at an offense into a helpless slave trembling with desire.

Silk brushed aside a stray curl on Phaleg's forehead. "You look a bit flushed, Major. Maybe you're dehydrated. I have something you can suck on to get a little fluid into you." Silk unfastened his slacks.

Phaleg hesitated only a moment before dropping to his knees. He was like a starved man, falling on the stiff cock and gobbling it in. Silk leaned back against the closed door, and Phaleg surrendered himself to Silk's direction, head loose in Silk's hands, letting him slick Phaleg's mouth up and down his length in a steady rhythm.

"Keep quiet," Silk ordered when Phaleg began to vocalize against him. "I've promised Anzhela you'll never make a peep while I'm violating you." It was all Phaleg could do not to let out a loud moan as Silk pushed him down deep. "We'll have to get creative about how to mute the sound of the various implements I intend to use on you. And in you. Perhaps we ought to think more in terms of ropes and knots than striking implements. Pull things tight." Silk bobbed against his lips while Phaleg struggled to stay silent. "See how much I can hurt you without hitting you at all."

An involuntary groan escaped him, and Silk pulled him off. "If you're going to make noise, I may as well work myself." He wrapped his fist around his spit-slick cock and made good on the threat, and Phaleg bit his lip to keep in a whimper of desperation. "What's the matter, angelwhore? You want this?"

Phaleg nodded, squirming. Silk teased the tip between his lips and pulled it away again several times until Phaleg was shocked to feel tears of frustration on his cheeks.

Silk rubbed his cock against the tears, his usual expression of wry amusement absent as he cupped Phaleg's chin. "Do you want me so badly?"

"Yes, please," Phaleg breathed. He'd lost all dignity, ready to beg, to be beaten, to grovel like a dog. He was ashamed of himself, and yet the shame aroused him beyond reason. "Please use me."

Silk cupped his face in both hands. "You're very pretty when you beg." His voice was soft. "Open. Eyes on me."

Phaleg obeyed, grateful.

Silk nodded approval and began to fuck him. "I like the way you want me," he said, getting into a rhythm. "The way you enjoy how I use you rather than enduring it. And I love watching your delicate angelic cheeks flame red as a firespirit's when you realize I know how much you want it. Are you shameful, pretty angelwhore?"

Phaleg nodded, his eyes smarting as he struggled to keep his throat relaxed.

"Are you a dirty, pathetic fuck toy, good for nothing but the sexual amusement of a demon pander?"

Phaleg nodded again, his face hot at the demeaning words and his cock harder than a crystal facet. He wished Silk would throw him over the end of the bed and fuck him without mercy. Silk wasn't one to do things roughly. Every action was smooth and sensual, yet commanding. But Phaleg yearned to be thoroughly taken, to know Silk wanted him as much he wanted Silk.

Silk stilled, his body tensing, and Phaleg waited for the hot spurt in the back of his throat, panting around his mouthful in anticipation. Instead, Silk pulled out unexpectedly, gripped Phaleg's curls at the hairline, and shot against the crisp emerald-green collar with a long groan of delight.

Phaleg stared, horrified, at the stain on his jacket.

"Tell everyone it's icing from a pastry you stuffed into your mouth too greedily." Silk relaxed against the door with his characteristic smirk. "But you can't leave this room with that granite pole in your pants. Take it out and take care of it."

Still mortified and disappointed that Silk didn't want to help him with his own erection, Phaleg unlaced and released himself.

"Eyes on me," Silk snapped. "Get to it. We don't have all day."

Phaleg jerked himself with swift efficiency. If this was going to be nothing more than humiliation, he would get it done quickly so he could take his leave. Silk was confusing him again. Phaleg wanted more of him, and that frightened him. He was an angel. He couldn't be with a demon. He'd only agreed to be a demon's toy.

Silk watched him passionlessly, arms folded, as if he were counting time in his head. Phaleg closed his eyes for a moment to try to replace the disappointing scene with an internal play in which Silk was making him come for a room full of strangers.

The fantasy worked, but as he was about to come, Silk's hand struck his cheek.

"I told you, eyes on me."

"I'm sorry—"

"You're sorry. Dirty little pervert. Get up off your knees and finish yourself."

Phaleg stumbled to his feet, his face now flushed with shame that had no component of arousal. Why had he trusted Silk again? What the hell was he doing here debasing himself, letting Silk make him a fool?

"Kneel on the bed, facing me." Silk shoved him toward it.

The rough push reminded Phaleg of the fantasy he ached for. When he positioned himself on the mattress, the soft leather of his pants tight beneath his exposed balls, the thought of that secret desire and his hard strokes brought him once more to the brink.

He gritted his teeth to stay silent, and as he came, Silk unexpectedly dropped to his knees before the bed and took it all in his mouth. Phaleg groaned with relief, his cock quivering at the touch of Silk's tongue. But before he could relax, Silk rose and pushed Phaleg onto his back and kissed him with the spunk still in his mouth, giving it back to him.

Silk had never gotten this close to him before. It had always been about enjoying the view of Phaleg's torment and obedience from a superior position. Now Silk held him down with his lithe body and kissed him, the taste of Phaleg's semen shared on their tongues. Silk had never really kissed him before either. Not like this. Phaleg forgot himself and slipped his arms around Silk's slender waist, savoring the feel of him.

"Dirty angelwhore." The murmured words didn't sound like debasement. They sounded like a term of endearment. "When you return to Elysium, I want you to come straight here. I want to have you all night."

Phaleg shivered. "All night?"

"If you think you can handle it." Silk rolled onto his side, propping his head on his hand. "We'll need to establish that word. Did you have one with Belphagor?"

Phaleg nodded. "*Pozhaluista*. It means 'please' in—"

"I know what it means. I don't think that will work for us. I like it too much when you say 'please,' and if I heard it in the peasant tongue, it might incite me to do more rather than stop. Let's make it . . . 'Arkhangel'sk.' The name of the other master you serve."

An altogether different surge of shame washed over him as Silk kissed his throat without any inkling of how Phaleg was serving his master even now.

While Phaleg put the "Iriy Contingent" of the game into play to determine to what extent Grand Duke Lebes might be involved in the conspiracy, Belphagor had agreed to stoke the fires of discontent among the Fallen. The problem was, he had a reputation for not giving a damn about celestial politics or the grand ideas behind the movement for demon rights. He'd seen enough bullshit in the world of Man, seen enough rulers and governments come and go. Little changed when a regime did, other than the peasant class getting shafted no matter who was in control.

The idea that his part in this scheme would be to make the reigning principality less trusting of demons didn't sit well with him. The Fallen were too often scapegoats for the failings of angels as it was. Further, he'd met Helison and found him to be a kindly, well-meaning sort. He was much like his doppelgänger, Russia's Tsar Nicholas, whom Belphagor had met through a bit of trickery and luck many years ago.

Nicholas's failing had been his naïve idealism, which Helison seemed to share. Perhaps the disillusionment inherent in this plan would do the principality some good. Or perhaps it would quash the best instincts of a decent angel forever. Either way, Belphagor doubted it would matter to the Fallen. The Liberation Decree had been dangled before them like a carrot to the angels' authoritative stick for decades.

Whether he managed to feign interest convincingly in the cause of liberation, he intended to leave the tables this evening with debts owed to him by every demon who dared to challenge him. Debt was a language universally understood, and leaving the door open to collect on it later would be more valuable than any idle shit-stirring Belphagor might do.

He was counting his facets after a number of satisfying rounds when the next player to advance from the table beside him took a seat to challenge him.

"Sorry, friend." Belphagor didn't glance up. "I'm about to turn in for the night. But you're welcome to defend the table as champion for the remainder of the evening."

"That's a shame." The smooth, familiar voice made Belphagor's skin prickle with misgiving. "I was hoping to offer you a wager that would make things interesting."

Belphagor tied off his purse and gave Kezef a dismissive glance. "Nothing you could wager would make things interesting enough to abide your presence."

Kezef leaned back with his fingers clasped behind his head. "You realize refusing a challenge automatically forfeits your title as master of the game."

Undeterred, he pushed back his chair. "Not if I'm turning in for the night, as I said. You'll have to amuse yourself with someone else."

"Run and hide if you wish. You're still required to play me tomorrow."

Belphagor shrugged. "If you manage to hold the seat tonight. Be that as it may . . ." He rose, not bothering to finish the sentence.

"The wager I intend to put forth is information I believe you have an interest in."

"Wager it tomorrow."

He turned, but Kezef's next words stopped him in his tracks.

"I recently learned some interesting news about the girls from the Fletchery."

Belphagor's fists curled at his sides. When they'd rescued Anzhela and the Lost Boys from demon traffickers in the world of Man, they'd been too late to save the underage girls, whose "unspoiled virtue" had apparently been a quick sell within Heaven. "What news?"

"I thought that might give you pause." Kezef's smile as Belphagor turned back toward him said he knew he'd already won the first round. "What will you wager?"

"You intend to use this information as ante in a card game?"

Kezef unclasped his hands and took up the deck. "Information has value. Why shouldn't I profit from it?"

"You're a pig."

"You're a hypocrite. Are we playing or not?"

Belphagor hesitated. It had been weighing on him that he'd failed the girls—and that Anzhela carried the burden of having been unable to protect them as well, though she never spoke of it. "I could pay you for the information, as despicable as I find the prospect. No need to waste time gambling over it. Name your price."

Kezef shuffled. "But gambling is so much more fun. Have a seat, Belphagor, and earn your title."

Both literally and figuratively, the bastard held all the cards. Belphagor ground his teeth and returned to his chair.

Kezef dealt. "What will you put up against my wager?"

"As I said, name your price, and let's get this over with."

Kezef picked up the cards he'd dealt himself, perusing them with a calculating eye. "I'll have your boy."

Belphagor nearly toppled the marble table as he jumped up. "*Idi k chertu.*"

Kezef laughed. "Go to hell? Is that the best you could come up with? Really, Belphagor, I'd heard you were such a skillful player, but I've never seen any evidence of it. Why don't you sit down and stop acting like a halfwit before the den manager thinks someone's cheating at the master table?"

"I'm not going to play your fucking game, Kezef."

"But you're usually so certain you'll win. Is your faith in your own skill so poor you won't wager anything you value?"

"Only a fool or a cretin would wager what he cherishes most."

"And yet you auctioned off his ass to anyone with a purse full of facets. Tell me, did you watch the winner pound him? Did you make your boy beg to be drilled by a stranger to get your rocks off?" Kezef set the die in the center of the table. "It's your cast, Belphagor. Stop making a spectacle of yourself."

Belphagor gripped the edge of the wingcasting table and leaned across it. "Listen to me carefully, you repugnant swine. I will not play your game. You want my title forfeit? So be it. I fold. The title's yours."

Kezef smiled with infuriating calm. "I suppose you're a little touchy about the subject, seeing as the merchant who nearly bankrupted himself bidding on him that evening has been courting him ever since. From what I hear, his advances haven't been rebuffed. Your boy has been willingly entertaining him. Repeatedly."

Belphagor peeled his grip from the table and straightened, forcing himself not to react. "Since you've been banned from the Stone Horse, I can only assume you enjoy talking out of your own ass." He lifted his hand to call the den manager over to acknowledge Kezef's status as master player.

Kezef gathered the cards once more. "Relax. Your title's safe for now. We'll play tomorrow, when your disposition has improved with a little sleep. I know how much you older demons need it."

Belphagor hadn't wanted to let Kezef get under his skin, but he could think of nothing else. Vasily hadn't come home yet. He was probably with Silk. Regardless, Belphagor had told him to keep an ear out for information however he had to. He was *not* jealous of some repressed merchant.

Yet he could only picture one thing when he closed his eyes: Vasily on his knees before the merchant, giving him his special brand of oral pleasure. The idea had aroused him before, sending Vasily off to suck cock because he said so. Now, on his cold, hard cot, it seemed idiotic. Why in Heaven's name had he thought it would be hot to let someone else have his boy? *His* boy, damn it. Never mind that he refused to acknowledge it for the sheer, perverse pleasure of tormenting him, Vasily was his.

Belphagor lay awake for hours, telling his brain to shut up. He was being ridiculous, playing Kezef's game. When had he become so easily influenced? He suspected it might have been around the time a lanky, flame-haired thief had made the worst attempt ever to cut his purse.

Vasily had made him soft. It was hard to fault him for it.

When Vasily finally came in, he tried in vain to be quiet. He'd obviously had far too much to drink. Seriously misjudging both distance and his own strength, he stumbled over the chair and knocked it halfway across the room before he managed to right it and fumble into bed. If Belphagor had been asleep, the heavy drop of Vasily's body beside him and the thud of the wooden cot against the wall would have remedied that for certain.

Belphagor rolled over and slid his arms around him, and Vasily jumped. "Have a good night?"

"Thought you were sleeping."

"I was," Belphagor lied. "But you were a bit noisy."

"Sorry. Guess I had more to drink than I thought." Was it his imagination, or was Vasily not responding to his embrace?

"You and Silk have fun?"

"Not exactly." Vasily fidgeted. "I spent the evening with Gaspard."

"Oh." So damned Kezef had been right. "The whole evening?"

Vasily turned toward him, finally. "You told me to 'make friends.' Now you're pissy about it?"

"I'm not *pissy*, I'm surprised. What did you manage to spend the whole evening doing? I thought he was something of a one-trick pony."

"You *are* being pissy."

Belphagor grimaced. "Maybe a little. So what did you do?"

Vasily rested his elbow on the bed and propped his head on his hand. "I meant to tell you in the morning when I'm not so drunk. He's drawing me."

Belphagor blinked, trying to make sense of the words. "He's what?"

"Drawing me. He draws. He asked me to sit for him."

"Drawing? With a pen?"

"Some kind of charred wood, actually. He has dozens of drawings at his studio. He paints, also, I guess. And then he sells them." Vasily's cheeks were a tad ruddier than usual.

"I take it these drawings—he does nudes?"

"Nudes?"

"Naked. He's drawing you naked."

The ruddy cheeks got pinker. "Mostly, yes. He draped this cloth over one shoulder and across my stomach, sort of artsy-like, and had it pooled around me."

Belphagor eyed him shrewdly. The level of embarrassment seemed to be about something more. "Vasya. Is this an erotic drawing?"

Vasily dropped his arm and reclined on the cot, rolling slightly away from him. "I don't know. What do you consider erotic?"

"Does it require you maintaining an erection with that magnificent cock of yours?" He stole his hand over the upturned hip and found the cock in question, not quite hard but showing apparent interest at his touch. He wrapped his fingers around the shaft, and the tentative expression of interest became firmer. "You didn't answer."

"I don't know why I go to bed naked—*nude*—with you," Vasily growled instead of answering. "You always take it as an invitation to molest me."

Belphagor laughed and kissed a warm shoulder. "Yes, I can see how you hate it." He stroked the now undeniable erection. "Shall I stop?"

"You're just mean enough to do that, aren't you?"

"I am, indeed. But I'd prefer to watch you come while you tell me about this session." He moved his hand slowly up to the head, enjoying Vasily's little shiver when his thumb traced the rim. "Did he have you lying on your side like this?"

"Sort of." The words were breathy. "Leaning on my shoulder with one knee up. Ohhh, *bozhe moi*."

Belphagor smirked at the exclamation and prodded him into the position he described, threading his arm beneath Vasily's raised knee to get a better grip. Fondling Vasily's balls in a bit of misdirection, he used his other hand to whisk the almond oil from the nightstand and emptied the last of the bottle onto Vasily's cock. Vasily yelped at the cold but was soon groaning with pleasure as Belphagor—and his own skin—warmed it up.

"So, how did you maintain the required erection?" Belphagor rested his chin against Vasily's shoulder, enjoying watching his face. "Did he help you with it like I am?"

"N-no," Vasily managed. "He wanted to watch me jerk off."

Belphagor dropped his hand, and Vasily whimpered. "Go ahead, then. Show me."

Reluctantly, Vasily worked himself with rapid efficiency.

"I don't imagine you kept it hard for long doing that."

"No." Vasily slowed with a sound of frustration. "I only topped it off, so to speak, whenever it needed it, until he finished."

"That's how you'll do it for me, then." Belphagor had stroked the abundant oil over his own cock while he spoke, and with Vasily's upraised knee, it only took one swift, smooth thrust to enter him. Vasily had let his eyes close, and he opened them with a gasp, which was rather charming, as if he didn't know Belphagor as well as he did. Belphagor drove in deep, pleased that Vasily's nipples went hard. "Was he a fast sketcher, or did he take his time?"

Vasily arched back to meet his thrusts. "He sketched the outline fast. Then spent more time on the details."

Belphagor held on to Vasily's locks and fucked him fast and deep, and Vasily took it passively, moaning in staccato, his face and cock both pink. When his hand stole toward the latter, Belphagor slapped the blushing head to let him know he'd noticed, making Vasily hiss and tighten his muscles as if that single strike had almost made him come. Belphagor slowed, getting to the "detail of the drawing," and stroked one finger up and down Vasily's shaft. Vasily sucked air through his teeth as he rocked his ass against Belphagor, who was thrusting and withdrawing with excruciating patience.

"Do you want to come?" Belphagor murmured at his ear.

"*Da, ser.*" There was nothing like hearing those words uttered in that deep gravelly intonation.

"What a good boy you are to remember the rules." Belphagor withdrew again and then slowly drove himself in while Vasily whimpered. "I think you've earned the right to 'top yourself off,' although you clearly don't need it."

With a grateful sigh, Vasily wrapped his hand around his cock, and Belphagor picked up speed as Vasily did the same.

"That's it, boy. Come for me." He was pounding him now, eliciting sharp grunts, and he knew the harder he fucked him, the hotter Vasily would become until he finally burst. He tilted Vasily back and drew the upraised leg over his thigh to spread him wider, twisting his fingers in the locks to force Vasily's head back. Gasping and arching, Vasily practically choked his own cock, and the hot, pearly fluid shot upward from it like a faithful and thoroughly marvelous geyser.

Belphagor took the opportunity to fuck him harder still, both of them groaning and growling as they slipped and slapped together. When he couldn't hold back a moment longer, Belphagor closed his mouth over the piercing on Vasily's neck to muffle an irrepressible roar as he spilled into him.

As they wound down, basking in the afterglow, with Vasily's head turned to the side so Belphagor could kiss him, a loud, angry pounding on the wall beside them broke the silence.

"All right!" the tenant shouted through the wall. "We get it! You like fucking! Now shut the fuck up!"

They melted into one another, collapsing in giggles muffled into one another's mouths. Belphagor was fairly certain he'd never giggled before, but what the hell. There was a first time for everything.

In the morning—or what was left of it when he woke—Belphagor found Vasily already up and getting dressed. In the annoying manner of the young, he wasn't the least bit hungover.

"Where are you off to so early?"

Vasily snorted. "It's nearly noon." He put his boot on the chair and laced up. "Gaspard invited me to his house for an artists' salon. Strange things these upper-class demons get up to. I had no idea anyone but angels held 'salons.' Not really sure what one is."

Belphagor drew his knees to his chest and hooked his arms around them—a gesture he knew was defensive, as if he expected Vasily to kick him in the nuts. "Now you're going to salons with him?"

"You're pissy again." Vasily took his fancy coat from their makeshift wardrobe. "I thought I might learn something there. Gaspard is always going on about how liberationists are fools. I think he might be a Lebes supporter." He was animated and cheerful—not an ordinary state for him.

"You're wearing the coat?" Belphagor was full of witty repartee this morning.

Vasily glanced down at the velvet garment as he buttoned. "You think it's too much? I didn't really know what to wear. I don't have anything else nice."

Belphagor swallowed his irrational annoyance. "I'm sure it's fine. You won't have it on that long anyway, will you? I suppose he wants you to 'sit' for him after." Belphagor's gut twisted at the guilty look that clouded Vasily's features. He had the overwhelming urge to cover his nads.

"Beli . . . do you not want me to go?"

The pitying look was almost more than Belphagor could take. His brow creased with irritation. "Why wouldn't I? Of course you should go. Find out anything you can about the Lebes faction. I'd be curious to know how many demons are actually against their own liberation. I imagine it's confined to those making good facets in 'respectable' trades."

Vasily shrugged. "I guess. I'll try to keep track of who's who."

As Vasily headed for the door, Belphagor bounded out of bed and pulled him back for a kiss, rather forcefully reminding him whose boy he was, even if he wasn't going to give Vasily the satisfaction of saying it.

"Don't spend all your time with Gaspard." He tried not to grumble the admonition. "Remember, you're supposed to be making friends with the rent boys too. We need to know if illicit rendezvous are indeed happening at the Horse."

Vasily nodded. "*Da, ser.*" The rumble simultaneously soothed and riled Belphagor's passion.

As he closed the door behind Vasily, Belphagor's stomach soured. He still had Kezef to deal with.

# CHAPTER EIGHT

Kezef was waiting for him at the master table with a smug expression. "Saw your boy on his way out. He cleans up well. I can't wait to dirty him."

Belphagor counted in his head, forcing himself to breathe normally—and not to kill Kezef—before he put his hands on the back of the master chair. "Since it seems you must be hard of hearing, I suggest you listen carefully. I have no intention of betting my boy. By the rules of the house, the reigning champion must accept all challengers or relinquish his title. It does *not* say he has to agree to any asinine betting terms a challenger proposes."

Kezef adjusted his cuffs. "Fair enough. But my proposed bet is also rescinded. We'll play for facets."

Belphagor nodded and took his seat as Kezef began to shuffle the wingcasting deck.

"It's a shame, of course. The information I offered you would be of great interest to a demon who holds himself in such high esteem when it comes to the welfare of innocents."

He wanted not to ask. He wanted to be beyond the bastard's manipulative influence. "And what 'welfare' would that be?"

Kezef took up his cards. "Well, now. If I told you, there'd be no value to the information. You'd have no reason to meet my challenge."

"I'm not going to play your game, Kezef." He was becoming a broken record, and it was pissing him off. Belphagor cast the die, and Kezef called out, "Ptarmigan," while it snapped against the table's corner. It landed on Ptarmigan. He was already playing

Kezef's damned game, and they both knew it. He surrendered a card to the pile, and Kezef took it up.

"Tell you what, Belphagor. I'll modify the challenge. I'll still wager my information, and you wager your boy for an evening, which he may take or leave as he chooses. So long as he entertains my offer, he'll be free to go, but I'm quite certain he'll be unable to deny himself what I provide. A single evening, no strings attached, at your boy's sole discretion in exchange for the fates of five girls who are little more than children. You can accept the simple challenge—assuming you have any faith in your own abilities—or you can leave the young girls to their lot." He cast the die against the opposite corner of the marble table.

"Serpent," said Belphagor. The face of the die stopped on serpent. They were well matched. It was going to be a long game.

Kezef put down his discard, and Belphagor took it up. "What do you say? Is your boy's already much-tattered virtue worth more than that of any other demon's?"

Belphagor gritted his teeth and held on to the die, though it was his cast. "How do I know you have this information?" He could feel Kezef radiating triumph from across the table, knowing he'd reeled Belphagor in.

"If you win, you'll be able to confirm the information, but I understand your concern." Kezef studied his cards. "You're wondering what happens if you lose. Perhaps my information will prove to be complete invention, and on such a false pretext, you'll have surrendered your dearest possession for a night at my mercy, but you'll never know for certain." He smiled at Belphagor over the cards. "Let me set your mind at ease. When I win—and I *will* win—I'll forfeit my wager anyway. You'll have the information, which you may verify before I have my way with that ferocious firespirit." He shifted his gaze to Belphagor's hand, still holding the die. "Are you going to fondle that thing all night?"

If he cast now, it meant he agreed to the terms, and the first round would officially begin. There would be no turning back. "Let me discuss it with Vasily."

Kezef shook his head. "The deal is on the table now. Negotiating it with the prize is out of the question. Take it or leave it. This is the last time I'm going to offer."

His stomach churned. Vasily would never forgive him if he knew he'd made such a bet. There was no way he'd lose, but the principle of the thing was beneath contempt. Kezef had him in a corner as tight as the sharp-edged marble ones of their playing surface.

Belphagor cast.

Kezef laid his cards on the table without bothering to call the die. "Scarlet wing."

He'd played a nearly impossible hand, and the odds that he would have managed it after a single turn were astronomical. Kezef was either the best player Belphagor had ever seen or extremely adept at magical manipulation. And Belphagor had just wagered his boy.

Gaspard, of course, didn't advertise his sexual proclivities—or the subject of his art. Vasily would have to be discreet at the salon about their involvement. With his rough looks, Vasily couldn't possibly be taken for a peer. Gaspard introduced him to his guests as a reformed pickpocket he'd taken on as an apprentice at one of his warehouses.

Since none of them had knowledge of the day-to-day operations of Gaspard's trade, there were no suspicions about why they'd never seen him before. Gaspard also presented Vasily as a budding talent he was cultivating. Apparently, he *did* have a reputation for painting, but not the sort of paintings Vasily had sat for.

Gaspard's friends observed him with interest, a sort of "wild boy" oddity whom one of their peers had managed to tame. It was incredibly condescending but made it all the more satisfying when they jumped at his gruff voice or when he belched and let off a little steam. Literally.

As for what a salon consisted of, if this one was anything to go by, it seemed to be nothing more than a handful of demons trying to impress one another with how well they had integrated into angelic society. Not one of them had the fair coloring of the Fourth Choir angels, so there was no question of passing. But they'd made it their business to be accepted through their assimilationist behavior, making sure never to transgress against angelic law or etiquette.

Which made Gaspard's secret desires all the more scandalous. Vasily wondered what would happen if he got down on his knees right here in the parlor and swallowed his cock. Gaspard would be ruined, of course, but it was a rather thrilling thought.

"Liberation is not the way forward for the Fallen."

Vasily paused in poking at the tiny sandwiches on his plate as the conversation drifted toward him from the two merchants on the settee across from him.

"It's a mirage to pacify the peasant class," the merchant continued. "Always just beyond reach. A promise that will never happen."

"Of course, Barakel," the other replied. "We're already liberated." The merchant swirled the bowl-like glass resting in his hand and took a delicate sip of caramel-colored liquor. Typical angel tipple. They didn't have the stomach for real spirits. These demons had even adopted angelic affectations. "We make a good, honest living and have every opportunity to prosper. Those who remain impoverished merely lack the fortitude to make something of themselves and prefer to blame it on the angels."

Vasily stifled a growl by stuffing a finger sandwich into his mouth. What bollocks. But this was precisely the sort of thing he ought to be listening for, so he leaned in a bit, pretending to be fascinated by the brocade upholstery on his chair.

"Too bad the current principality has let the bleeding hearts bend his ear with all their whinging about demon rights. All his programs of reform have done is make a discontented, entitled, shiftless class of demons. His father would never have been that sort of spineless ruler. They say he was built like a firespirit: gruff and broad, and brooked no nonsense. I wouldn't be surprised if the liberationists were behind the 'accidental' fall that placed his weaker son on the throne."

Barakel lowered his voice, and Vasily had to strain to hear. "Between you and me, they say the younger brother is more like the father."

The other demon set his glass on the table, leaning forward with interest. "I heard talk of a movement to encourage him to challenge the principality."

"Not mere talk, my friend. He has a solid following, and I'd say solid grounds to replace his incompetent brother. Word is, he's promised to be a friend to the merchant class. He's no liberationist. He believes in rewarding those who are industrious."

"I'd back him in a minute."

"Talk to Gaspard later. He'll set you up with a group of the grand duke's supporters, both Fallen and Host."

"So, young Vasily."

Vasily jumped at the sound of Gaspard's voice behind him.

"Are you enjoying the salon? Sorry to have left you alone so long."

Vasily turned. "Oh, I've been amusing myself with these little sandwiches." He nodded toward the four he'd pushed together to form a more respectable meal.

Gaspard laughed and held out a hand. "Let me find something more entertaining for you. I received a shipment of pigments I wanted to show you. Very fine, rich colors from the cliffs of the Samudran Sea in the southern tip of Vilon."

Vasily went with him to his studio on the second floor of the house, where Gaspard closed and locked the door.

Vasily tilted his head with a sly smile. "There aren't any pigments, are there?"

"Oh, there are, but that's not why I wanted to bring you up here." Gaspard crossed to the covered easel and drew the sheet off to reveal a finished sketch. Vasily's cheeks heated at the way Gaspard had drawn his erect cock almost absurdly beyond scale. "Do you like it?"

Only a croak came out when Vasily tried to speak. He cleared his throat and tried again. "It's very well done."

"But you don't like it."

"It's not that I don't like it." Vasily's voice was raspier than usual. "I suppose I don't really feel comfortable viewing myself that way."

Gaspard let the sheet fall back over it. "I see. I didn't mean to insult you."

"No, that's not it at all. It's very flattering. It just makes me feel a bit bashful." His cheeks were definitely flaming now.

"Bashful?" Gaspard observed him with a look both amazed and amused. "You? You do those performances for the entire Stone Horse."

"Sure, but I don't have to watch myself do it, if you see what I mean. In the world of Man, they have magic that allows you to capture a moving image. If someone captured my image that way during my performance, I'd be mortified if I had to see it. Does that make sense?"

Gaspard tilted his head as if considering it. "I suppose it does. Should I not have done the sketch?"

"No, really, it's fine. I'm happy to pose for you. But I feel a little silly faced with the completed work."

"Oh, it's not completed." Gaspard moved aside a stack of metal boxes on the worktable and opened one. "These are the pigments I told you about. I'm going to use them to paint your likeness from the drawing."

Jars containing varying hues of bright reds and oranges filled the box. Vasily couldn't help but smile at the selection. "I've never seen such vivid paints. Where do you get them?"

"They're not contraband, if that's what you're thinking." Gaspard sounded a bit put out, but he went on before Vasily could assure him he hadn't meant anything by it. "I've arranged a bit of trade with a merchant in Arcadia. He gives me access to a selection of Vilonese pigments." Gaspard looked pleased with himself as he set the box aside. "The very same used by the official portrait painter of the House of Arcadia himself."

"What do you trade him for it?" It was an idle question, an attempt to show interest, but the answer made Vasily take note.

Gaspard gave him a sidelong look. "I keep him apprised of certain developments from some of my benefactors with connections to the supernal family."

Vasily had never paid much attention to the political intricacies of the various houses of Heaven, but he remembered something Belphagor had said. Queen Sefira was from the House of Arcadia. And she would return to her family home to raise her children as Arcadians if Principality Helison were to die before an heir was born.

As Belphagor had predicted, the game showed every indication of going on indefinitely. A champion couldn't be declared until a player won three consecutive rounds. Neither he nor Kezef intended to let the other do so anytime soon, and both had the skill—and other means—to ensure it. After a week of defending his title nightly, with crowds of onlookers now placing bets on who would prevail, Belphagor was no closer to discovering the fate of the missing girls.

As they closed out for the evening, he offered Kezef a proposal. "What do you say we engage in a formal tournament? We can reconvene after a temporary truce and play until one of us wins. No one leaves the table until it's done."

Kezef yawned as he gathered the cards. "I must admit, these endless matches are growing tedious, and I have other business I've been neglecting." He rose and stretched as if he hadn't a care in the world. "All right. We meet again in a week's time. One game. Winner takes all." He held out his hand, and Belphagor shook it, feeling dirty.

Vasily, meanwhile, had been gathering information. Belphagor tried not to think about how. Both of them were tired when they turned in, or one of them turned in after the other had gone to bed, so their usual sexual fervor was lacking. At least, Belphagor tried to tell himself that was the reason. For his part, guilt weighed on him about the wager. He doubted guilt factored into Vasily's lack of enthusiasm—or maybe he *hoped* it didn't, come to think of it.

But the upshot was that for the first time since they'd been together, except for their brief separation, they'd gone several days without fucking. Or fucking each other, at any rate. Vasily was clearly enjoying the attentions of his merchant. Belphagor hated the petty jealousy percolating inside him as he imagined all sorts of scenarios wherein Vasily might be achieving satisfaction.

With his time temporarily freed up, Belphagor had hoped to fill it with Vasily—and to fill Vasily—but it was the following morning before he made an appearance.

Belphagor was already awake when he stumbled in. "Well, look who it is." He smiled to soften the sarcasm, though he wasn't quite feeling it. "I was beginning to think you'd taken a permanent room at the Horse."

"Sorry. One of the working boys had a birthday celebration, and it's kind of still going." Vasily stripped out of his clothes, which cheered Belphagor immensely until he noticed the distinctive red marks of an open hand on Vasily's ass.

He grabbed Vasily's arm and turned him about to take a closer look, instantly sober. The marks were well placed, and the skin had the bright flush of having taken several strikes in succession in the same two spots. "What the hell is this?"

Matching blotches formed on Vasily's upper cheeks. "Silk wanted to spank the birthday boy—someone said it was a custom from the world of Man—but he couldn't take more than a couple of swats, so Silk decided to make me his 'proxy.'"

Belphagor had to take a step away to control the surge of anger that nearly choked him. Beneath it throbbed a hollow pain, like he'd been punched in the gut. "I know you're not officially my boy." He spoke carefully, making sure his voice didn't catch. "But you belong to me." He put his hand around the back of Vasily's neck and dug his thumb against the piercing on the left, though the spike made the action more painful for him than it would be for Vasily. "Have you forgotten that?"

Vasily looked crestfallen. "*Nyet, ser.* I'm sorry. I didn't think you'd mind. You let me play with Silk before, and this was only a spanking, not sex."

Belphagor yanked him closer, bringing them face-to-face. "Only a spanking? Is that all they are to you? Do you think all we're doing is playing a game?"

"No!" Vasily squirmed under his steely gaze. "Not with you, Beli. I meant with *Silk*, it's nothing."

He and Vasily had begun with a spanking. Vasily had tried to cut his purse, and Belphagor had given the skinny young thief a thrashing to remember. It had turned out to be one Belphagor would never forget. That night, Vasily had become his, though it would be another year before he realized it. Belphagor had finally, truly fallen, bound to this demon as surely as if a serpentine chain passed through one of Vasily's piercings instead of the steel bar—a chain lodged with a hook in Belphagor's heart.

He steered Vasily roughly toward the bed. "On your knees. Face the cot." Alarmed enough, or penitent enough, Vasily obeyed without question. "Clasp your hands behind your head and bend over."

Vasily's long legs and the short height of the cot made it perfect for him to stretch over it and expose his reddened ass. Belphagor stared at the inflamed skin for a long time, struggling with unfamiliar emotion. He was angry with Vasily and angry with Silk. He felt betrayed, though he knew Vasily hadn't meant it that way. But how could Vasily not feel the special, sacred thing this was between them? How had Belphagor never managed to convey that?

He calmed his breathing and swallowed his irrational emotion. "How many times did he strike you?" He knew the brusque, dispassionate tone would provoke an involuntary response in Vasily. His heart would beat faster. Fear would settle in the pit of his stomach. And his cock would rise. Through Vasily's spread thighs, he could see evidence of the latter. For once, this evoked no similar response in himself.

"It's a birthday tradition." Vasily's voice was sullen and muffled against the cot. "One for every year. Sasha turned twenty-two so I got twenty."

"Twenty." Belphagor bent and stroked the marks, raising gooseflesh on Vasily's skin. "Twenty times you gave to someone else what is mine."

"I didn't think—"

"Silence!" He crossed to the vanity, and from the special drawer, he took the paddle reserved for actual discipline. Vasily had rarely needed it. "I've failed to enumerate certain rules that I took for granted you would follow. Let me make this one perfectly clear right now." He struck Vasily over one of the marks, a spot that was obviously bruised deep and had to sting after taking ten solid open-handed swats the night before. Vasily made a soft noise of discomfort against the blanket. "A bare-handed spanking is for no one but me to administer, unless I've ordered it." He struck the other side, and Vasily managed only a muffled grunt. "Does that hurt?"

"*Da, ser.*"

"Good." He struck both cheeks again with unrestrained force, and Vasily moaned with his lips shut tight. "For both your failure of judgment and my evident failure to make it clear what such discipline signifies to us both, I'm going to match the strikes you took without permission. And I promise this will be a lesson you remember."

It took only a few more swats before Vasily was unable to keep from crying out. When Belphagor had reached twenty, he added two more on each side before stepping back.

"Next time you try to sit, I imagine you'll remember whose ass that is."

"*Mne zhal.*" Vasily's characteristically gruff voice against the bedspread was a miserable whisper. "*Prostite menya.*"

"Forgive you?" Belphagor set the paddle aside and stroked a hand across the heat radiating from Vasily's penitent flesh. "Sweet boy. You need never be forgiven for an unintentional transgression. That's what the discipline is for. Now we both understand where we went wrong, and the lesson has been learned." Unintentional or not, it still stung to see someone else's handprints marking Vasily's skin. Belphagor took his coat from the back of the chair and pulled it on. "Get some rest. I have a few things I need to do."

Vasily had returned to catch up on his sleep before heading to a secret meeting to which he'd managed to secure an invite. Pretending to let Gaspard convince him Lebes would be a better ruler for demonkind had finally paid off. Gaspard was eager to introduce Vasily to what he called "enriching discourse." Vasily had meant to tell Belphagor all about it before grabbing a quick nap, but he hadn't considered that waltzing in sporting Silk's handprints would throw Belphagor for a loop.

And to say to Belphagor that it was only a spanking—he'd wanted to bite his tongue as soon as the words were out. To Belphagor, sex was the impersonal activity; spanking was intimacy. Vasily could have bent over the bar while every demon and angel in the Stone Horse lined up to have their way with him, and Belphagor wouldn't have cared, so long as Vasily wanted it. If he'd stopped to think—or been a little more sober—he would have realized it was something he'd never done with anyone else, and there was probably a reason.

He climbed into bed, lying on his stomach, but he was too awake for sleep. He'd hurt Belphagor—unintentionally but carelessly. And the knowledge stung worse than the spanking itself.

Belphagor still wasn't back by the time he had to head out. Vasily's attendance at the meeting was likely to put the angels off, so Gaspard had told him to arrive early. He wanted him to absorb what information he could while playing the part of his houseboy—something Vasily was sure Gaspard would prefer to be more than an act.

Gaspard greeted him with a kiss on each cheek, an intimate gesture he hadn't been afforded before, and provided him with a uniform. How Gaspard had managed to find one in his size, Vasily had no idea.

Gaspard briefly instructed him in how to behave as a houseboy: being seen and not heard was key. As the guests arrived, Vasily opened the door with his head bowed and stepped aside. The demons paid him no attention, as Gaspard had informed them of Vasily's role in advance, but the angels started visibly. These were not the sort who frequented the Stone Horse, nor were they like those he'd briefly encountered at Duke Elyon's affairs. They were true aristocrats from the upper echelon of society, along with a number of military Powers and even a Virtue from the Princedom of Aravoth.

Vasily found it difficult not to stare. He'd never seen a Virtue before. They seemed to be as different from the other orders as the elemental firespirits. The angel had snowy white skin with a luminous quality—not the glow of fire but a kind of sheen when the light caught it—shimmering silver eyes, and a stunning length of smooth platinum hair. He called himself Auria.

He was the only angel who smiled and nodded at Vasily in greeting, as if Vasily were nothing out of the ordinary. Auria moved with extraordinary grace, and his voice was as sexually indeterminate as the rest of him, including his long white gown. It reminded Vasily of the paintings of angels he'd seen in the cathedrals of the world of Man. Perhaps the painters had seen a Virtue once, though he couldn't fathom one falling.

Once the guests had been seated in the parlor, Vasily stood off to the aside to await instruction. He realized he'd been listening to Auria's voice without hearing his words until a startling phrase registered.

"Sefira must not carry this child to term."

One of the Powers leaned forward. "Surely, you're not suggesting—"

"I'm not suggesting anything." Auria smiled disarmingly. "I'm merely stating a fact. If the queen delivers an heir, there will be no support for Lebes's ascension. The Traditionalist mission will be rendered moot."

"We have no reason to believe it will be an heir. She's failed three times already."

"Are you willing to take that chance?" Auria smoothed his gown, his long, slender fingers mesmerizing. "Either way, swift action is imperative. We cannot expect Lebes to move against his brother without encouragement."

"And what is that supposed to mean?" asked another angel.

"He needs a compelling reason to believe that deposing Helison is vital for the good of Heaven. He must be made to see what comes of having sympathies toward the wrong sort of demon."

# CHAPTER NINE

Phaleg had always found Iriyan architecture fascinating. It was distinct from anything in Elysium. The little duchy had a quaintness to it, like a village from an earlier time, the Ereline Palace situated like a miniature fortress, with stone walls surrounding it. Yet the space where a gate might once have kept marauders out now welcomed visitors onto a broad palace courtyard from the marble setts of the highway beyond. Phaleg's coach wasn't challenged as they passed through. He supposed the likelihood of trouble coming in a supernal coach was slim.

Ruslan had watched with fascination through the window as they traveled, having seen little of Heaven, but as they drew close to the palace, he sat back primly with his hands in his lap. His role had been well rehearsed. The idea was to make it seem Soluzen had raised Ruslan in his household with the same expectations as his legitimate children.

The grand duke, who came out to meet them as they stepped down from the coach, bore a great resemblance to his elder brother, lacking only the beard. As Phaleg straightened from his bow, he saw Lebes was also a few inches taller.

"Welcome to Iriy." Lebes was gracious. "I trust your travel was pleasant?"

"Indeed, Your Supernal Highness. Nothing like the smooth marble of the Eastern Road."

"Ah, of course, you've been through Iriy before on your way to the academy in Asphodel. All roads lead to Elysium, as they say." Lebes glanced at his companions with interest. "My brother sent word you'd be coming with the tutor for Kae, but who else have we here?"

Soluzen stepped forward and bowed once more. "May it please Your Supernal Highness, upon His Supernal Majesty's advice, I've brought a handmaiden for the grand duchess to help in her confinement. Anzhela is a member of our household staff. Her family has been with us for generations, and I believe you'll find her capable and trustworthy."

Anzhela curtseyed, and Lebes nodded his approval as he looked her over. "Send my thanks to the principality, Major Phaleg. Very thoughtful of him. And this young man?"

Ruslan's graceful bow made it seem as if he'd been in the company of royalty all his life.

"My son Ruslan," said Soluzen.

Lebes lifted his eyebrows.

"His mother was a youthful dalliance of mine. He's been raised as a companion to my other boys, but as I'm sure you understand, his presence has become more difficult for my wife to tolerate as he grows older. With your permission, I present him to you as a companion for the little grand duke. He'll make a fine page."

Lebes's brow winkled in thought. "Come here, boy."

Ruslan stepped forward, and Lebes inspected him as one might a horse, opening his mouth to check his teeth and feathering his hands through the boy's hair. This latter action puzzled Phaleg until he recalled with a slight blush what Belphagor had told him about the parasites demons sometimes carried when they lacked access to proper sanitation.

Soluzen looked perturbed. "As I said, Your Supernal Highness, Ruslan has been raised in my household among my own boys."

Lebes dismissed Ruslan with a glance and nodded to Soluzen. "We all have our indiscretions, I suppose. I'm sure my son will enjoy the company of someone close to his age."

Phaleg let out the breath he'd been holding.

"My wife is confined to her bed at the moment," Lebes continued. "Physician's orders. She's had some swelling in her feet." He snapped his fingers, and a servant appeared. "Escort the young lady to Her Supernal Highness, and inform her the girl is at her disposal."

"Very good, sire." The servant bowed and turned toward the palace, and Anzhela fell into step behind him.

"My son, however, is anxiously awaiting your arrival." Lebes gestured to Soluzen. "Come. We'll see what he makes of your Ruslan." He inclined his head toward Phaleg as he headed inside, and Phaleg hurried to keep up. "Major Phaleg, will you dine with us? We're about to have tea."

"I'd be honored, Your Supernal Highness. Though I regret I must head back to Elysium afterward. I'm afraid the principality can't spare me any longer."

"No need for formalities, Major. Call me Lebes."

Inside the grand foyer, a young boy with wispy curls a shade pale of the hallmark of the House of Arkhangel'sk stood at attention. His gray-blue eyes widened as Ruslan came into view behind the tutor, and he stared with frank fascination.

"May I present my son, Grand Duke Kae." Lebes regarded him fondly, putting a hand on Kae's head. "This is your tutor, Master Soluzen. He's brought a companion for you." He glanced at Soluzen. "What was his name again?"

"Ruslan, Your Supernal Highness." Soluzen pushed the boy forward, and Ruslan bowed as he'd been instructed.

Kae stepped closer. "How old are you?"

Ruslan answered without hesitation. "Ten, Your Supernal Highness."

"Are you a demon?"

Ruslan glanced at Soluzen as if uncertain of his own status.

Lebes frowned at Kae. "What have I told you? Is that a polite term?"

"Sorry, sir." Kae cringed. "I meant Fallen."

"Ruslan is of mixed blood," said Lebes in a kinder tone. "So, yes, that makes him Fallen. Why don't you show him your rooms while I discuss your curriculum with Master Soluzen?"

Kae shrugged. "Come on, then." His tone was rather supernal, and he turned toward the corridor without waiting to see if Ruslan would follow.

Lebes seemed satisfied. "I think they'll get on excellently."

By the time tea was served, Lebes's prediction proved correct. Kae and Ruslan arrived at the table giggling, though Ruslan quickly silenced his laughter, shy in the elder grand duke's presence. Kae proudly showed his father the gift Ruslan had brought him: a lovely jade keepsake box. Phaleg couldn't imagine where Ruslan had obtained such an object, but he suspected he'd been picking up tricks from Belphagor. Wherever it had come from, Kae apparently adored it, and Lebes looked pleased that Ruslan had been so thoughtful.

Afterward, Phaleg looked in on Anzhela and found her helping Grand Duchess Tsirya with her layette. Tsirya paused in her embroidery and held out a hand to Phaleg as he bowed to her in the doorway.

"Major Phaleg, please come in." Her warmth was infectious. Queen Sefira had a tendency toward introversion, only letting down her guard to reveal her playful nature among close family, which had given her a reputation for dourness. It wasn't surprising that Lebes's wife was the more beloved in the princedom. "Thank you so much for bringing Anzhela to help me. We're getting along famously already, aren't we, dear?" She beamed at Anzhela, who sat on a stool beside the grand duchess's bed, and Anzhela nodded.

"It was the principality's idea," said Phaleg. "I can't take the credit."

"Ah, but you found the tutor for my son, and had you not, there would be no Anzhela for Helison to send." Her gray-blue eyes twinkled beneath the same fair curls as her son's as she took up her embroidery once more. "It was very kind of Master Soluzen to bring his boy here to keep my little Kae company. I'm afraid he hasn't many peers in Iriy, and with me confined to my bed, he's been rather lonely. He misses his little cousins."

"I'm sure they'll be glad to see him when you return to Elysium."

Tsirya patted her round belly. "That all depends on this little one. If he makes an early appearance, we may be delayed."

"Of course. Well, we hope to see you soon." Phaleg bowed. "It was a pleasure meeting you."

"And you, Major Phaleg. My brother-in-law is obviously well served by your loyalty."

The phrase struck him as unusual as he headed back downstairs. Had there been an implication she suspected him of planting spies on Helison's behalf?

At the bottom of the staircase, Lebes awaited him. "Major Phaleg, if you might pass along a message to my brother, I'd appreciate it."

He paused. "Certainly, my lord."

Lebes fixed him with a shrewd gaze. "Whatever it is he suspects me of, he needn't worry. I have never had any designs on the throne."

Phaleg paled, uncertain how to respond.

Lebes's smile was strained. "You have no idea how freeing it is *not* to be saddled with supernal responsibilities. I wouldn't trade what I have for anything."

"My lord, I don't think—"

"Don't be disingenuous, my dear fellow. I'm not offended Helison wants to keep an eye on me. His position isn't any easy one. I'd simply like to set his mind at ease if it's at all possible. I'm his loyal subject, as you are."

"Of course, my lord."

Phaleg pondered Lebes's response on the tedious journey back to the capital. He'd given no indication of being party to anything his supporters might be planning.

But as he drew closer to Elysium, his thoughts were less on the sons of the ruling house of Heaven and more occupied with a demon. Silk had essentially given him a command to report to him as soon as he arrived. And he wanted to keep Phaleg all night to do with as he pleased. By the time Phaleg reached the bridge over the Acheron to Raqia, he was trembling with anticipation and fear, imagining himself tied down—naked and at Silk's mercy, a sex toy for a demon whore.

Belphagor had mentioned nothing more about the spanking incident in the past week, and Vasily was afraid to broach the subject. Since Belphagor was behaving as if it hadn't happened, he supposed he'd have to do the same. Nonetheless, Belphagor seemed tense, though it appeared to have nothing to do with Vasily. He'd passed on the information he'd obtained from Gaspard's salon that at least some of Lebes's followers clearly intended harm to the queen. Perhaps carrying the burden of that knowledge without being able to do anything about it until Phaleg returned was weighing on Belphagor.

He had some kind of special wingcasting match planned for the evening, however, so Vasily was on his own. He headed to the Stone Horse, hoping to play with Silk—and to set out clear rules about what they could and couldn't do—but Phaleg had returned, and Silk had taken the night off. Gaspard hadn't yet made an appearance either, so Vasily hung about with the demons who were between clients, which turned out to be fortuitous. A number of them had engagements with anti-Helison sympathizers, deliberately arranged while Silk was away, which confirmed what Vasily had begun to suspect: Silk was unaware of these secret meetings. Belphagor would be happy to hear it.

Gaspard at last made his appearance, pleased to see Vasily, and was in the mood for something daring. He wanted to be pleasured beyond the confines of the Stone Horse for a change. The Brimstone seemed the safest place. The dark interior, drunken clientele, and the distraction of the games were the perfect cover for a toss-off beneath a table. Gaspard wanted the thrill of exposure without fear of truly being exposed.

When they arrived, a crowd had gathered around the master table, and Vasily saw with an unpleasant start that Belphagor sat opposite Kezef. Intently focused on their game, neither looked up. Vasily led Gaspard to a bench table below the front windows of the tavern, an ideal spot for not being seen while giving the feeling of being right out in the open. Why hadn't Belphagor told him he was playing that piece of shit? To keep him from worrying or getting pissed, Vasily supposed. Which was precisely what he was doing now, in alternating waves.

He tried to ignore them, but the gasps and hoots from the spectators at the end of each move made it difficult. Once their drinks arrived, Gaspard drew Vasily's hand beneath the table and guided him to his eager erection. Vasily unbuttoned the pants with deft fingers and closed his warm palm about the exposed cock. Gaspard covered his reaction with a quick sip of brandy.

"Looks like demons are placing wagers on the game your Belphagor is playing," Gaspard managed. Vasily stroked, and Gaspard gripped the edge of the table. "Perhaps we should lay odds."

"Easy odds." Vasily shrugged. "Belphagor always wins." He took a swig of his mead while he pumped his fist in Gaspard's lap.

Gaspard groaned softly and grabbed his drink again, only able to speak after he'd taken a large swallow. "All the more reason to lay— Oh, sweet Heaven." Sweat had broken out on his lip. "You have to let up. Someone will see."

"No one cares what we're doing over here. I guarantee it." Vasily slowed his motions. "Do you really want me to let up?"

Gaspard dug his hand into Vasily's thigh beneath the table. "Please, for the love of Heaven, no."

Vasily worked him expertly, and Gaspard grabbed his snifter and held it to his lips, moaning into it helplessly as Vasily's efforts paid off, but a loud cheer from the wingcasting tables drowned him out.

As Gaspard sank back with a relieved sigh, Kezef's voice carried across the den. "You keep playing like this, Belphagor, and I'll have your boy before the night is out."

By the time Phaleg arrived at the apartment, nervous excitement had wiped out any weariness he ought to feel from his trip. The older boys had taken the others out for the evening to practice their "thieving" skills in the Demon Market. Apparently, this was indeed something Belphagor had been teaching them. The flat was empty for the next few hours except for Phaleg and Silk.

Silk wasted no time, taking a length of rope from a secretary drawer. "I've been working on some knotting techniques." His tone was casual. "Take off your clothes so I can truss you."

Phaleg's heart pounded as he disrobed. Silk wore a long dressing gown in Vilonese fabric to match his name, red peonies blooming across a cream drape. Next to Silk's casual, almost regal elegance, Phaleg felt doubly exposed. It was impossible to be elegant or regal while standing in the middle of a sitting parlor completely in the buff, sporting a massive erection. Perhaps *massive* was a bit self-aggrandizing. Phaleg couldn't help but smile.

Silk frowned and paused in fussing with his ropes. "Something funny, Major?"

Phaleg's cock twitched visibly. "No, sir. Nothing funny."

Silk continued to frown for a moment before turning him about and wrapping the rope around his wrists in a figure eight. "Spread your legs."

Phaleg quickly obeyed, gasping as Silk passed both ends of the rope between his thighs and bound his cock and balls with a similar configuration.

"Uncomfortable?" asked Silk.

"A bit," Phaleg admitted. It also had him more than a little aroused.

Silk shrugged and brought the rope forward at waist level. When he tugged on it lightly, Phaleg made a noise between a yelp and a groan. The sensation was intense, but he couldn't decide whether it was pleasurable or horrible.

Silk continued his methodical weaving as if Phaleg's responses merely formed the basis of an interesting scientific observation. He fashioned a fancy knot below Phaleg's navel, crossed the two ends, and brought them around Phaleg's waist. With a jerk that made Phaleg's knees buckle, he pulled them tight.

After working his way up Phaleg's body with a series of elaborate knots, Silk made a final, thick mat knot over Phaleg's sternum. From Phaleg's vantage point, it looked like a rose. He'd seen this knot before—in fact, he'd seen them *all* before. Silk had gone to great lengths to learn the official knots of the Supernal Navy.

When Silk finished with his artistry, he pulled the whole thing tight once more at Phaleg's back, wrapped it through the bonds at his wrists, and yanked up, forcing his elbows out.

Silk stepped back to admire his work, letting his robe fall open to reveal his stiff cock in its anchor of dark curls. Phaleg instantly regretted his sharp inhalation; everything seemed to tighten at once.

The corner of Silk's mouth turned up while he stroked himself. "On your knees."

Phaleg obeyed, groaning as the motion tugged at the bonds around his genitals.

"If that's too tight, you're to tell me. You remember the word we agreed on?"

Phaleg nodded.

"Say it, so I know you remember."

"Arkhangel'sk," Phaleg managed.

"But you're not saying it because the rope is too tight."

"No, sir."

Silk pondered him for a moment. "Your servility pleases me, but it's a bit militaristic. I've decided you will call me 'milord.'"

"Yes, milord." Phaleg was shocked at himself. Calling a demon *sir* was bad enough, but implying a demon was worthy of the address of nobility was utter perversion. Phaleg looked down at his prick, bound in knots and standing at attention. He was so far beyond utter perversion it was almost laughable that mere words could unnerve him. The realization made him gasp as more blood rushed to his groin, and he looked up into Silk's lovely eyes. "Yes, milord," he said again, almost breathless. "Do what you want to me, milord."

Silk bit his lip and blinked rapidly, slipping out of character for a moment. He put his hand on Phaleg's head, holding himself in the other. "Swallow me."

Phaleg eagerly complied. Discovering that his bindings made it difficult to go at it with his usual enthusiasm, he surrendered himself to Silk's mercy and held still while Silk fucked his mouth, fingers twisting in Phaleg's hair for leverage.

Far too soon, Silk pulled out, and Phaleg grasped for him hungrily.

"I don't want to come yet," Silk explained. "I want to do more to you. We have until at least midnight before the boys return." He picked up Phaleg's clothes from the floor and headed for his bedroom, leaving him on his knees in the center of the parlor. "And you won't be needing these until tomorrow."

Phaleg shivered with delight, savoring the ache and tug of the rough fibers against his flesh. *All night*, Silk had promised. He'd really meant it.

Silk returned with a chain on a short lead, dropping it over Phaleg's head and then pulling it tight around his neck. Without giving him direction, Silk walked toward the bedroom, and Phaleg scrambled to his feet and followed before the chain collar could choke him, mesmerized by the way the dressing gown caressed Silk's pert ass.

When they'd reached the room, Silk pointed to the floor. "Kneel."

Phaleg dropped to his knees.

"Open your mouth."

Phaleg complied, a bit startled when Silk placed the lead between his teeth.

"You will hold the leash while you're at rest."

Phaleg bit down on it. He'd seen angels training their dogs similarly. He supposed he ought to feel humiliated and ashamed. But he'd begun to imagine Silk fucking him at last, bent over the end of the bed, and he didn't care what debasement preceded it. He would be used by a demon. Silk owned him, and he'd never been so happy in his entire life.

Silk reclined on the bed, letting his dressing gown fall open. The décor of the room was like Silk himself, all smooth lines and soft, draped fabrics, and slightly exotic. He looked like a painting by one of the angelic masters. Phaleg longed to touch his skin.

Silk played with himself, making Phaleg's mouth water. "You may have noticed the more aroused you are, the tighter the knots become around your balls. The knots are designed, in fact, to keep you erect." He patted the bed, smoothing his hand in a circle over the velvety purple bedspread. "Kneel here beside me so I can play with you."

Phaleg struggled to his feet and climbed onto the bed. Being without the use of his arms was more challenging than he'd expected. He knelt where Silk had directed, the lead still in his mouth, his ass resting on his heels.

"What would your men think if they saw you now?" Silk stroked his finger up the length of Phaleg's cock, and Phaleg could only moan helplessly around the leather strap. "Do you think they'd all want to have you in turns once they knew what you were?"

Phaleg gasped, the sharp intake of breath pulling every knot so tight it made him shudder.

Silk's eyes sparkled. "Ah, you *do* think of it, don't you? Trussed up and passed about, unable to fight it, unable to speak because they've put a gag in your mouth, taking it out only to fill it with dick and loads of come. No safeword for you, then, eh? You think about that when you pleasure yourself, don't you?"

Silk watched his reaction, and Phaleg tried to still his pounding heart. He'd been found out. With an unreadable expression, Silk rolled over onto his stomach, propped on his elbows. "Spread your legs."

Phaleg moved his thighs apart, tightening the rope about his scrotum. He was almost in an altered state now, as if he'd taken some drug. His body hardly felt like his own, and his cock was so engorged he thought he might come without being touched. But he desperately wanted to be touched.

He closed his eyes, breathing the way Belphagor had taught him as a means of enduring pain or endless teasing. His eyes flew open when he felt Silk's mouth on his balls. Silk smiled up at him, sucking them in one at a time, circling them with his tongue. Phaleg groaned and swayed, biting down on the strap in his mouth.

"I'd love to take you out on that lead," murmured Silk against his sensitive skin. "Make you follow me with it in your mouth like that so everyone knows I don't need to hold the leash to control you."

He moved his mouth to Phaleg's cock, sliding his lips down the length of it as he took him in. Phaleg moaned around the strap, fully at Silk's mercy while he went down on him for several agonizing, wonderful minutes. He pulled away when Phaleg was close to coming, and Phaleg groaned.

"Aw, poor dirty angelwhore." Silk rose onto his knees and pressed his groin against Phaleg's, letting their hard flesh rub together. He moved his hands over Phaleg's skin, stroking his shoulders and arms, caressing his abs between the knots, running over his hips to grab him tight. "You can't come yet. You're my toy. I want to play with you." He climbed off the bed and went to his wardrobe. "Bend over with your forehead on the bed and your ass in the air. Let's see what I have in here."

Phaleg got into position, his pulse quickening as he wondered what Silk might do to him.

"We can make a bit of noise after all." Silk returned with whatever he'd been searching for. "Since the boys aren't home." Without warning, he struck both cheeks in one blow with something thin and stinging. *The cane.* Silk struck him again, and Phaleg cried out around the strap, his cock throbbing in its bonds. "Spit that out. I'd like you to count the strokes." He tapped the cane against the inflamed stripes he'd made while Phaleg dropped the leash. "When I strike you, you will count, followed by 'Thank you, milord. I deserve this, milord.'" The cane moved away from his skin, and Phaleg braced for the blow as he heard it hiss through the air.

"One!" he cried. "Thank you, milord. I deserve this, milord."

Silk smoothed his palm across Phaleg's throbbing flesh. "That's actually three. I thought they taught you how to count in your fancy schools." The cane struck again.

"Four!" Phaleg gasped. "Thank you, milord! I deserve this, milord!"

"That's better." Silk continued, while Phaleg soldiered on with his counting. By the time they'd reached ten, he was groaning out his thanks between hitched breaths.

"What a marvelous color. You're going to bruise so beautifully." Silk tossed down the cane and touched Phaleg's hands, stroking his fingers. "No numbness, I hope?"

"No, milord," Phaleg panted.

Silk climbed up behind him, and Phaleg's heart beat faster at the thought of how Silk's cock would feel inside him while the stripes of the cane burned on his skin. He pictured his men watching while Silk pumped in and out of him, and shivered with the thrill and horror of the idea.

But Silk rolled him over and wrapped his arms around him, rocking them onto their sides. He bucked lightly against Phaleg, making the rope twist and tug. "I could torture you for hours and then fuck your mouth until I come and make you get back down on the floor with your leash in your mouth without allowing you satisfaction. Make you stay there all night while I sleep and use you again in the morning."

Phaleg groaned softly. Part of him wished Silk would do it.

"Couldn't I?"

"Yes, milord."

"And you'd love it, wouldn't you, you filthy little pervert?"

Phaleg moaned. "Yes, milord."

Silk squeezed Phaleg tight against him, bringing their mouths together, and kissed him as he had the last time they'd been together. Phaleg was slightly alarmed at how good this felt, how soft and sweet Silk's lips were, how his tongue tasted of Phaleg's own cock, and how Phaleg didn't want to let go of it. It was one thing to derive pleasure from his debasement, but this—it filled him with need and desire and longing that an angel shouldn't have for a demon. *Couldn't* have. It made his heart ache.

Silk let go of his mouth and whispered, "What do you want?"

"Milord?"

"Tell me what you want, my dirty angelwhore. I want to give you pleasure."

Phaleg closed his eyes and leaned his forehead against Silk's shoulder. "Please, milord." He was almost ashamed of what he wanted now that he had to say it aloud. It was different when he was being used without being asked. Admitting his desire made him feel more naked than he did in disrobing, more vulnerable than being immobilized in a garment of rope. "Please. I want you to fuck me." His body prickled with anticipation. Now Silk would take him the way he longed to be taken.

But Silk had gone still. And quiet. Too quiet. Phaleg was afraid to open his eyes. Had he gone too far after all? Did Silk not want him that way?

Silk withdrew his arms and rolled onto his back, and Phaleg groaned inwardly. *Damn it.* That wasn't what Silk had meant. He'd been expecting Phaleg to ask to be beaten or forced to suck him off.

When Silk spoke at last, the words threw him completely. "Did Belphagor tell you to ask for that?"

Phaleg opened his eyes, baffled. "Belphagor?" Silk was regarding him with cool mistrust. "Why would Belphagor tell me anything?"

"Do you think I don't know you're using me for your own pleasure?" Silk jumped up from the bed and paced away from him. "You come to dip your prick in the filthy waters of Raqia and get your rocks off like the rest of the angel rabble. It's not a fucking amusement park."

Phaleg struggled to sit up, mystified at this sudden change of mood. He'd obviously asked for the wrong thing, but Silk's response made no sense. "Silk, what did I do?"

"Don't you mean '*milord*, what did I do'?" Silk uttered the words in a mocking nasal tone that made Phaleg's face burn.

"Stop it. Untie me."

"What's the matter? You only like it when the humiliation suits your fetish? So long as the demons are the real dirty whores?"

Phaleg jerked at the ropes, sweat breaking out on his forehead as he began to panic. And then he remembered. "*Arkhangel'sk.*"

Silk froze, and the color drained from his face. The mocking contempt had gone out of his eyes, and he looked as frightened and ashamed as Phaleg felt. He wrapped his dressing robe around himself and tied the sash, coming to Phaleg's side without a word to work the knots loose. It took far longer to undo his handiwork than it had to create it. Or maybe it only seemed longer with the sick lump churning in Phaleg's stomach.

The rope around his cock and balls had to come last since Silk had done it up first, which had the unfortunate effect of keeping him hard when he was no longer mentally aroused.

Silk freed him at last and handed him his clothes. "It's probably best you don't come back." The words were devastating, despite the fact that Phaleg had made up his mind he was done with Silk once and for all. There was something in Silk's demeanor that didn't fit his sudden burst of unerotic cruelty.

Phaleg pulled on his pants, grateful he hadn't worn his dress leathers, which would have taken time to work himself into. "Are you going to tell me what I did?" He needed to know, even if they were through. This was too unsettling.

"You didn't do anything, Phaleg." His name sounded strange on Silk's tongue. "I obviously can't do this."

An unexpected surge of anger took hold of him. "'This' what? Caning me? Or fucking me?"

Silk's eyes flashed a warning, and he drew in a hissing breath through his teeth.

"That's it, isn't it? I'm good enough to be your pathetic clown, but not good enough to fuck." He'd never spoken like this to anyone before. It was alarming. And freeing.

Silk looked shaken. "Shut up."

"I'll shut up as soon as you admit it. In your twisted conception of Host and Fallen, you think you're superior to me because you weren't born to privilege. That because I was, I deserve nothing of what I have. You think of me what you think of all angels, that I'm pampered and simple and weak. The idea of actual physical intimacy with me fills you with scorn and revulsion."

"Phaleg—" Silk had taken a step back from him, arms stiff and hands clenched at his sides. "You have no idea what you're talking about. Go back to your safe, sterile world."

Without thinking, Phaleg advanced, as if Silk were an opponent in a fencing bout. "Not until you tell me why you won't fuck me. Tell me to my face you think you're too good for me."

"Too good?" Silk had backed into the bureau, and he gripped the edges of it behind him. "What the hell are you talking about? What is *good* about that?" He was shouting suddenly, only he didn't seem angry as much as he seemed afraid, as though Phaleg had cornered him.

Phaleg stopped in front of Silk. "What do you mean, what's good about it? About what?"

"*Fucking!*" Silk hurled the word at him as if he'd vomited it, his hands white against the bureau and his whole body tense with resistance.

The realization struck Phaleg that his outburst about Silk's prejudice against his privileged status as an angel was absurd. Silk had been sold to a brothel as a child. Phaleg truly had no idea what he was talking about.

He put his hand over one of Silk's, and Silk flinched. "Did someone hurt you?"

Silk laughed, the sound verging on hysteria. "Did someone hurt me? Who do you think you're talking to?" Though his demeanor radiated scorn, there was an edge of terror in his laughter, and he looked ready to bolt.

Phaleg dropped the shirt and jacket he still clutched and wrapped both hands around Silk's arms. "You can trust me. I'd never hurt you."

Silk began to shake. "You don't know me. You don't know anything about me."

"So you keep telling me." Phaleg enveloped him in his arms, and Silk collapsed against him, knees buckling so violently they both slid downward to the floor. Silk sat roughly against the bureau drawers with his knees drawn up, while Phaleg sank to his. "It's all right. You don't have to say anything. The safeword is yours too." He dared to kiss Silk's damp lips, tasting the salt on them.

Silk stared at him as if he couldn't quite comprehend what was happening. "Why aren't you leaving?"

"You said I could stay. All night. And I mean to." He took Silk by the hand and drew him to his feet. "Come on. Let's just sleep." Silk followed him to the bed with a look of bemusement, and they climbed into it, Silk in his dressing gown and Phaleg in his traveling pants. Phaleg curled himself around Silk and held on to him.

Their roles had reversed, and yet they hadn't. He still longed for Silk to abuse him, and the memory of being Silk's helpless toy made his skin tingle. Not to mention the throbbing marks from the cane. He winced as his pants chafed against the stripes.

Silk noticed the motion. "You all right?"

Phaleg shrugged. "My ass is on fire." He could feel Silk's satisfaction in the set of his shoulders.

"Good." Silk pulled Phaleg's arms tighter around himself, his next words almost too quiet to hear. "Dirty angelwhore."

# CHAPTER TEN

G aspard seemed to have noticed nothing at the master table, which Vasily took as a testament to his own skill. He was happy to slip out of The Brimstone once he'd recovered enough to stand, and Vasily managed to maintain a somewhat normal demeanor as they walked arm in arm toward Gaspard's cab. It was a common enough occurrence in Raqia for men who had been drinking to be chummy and unlikely to make anyone think twice, but it was rather daring for Gaspard.

"Why do you let him treat you that way?" Gaspard asked as they reached the conveyance. Apparently, he'd noticed more than Vasily had guessed.

"What way?"

"Don't be coy. He was betting you, wasn't he?" Gaspard shook his head. "First he auctions you off, now he uses you like currency in a game."

Vasily unhooked his arm from Gaspard's. "*You* offered to play him for me, if you recall."

"So I did. That was in poor taste. I apologize." Gaspard opened the door of the cab and stepped up. "You shouldn't go back to his bed after that display. Come home with me. No services required, just a place to sleep."

He wouldn't normally have accepted, but the more he thought about it—Belphagor betting him was bad enough, but to *Kezef*, of all people. He was livid and humiliated. And hurt. He took Gaspard's hand and climbed into the carriage.

The game went on all night. Kezef confounded his influence, and Belphagor blocked Kezef's numerous attempts to rig the game through whatever magical charm he was invoking. It was exhausting playing on two levels with equal concentration devoted to each. Kezef also played very well, magic aside, and for every hand Belphagor won, Kezef would win the next. But there was no way Belphagor was losing this game.

As the darkness began to pale to gray through the windows facing the street, one of the onlookers proposed they play a final sudden-death round to decide the winner, and the rest of the crowd took up the call. Nearly every demon in the house had wagered facets on the outcome, and they wanted to go home to their beds.

Kezef studied him as he shuffled the deck. "I'm game if you are."

Belphagor called for another pint of mead and downed half of it. Belching, he set the glass on the side table. "If you think you can abide by the outcome, deal the cards."

Because the rules of wingcasting allowed for any number of cards to be maintained in a single hand after the initial seven were dealt, part of the art of bluffing included taking cards one didn't need. It was a careful balancing act. Take too many with no obvious connection and you might tip your hand. Adding influence to the mix could only take you so far. With an audience present, tricks like altering the way the die landed and palming cards became more difficult to pull off.

But Belphagor couldn't afford to lose this round.

Since their tournament had begun, he'd been training Kezef with every hand he played to read him incorrectly—inventing a false tell, missing a call deliberately when he knew it wouldn't affect the outcome of a round—just enough to let Kezef become overconfident. Kezef had been playing an invented opponent for the entire tournament. Now to confound him by letting him play against the true master of the game.

Belphagor dealt, and as the spectators held their breath in anticipation, every card dropping onto the table was audible. After perusing his cards intently, Kezef set them facedown, cracked his knuckles, and picked up the die. The snap of it against the marble corner and Belphagor's call were eclipsed by a sudden uproar from the front of the tavern.

Belphagor tried to ignore it. He couldn't afford any distractions. Maintaining an acute awareness of Kezef's demeanor without seeming to, he examined his hand and selected his discard just as the commotion out front spilled into the gaming room. The table was nearly upended as demons jostled to get to the rear exit. The Brimstone was being raided.

Kezef, who had been as intently focused on the game as Belphagor, rose calmly and stepped out of the way, still holding his cards to his chest. His eyes were on Belphagor's hands to ensure he didn't try anything during the distraction.

Shrieks rang out from the entrance. The Ophanim had arrived on the heels of the supernal officers, and demons were being arrested. The game was over.

"We'll have a rematch," said Kezef. Belphagor had opened his mouth to say the same. He nodded, and they laid their cards on top of the deck in near unison.

He recognized an officer marching into the gaming room as one of the angels he'd solicited two winters ago. It had been part of his plan to get Vasily back after he'd been abducted by Duke Elyon. It was after Belphagor had serviced the angel along with Phaleg and another officer that Phaleg had stayed behind in the rented room and fallen from grace—straight onto his knees, with his mouth full of Belphagor.

Belphagor rose and stepped in front of the angel. "Lieutenant Phanuel."

Phanuel stopped short with a scowl. "How do you know my name, demon?"

"I've made your acquaintance."

Phanuel sniffed. "I highly doubt that."

"Two years ago. In the Demon Market. With your friend Phaleg."

Phanuel's face went white, followed swiftly by a brilliant shade of red. His gaze darted about the room, likely assessing whether any of his fellows were within hearing range. "I could have you arrested for harassment of an officer of the Supernal Army."

Belphagor raised an eyebrow. "For saying hello to you? You mistake my intent. I merely want to know what's going on. Why are these demons being arrested?"

"On suspicion of conspiracy to incite a rebellion. Authorized by Major Phaleg, in fact."

So Phaleg was stirring the hornet's nest because Belphagor hadn't been stirring it enough himself. He kept his expression neutral, but they were going to have words. Not only would it set back any reasonable hope for the peaceful demonstration Phaleg envisioned, but it was already putting demons in danger, when Phaleg had promised to ensure their safety.

Phanuel took a clipboard from under his arm. "What's your name, demon?"

"Belphagor." He bowed extravagantly. "The one and only."

Phanuel scrutinized the clipboard, running his finger down a list of names, and then frowned with apparent disappointment. "You're not a suspect. Yet."

Belphagor shrugged. "Ah, well. Rebellion isn't what I normally incite."

Phanuel blushed again and hurried off to supervise the roundup.

When Belphagor turned back to the wingcasting table, Kezef had gone. Just as well. He'd seen enough of him for one night. And it was no longer night.

Frantic pounding on his bedroom door woke Silk from a dream in which Phaleg had been the principality and Silk, his queen. It had been absurd and delightful. His near breakdown the night before rushed back to him as the pounding came again. He wanted to return to his dream and to wearing silk corsets and velvet gowns, to feel as if he deserved Phaleg's arms around him.

"Silk? Are you in there?" It was Tilli, the eldest boy. Silk started with guilt as he realized he'd gone to sleep without waiting to make sure the boys arrived home safely.

He pried himself from Phaleg's sleepy embrace and jumped up, tying the sash on his dressing gown before he threw open the door. "Tilli? What's wrong? Is everyone okay?"

"It's the Stone Horse. They're raiding it again."

*Damn those bloody angels.*

Phaleg, now wide awake, came to his side. "Raiding it? Under whose authority?"

Tilli scowled at Phaleg. "Yours, of course."

"*Mine?*" Phaleg met Silk's questioning gaze with an adamant shake of his head. "I haven't authorized anything. I haven't even been back to the palace yet to let the principality know I've returned. How could I have authorized a raid?"

Tilli crossed his arms over his chest. "The angels say you did."

It wouldn't be the first time Phaleg had raided one of his own brothels, but Silk decided to reserve judgment. There had to be some explanation. "Thanks, Till. I'll take care of it. Everyone else okay? You boys didn't get mixed up in anything, did you?"

"Everyone's fine. They're watching through the attic windows."

"Go back and join them, then." Silk gently prodded him out and closed the door before going to the wardrobe and pulling out his best suit. Whoever had authorized it, he wasn't going to stand for his boys being rounded up like common street whores.

Phaleg gathered the rest of his clothes. "If you're going over there, I'm going with you."

Silk paused in shimmying into his pants. "You can't show up there with me. Do you want to lose your commission?"

"They don't have to know I came from next door with you."

Silk shook his head, slipping into his white shirt and hurriedly fastening the pearl buttons. "If it's anything like last time, they'll be rounding them up in the street. They'll see you, and they'll know exactly where you came from, especially in those wrinkled pants. Stay put until they've cleared out."

Phaleg watched him dubiously, and when Silk looked about for his socks and shoes, Phaleg fetched them and knelt to put them on him. Silk stroked his hair, touched and yet uneasy that Phaleg showed him such deference after he'd lost control again. Why the hell wasn't Phaleg running the other way? After Phaleg helped him into his jacket, Silk drew him close and kissed him. He couldn't help it. It was foolish. Angels didn't have feelings for demons. This could only end badly. But his heart wouldn't listen.

At the Stone Horse, things were worse than he'd feared. Several patrons knelt in the street in the custody of angelic officers, and all of his boys were lined up outside in various states of undress. A writ citing some archaic anti-soliciting law that was obvious bullshit was being nailed to the door, declaring the brothel's business illegal. There were a dozen houses of ill repute in the Demon District, and the law had never been invoked for any of them.

"What are the charges against these gentlemen?" Silk demanded. "No one has been 'soliciting.' All of our clientele come to us in need of custom services."

The angel in charge spat on the ground. "*Gentlemen*. You have some nerve applying that term to a bunch of whores and perverts." He showed Silk a list of names. Most were patrons, but three of his boys were on it. "Your whorehouse is shut down. Your stable of 'stallions' can go back to doing back-alley business. They aren't worth the bother of arresting, but I've been authorized to bring in the names on this list for conspiracy to incite rebellion against the Crown. Now move aside unless you plan to join them."

Silk stepped back to the curb where the rent boys were lined up. It was far too cold out for them to be standing in this weather with so little covering. He took off his suit jacket and put it around the shoulders of Sasha, who wore nothing but his drawers.

Sasha drew it tight around himself. "Thanks. They wouldn't let us grab our clothes."

"Bastards." Silk tucked his hands under his arms.

"I warned Arkady about doing that kind of business here, but he wouldn't listen."

"What kind of business?"

"Passing information for those 'liberation' types for extra facets. As if angels are ever going to do anything for us."

Silk narrowed his eyes and lowered his voice. "You mean to tell me Arkady is actually guilty of what he's being accused of?"

Sasha shrugged. "If that amounts to 'conspiring to incite rebellion,' then yes. Apparently, that officer you used to spank has had a spy here ever since the last raid to see if you were setting up the meetings. Good thing you kicked that little fascist to the curb."

The feeling he'd been punched in the gut was so strong that Silk nearly clutched his stomach. Phaleg had been spying on him? The momentary feeling of safety he'd had in his arms last night dissolved like a sculpture made of sugar in an autumn rain. How could Silk have been such a fool? He glanced up at the apartment. Phaleg's silhouette was visible at the attic window.

The accused conspirators were prodded to their feet, and the three demons who'd been consorting with them were dragged forward for the march of shame to Elysium.

"The rest of you, clear out," barked the officer in charge. "You're through doing business here."

"This is my building," Silk objected, though technically, it belonged to Phaleg. "If I want to let them sleep here, I have every right."

The angel curled his lip. "Suit yourself. But this property is under surveillance, and if any further business continues here, you'll all be rounded up and shipped to the mines in Eastern Zevul. And that notice had better stay in place." He shoved a copy of the writ at Silk and strutted away.

Folding the notice and stuffing it into his pocket, Silk headed inside with the others, who were visibly discouraged. "Don't worry." He fabricated a confident air. "We'll figure something out." His thoughts, however, were preoccupied with Phaleg's betrayal, and he avoided going back up to the apartment until one of the boys came to see if he was all right.

He said nothing in front of the boys, waiting until he and Phaleg were alone in his room. Phaleg reached for him, but Silk took a step back.

"Is everyone all right?"

"*Is everyone all right.* That's a very interesting question, Phaleg."

He flinched at the use of his proper name. "What's wrong?"

"What's wrong is that you've apparently been spying on me. That you suspected me of being behind a conspiracy against your precious principality."

The color drained from Phaleg's face. "Shit."

"*Shit.* That's your response."

Phaleg put his hands into his pockets. "Stop repeating everything I say back to me."

"Then stop saying stupid things!" Silk turned away and folded his arms on top of the bureau, staring at his reflection: a demon fool who'd allowed an angel to humiliate him instead of humiliating the angel. "You got the Stone Horse shut down for good."

"*What?* Silk, I swear to you, I knew nothing about the raid this morning. I never authorized anyone to shut you down."

"Then what did you authorize? You haven't denied having me spied upon. Or suspecting me of sedition against the Supernal Crown."

"Silk . . ."

"Did you or didn't you have me spied on?" Silk met his eyes in the mirror.

Phaleg ran his fingers through his fair curls and sighed. "Yes, I did. There have been threats made against the supernal family that couldn't be ignored. I asked Belphagor to keep an eye on what was happening here."

"Belphagor?" Silk whirled about.

"I didn't know what else to do. I knew he'd be discreet."

"You could have spoken to me!"

Phaleg folded his arms. "We weren't exactly on speaking terms at the time."

"Is that what this is about? I humiliated you, so you decided to take revenge?"

"*No*. This wasn't about you. Please believe me. I wanted Belphagor to tell me you weren't involved."

Silk resisted the urge to fly at him and scratch out his eyes. "And if I had, if I'd been doing a little side business setting up meetings for liberationists, I'd be on my way to Palace Square to be hanged right now."

"No one's going to be hanged. It's the supporters of Grand Duke Lebes who've made the threats. I needed to show the principality he couldn't trust—"

"Couldn't trust whom?"

Phaleg swallowed. "Demons."

"Get out."

"You don't understand—"

"Get OUT!" Silk sprang forward, propelled by fury, and Phaleg took a step back with a look of alarm. "Are you an imbecile? Take your precious angelic ass out of this *demonic* apartment. And stay out of the fucking Demon District. Go find yourself a lily-white, gilded, squeaky-clean officer to fuck you in the ass."

Phaleg's expression had gone stony and supernal. He picked up his coat from the bed and let himself out without another word.

Silk slammed the bedroom door and turned around to push back against it, seizing his hair at the roots. He wanted to tear it out, wanted to beat himself for being such a pathetic fool. He slammed his head back against the door and then slumped to the ground with tears springing to his eyes. But it wasn't the throbbing in his skull that had stunned him, it was the twisting in his gut and the sharp ache in his ribs. It sure as hell wasn't his heart.

Vasily stretched under the soft sheets in Gaspard's guest bed, relishing the feel of the expensive fabric slipping over his bare skin and his morning erection. But what he'd heard at The Brimstone the night before came back to him, swiftly diminishing it. He sat up, swinging his legs over the side of the bed and gripping the mattress. Maybe he'd misunderstood somehow, misinterpreted Kezef's words. Kezef was a conniving bastard, after all. His gut, however, said he'd understood perfectly. He wondered if Belphagor had "lost" him last night.

Vasily gripped the sheet beneath him more tightly and felt it rip. *Shit*. He'd have to reimburse Gaspard. But whatever the outcome of Belphagor's disgusting "game," he damned well wasn't going to present himself to Kezef to be violated. They could both go fuck themselves.

Not wanting to go home, he opted for Silk's place. Gaspard was reluctant to see him go, as though he'd imagined this had been the start of something more. He kissed Vasily on the cheek with far greater intimacy than he'd demonstrated before, making Vasily a little uncomfortable. Had he inadvertently led Gaspard to believe their association was something more than professional? He'd have to make things clear to him next time they met.

But when he arrived at the apartment and heard the news about the raid, he forgot all about Gaspard. He hovered inside Silk's bedroom door while Silk sat on the edge of the bed looking defeated. "Why would Phaleg raid the place again?"

Silk narrowed his eyes. "What do you mean *again*? You knew it was him behind it before?"

Vasily cringed. "I—I'm just assuming—"

"*Ruby*." The ice-hard voice silenced Vasily's stuttering. Silk searched Vasily's eyes, his expression betrayed. "You were the spy, weren't you?"

Vasily rubbed at his arms, wishing he could disappear into the floor. "Belphagor asked me to keep an ear out."

"Did you give Phaleg a list of names?"

Vasily shook his head. "No. I mean, Phaleg was away. I told Bel . . . phagor." His voice fizzled out in a deflated rumble.

"Oh, Ruby. How could you?" Silk looked like he might cry.

"It wasn't to hurt you, Silk."

Unshed tears brightened his gray eyes. *Damn it.*

Vasily went to him, sinking to his knees beside the bed. "I'm so sorry. I should have told Bel no."

"Oh, hell, Ruby. How could you possibly have told Belphagor no?" He swiped at his eyes, his expression hard. "I suppose Phaleg put him in a tight spot."

Vasily rubbed Silk's arm. "Where *is* Phaleg? Wasn't he with you?"

Silk's arm rippled with tension. "He was. He spent the whole night here, acting as if nothing was going on. Taking from me, like the selfish angel he is. He had the gall to act surprised when the raid went down."

"Are you sure he was behind it?"

"Who else would have been? He was spying on me, using my own friends to do it. Anyway, the officer in charge of the raid confirmed it." Silk pressed both palms against the ridge of his brow. "But that's not the worst of it." Vasily waited while Silk remained silent for a moment, scrubbing his hands down over his face before he went on. "The Stone Horse is closed. We're done."

Vasily's stomach tightened. "What? What do you mean? How can it be closed?"

"Phaleg's men—they brought a writ of prohibition. Claimed the brothel's activities were illegal. The writ's posted out front. If a single patron steps through that door, we'll all be sent to the mines."

Vasily let out a low growl. So that was why it had seemed so quiet. Even this early in the day, there were always a few customers.

"All those demons were depending on me." Silk's shoulders slumped. "Things have gotten bad on the street, and this was their only safe haven. They're down there right now waiting for me to come back and tell them it was all a misunderstanding and they still have jobs. And a home."

"Belphagor won't let this happen."

Silk stared at him with disbelief. "Won't let it happen? It's happened, Ruby. It's done. And you and Belphagor helped. Without facets coming in, I can't pay Belphagor his rent. And as much as he'll probably protest that I don't need to pay, that he'll keep me and the boys here, what am I now? A washed-up, *used-up* sissy whore at twenty-two."

"I thought you were twenty-one." Vasily cringed at the black glare Silk gave him. "You're not washed up *or* used up. Don't say that."

"You're impossibly naïve. Why is everyone I know impossibly naïve?" Silk shook his head with disgust. "It's not my problem if you can't deal with reality. I might as well pack up and head for outer Zevul on my own. Maybe I can play the boy for those fucking pedophiles we got shipped out there."

Vasily had to curl his fists at his sides to keep from boxing him. But before he could tell Silk exactly what he thought about that nonsense, a knock came at the door, and Belphagor entered without waiting for an answer. He glanced from Vasily to Silk and back again as if to ask Vasily whether they'd spent the night together. Vasily was still on his knees. He started to edge himself up onto the mattress and then decided Belphagor could bite himself.

"I heard about the raid, and I came straight over. The Brimstone was raided too."

"The Brimstone?" Vasily gaped, forgetting he was pissed. "When did that happen?"

"Early this morning, around the same time as the raid on the Horse, I gather." Belphagor regarded Silk, who still hadn't said a word. "Are you all right?"

"You mean why haven't I been dragged through the streets as an accomplice? Well, surprise, Prince of Tricks, I had no idea what had been going on at the Stone Horse right under my nose." He glared at Vasily. "*Any* of it." He rose, tightening the sash on his dressing gown. "If you'll excuse me, I need to pack."

"Pack?" Belphagor threw a baffled glance at Vasily. "Where are you going?"

Silk began opening drawers and tossing things onto the bed. "With the Stone Horse closed, I'll have to find somewhere else to peddle myself."

"Closed?" Belphagor put a hand on his arm to stop him, and Silk jerked from his grasp with a dangerous look. "Sorry. Please—slow down a minute and tell me what's going on."

"What's going on is that you and your self-righteous angel got your own brothel shut down. Congratulations."

"That doesn't make any sense. Phaleg had it closed?"

Silk smirked. "How telling. You recognized him from the description without missing a beat. He ordered the raid, and the raid came with a writ of prohibition." He picked up a wrinkled sheet of parchment from the bureau and handed it to Belphagor, who perused it with a frown.

"When did Phaleg get back?"

"Last night. But you knew that already. You gave him the names Vasily provided."

Belphagor's head shot up. "No, I didn't. I haven't spoken with him."

"Don't treat me like I'm stupid. Vasily came by last night, and I told him I was busy with Phaleg. He wouldn't have kept that from you."

Vasily cleared his throat, but Belphagor said it first. "Vasily wasn't with me last night. I thought he spent the night with you." He met Vasily's eyes with his "wingcasting face" firmly in place.

Vasily crossed his arms. "I slept at Gaspard's." He wasn't about to offer him anything more. Let Belphagor think what he liked. Let him imagine Vasily bent over a fancy chaise longue, taking it up the ass from Gaspard all night long for all he cared.

"I see." Belphagor glanced at Silk, who'd taken a satchel from his wardrobe and was filling it with clothes. "Stop packing, damn it. Please. I'm going to get to the bottom of this, and we are *not* giving up the Stone Horse. There's no law against prostitution."

Silk shrugged. "Writ says there is. 'Public solicitation.' I don't see how the inside of a brothel is public, but I guess if anyone can enter . . ."

"Public solicitation." Belphagor had that calculating expression. "There may be a way around this. Promise me you won't do anything rash. Stay put until I have a chance to mull this over."

Silk shrugged again and sank into the pile of clothing. "Mull all you want. I don't have anywhere to go anyway. I can't leave them—my Lost Boys—until they have a new situation somewhere. They've been through too much."

"They will *not* need a new situation. I'll figure this out. Trust me."

"Trust you?" Silk shook his head, incredulous. "Belphagor, go away."

The walk back to The Brimstone was tense. Vasily was obviously furious with him for reasons that had nothing to do with Silk, and Belphagor had no idea what they were. He tried to think of something to say that wouldn't seem like jealousy of Gaspard, but Vasily broke the silence.

"So are you still master of the game?" There was a snide tone to the question.

Belphagor was careful with his answer. "The game was interrupted by the raid. We'll have a rematch."

"Well, that's good, then. No need for me to pack my things just yet."

"Pack your things?" Belphagor slowed his steps. "Where are *you* going?"

"Anywhere, Belphagor." Vasily stopped to deliver his name with a growl that made it clear Belphagor was in hot water. "Anywhere but here, where I'm nothing but currency in your game."

*Oh, crap.* He considered playing stupid—but he'd already done that. "Vasya, listen—"

"*Listen?*" The ground almost rumbled under their feet. "Now you want to talk to me? You cavalierly bet me, like a *thing*, without so much as bothering to tell me you're playing a tournament against *Kezef*, of all demons! And now I'm supposed to listen to you?"

"I did not bet you cavalierly."

"Ha!" The heat that came off him as he expelled the word could have singed Belphagor's eyebrows.

"I didn't have a choice. Kezef put the lives of the girls from the Fletchery on the line."

The flame crackling in Vasily's pupils faltered. "The girls?"

"He claims to know what's happened to them and is holding the information as his wager."

Vasily paced in a circle. "Goddamn him. But you *bet* me, Belphagor. To *Kezef*."

"I'm sorry you had to hear that from him, but it's not as dire as it sounds. He promised all you'd have to do is show up at his place, and it would be your choice whether you wanted to stay for the night and abide by his rules. He thinks he'd be irresistible to you."

Belphagor held up his hand as Vasily started to form an angry retort. "But one thing I've tried to teach you at the tables is that I never play a game I'm not certain I'll win. And I will *never* lose you. Do you understand me? You are *mine*, and I would never let anyone else have you without your consent. Certainly not Kezef. You should know that by now. Or don't you trust me after all?"

Vasily blinked, the fury abating somewhat, but his expression was troubled. "It's a two-way street. You promised to tell me the truth instead of keeping things from me because you think you know best."

Belphagor blanched. Vasily was right. He'd known it was a violation of their contract with one another, but he'd assumed he wouldn't get caught. "*Shit*. As usual, I shut you out after I'd promised not to." He ran his fingers through the spiked tips of his hair. "*Fuck*. What the hell is wrong with me?"

They started walking again, and Vasily kept his head down, hands in tight fists in his pockets.

Belphagor cursed himself. It was little wonder Silk had lost confidence in him. He couldn't keep from fucking up long enough to maintain the trust of his boy. The door of communication had to remain open. He'd said so to Vasily himself. And yet he'd—

He stopped in his tracks. "That's it."

Vasily eyed him as if he'd gone soft in the head. "What's it?"

"The door. Come on." Belphagor grabbed Vasily's hand. "We have to go back."

"What are you talking about?"

"Shhh, I have to work the problem." He pulled Vasily along with him back to The Boudoir, going over the idea in his head, while Vasily sighed with exasperation, the heat from his exhalations warming the back of Belphagor's neck. The idea was absurdly simple, but it would work.

He took the stairs two at a time and pounded on the door so hard that Silk was holding a shoe when he peered out, heel raised, ready to strike.

"Belphagor? What's wrong now?" He backed up, and they stepped inside.

"Nothing's wrong. It's the door. The key is in the door."

At Silk's glance, Vasily shrugged and threw his arms in the air.

"The writ cited public solicitation," Belphagor prompted. "So what makes it public? You said it earlier."

Silk threw a pointed look at his own door and glared at Belphagor. "*Anyone* can enter."

Belphagor grinned. "Anyone can enter."

Silk crossed his arms and addressed Vasily. "What in Heaven is he on about?"

"Hell if I know. When he gets like this, it's best to stand back and let him rave."

"Anyone can enter," Belphagor repeated. "The Stone Horse is open to the public. But if membership were exclusive, not just anyone would be allowed in."

"Membership?" Silk tossed the shoe aside.

"What if we close the Stone Horse *brothel*, abiding by this writ, and next week, we open the Stone Horse, gentlemen's entertainment club?"

"We *were* a gentlemen's entertainment club."

"Yes, but there would be no solicitation at this club. No one would be paid for sex."

Silk's normally well-groomed hair hung in his face, and he blew at it with irritation. "What point would there be in giving it away for free?"

Belphagor smiled. "The gentlemen admitted would pay a monthly membership fee, giving them access to the facilities to engage in whatever consensual activities they please. If that happens to include letting the club's entertainers suck their cocks or going downstairs to enjoy some time at the whipping post, it's all legal."

Silk sat on the edge of the armchair cushion, considering. "A private club with an exclusive clientele."

"The entertainers would never solicit a member, never take facets from one. Their time would be booked by members and their salaries paid by you for unrelated services. In fact, members would be under no obligation at all to book the company of an entertainer. Once they've paid their fee for use of the facilities, they can do what they like, even with a companion they've brought with them. I'm sure there are plenty of demons—and angels— who would be willing to pay a decent fee to have someplace where they could be free to be themselves, someplace besides the rent-by-the-hour tenement rooms in the Devil's Doorstep."

Vasily caught Belphagor's eye with a little flash of fire. "With the ability to choose who's allowed membership and who's not. Like Kezef."

Belphagor nodded. "Exactly."

Silk leaned back and crossed his ankles, swinging them in a boyish manner. The chair had been a gift from Belphagor, sized to Vasily's proportions. "You beautiful bastard. I have half a mind to get down on my knees and polish your knob for free, right now. Except I'm still mad at you for sending Ruby to spy on me." He pouted, but it was clear that Belphagor had won him over.

Vasily was quiet beside him, watching his steps melt the snow as they headed back. He obviously hadn't forgotten what they'd been arguing about.

As they neared The Brimstone, he finally glanced over. "I have to admit, that was kind of amazing. The Stone Horse will be even better than it was before. But I haven't forgiven you for what you did. It was pretty awful."

"I know, love. And I'm sorry." Damn, he was tired of saying those words. "I don't know how to—"

"Which means you've earned a pretty awful punishment."

Belphagor fell in love with him all over again with that single sentence. "Pretty awful," he agreed. "It might take me days to atone."

A visible shiver ran down Vasily's spine. He nodded. "Days."

Belphagor held the door open for him, following him down the stairs into the dark, warm interior. When they reached their room and he'd unmagicked the lock, he let Vasily enter ahead of him once more, cupping the shapely posterior as he shut the door and enjoying the little jump this elicited.

"How's your ass, sweet boy?" He pulled Vasily back against him and wrapped his arms around the broad chest. "Still bruised?"

"Only a little." The words crackled like tumbling embers in a fire.

"I was hard on you. And you took your punishment without complaint." Belphagor moved his hands to Vasily's waist and slipped the belt from its buckle. Vasily inhaled, breath suspended in anticipation, as the jeans slid over his thighs and Belphagor dropped into a crouch. He peeled the shorts down to bare Vasily's exquisite ass and slowly licked one of the fading bruises, earning a soft gasp. "We'll start my penance here."

# CHAPTER ELEVEN

Phaleg might still be the owner in name of the Stone Horse—successfully reimagined as Raqia's first establishment dedicated to sexual entertainment without solicitation—but he wasn't welcome there. In his investigation into the raid, Phaleg had found an overzealous captain climbing the ranks had overstepped his bounds, hoping to impress the principality. An angelic patron arrested for public drunkenness had overheard some of the conspirators in conversation and had been all too eager to name names in exchange for keeping his own untarnished.

While the raid had planted seeds of doubt in Principality Helison's mind, which had been Phaleg's aim all along, shutting down the Stone Horse had never been his intention. And hurting Silk? He deserved his scorn.

But it was just as well he'd been cut off. He'd put off selling his interest in the place for too long. Cavorting with demons and indulging his secret perversions was not the job of a senior staff officer of the Supernal Army. His responsibility was to his principality and his queen, and he had to focus on their safety to the exclusion of all else. As Silk had once said, his loyalties lay with the House of Arkhangel'sk.

*Arkhangel'sk.* The thought of the safeword made him feel hollow inside, as though Phaleg were a hole that could never be filled.

He had to stop thinking about Silk and put all that nonsense behind him. The prelude to Elysian winter had begun, and with the heightened revelry and temporary swell in population, security in the capital was on high alert. Phaleg hadn't quite persuaded the principality to give up his plans to endorse the Liberation Decree, but Helison had at least agreed to be cautious.

After cutting short his holiday at the Summer Palace to welcome Lebes—who'd arrived last night with his family for wintering at his Elysian domicile—Helison had consented to keep Phaleg at his side with a small unit of bodyguards in addition to the Seraphim Guard who accompanied him everywhere. *"If a pair of flaming Seraphim aren't going to keep me safe,"* he'd grumbled, *"I don't see how the added presence of a few mere waterspirits is going to make a difference."* Nevertheless, he'd agreed.

Phaleg was anxious to hear what the others had learned at Iriy, but they'd already departed for a visit to Raqia. He'd have to wait for news from Belphagor. At least Belphagor was still speaking to him.

One of the Lost Boys had been dispatched to The Brimstone at last with the happy news that Anzhela and Ruslan had returned to Elysium with Lebes's entourage and were home in Raqia for the day. Only one thing marred the homecoming: Vasily had been invited to another "secret salon" with Gaspard. Belphagor was on his own.

The match with Kezef hadn't yet been rescheduled, but there was a tense, silent acknowledgment between Belphagor and Vasily that the game would soon continue. When it did, it would be up to Belphagor to keep Vasily safe as he'd promised. Not to mention the girls, whose fates Belphagor still didn't know. He'd hoped to have news for Anzhela by the time she returned, but after all his posturing, Kezef had made himself scarce. Belphagor was beginning to fear that either his claims about information had been invented or, for some reason, he'd decided not to share what he knew.

At the apartment, Ruslan was the star of the day. Dressed in his finery, he looked like a proper little angel. Or at least a proper little angel's bastard. He was brimming with pride and excitement.

"I'm even farther along in my studies than Grand Duke Kae," he announced as the other boys crowded around him. "Of course, he's younger than me," he amended graciously. "I'm sure he'll be smarter than I am when he catches up."

After a few minutes of Ruslan's tales of the splendor of Iriy, Anzhela announced she was putting on tea. Belphagor took this as his cue to head downstairs with her to find out what she and Soluzen had discovered. The tutor was already waiting in the kitchen.

Belphagor sat at the table and waited for the water to boil. "So what conspiracies did you two uncover?"

Soluzen shrugged. "Frankly, none. I wasn't privy to the grand duke's private audiences, of course, but I didn't hear so much as a whispered word against the principality. I believe Anzhela's experiences with the grand duchess have been the same."

"Not exactly the same." Anzhela spooned tea leaves into the warmed pot.

Belphagor lifted an eyebrow. "Oh?"

"Tsirya seems to think there's a conspiracy against her husband."

"Tsirya?" Belphagor smiled. "We're on a first-name basis with the Grand Duchess of Iriy?"

Anzhela blushed as she put up the tea tin. "She said I should call her that. She's been very nice to me."

"I'm teasing. Go on."

"She doesn't trust the principality. Thinks he's behind a plot to make the grand duke look like he's trying to steal the throne. She also believes the queen resents her for having produced a son while she's been unsuccessful." The kettle whistled, and Anzhela took it off the stove and filled the teapot.

Belphagor pondered her report. "Not an altogether unreasonable assumption—at least the last bit. According to Phaleg, Queen Sefira is afraid her cousin will have another boy and the people will take it as a sign Lebes was meant to be principality."

"It's more than that, though." Anzhela's tone was troubled. "I think one of her ladies-in-waiting may be filling her head with such fears. And I've only been with her a month, but I think the pregnancy might be affecting her mind. Her fears and obsessions border on paranoia. When the grand duke insisted she and Kae come with him to Elysium after she begged off, citing her physician's orders of bed rest, she told me in private she wouldn't have any of the queen's attendants or physicians touching her because she fears they'd harm the baby on the queen's orders. She doesn't want anyone at the birth except me." The blush crept up her cheeks again as she poured the tea. "I told her I'd attended a few births—didn't tell her where, of course—and she insisted I should be her midwife."

Belphagor dropped a sugar cube into his tea, watching it dissolve. "The lady-in-waiting whom you suspect has fueled her paranoia ... I wonder if she could be a Traditionalist trying to stir up mistrust of the supernal family."

Anzhela nodded. "I thought that too." She joined them at the table, warming her hands with her cup. "I have an idea who it might be, so I'll keep my eyes and ears open."

"Excellent. And stay close to the grand duchess. Perhaps you can keep this bad influence at arm's length if you make yourself indispensable to her. Maybe undo some of the damage by giving her more rational counsel." He sipped his beverage and glanced at Soluzen. "How is Ruslan getting on with the little grand duke?"

"Even better than we'd hoped." He set down his cup. "I think he'll prove very valuable. Adults tend to say things in front of children they wouldn't otherwise reveal, discounting their intelligence and attention. But Ruslan is nothing if not intelligent and attentive. If any conspirators visit the grand duke's residence, I'm confident he'll be well placed to obtain the information you need."

They were as embedded within Lebes's domain as they could be. Now it was up to Vasily to see what he could glean from the Traditionalists. Belphagor hoped they could come up with something concrete soon to ensure Sefira's safety. Not only for her sake, but, selfishly, for his own. He was tired of letting another demon dominate Vasily's attention. He would happily admit it now, if only in his own head: he was jealous, and he wanted his boy to himself.

Vasily tried to remain as unobtrusive as possible—or as unobtrusive as a six-foot-five firespirit with flame-red locks and piercings in his neck could be—while playing Gaspard's houseboy once again. As before, the mysterious Virtue was in attendance, along with a heavyset Dominion and a pair of Powers who seemed fairly high up in the military. He listened attentively for their names, but they were never used, only their ranks: a brigadier and a major general, whatever those were. Perhaps there weren't many officers at their level and Phaleg would be able to identify them from their descriptions.

The Virtue, Auria, wasted no time in returning to the subject he'd broached at the previous salon, and this time he was less subtle in his intentions.

"There are a number of ways our aim might be accomplished," he said as Vasily served them afternoon tea. "None need go so far as to risk harm to the queen herself. It's the birth we want to prevent."

He smiled as he spoke, nibbling one of the little sandwiches, as though what he was talking about weren't both treasonous and demented. "This could be accomplished with a simple herb tincture introduced gradually into her food to induce an early labor. Even the most uneducated and shiftless demon knows how to make the preparation. It's used to terminate pregnancies by these common demons when they've overproduced due to their lack of restraint in their carnal appetites. Or, if you'll excuse the indelicate reference, by *whores* who've failed at the various demonic methods of contraception."

Vasily swallowed a growl. Who the hell was this pompous Virtue to make such assumptions? A forthright one, he supposed. Given the nods of affirmation from the rest, the other angels Vasily'd met probably believed as Auria did but kept it to themselves. It was eye-opening to hear what they actually thought of his kind. The fact that Gaspard and the other demons in attendance seemed to assume Auria wasn't referring to any of their class was also telling. And extremely insulting that they considered him such a nonentity that it didn't occur to them to be more restrained.

Since his own mother had been a whore who'd abandoned him before he could remember, it was a sensitive subject. Belphagor had helped him to see that women in his mother's position might have little choice. Vasily couldn't forgive his nameless mother; he didn't care what her choices were. But he could be more sympathetic to strangers.

He realized he'd stopped listening when one of the Powers spoke in his deep, booming voice. "The queen is due to deliver in a month. What if the herbal tincture induces premature labor yet the child manages to survive? I think this is cutting things too close for such methods."

"What would you suggest, Major General?" Auria smiled sweetly, but the luminous silver of his eyes didn't share in the expression. "Spearing it on your sword as soon as it breathes air? That would be a bit obvious, don't you think?"

The others laughed nervously, as if they weren't quite sure whether Auria was serious.

"If it cannot be accomplished in an efficient, discreet way, we will have to take more drastic measures. An assassin must be hired." For the first time since he'd arrived, Auria glanced at Vasily, acknowledging his presence. "Perhaps your houseboy, Gaspard. He seems particularly suited to the task."

Vasily froze, not knowing how to play this one, but Gaspard answered before he had to think of anything. "He's far too conspicuous to expect him to be able to get anywhere near the queen."

Auria inclined his head in acknowledgment and went back to his fussy sandwich. Vasily had never seen anyone spend so much time consuming such tiny food. "It was only a thought. I'd still much prefer we find a less drastic method of stopping the birth. But whatever move we make must be soon, while Lebes is in Elysium. The people can call for him to take the throne in the aftermath while worry for the stability of the princedom is at its height. I will abide by the group's decision—the larger group, of course. We should be convening in the next day or two, once they've all arrived in the capital for the winter festivities."

This was the first Vasily had heard of a larger group. He tried to keep his face neutral, refilling the teapot with hot water from the warming stove.

"Could we induce an accident?" It was the first time one of the demons had spoken up. "A runaway horse drawing the supernal carriage? The roads will soon be icy, and the days darken early."

"Or a soft spot on the river's ice if she were to cross it," offered another.

All manner of conveyances used the frozen rivers in winter as a sort of high-speed thoroughfare. Sleds and skaters predominated, but it wasn't unusual to see a full set of horses drawing an aristocrat or two across the Neba as a shortcut.

"Oh, I like that." Auria had finally finished his sandwich. "The freeze is bound to be incomplete in certain areas. We could have someone scout it out to find a sure spot. If she were to go under in her condition, I'm sure there would be no question as to the outcome."

Gaspard spoke up in the thoughtful, silent agreement that followed. "What if we simply waited for the grand duchess to deliver first? She's bound to do so before the queen, and my sources say the child's sex has been divined. She's carrying a boy. With two healthy sons produced, Lebes will be the certain favorite."

"I'm afraid we can't take the chance." Auria was firm, and despite his insistence that he intended to abide by the group's decision, he was clearly the authority here. "If Queen Sefira manages to give Helison a son, it won't matter that his brother has two. The citizens of the Heavens will at last rally about the supernal ruler." With impossible grace and elegance, he shook his head and rose. "I will carry our proposal to the larger group, but I'm certain they shall be amenable. Let us reconvene at my villa at the same hour in three days' time."

Gaspard stood, a frown creasing his forehead. "I'm sorry; what proposal is that?"

Auria regarded him with a look of tolerant disdain. "That the queen of Heaven shall meet an untimely end beneath the Neba due to an unfortunate accident, of course."

Gaspard gave him a clipped bow. "Of course."

When the others had gone, Gaspard poured two generous servings of brandy from his fancy decanter, downing his drink swiftly instead of sipping it as usual. Then he poured himself another. It was as though his nerves had been rattled by the turn the meeting had taken. Vasily didn't care for the fruity stuff, but he drank what he was given, not wanting to be rude.

When the decanter was empty, he stepped into the pantry to change into his street clothes, anxious to get back to Belphagor, but Gaspard stopped him with his hands on Vasily's biceps before he'd pulled his sleeves all the way on. Vasily regarded him. It was unlike Gaspard to be so physical. The brandy had evidently emboldened him.

"Must you leave so soon?" Gaspard slid the shirt down to Vasily's elbows, admiring his pecs. "I was deprived of your company the other morning when you ran off, and I hoped to enjoy looking at you a little bit longer. I meant to show you something."

Vasily pulled the shirt back up but left it unbuttoned, tucking his hands into his pockets. "What is it? More pigments?"

Gaspard smiled. "You'll see." He went up the stairs, and Vasily followed, not especially interested in seeing any more art with himself in it. In the studio, Gaspard approached a large canvas draped in a drop cloth and unveiled it.

Vasily almost choked on his spittle.

"What do you think? Still bashful?"

If the proportions of Vasily's endowment had been a bit unrealistic in the drawing, they were utterly fantastic in the painting. A phallus so large it would no doubt ruin any recipient of its attentions dominated the painting in vivid vermillion. But it wasn't merely the proportions that were alarming. Gaspard had painted him ejaculating a gush of lava. Drops of the glowing orange emission spattered the sheet on which Vasily's form lay, and where they landed, the fabric smoldered and burned. With his head tilted back and lips parted, Vasily's image looked both wild and alluring.

Gaspard was staring at him, waiting for his reaction.

"That's . . . *bozhe moi.* That's something."

"It's how I see you." Gaspard stepped closer to him, dropping the cloth. "I see you when I close my eyes at night. I can feel your heat." He ran his palm down Vasily's bare chest, and Vasily jumped.

"Gaspard."

"I would take such care of you. Forget about that wastrel, Belphagor." He was touching Vasily again, resisting Vasily's attempts to hold him at bay, one hand sliding around his waist and the other dipping into the top of his jeans. "These body-hugging garments from the world of Man make me want to peel them off you to reveal the virility barely hidden beneath them."

Vasily grabbed his wrist, eliciting a yelp of surprise. "*Gaspard.* I'm sorry if I've given you the wrong impression, but I have no intention of leaving Belphagor. And he is not a *wastrel.*"

Gaspard's eyes went hard. "He beats you. I can feel the marks on your back. Do you think that's love?"

Vasily wrested himself from Gaspard's grip, holding him away. "It's none of your business what Belphagor and I do, but I assure you, it's not abuse. And you need to back off."

"Back off?" Gaspard yanked his hands from Vasily's grasp. "You came here to my house—wearing *that*—and you expect me to believe you don't want my attentions?"

"This is how I always dress. I don't want to hurt your feelings, Gaspard, but I'm sorry. The attraction isn't mutual. You're a very nice demon, but I—"

"A nice demon!" Gaspard's face blazed. "And you don't like them nice, do you? You like that prissy Silk who doles out whippings to you like a schoolmaster, and your precious rogue,

Belphagor, who sells you, bets you, and physically assaults you on a regular basis."

Vasily clenched his jaw. "You're out of line. I'm afraid I'm going to have to decline any future engagements with you."

"The hell you will." Gaspard had the audacity to grab him by the hair. Closer to Vasily's height than Belphagor was, Gaspard didn't need to pull him down to reach his mouth.

Vasily stood frozen in shock for an instant with Gaspard's tongue trying to force its way in before he pulled away in outrage. "What the fuck do you think you're doing?"

"You know exactly what I'm doing. You've been asking for it." When Gaspard tried to move toward him once more, Vasily acted on instinct and swung at him. He clipped him on the cheek, and Gaspard stumbled back in shock.

Vasily opened his mouth to apologize but then closed it. Gaspard had essentially assaulted him. He had nothing to apologize for. He buttoned his shirt and went past him to the door.

"Vasily—"

"Save it, Gaspard. The only reason I'm not pummeling your face right now is that I'm giving you the benefit of the doubt that this was an error in judgment. But if I ever find out you've treated any of the boys at the Horse this way, I *will* bloody you."

Gaspard shouted down the stairs after him from the studio doorway. "I should have known better than to waste my attentions on a demon of your poor breeding!"

"Yeah, you probably should have." Vasily let himself out.

He fumed as he headed back to The Brimstone. He could still feel that clammy, unexpected kiss being forced upon him, and he wanted to wash his mouth out with soap. If he'd been anyone else, he wondered whether the kiss would have been all he suffered. And if this had happened when he'd been a few years younger, he doubted he'd be walking away from it right now.

Vasily sighed and shook it off. At any rate, his career as a spy was over. There would be no more salons, demonic or angelic.

He hoped what he'd already learned was enough to stop them from carrying out their plan.

Looking grim when he returned, Vasily shared what he'd discovered.

Belphagor paced in front of the vanity. "You're sure it wasn't just talk?"

Vasily shook his head. "'The queen of Heaven shall meet an untimely end beneath the Neba' sounded pretty definitive."

"Damn." Belphagor studied him as he considered what to do. Although this development was reason enough to be grim, he had the distinct impression Vasily was keeping something from him. Belphagor didn't press, though he intended to later. For the moment, protecting the queen was paramount.

"I'll send a messenger to Phaleg to meet us this evening." Such sensitive news couldn't be delivered in the gaming room, and for an angel of Phaleg's stature, escorting him back to his room for a private discussion wasn't an option. The atmosphere in Elysium had changed drastically since the last time he'd had him there.

*Had him there.* Belphagor smiled to himself at the phrase. He certainly had. Watching Vasily's generous cock being swallowed up by Phaleg's sweet ass while his mouth was busy swallowing Belphagor had been one of the highlights of his life.

Delicious memories aside, a den of iniquity was far too public a place, and rumors would spread. They had no other option but to meet at the Stone Horse, as uncomfortable as it might be for Phaleg.

Belphagor let Silk know Phaleg would be coming. Silk said nothing, giving Belphagor a sharp nod with his lips pressed together in a thin line. He understood the importance of the information.

But if Belphagor thought Silk wasn't anticipating Phaleg's arrival, acutely aware of the moment Phaleg entered, any such notion went out the window when Silk had a perfectly timed and enthusiastic orgasm standing right out in the open in the parlor, with Khai kneeling before him reaping the rewards of his oral attentions.

Phaleg kept his eyes fixed on the far end of the club, willing down the heat in his cheeks and the sick feeling in his stomach. As Belphagor ushered him past the parlor to a private room, he motioned to Vasily to join them.

"Sorry about that." Belphagor grimaced once the door was closed behind them. "I warned him you were coming. I didn't know he was going to put on a show."

Phaleg tried to shrug, but the motion felt stiff and awkward. "That's his specialty, isn't it? Getting attention." He remained by the door while Vasily and Belphagor sat on the bed. He couldn't help but recall the first time the three of them had been alone in a bedroom. Despite his understandable resentment of Phaleg, Vasily had demonstrated surprising enthusiasm about . . .

Phaleg cleared his throat. "So, you said Vasily has vital information?"

Vasily, who'd looked as if he approved of Silk's antics, grew serious. "The Traditionalists are planning to stage an accident. The next time the queen goes out, they're going to make sure her carriage will cross the Neba at a weak spot."

Phaleg scowled. "Despicable cowards. But that's easy enough to prevent. I'll advise the principality not to let her go out by carriage, and certainly not to cross on the ice."

Belphagor's expression was amused. "Most husbands don't get to 'let' or 'not let' their wives do anything. Not even the principality of the Firmament of Shehaqim and All the Heavens."

"It's for her own safety. I'm sure she'll heed his counsel."

"All the same, try to come up with some other method to ensure she stays out of harm's way. These angels are determined."

"A pair of Seraphim will be with her at all times. It's tradition. I don't see how they can execute something like that in plain view of two elemental firespirits."

Vasily made a derisive sound in his throat. "Firespirits don't like water."

Belphagor nodded. "And they like ice even less."

Phaleg was unconvinced. "So what are you saying?"

"I'm saying an accident on ice is probably the most ingenious plan they could have come up with. The moment the horse team drawing the queen's carriage sets hooves on the ice, the Seraphim will take wing and circle overhead, observing from a comfortable distance. It would be a simple matter to distract the Seraphim for a moment, taking their attention just long enough to pull it off."

Phaleg knew little about Seraphim other than the fact of their origins in the molten river of fire that circled the tip of the Heavens, but he was certainly more familiar with them than demons. "How do you know what a Seraph would do?"

"I would venture to say, my dear boy, that I've been in much closer proximity to Seraphim than you have." Belphagor's tone said Phaleg had stepped in it.

He had to resist the conditioned response of dropping to his knees at that tone. "How? When have you been around Seraphim?"

"I have been tracked and arrested by them in the world of Man. The supernal family uses them to protect Heaven's interests by ensuring demons who fall are swiftly dealt with when matters of human law are in play, and they are far more elemental in the terrestrial sphere. Being at the mercy of an earthbound Seraph is an extremely unpleasant experience." Belphagor's expression was dark. "One I wouldn't recommend even to a masochist such as yourself."

Phaleg felt heat rise from his throat to the tips of his ears. "I'll take your word for it. I still find it hard to credit the idea that the conspirators could manage to lure the queen's carriage onto the precise spot required to carry it off. It would take incredible planning and coordination. I don't see a bunch of aristocratic angels of the blood being that clever and calculating."

Vasily looked puzzled. "What's 'of the blood'?"

"Of the same element that flows in the Principalities' veins. The waterspirits. The Fourth Choir."

"I know what damned choir you're in," Vasily growled. "The Fallen aren't simpletons."

"Sorry." Phaleg hated sounding like an ass. "I don't really know what demons know. I'm not trying to be condescending."

Vasily shrugged. "So you're assuming all the conspirators are of the blood."

"I can't imagine the higher orders taking an interest in who sits on the throne, and the firespirits are sworn to protect the House of Arkhangel'sk."

Belphagor's eyebrow flicked upward. "Tell that to the Cherub assassin Duke Elyon hired."

"Point taken." Phaleg shuddered at the memory. "But surely he was an exception."

Vasily drew one knee up onto the bed frame and hooked his arms around it. "The Virtue wasn't the only earthspirit at the gathering I attended. I saw at least one Dominion and two Powers, and there was mention of a 'larger group,' though I didn't get a sense of how large it might be or who belonged to it."

"Powers?" Phaleg stared in dismay. As a military officer, he'd been trained to have the utmost respect for the order of angels bred to lead the Host in battle.

"And the angel who appears to be the mastermind of the whole thing?" Vasily held Phaleg's gaze. "He's a Virtue."

The blood drained from Phaleg's face. For a Virtue to conspire against the throne of Heaven was unheard of. And conspiring to murder Heaven's pregnant queen? Unthinkable. "You're certain there's a Virtue involved?"

The look Vasily gave him said he thought Phaleg was stupid. "It's kind of impossible not to notice when one's in the room."

"Did you catch any names?"

"Not of the others. But everyone called the Virtue Auria."

"Auria. That's not one I'm familiar with, and I'm acquainted with all the Virtues currently in the capital. He must be using an assumed name." Phaleg shook his head. Heaven had ceased to make sense to him. "This goes so much higher than I imagined. I was thinking in terms of the Union of Liberation, a secret society to be sure but restricted to an elite membership within the

Supernal Army." He pushed his curls back from his forehead and flattened them with his palm. "If only we could find a way to delay their plans a little longer until I can convince the principality of the seriousness of these threats."

Vasily was thoughtful. "There might be a way to buy some time."

"What way?"

"They need Lebes to be in Elysium when they make their move so he can be convinced to take the throne immediately."

Belphagor nodded, pondering. "So if Helison were to send Lebes on some sort of diplomatic mission—brief enough that he wouldn't be concerned about missing the birth of his child, of course—"

"Then Lebes wouldn't be in Elysium." Relief washed over Phaleg. "That's perfect. There's been some squabbling among the nobility in Arcadia; I can recommend the principality let his brother handle it. And while he's away, if there happened to be a demonstration that got a little out of hand—some rock-throwing at the palace windows, nothing too violent—Helison might come around."

Belphagor frowned. "Wouldn't it be better to try to expose these Traditionalists as we did with the Union of Liberation? They're the ones who pose the threat, not the Fallen. I'm still bothered by the idea of convincing the principality not to sign the decree."

"If we *could* expose them, and if the principality could be convinced of their guilt, yes. But this goes too high up and too deep." Phaleg chewed his lip. "If a Virtue is behind it, this conspiracy may be impossible to thwart. The Virtues are the angels who investigate such claims and ensure the tenets of angelic law are followed, while the Dominions make and interpret the law. And Powers? What is that phrase you demons are so fond of? *Bozhe moi.* There were two Powers at that small gathering alone. Depending on their rank, they could influence a great number of supernal soldiers."

"A brigadier and a major general," Vasily supplied.

Phaleg's heart sank. "There are five thousand soldiers in a brigade. A major general commands an entire division. We could have a civil war on our hands." He paced before the door. If this was true, half measures wouldn't be enough. "I've been working on several proposals the principality might introduce to improve the lot of the Fallen. Something the majority of the Host couldn't possibly begrudge the less fortunate among them. Small steps, but a beginning. If the principality signs that decree, however, it will end in bloodshed on a scale you can't imagine. I fear for what a Traditionalist Heaven would mean for the Fallen."

Belphagor considered. "I don't like it, but I can't see any other options. You'll have your demonstration. Tell me when, and I'll make it happen. But I want your word that the demonstrators won't be arrested or face violence at the hands of your 'peacekeepers.'"

"You have it."

On his way out, Phaleg tried not to look around for Silk, but when he reached the exit, he made the mistake of glancing back. Reclining on one of the settees with his arms stretched across the back to reveal his sleek torso through his open shirt, Silk looked like he was holding court. Khai knelt beside the couch, and a pair of angelic soldiers from Phaleg's own unit cuddled Silk on either side. What happened at the Stone Horse stayed there; he wasn't worried about being outed. Nevertheless, seeing Silk dominating other angels was a hard blow.

But Phaleg had more important things to worry about. Like protecting the queen and preventing a war.

When Phaleg had gone, Belphagor closed the door and stood in front of it, staring at Vasily. "So when are you going to tell me what happened at that salon?"

Vasily narrowed his eyes, letting his propped-up leg drop back down to the floor. "What do you mean? I told you what happened."

"Let me put it this way. Will you be joining your friend Gaspard at his next soirée?"

"What's a soirée?"

"Vasya."

"I don't know what a damned soirée is!"

"It's a party. Are you angry with me?"

The flickering fire in Vasily's eyes suggested he might be, but Vasily sighed. "I don't want you to make a big deal about this."

His pulse quickened. "About what?"

"Gaspard got a little carried away." Vasily clearly didn't want to tell him how. Belphagor took a step toward the bed, and he must have had menace in his eyes, because Vasily blurted it out. "He wanted more intimacy with me than I was prepared to give, and when I told him no, he tried to take it."

If Belphagor had possessed the element in Vasily's veins, his eyes would be shooting flames. "He tried to rape you?"

Vasily blanched. "No, nothing so brutish. He grabbed my hair the way you do and kissed me without my permission. I had to shove him off. More than shove him, actually. I punched him."

Blood pounded in Belphagor's head. "I may kill him."

"Beli, don't make a big deal about this, please. It's over, and he couldn't have forced me to do anything. He doesn't have the strength."

"That's not the point. The fact that he tried—"

"He didn't try anything else. I think I may have given him the wrong idea, and he thought being dominant would excite me."

"You're blaming yourself because some *ebanniyi zasranets* demon merchant tried to force himself on you?"

"I'm trying to explain that this isn't as one-sided as you're making it out to be."

Belphagor was careful to respond evenly so Vasily wouldn't feel the anger was directed at him. "Rape is always one-sided, *mal'chik*."

He hadn't meant to say it now, in conjunction with such an unpleasant truth, but emotion had propelled the word out of him. And with that single word, the tension of the argument fell away.

Vasily searched his eyes. "You said '*mal'chik*.'"

"So I did."

"Does that mean . . .?"

Belphagor  pushed Vasily's knees apart with his legs as he stepped in close. "It was a slip of the tongue." He ran his hand up the side of Vasily's neck, enjoying the roughness of the metal as his palm passed over it, and stopped at the jaw, tracing his thumb along the rough edge of beard. "But I expect my tongue will slip again." He bent and let it slip over Vasily's full lower lip while Vasily closed his eyes with a soft inhalation. "You know you're mine, though, regardless of whether I ever manage to earn you back as my boy." He gave him a proper kiss, taking his time to enjoy the smoky taste and the softness of the firespirit lips that always surprised him.

Breathless when Belphagor released him, Vasily gazed at him with eyes like kindling. "Don't you think you've been punished enough?" His voice was fiery gruff.

Belphagor tugged at Vasily's sideburn. "I decide when it's enough."

Vasily's eyes smoldered. "Fucking masochist."

Belphagor pushed him back onto the bed and crawled over him. "Damned right I am."

# CHAPTER
# TWELVE

Belphagor received word from Phaleg the following day. The principality had been receptive to his counsel. He'd presented the idea of sending Lebes to Arcadia as a means of demonstrating Helison's trust in his brother. It was considered an honor to serve as Helison's ambassador in securing the loyalty of the house from which both the queen and Lebes's own wife hailed. The grand duke would leave immediately and be gone less than a week. Belphagor would have to work quickly.

He'd never been one for demonstration or protest, not even during the Bolshevik Revolution in the world of Man. Political idealism and faith in any sort of government was something he had no time for. But sowing chaos he excelled at. And if he was going to stir things up among the Fallen, The Brimstone was the place to start.

But when Belphagor entered the gaming room that afternoon, Kezef, who hadn't made an appearance since the raid, was seated at the master table, as was expected of the challenger when the reigning champion was absent.

With a brief glance in Belphagor's direction, Kezef called his opponent's cast without missing a beat. "If it isn't the elusive Belphagor." Well that was rich. Kezef continued perusing his cards while his disappointed opponent surrendered one. "I hope you haven't been hiding from me."

Belphagor decided to play along. "Oh, I have." He held a lighter from the world of Man to the cigar he'd put in his mouth, puffing until it was lit. "I find your company a bore."

Kezef laughed good-naturedly. "Refreshingly honest. Though I suspect that's merely a partial truth. I think you're afraid of losing your boy."

"Impossible. I could never lose my boy." Belphagor remained standing as Kezef's opponent rose to give over his spot, having lost while they were trading barbs.

Kezef gathered the cards. "Take a seat, Belphagor."

Belphagor turned his cigar, enjoying the scent. "I'm not here to play this evening."

"You're obligated to play me. We agreed to a final match. Winner take all. If you're refusing to play, I am that winner."

"I'm not refusing to play you." Belphagor took another puff. "I would have played you any night over the past three weeks. Tonight, as it happens, there's going to be another raid."

Several players tensed and turned in their seats, and the tables in the immediate vicinity quieted.

"I thought it was only fair to warn you all."

Kezef shuffled the deck. "You would know this because . . .?"

Belphagor let him wait a moment for the answer. The quiet in the den spread like ice across the Neba. He smiled. "I beat it out of a young soldier earlier this evening at the Stone Horse. It's remarkable what these angels will tell you for an orgasm."

One of the gamers near him spat on the floor. "You're disgusting."

Belphagor rolled his eyes, his cigar clenched in his teeth. "Demon spits on the floor an' calls *me* disgusting. I was merely bringing this information as a courtesy, but if the lot of you want to sit here while the Supernal Army tramples all over demon rights, that's your prerogative."

A few chairs scooted back as some of the wiser patrons prepared to leave.

"Running and hiding like cowards is an option, I suppose."

One of the players who'd risen turned around. "Who are you calling a coward?"

"Well, how would I know?" Belphagor shrugged. "I can't be expected to remember all your names."

The demon advanced on him, while a few others looked ready to do the same. He dodged the first punch with an airspirit cheat. With the next, he wasn't so lucky, but he managed to hang on to his cigar. He could have wiped the floor with either demon, but it was a really good cigar.

"Am I the one you're angry with?" He dodged another, who stumbled into the table behind him. "Or is it the principality? Are we all going to squabble here amongst ourselves and wait for the gendarmes to arrive, or are we going to take this fight to where it rightly belongs—the principality's doorstep?"

"Fuck the principality!" someone yelled, and a chorus of agreement followed in yet more colorful language.

The previous raid on The Brimstone had been a tipping point, and it didn't take much to push them over it. Angelic thugs picking fights in the streets were one thing, but they had entered one of Raqia's most cherished establishments and harassed its patrons without cause.

"I say we march on Elysium, surround the Winter Palace, and demand an end to the presence of the Supernal Army in Raqia and to Ophanim Guard brutality." Belphagor raised his fist toward the door. "Who's with me?"

Shouts of agreement filled The Brimstone, with demons charging up the stairs to take to the streets of Elysium.

As the place cleared out, he glanced at Kezef, still seated at the master table. "Not coming?"

"To protest an imaginary raid?"

Belphagor feigned shock. "You doubt my word?"

Kezef sat back, pocketing his pouch of facets. "Carry on with whatever you're up to. I'm sure the girls can wait."

Belphagor swung the door shut and stepped back down into the gaming room. "Are you suggesting we continue the tournament without observers?"

"Heaven forbid."

Belphagor frowned. "Then what is this about the girls?"

Kezef placed the deck on the table. "Over the past few weeks, I've been otherwise occupied with breaking the will of a young soldier—something I'm sure you can appreciate." He smiled as if they shared some kinship, but Belphagor didn't return it. "This soldier is the source of the information I've wagered, and I've come upon some additional facts that you may wish to know."

Belphagor looked out the windows at the demons leading the charge. They were bound to pick up supporters while they marched. Belphagor had enlisted the aid of the girls at The Cat to rally their demonic patrons and employed the Lost Boys to stir up trouble in the Demon Market. They would have to do without him.

He remained standing, arms crossed. "If you intend to extort something else for this information—"

"Not at all, Belphagor. I merely want to engage you in a friendly game for facets, unrelated to our tournament. I'll share this new information with you free of charge."

There was no way Kezef was offering *anything* free of charge, but Belphagor sat. It would give him a chance to observe Kezef's tells free from the pressure of their wager. Which perhaps was Kezef's aim as well.

Kezef pushed the deck toward him. "Why don't you deal?"

Belphagor shuffled, sliding the cigar in his teeth to the side. "Your new information?"

Kezef perused his cards as Belphagor dealt them. "I've discovered that the fates of our young demonesses may soon change."

"Change how?"

Kezef cast the die and waited for Belphagor's call before he replied. "Until now, their safety has been assured, but recent developments jeopardize that safety."

"I swear to you, Kezef, if we conclude our tournament only for you to tell me *you* purchased the girls—"

"Of course not." Kezef called his cast perfectly, and Belphagor surrendered a card. "Don't be absurd. I do know who did, however. And I assure you, I have no influence over this individual."

"Yet you know they're suddenly in jeopardy."

"I do." Kezef had cast while he was speaking, and Belphagor realized he'd missed the call altogether, like a complete amateur. He had to surrender one of the cards that he needed to win.

He set it down casually, but he suspected he'd shown his hand with his aggravation at the blunder. "How so?"

Kezef picked up the card. "If I tell you any more, it will give away the information I hold as stakes in our tournament."

"Then why tell me this at all?" Belphagor cursed as Kezef set down a scarlet wing and won the hand.

Kezef's smile as he gathered his facets said he'd gotten everything he wanted out of this one-off, and Belphagor had walked right into it. "It's been a pleasure, Belphagor. I'm looking forward to your ultimate defeat. Shall we say tomorrow evening? I can't tell you how delighted I will be to bend your boy to my will."

It took every ounce of control Belphagor had not to take a swing at the bastard as he walked away.

In the morning, The Brimstone was rumbling with talk of the demonstration. Predictably, it had turned toward rioting, but the Ophanim Guard had been disinclined to break it up because of the heavy snowfall. Like the Seraphim, Ophanim weren't fond of water. Belphagor suspected it had something to do with their electrical qualities. They'd stood in formation beneath the eaves of the palace, surrounding it on all sides to keep the supernal family and the wealth of Heaven safe, but had come no farther.

Their reticence encouraged the throwing of projectiles and resulted in more broken windows, until the Supernal Army was called in. But to Phaleg's credit, they'd dispersed the protestors without violence, eventually employing a hose attached to a water pump. Unlike fire hoses in the world of Man, these lacked the sort of pressure required to cause physical injury or beat back the crowd, but in the freezing weather, it was incentive enough.

Anxious to be sure the boys hadn't gotten into any trouble, Belphagor and Vasily made their way to Silk's place after lunch. The precipitation hadn't let up, and gusts of wind picked up the falling snow in bursts, as though the Snow Queen herself were trying to manifest.

Belphagor had always liked the idea of the "snow bees" in the Hans Christian Andersen tale, and these sudden squalls seemed to be precisely what the Danish author had in mind. He and Vasily plowed arm in arm through buzzing swarms of white. No one was around to look twice at them about it. Not that Belphagor would have cared, but it was nice to be able to indulge in the comfort of touch.

They arrived at the apartment in high spirits, flushed from the cold. Vasily was laughing in his deep rumble at Belphagor's teasing about snow bees being after him as they threw open the door. It took them a moment to transition to the dramatic difference in mood inside.

Anzhela, seated at the kitchen table with Silk and the boys huddled around her, was weeping and covered in blood.

Belphagor shook himself and shut the door. "What's happened?" He hurried to her side and crouched by her chair. "Anzhela, who hurt you?"

She shook her head violently, crying too hard to answer.

"It's the grand duchess," said Tilli. "It's *her* blood."

A chill ran up Belphagor's spine. "The grand duchess?"

Silk stroked Anzhela's bloody hand. "She went into premature labor. Anzhi was the only one there." He lowered his voice. "The grand duchess is dead and the baby with her."

As Anzhela's sobbing intensified, Belphagor rose and gently persuaded her from her seat. "Hush, dear heart. Let's get you cleaned up. Silk, put on the kettle, would you?"

Vasily, standing frozen by the door, took a step forward. "Can I do anything?"

"Help Silk with tea." Belphagor led Anzhela to her room.

Her tears were replaced by uncontrollable trembling as Belphagor helped her out of her clothes and dipped a flannel into the basin to wipe the blood from her skin.

"It's all right, Anyushka." The fond Russian nickname Anzhela's grandmother had given her came more naturally to him than "Anzhi." "My inclinations are firmly one-directional. You don't need to worry about me."

Unexpectedly, Anzhela giggled and then covered her mouth with her hand, to renewed weeping. But these were calmer tears, and after he'd wrung out the cloth a second time, she took it from him. "I've got it. I'm okay."

He nodded and fetched a generous Aravothan bath towel for her—Silk was one for luxuries—wrapping it around her when she'd finished. She sat on the vanity stool, eyes heavy with exhaustion, and stared at the floor.

"You've got a little on your cheek." Belphagor scrubbed it for her. "Do you want to talk about it yet or maybe get some rest?"

"She'd been in labor for more than a day, and somehow she kept it from me." Anzhela apparently wanted to talk about it. "We were watching the protest from the window. You can see all the way to the Gulf of the Firmament from the Duke's Hall. Her water broke. It was pink. She said it was only the bloody show, but it's not like that. I've seen it enough times to know. I wanted to go for the queen's physician immediately, but she was terrified and begged me not to leave her. I told you she'd dismissed all but a few of the servants." Anzhela looked at him, guilt apparent on her face. "Should I have gone anyway? I didn't know what to do."

He took her hands, leaning in as he sat on the edge of the vanity. "This wasn't your fault. I'm sure you did everything you could. Some lives aren't meant to be."

Anzhela sighed. "No, I know. The babe was dead inside her. I think she'd known for days but kept it to herself because saying it aloud would make it real. Maybe it was the cause of all her odd behavior, trying to deny what was happening and wanting to blame some outside force at the same time. I sent Ruslan for help and stayed by her as long as I could, but he didn't come back." She closed her eyes. "She was bleeding something awful by then. She kept calling for the grand duke, and I kept telling her he was away, and then she finally said, 'Bring me my boy. I want my Kae.'

"I wouldn't have done it. Maybe I shouldn't have. But I knew she was in a bad way, and I couldn't bear the thought he might not see his mother again. I cleaned her up as best as I could and let him come in and hold her hand. I didn't realize what a fright I looked. That's when I went for the physician myself. I told the little grand duke to count between her pains to give him something to do, something else to dwell on, and told him if they got close to a minute between to get the chambermaid to help his mum whether she wanted her or not. And I left." Anzhela pulled away from Belphagor and put her head in her hands. "But it was chaos in the city, and I couldn't . . ." Her voice hitched and trailed off.

Of course there was chaos. The chaos he'd fomented. Belphagor felt sick.

After a moment, Anzhela gathered herself and went on. "I couldn't get to the palace. It was impossible. It took me ages to get back through the crowds. The little boy was alone with her. I think she died as soon as I left."

"Oh, sweetheart." He moved his hand in gentle circles on her back, troubled that his actions had inadvertently led to this tragedy. He hadn't caused the grand duchess to miscarry, of course, and he couldn't have known it would happen on this night of all nights. From the sound of it, her death had likely been a foregone conclusion. Nevertheless, the thought that'd he'd put Anzhela in such an impossible position made him ache. And he was sure the image of the little boy at his mother's side would haunt him—as it would no doubt haunt Anzhela. "I'm so sorry." Something else she'd said finally registered. "Ruslan—we need to find him."

Anzhela sat up, drying her eyes. "He's all right. He found his way back right after I did. He brought the physician." She shook her head. "I don't know how he managed to find him. I'd tried to take little Kae out of the room—he didn't want to leave his mother. But Ruslan arrived, and Kae took his hand and went with him without a word. They're both at the palace now. Kae refused to be separated from him. Soluzen's gone with them. Kae's to stay there until the grand duke's return."

The terrible news reached Phaleg before he'd reported to the principality in the morning. It seemed all of Elysium was repeating it in hushed tones—but with a sickening air of eagerness, as though the tragedy of the supernal family were a kind of entertainment. Almost in the same breath, angels began to whisper of a conspiracy by the principality to send Lebes away and poison the grand duke's wife because of the queen's jealousy.

"They can't really think that, can they?" Helison slumped over the large walnut desk in his study, elbows on the polished surface and hands clasped in front of him. His face was troubled within the frame of his fatherly beard and whiskers, and the bright celestine of his eyes was tired and dull, like Elysium's wintry sky.

Phaleg stood with his hands locked behind his back. "I think people love a scandal, sire, and will repeat anything that smacks of one. But I don't think we can afford to ignore the rumors. It's the sort of thing Grand Duke Lebes's supporters will pounce upon in their efforts to oust you."

The principality looked up with a sharp frown. "I've told you, Major. My brother has no designs on the throne. I don't want to hear any more about it."

"I'm afraid you must hear about it. I don't mean to be impertinent, but the threat is very real, and it isn't your brother it's coming from but those who would use him to further their own aims. Only yesterday, I learned of the involvement of two members of the Supernal Army leadership, as well as a Dominion and a Virtue, in a conspiracy to do harm to the queen to prevent the birth. And they're quite serious."

Helison's expression darkened. "And you're just telling me this now?"

"I had to be certain of my source before I came to you with it, and I have no names of those involved, only their ranks. I would have brought this news to you last night, but—"

"But the square was full of angry rioters." Helison sighed and shook his head. "How can all of my subjects have misunderstood me so? The Fallen believe I mean to rule them with an iron fist, and the Host think I'm unfit to rule because I'm too soft on the Fallen."

"If you want my recommendation, I would suggest this is not the time for grand gestures toward a people who are clearly unappreciative. Would it not be better to capitulate to the Host than to the Fallen? For the sake of Her Supernal Majesty's safety and that of your unborn child, let the Liberation Decree go."

Helison regarded him icily. "As it happens, I do not want your recommendation, Major. You may leave me."

Phaleg bowed and went out, cursing himself for being so blunt. Helison was invested in an idealistic fantasy of what the ruler of Heaven ought to be, and opposition to his ideas couldn't be forced upon him. He saw himself as a paternal figure to his subjects, and despite the evidence of percolating rebellion and insurrection, he imagined a father's firmness was all that was needed to keep Heaven in line.

It would be up to Phaleg now to be on the alert and ensure the queen's safety. In the wake of the grand duchess's death, and with such ugly rumors flying, he couldn't take any chances. At least he'd managed to persuade the principality to send a full platoon as escort for the queen and the young grand duchesses on their return from the Summer Palace. Phaleg couldn't imagine anyone being so base as to take the lives of young girls to achieve their political aims, but these Traditionalists were already willing to murder a pregnant woman.

Phaleg's sense of urgency increased that evening when Lebes returned early, having received a message from the palace almost as soon as he'd arrived in Arcadia. The queen and the little grand duchesses were expected the following morning. If the Traditionalists were going to act, it would be on the road to Elysium or swiftly following her arrival.

Phaleg rode out after dark with his most trusted men to meet the queen's coach, appointing himself as her personal escort. The coach had stopped at an inn for the night, hours north of the city, and Phaleg sought a private audience with the queen to tell her of her cousin's death.

Sefira's hands went to her round belly at the news, instinctively protecting the baby within. "Sweet Heaven, no." Tears ran down her habitually stoic face. She might have had a rivalry with her cousin, but it was clear she had also cared for her. They had, after all, spent their girlhoods together in Arcadia. They both had the same delicate grace, though Sefira's features were less soft, and her hair was the darker golden shade typical of Arcadian nobility. "And the baby?"

"Stillborn."

The queen lifted one hand from her belly to cover her mouth. She looked faint, and Phaleg led her to a chair. "Do they know, was it . . .?"

"A boy," he said quietly.

She shook her head, wringing her hands. "Poor Lebes. And little Kae! Oh, how cruel! This doesn't happen to the Host. Does it?" Sefira was becoming overwrought. "Oh, it's horrible, *horrible* that it should happen to anyone. But pure blood is healthier— that's what they always say." She pinched her cheeks sharply as though trying to calm her own hysteria. "No. I've always thought we'd fall to violence, not to frailty."

It was a disturbing sentiment and reminded him why he'd come. "I don't want to alarm you, but I feel it's my duty to warn you. There has been unkind slander against you and the principality. I suppose it's angelic nature to seek some cause, some blame, for events that have none."

Sefira's agitation stilled, and she stared at him, shrewd eyes still damp with tears. "They're saying I did something to harm her, to bring this on." There was no question in her voice. "I never wished her ill."

"Of course you didn't, Majesty. Please don't take it to heart. I only wanted you to be aware so it wouldn't come as a surprise should any unkind words reach you." He lowered his voice. "I'm also concerned for your safety. There are some among the Host who . . ." He paused, trying to find a way to put it delicately.

"Who would rather see my brother-in-law on the throne than my husband." Sefira was no fool. "And they would come at him through me?"

Phaleg unfolded and refolded his gloves in his hands. "My intelligence suggests they seek to prevent the birth of an heir so

Grand Duke Lebes will seem the more viable ruler. His Supernal Majesty would not have had me tell you of this. He dismisses it as the grumblings of detractors who would not dare to act against the throne. But I believe they are in earnest, and I cannot in good conscience stand by and keep this from you after what I've uncovered. They seek to get you alone in your carriage on unsafe ground—a muddy road or weak ice on the river—and stage an accident."

Sefira contemplated her hands in her lap, seeming to consider his words, before gathering her reserves and regarding him with her usual staid composure. "You are my husband's Chief of Security."

"Yes, madam."

"And you are loyal to him—yet not so loyal that you would follow his word on this matter."

Phaleg swallowed. "Your Supernal Majesty—"

"If my husband has seen fit to dismiss these concerns, I will abide by his wisdom. The wife of a principality has social obligations. I cannot hide inside the palace." She let the proper veneer slip for a moment with a kind smile, one gloved hand absently stroking her belly as if to calm the child. "Your intentions are unimpeachable, Major Phaleg. I appreciate your warning. I won't mention this to my husband." This last sentence bore a tone of dismissal.

Phaleg bowed. "Of course." He had done all he could on this front, and her rebuke wasn't so much a refusal to heed his warning as it was decorum. His only recourse now was to try to prevent any threat from reaching her.

In the morning, he rode ahead to scout the way, with his men following at the rear to ensure no one overtook the party from behind. Steady snowfall followed them southward, with increasing flurries and gusts of wind across the icy highway that made the going slow. But it also likely deterred any plans for ambush.

Dusk fell early as a sudden squall ushered them into the supernal city. Phaleg dismounted inside the courtyard gates to help Sefira and her young daughters from the coach. The mood among the waiting servants in the courtyard was tense as they stamped their feet against the cold. Phaleg attributed it to gossip over the deaths until the hostler gave him more unsettling news.

"Terrible about the principality's sister-in-law and the baby." The hostler shook his head, taking the reins from Phaleg. "And now the little grand duke has gone missing with that half-demon boy."

After staying late at The Boudoir to comfort Anzhela and calm the boys, Belphagor spent the night sleeping on the floor of the parlor with Vasily. In the morning, a meager breakfast of porridge and butter revealed that the kitchen hadn't been as well stocked as it ought while Anzhela was away.

Anzhela offered to go out, but Belphagor insisted she stay put. "You've had enough to deal with in the past twenty-four hours. Bundle up and stay warm. I'll take care of it."

With his rucksack stuffed with groceries from the Demon Market, he started to head back when a commotion broke out near the riverbank. From the looks of it, some pickpocket had been apprehended. For a moment, Belphagor thought he heard Ruslan's voice. But that was absurd. Ruslan was safe and sound at the palace with his little grand duke.

He wondered if he ought to investigate, but the boys would be getting hungry, and he wanted to stop in at the bakery and fetch some sweets he'd seen in the window. The baker had spent some time in the world of Man, and a tray of delicious-looking Russian hand pies, advertising creamy imported Aravothan cheese for the filling, was sure to go fast.

At the bakery, a stout demoness matron stood chatting with the baker's daughter as she boxed up her order while Belphagor waited for his *vatrushki*. "My girl works at the palace," she said proudly. "They're all in a tizzy there this morning. Seems the principality's nephew has run away."

Belphagor paused in shaking out a couple of facets from his purse for the pastries and raised his head.

The baker's daughter clucked her tongue. "You'd think he'd want for nothing."

"It's all on account of the grand duchess I'm sure. They say he was there with her when she died."

The younger woman tied off the twine in a carrying handle at the top of the patron's box and passed it over the counter. "I suppose even an angel feels the loss of his mother."

Belphagor set his facets on the counter, took the box of pastries from the baker, and hurried out. If Kae had run away, chances were good that Ruslan had gone with him. It *had* been his voice. Belphagor should have trusted his instincts.

Upstairs, he dropped off his purchases and made an excuse about having forgotten to get eggs. No point in getting everyone anxious when there was nothing they could do.

The crowd in the market had dispersed, but the demon who'd been stolen from was dragging a golden-haired child by his ear with Ruslan hurrying along behind him.

The demon shook Kae roughly. "Your kind hasn't taken enough from demons? You think you can just walk into Raqia and help yourself to whatever you like?"

Ruslan pleaded his friend's case. "He wasn't stealing. It's my fault. I didn't explain to him how the market worked."

"Didn't explain to him how not to get caught, you mean."

Belphagor approached, deliberately ignoring Ruslan. "What's he stolen?" He reached to untie the purse on his belt. "I'll reimburse you."

The demon scowled at him. "It's not the cost, it's the principle. He needs the sort of beating his people no doubt dole out to their demon servants on a daily basis."

Kae appeared to be taking this calmly, although his eyes were as wide as saucers.

Belphagor pinned him with a hard gaze. "What did you steal, boy?"

"I ate a meat pie." There was no defiance in his tone, and no real fear, only a sort of surprise that he was being treated so brutishly.

Shaking out a few facet chips that were more than generous for a single meat pie, Belphagor handed them to the vendor and took Kae by the collar. "These are my boys. I own the demon, and it seems he's brought me another houseboy. Not my fault if the Host can't keep track of their brats. Good work, Ruslan." He turned Kae's face to his with a rough hold on his jaw. "If you're as good at scrubbing floors as you are at arrogant entitlement, I'm sure we'll get along nicely." Snapping his fingers at Ruslan, he turned Kae about and led him along one of the cobblestone streets without looking back.

When they were well enough away, he paused and took off his coat to put it on Kae. The snow wasn't falling this morning, but it was far too cold outside for the fancy indoor jacket the boy had on.

"Sorry about that." Belphagor buttoned him up. "It seemed the easiest way to get you out of your predicament. And I'm very sorry to hear of your loss."

Kae acknowledged the condolence with a nod of uncanny adult grace.

Belphagor turned to Ruslan. "Exactly how did you two get into this predicament?"

"I ran away," said Kae.

Belphagor raised an eyebrow and glanced once more at Ruslan.

"He overheard the grand duke telling the principality he couldn't take proper care of a boy all alone. He wants Kae to stay at the supernal palace with his cousins."

"And you don't care for your cousins?"

Kae shrugged. "They're all right for girls. But Ruslan told me all about Raqia and the Demon Market. He said he knew of demon boys who live in a house together and get to do as they please."

Ruslan looked chagrined. "I didn't mean for him to try to come here. He snuck out, and I came after him."

Belphagor sighed. They didn't need any more Lost Boys, and they certainly didn't need any runaway royalty. "Your father must be very worried. I'll have Major Phaleg return you two to

Elysium. I'd take you myself, but I doubt having a demon of my ilk as an escort would be viewed with anything but suspicion. In the meantime, we'll get out of this cold."

Though Silk had agreed to send Tilli and Danila to the capital to fetch Phaleg, his scowl as he sat hiding in the kitchen told Belphagor he was far from pleased at the prospect.

"I don't want him in my home." He peered through the kitchen door, open a crack. In the parlor, the boys surrounded Kae with fascination. "Phaleg, I mean. Not the little boy. I've nothing against *him*."

Belphagor sighed. "Are you never going to forgive him for doing his job?"

Silk's eyes narrowed. "Spying on me was doing his job? Lying to me was his job? Discrediting the Fallen is his damned job?"

Belphagor's mouth twitched. "I'm not sure if you noticed, but I've been involved in all three of those activities. And it's not for fun and games. We're trying to prevent an assassination and a bloody war that will do far worse than discredit our kind. Phaleg believes dissuading the principality from signing the Liberation Decree is the only way."

"That's complete bullshit. If he has such great rapport with his precious principality, why couldn't he find some other way that doesn't involve shitting all over us? Regardless, he didn't have to lie to me. Neither did you." Silk glared at Vasily where he crouched before the wood stove, stoking it with a few firespirit breaths. "Either of you. None of you trusted me. You made me a fool. Good enough to run your brothel and suck your cocks for a lark, or maybe stand there and look pretty—all of which I do damned well, make no mistake—but not good enough to treat me with respect. What am I, after all, but a sissy whore from the Fletchery?"

Vasily's eyes skittered with sparks. "Don't you say that—"

"It's true," Belphagor interrupted, and Vasily gaped at him while Silk looked ready to challenge him to a duel. "Everything you've said about me is true. I've treated you shabbily. You're my business partner and an adult—and my friend, if I may be counted as such—and I treated you like a child who couldn't be trusted. I'm sorry."

Vasily's jaw went slacker.

Silk blinked as if he had something in his eye. "Damn right you have. You're a shit."

"Yes."

Vasily coughed harshly as if he'd breathed in wrong.

"And given what a shit I've been—"

"*Are*. Are a shit." Silk's eyes were still smoldering.

Belphagor cleared his throat. "Given what a shit I am and what my part has been in all this, your anger seems disproportionately directed toward Phaleg."

Silk rolled his eyes. "Yes, well, had we been sleeping together at the time, you'd be out on your ass too. I don't care if you *are* my landlord."

Vasily closed the stove door. "You were sleeping together?"

"It's a figure of speech."

Vasily stood, brushing off his hands. "Not one I've ever heard you use before. And I've actually slept with you. Several times."

Silk began setting the table, placing the plates heavily against the wood without responding.

Vasily traded knowing looks with Belphagor. "As little as I care for Phaleg personally—and I can't believe I'm saying this—I think he was good for you. And I think you're being too hard on him."

Silk dropped a plate on the table from too great a height, and the porcelain cracked. "What is *with* you two?" He pressed his back against the table, looking like a cornered wildcat. "Why do you care what goes on between Phaleg and me? How is this any of your business?"

"We're concerned," said Belphagor. "You've seemed unhappy lately."

Vasily nodded. "And you seemed very happy when you were tormenting that insufferable angel."

Silk laughed humorlessly. "Let's drop the subject, shall we? I don't want to hear anything more about him."

When Phaleg arrived, Silk escaped to his room and shut the door. Phaleg pretended not to notice. Before he left with the boys, Belphagor took him aside to find out whether the evening's events had resulted in the outcome he'd hoped for.

"Despite being disillusioned and disheartened by it all, the principality still insists that signing the decree is the right thing to do."

Belphagor clenched his fists at his sides. "So all of that chaos—putting lives in danger—was for nothing."

"Not for nothing. I think his eyes are opened now. He acknowledges the threat of conspiracy. But he's stubbornly committed to making the decree his legacy. He wants to be seen as a just ruler." Phaleg raked his fingers through the curls at his forehead and let out a tired, hopeless laugh. "He wants to be *loved*."

Belphagor lifted an eyebrow. "Don't we all."

"Heaven help me, I'm beginning to think he's right about the decree. Muleheaded and misguided, but right."

"What happened to 'it's the wrong time'?"

"Oh, I still believe it is. But maybe you're right, and there will never be a right time. Maybe the principality is obligated to do what is just and not what's expedient, regardless of the consequences."

"Well, listen to you, Major Phaleg." Belphagor smiled bitterly. "Don't tell me our noble principality's ideals are rubbing off on you?"

Phaleg shrugged, his shoulders heavy. "Ideals won't make a bit of difference when civil war erupts."

"Perhaps it won't come to that."

"If the Traditionalists manage to carry out their plan against the queen, Helison will act." Phaleg shook his head. "It will be too late, but he'll act."

# CHAPTER THIRTEEN

After Phaleg had departed with Ruslan and Kae, Belphagor headed back to The Brimstone with Vasily. Whether or not celestial stability was about to go to hell, he was finishing the game once and for all.

It was standing-room only in The Brimstone as demons crowded around to see if their bets would pay off. Belphagor arrived at the table with Vasily at his side, and Kezef cut the wingcasting deck with a smirk.

"Very considerate of you to bring the currency right to the table. Saves me the time of having you fetch him after I win." He winked at Vasily, as though thoroughly convinced of his own irresistibility.

Vasily's eyes kindled, and he made a threatening move toward Kezef, but Belphagor stopped him with a hand against his chest. "Keep still, boy."

When Vasily turned his outraged expression on him, Belphagor gave him a significant look, reminding him of their agreement. Vasily sat without another word. Belphagor had allowed him to look on so long as he managed to sit quietly throughout the game. One word, and he'd be banished to their room to wait it out, no matter how long the game took.

Fortunately, Belphagor didn't intend for it to take very long.

Kezef dealt, and Belphagor cast. Kezef called the die accurately. Belphagor laid a card on the pile, and Kezef took it. Except for their calls, they played in silence, and the fierce concentration was infectious. Observers held their breath with every play, letting out a collective, audible gasp when Kezef handily swept the first two rounds. He had only to win three in a row to take the match and the tournament. Belphagor was counting on Kezef letting down his guard, and he wasn't disappointed. It wasn't much, a slight slip in concentration as Kezef prepared to declare victory.

At the opening of the third round, Kezef cast the die, and Belphagor deliberately missed the call, pretending to be flustered, as he'd been in Kezef's "practice game" the previous evening. Kezef raised his brow and watched Belphagor toss down a card, seemingly at random and born of frustration.

Kezef couldn't resist a dig. "I almost feel guilty taking your boy at this point. But I am looking forward to hearing him beg for the complete degradation he and I both know he desires."

Vasily half rose from his chair with a low warning growl, but before he could get into trouble, Belphagor cast the die, and Kezef's swift call drew everyone's attention. The die landed on a corner and teetered near the face matching Kezef's call before flipping to the adjacent one.

Kezef was obviously trying to keep his expression neutral as he studied his cards, but a slight muscle twitch gave away his tension. He had to be holding a near-perfect hand if giving one up would cost him the lead. He set one down and took up the die, but Belphagor had already taken the discard. For Kezef to hesitate over the loss of a single card, he could only have been nursing a scarlet or ebony wing. Belphagor laid his cards face up on the table: four of a choir. And fourchoir could only be beaten by a wing.

Kezef laid down his: fourchoir in the suit of facets. A rare tie. This meant Belphagor had another three rounds to win, as neither could count this one. They each rolled the die to see who would deal the next hand. Kezef won the deal with a fire-element creature to Belphagor's earth. He dealt. They perused their cards. Belphagor cast. Kezef lost his call and surrendered a card without hesitation; his choice of discard had been immaterial, which meant he had nothing viable. Belphagor ignored the discard to give Kezef the idea he was close to a winning hand already.

Kezef cast. Belphagor called and missed and surrendered a card with an air of misgiving to give Kezef the impression he'd been on the verge of completing a wing. The misdirection paid off. Kezef played his hand too quickly, putting down another fourchoir. Belphagor smiled and laid down a pristine ebony wing, a hand that needed one less card than a regular wing.

Kezef's eyes narrowed. The odds of being dealt a perfect ebony wing were absurd. Belphagor had influenced Kezef's shuffling. Which seemed only fair, considering Kezef was still using some kind of illegal charm.

As the loser, Kezef dealt the next round as well, and after a few casts, Belphagor won it handily, without tricks. Kezef's charm seemed only to work when the other player dealt. One round to go, and it was Kezef's to deal.

Kezef set his hand over the die once he'd dealt so he could examine his cards thoroughly before Belphagor could cast it. Technically, a player wasn't allowed to touch the die when it wasn't his turn to cast, but Belphagor sighed and overlooked it. He'd be done with Kezef in a minute.

When Kezef moved his hand away, however, and Belphagor cast, he realized his mistake. The charm wasn't in the dealing, it was in whatever Kezef laid his hands on. And yesterday had been his test. Belphagor hadn't been as off his game as he'd thought.

Throughout the round, when Belphagor cast, Kezef called it correctly without fail. It was a risky gamble with so many observers, but it seemed the majority were on Kezef's side. Most of them had been beaten by Belphagor on numerous occasions. Kezef managed to win the round with a full choir, and Belphagor was back to where he'd started.

"What do you say we make this round the definitive one?" Kezef smiled affably. "Whoever wins this hand wins the game. As much as I'm enjoying our time together, I don't relish playing until one of us dies of old age."

Objecting to this proposal would call attention to the influence both had been employing, but Belphagor wasn't about to give Kezef the advantage.

He nodded but raised his hand to call for the croupier. "Fresh deck and a fresh die."

Kezef frowned, but he couldn't very well refuse such a reasonable request. Circumventing Kezef's move to put his hands on the new set as soon as it was delivered, Belphagor took them from the croupier and murmured a neutralizing spell so no influence or charm would work on them. It meant he'd have to play this hand straight—but so would Kezef.

He passed the cards over. "Why don't you deal?"

Kezef pushed them back. "I'd rather you dealt." He held out his hand for the die. Belphagor shrugged and placed the glass dodecahedron in his palm. He dealt the cards and looked his over with a neutral expression. It was probably the worst hand he'd ever been dealt. Kezef scrutinized his with an equal lack of concern, but it was an instant or two longer than usual before he cast, which meant he'd likely gotten a shit hand as well. Hoorah for non-magical wingcasting.

"Eel," Belphagor called as the die tumbled from Kezef's hand. *Rook.* He took his time discarding, though he had nothing, to give the impression he might have. Kezef picked up his card with the air of a player who'd gotten a stroke of good luck. Which meant he hadn't. There was no penalty for holding extra cards. It was good strategy to take as many as one reasonably could without alerting the other player to the fact that they might be extraneous.

Belphagor cast, and Kezef's call also fell short. He ignored Kezef's discard. He still had nothing, but the card would have given him nothing better, and letting it lie said he had a viable hand. At Belphagor's side, Vasily shifted nervously at the slow progression.

Belphagor had noted the muscle twitch on Kezef's discard. It was time to take a risk.

"What do you say we make this worthwhile?"

Kezef observed him with mild interest. "Meaning?"

"I'll modify my wager. If you win, Vasily's yours for a week, and you keep your information. He still has the right to refuse you, but you'll have a full seven days—and nights—to persuade him otherwise."

Heat radiated toward him from Vasily's furious exhalation. It was like sitting next to a dragon. Yet, Heaven love him, the boy stayed quiet.

"And if you win?"

"You give me everything you have on the missing girls—no omissions, full disclosure. And you agree never to challenge my title—or my boy—again."

Without looking, Kezef transferred his cards to his left hand and held out his right. "Agreed." They shook on it, and Kezef made a movement toward the die.

It was all Belphagor needed to confirm his hunch. He dropped his cards face-up on the table before Kezef could cast. Vasily's harsh intake of breath was audible. The hand was pathetic: two of a kind and a partial sphere. But with a bet like that, if Kezef had held anything at all, he'd have shown his cards immediately, not wanting to wait to give Belphagor a chance. All the same, Belphagor's gut churned with anxiety as he waited for Kezef's reaction. If he'd guessed wrong . . .

Kezef displayed his cards. Three of a kind, and a pair of Seraphim. But they were in opposite-colored suits. Belphagor's cards were all in black. He'd won by a hair's breadth.

It was several moments before the uproar of demons bemoaning their lost bets and others demanding their payoffs died down enough for the two players to be able to hear themselves speak.

"Well played, Prince of Tricks." Kezef extended his hand in congratulation, but his eyes were on Vasily as they shook. "It's a shame I won't have the opportunity to lay you bare to your authentic self and force you to voice your basest urges before I exploit them."

Vasily lunged forward, but Belphagor gripped his thigh firmly while squeezing Kezef's hand until the compression of small bones was almost audible, and Kezef winced. "You don't speak to him."

"That wasn't a stipulation of the wager."

"Cross me, demon. See what happens."

Managing to retain his dignity, Kezef wrested his hand from Belphagor's. "You're only demonstrating your own insecurity that you suspect what I say to be true. But no matter. You won. I'll concede."

Belphagor ignored his posturing as he gathered the cards. "Pay up."

Kezef glanced about. Now that the game was over, no one was paying attention to them, but this evidently wasn't enough. "Not here."

"Are you trying to renege?"

"Don't be tiresome. It requires a more private venue."

"The taproom, then." Belphagor rose without waiting for Kezef's response, and Vasily rose with him. They made their way to a booth in the adjoining room, but Kezef took his time following, stopping off at the bar to get a pint. Belphagor took out a cigar while they waited, and Vasily lit it with the heat concentrated in his tongue. Which meant he wasn't holding a grudge over Belphagor's risky gamble.

"So where are the girls?" Belphagor demanded when Kezef sat.

"They've gone to the residence of an angel."

"An angel?" This wasn't the information he'd expected. "What angel?"

"A member of the nobility who hosts elite affairs that cater to particular tastes—more specifically, to dominants. He's a Virtue."

"A Virtue?" Vasily sat up straight. "Are you sure?"

Kezef took a sip of his ale, deliberately avoiding looking at Vasily before he answered. "He goes by the name Auria."

Belphagor spoke sharply before Vasily could give away what they knew. "So where do I find this Auria?"

"He rents a villa on the Left Bank of the Acheron. I've never been to it myself. He doesn't entertain demons at these affairs. All I know is what I've heard from angels who share our leanings."

Belphagor bristled at the idea that he shared anything with the sort of individuals, demon or angel, who would traffic in minors. "I think you mistake my leanings."

"You're absurdly self-righteous." Finishing his ale in one swallow, Kezef stood to leave.

Belphagor's boot blocked his path. "Where do you think you're going?"

Kezef stared at the boot for a moment before meeting his gaze. "I gave you the information."

"All you've said is that some Virtue in the Left Bank purchased the girls for parties."

"I told you all I know. Including his name."

"I suggest you plumb the depths of your knowledge and dredge up any other details you can recall, or we're going to have a problem."

"What details do you imagine I've left out?"

"Yesterday, you implied the girls were in imminent danger."

"Perhaps you didn't understand me, so I'll put it as plainly as I can. Auria has purchased these demonesses for a party—not 'parties'—an affair yet to be held. He's held such affairs in the past when he had access to a steady influx of girls from the Fletchery. Spoiled, to be sure, but not for his purposes." Kezef paused as if to see whether Belphagor was following, sighing when Belphagor continued to scowl at him. "As with the product at the Fletchery, these girls are only good for one use."

Belphagor's mind fought against grasping the significance, but his stomach seemed to know instinctively judging by the sick feeling in its pit.

"My understanding," said Kezef, in case Belphagor still had any doubt, "is that they place wagers on how long each girl will last under the lash."

Anger choked him, but Vasily voiced his disgust. "Sounds right up your fucking alley." The growl was so full of fire, the words were difficult to work out, but Kezef seemed to catch the meaning.

"Contrary to what that silk-tongued liar with whom the two of you cavort would have you believe, it has never been my habit to inflict violence for the sake of violence upon the object of my attentions. I find such practices contemptible."

Vasily's outraged and humorless laugh shook the booth like low thunder. "And what do you call what you did to me?"

Kezef's gaze traveled over Vasily with unmasked appreciation. "Precisely what you craved and deserved."

Belphagor leaned in with menace. "I warned you not to speak to him. Another word and you'll find out how I earned my ink."

Kezef rolled his eyes. "Your obsession with your petty glories among a bunch of pathetic humans in the world of Man doesn't interest me. But perhaps you should consider disciplining your overgrown boy. He does seem determined to engage me. Now if we're quite through—"

Belphagor jerked his elbow in an involuntary motion as though he meant to take Kezef down, and he couldn't help but take satisfaction in his slight flinch. "Not yet. I don't suppose you have any information on when this repulsive affair will be held?"

Kezef sighed. "Because this bunch was sold off before being put to use at the Fletchery, unspoiled in every way, they are rather highly prized. The buy-in is quite dear, and the Virtue has been hoarding his cache like precious gems until all the players were lined up. Which my information indicates that they now are. All I'm told is that it's imminent. So I suggest you stop wasting time needling me and go play the hero you so fondly imagine yourself to be." Kezef stepped over Belphagor's boot and took his leave without a backward glance.

While Belphagor stared at the table without seeing it, trying to decide what to do with the information, Vasily's hand slid across the varnished wood. Belphagor took it gratefully, glancing over at him.

"Kezef is scum."

Belphagor snorted. "That's an understatement."

They were both quiet until Vasily at last broke the silence. "I'm going to have to make up with Gaspard."

Belphagor jerked his hand back. "What in Heaven's name are you talking about?"

"The group is meeting again this afternoon at Auria's villa. If I can get Gaspard to take me there, I can find an excuse to look around and see if there's any sign of the girls. It could be our only opportunity to get that close."

"We'll find another way. You are *not* going anywhere near Gaspard."

"I can handle him, Beli."

"Don't 'Beli' me." Belphagor rose and headed back to their room, too angry to argue about it and too angry to see whether Vasily would follow. He arrived at the room alone but was inside for less than five minutes when Vasily entered and slammed the door behind him.

Fire crackled around his eyes. "You don't get to walk off because you think you're right and I'm wrong."

Belphagor dug his fingers into the back of the vanity chair. "Vasya—"

"You take risks all the time when the payoff is worth it. You risked *me* in your damned game."

"And I'm sorry. If I'd had any other choice—"

"I'm not asking you to be sorry, damn it. I'm asking you to trust me for once to be able to do something useful. *Do* you trust me? Because I trusted *you*. I let you bet me like a cheap purse to that vile demon because I believed you when you said you'd never lose me."

He'd rendered Belphagor speechless for once. There were few things Belphagor hated more than being wrong. And he was plainly wrong. When had his boy gotten so smart? It was probably all that damned Dostoevsky he'd been reading.

Vasily crossed his thick arms in front of his chest. "I'm going to do it. It's all we've got. You can do what you like to me, but it's happening."

Belphagor's eyebrow twitched, and he released his grip on the chair. "Oh, can I?" He stepped closer, and Vasily's face reddened, but he stood his ground. "Anything I like?"

"You always do, Beli."

Belphagor burst out laughing at the unexpected use of his pet name in the midst of Vasily's defiance, and Vasily glared harder. "I suppose I'll have to think up a uniquely appropriate punishment for your being not only stubborn as a mule but smarter than me." He could see the surprise at this statement warring with Vasily's nature; once kindled, his fire was difficult to extinguish. But his arousal at the idea of being punished seemed to win out over both.

Belphagor nodded appreciatively at the generous swelling beside Vasily's fly. He cupped his hand over it, relishing the warm exhalation this provoked. "You go ahead and play the game with Gaspard." He squeezed lightly. "Find out what you can. But do it using this"—he traced his fingers against the fabric—"and nothing more. Only your firespirit allure. You may touch yourself, but you will touch nothing of his and you will not allow him to touch you. Your cock, your mouth, and your ass belong to me."

Vasily's arms unfolded, his glittering eyes an extension of the heat Belphagor cupped in his palm.

Belphagor dropped his hand. "Later, boy. Go earn it."

Vasily stood outside Gaspard's house in the Merchant Quarter with his hands in his pockets, working up the nerve to ring the bell. He'd come up with his approach, but swallowing his pride was going to take some doing.

Before he'd climbed the steps, the door opened. Vasily dropped back, and Gaspard stared at him with an expression of disbelief, quickly replaced by outrage.

"What the hell are you doing here?"

"I came to apologize for overreacting."

Gaspard pulled his collar up as the wind whipped through the narrow street. "Overreacting. Is that what you call it? You physically assaulted me."

Vasily bit his tongue to avoid retorting that it was Gaspard who had assaulted *him*. He forced himself to breathe deep, the way Belphagor had taught him to increase his endurance during discipline. "I think we both had a little too much to drink that afternoon. I said things I didn't mean. I'm sure you did too."

Giving Gaspard an out for his own behavior seemed to do the trick. His demeanor visibly softened. "I suppose I did have a little more than I'm accustomed to." He stepped down past Vasily.

He'd have to lay it on a little thicker. "I don't blame you if you don't want to engage my services again, but I was hoping . . ." He let his voice trail off uncertainly, glancing away.

Gaspard paused. "Hoping what?"

"Well, I sort of need a patron. An actual patron, I mean, not a client. You were right about Belphagor." He growled the name as though he hated the sound in his throat. "He's worse than a wastrel. He almost lost me in his damned bet. He would have given me away permanently to be another demon's slave."

Gaspard straightened his lapels as he appeared to give it thought, clearly enjoying being in the position of power. "I did warn you. He's the sort of demon who gives the rest of us a bad name. Demonstrates perfectly the point the Traditionalists have been making that giving demons special rights would only lead to more entitled behavior without accountability."

Vasily nodded, looking down at his boots. "I've been thinking about that a lot. I think maybe demons like me—demons who don't make an honest living—ought to be subject to harsher penalties. It might have helped set me on the right path when I was younger if I'd had to consider the consequences."

The hard-luck angle seemed to win Gaspard over. "You mustn't blame yourself." He put a hand on Vasily's sleeve and stroked it fondly. "All you need is a decent role model. If you really want to become a more productive citizen, perhaps I could help you with that. I'm sure we could come to some kind of arrangement."

Bells tolled the half hour in the distance, the clear wintry air carrying the icy notes from Elysium, and Gaspard withdrew his hand. "I have an appointment to keep right now—with the Traditionalists, in fact—but why don't you come by at dinnertime, and we'll discuss this further?"

Vasily gave him a look that mixed disappointment with hopefulness. "Couldn't I go with you? I'd love to help the cause."

Gaspard considered. "Auria did say he wanted us to recruit a few trustworthy demons. And he's met you already. I suppose it's only natural my manservant and protégé would be such a recruit."

He smiled tentatively as though convincing himself. "All right, then. Why not?" He held out his arm companionably. "Come along."

As they set out for the Left Bank, Vasily found the route eerily familiar. He'd headed off to his ill-fated embroilment with Duke Elyon at one of these same villas two years ago, almost to the day. Auria's was a more conservative abode, not so much a villa as an ornate and elegant townhouse. Vasily couldn't imagine where he might be keeping half a dozen young girls in captivity.

The servant who let them in was a common angel and not a demon. Vasily had never seen an angel in a service capacity before, but then he'd never spent much time around angels outside of Raqia. He hadn't considered what place in society the lowest angels among the choirs might occupy. He wondered if their lives were much different than the average demon's.

The servant led them to a private parlor, scarcely sparing Vasily a glance. He was either well trained or extremely jaded. Auria and the others Vasily had met were already gathered, along with a handful of new faces.

Auria rose and greeted them with a sort of odd half curtsy that seemed to be the Virtuous equivalent of a bow. As before, Vasily was a bit mesmerized by his exotic appearance. In his own environment, the Virtue seemed more luminous, like a crystal facet turning in the light.

"I see you've brought us a recruit." There was no hint of disapproval in Auria's smooth voice.

Gaspard inclined his head. "Yes, I believe you've met my houseboy, Vasily. He's an eager student. I've been educating him in the inequities created by demonkind and the furthering of inequity that would be fostered by the handout system the Liberation Decree would usher in."

"Indeed." Auria smiled at Vasily. "I'm so pleased to see a demon of your generation taking an interest in the betterment of his kind through honest effort." Since all celestials—at least those who hadn't fallen—maintained the appearance of early adulthood until a swift and graceful decline at the end of life, the comment seemed an odd one.

"How do you know what my generation is?"

Auria's smile became indulgent. "I am a Virtue, my dear. It is in my nature to see things with clarity. Such as your mixed blood."

One of the merchants laughed. "I believe anyone could see that."

"The precise makeup?" Auria's gaze flitted over Vasily as though seeing straight through to the blood in his veins. "I rather doubt it. If you did, I would venture to say you'd stand a pace back." Vasily assumed Auria could somehow detect the potency of his element, but Auria didn't elaborate. "Now that we're all here, we need to move quickly. We have an agent among the supernal livery, but the driver he engaged for the queen's carriage has backed out, so we need a volunteer." Auria glanced at Vasily. "As Gaspard pointed out before, you'd be much too conspicuous in that capacity."

Well, that was a mercy. The last time he'd been coerced into a scheme to assassinate a member of the supernal family, he'd been "volunteered" to do the deed himself. His life had become exceedingly peculiar since he'd met Belphagor. He'd certainly never had a dull moment.

One of the merchants stepped up to take the job—a dangerous one, since the driver would have to steer the carriage toward disaster without raising suspicion, at risk to his own life—and it seemed a groom at the carriage house had already been bribed to loosen the rivets on one of the rear hubs.

Gaspard looked surprised as the planning escalated. "I thought we had some time to refine the plan. When are we doing this?"

Auria waived a hand dismissively. "Try to keep up. The death of Grand Duchess Tsirya has shifted the timetable. We make our move at dusk tonight."

*Tonight?* Vasily had hoped to find an excuse to slip away, but he had to do something to stop this. "What if she survives?"

The conversation halted, and all heads turned toward him.

Auria blinked. "How's that?"

"How are you going to ensure that she drowns?"

One of the Powers skewered Vasily with his gaze. "The river is extremely cold." The icy look and disapproving tone managed to convey that not only was Vasily obviously an imbecile, but he was expected to be silent.

He ignored the hint. "Yes, but it's no guarantee. She might be a good swimmer. And what if someone sees and tries to help?"

Auria smiled patiently. "The spot we've arranged is quite secluded. The driver will tell her he needs to take a detour because the ice isn't safe on the main path. The break in the ice will be a terrible irony."

The Power laughed, and Auria frowned.

"This is an angel's life we're taking," Auria reminded him sharply. "A member of the supernal family. Make no mistake, Major General, this is a somber necessity, a terrible thing that nevertheless must be done."

The Power went red in the face—an impressive thing to see on such a brawny, bearded angel. He cleared his throat, glaring at Vasily as though he'd been the cause of his blunder. "At any rate, she'll be bundled up in layers of heavy clothing and trapped inside the carriage as it goes under. She'll sink like a stone."

"Still," said Vasily, "things don't always go as planned. The ice might not break completely. The carriage might not fully submerge if any of the wheels are on solid ice. Someone should be stationed there to keep her from benefiting from dumb luck." He waited a beat while they stared at him as if he were a piece of furniture that had acquired the power of speech. "I'll gladly volunteer for that. I know some of you would be uncomfortable having to get so closely involved, but I have personal reasons for wanting to make sure this happens, no matter what."

Auria studied him with interest. "What reasons would those be?"

The volunteer carriage driver eyed him with a look of dawning recognition. "You're the demon they arrested for the attempt on the principality's life at the Council Square Uprising. But you were exonerated."

Vasily let a touch of fire show in his eyes, drawing a few gasps from among the angels in the room. "A member of the supernal family used me as a scapegoat in his own little scheme of advancement, and the principality was all too happy to have a demon to hang before the bastard confessed."

"Duke Elyon," Auria recalled. "So you're *that* demon." He nodded slowly. "I can see how you'd have a personal stake in this. You understand we aren't doing this because we have anything against the queen herself or the supernal family. It's for the sake of Heaven."

Vasily nodded gruffly. "All the same, I'm motivated."

"Indeed." Auria tapped his fingers against his lips. "Your protégé has good instincts, Gaspard. Yes. Let's station him under the bridge as our security should anything go wrong."

There was no time to get word to Belphagor, or to search for the girls, as Vasily was swept up into the planning. Barely an hour after he'd left the comfort and safety of the Demon District, he found himself standing on the ice beneath the Alimielov Bridge awaiting the arrival of the queen of Heaven.

Belphagor was putting another log on the fire at The Boudoir when the boys he'd sent to follow Vasily at a discreet distance reported back. He felt slightly guilty about the subterfuge. But it wasn't that he didn't trust Vasily; it was Gaspard and his angelic friends he was worried about.

He glanced up as Anzhela stopped the boys at the door and made them trade their muddy shoes for their *tapochki*. "What's the news?"

Olivier came to the fire to warm his hands. "He went with that stuffy merchant across the river to the Left Bank. We followed them to the angel's house and had to hide in a window well at the side of the building to wait for him to come back out. They were in there quite a while, and it was fuh-*reezing*."

Belphagor grinned. "Good job. Extra dessert for you both tonight. I think Anzhela's baking an apple pie. Giving the baker downstairs a run for his money." The scents of cinnamon and cardamom had been curling out of the kitchen all afternoon, mingling with the smell of burning wood. "Where did they go after?"

"The merchant went back home," said Danila. "Ruby headed toward the city with another demon."

"Toward the city?" Belphagor put the iron poker back in its stand. "Did you catch anything they said? Did they mention their business in Elysium?"

"Ruby growled something about not knowing the Alimielov Bridge from his asshole."

Belphagor laughed. His boy had a way with words. Heading for a bridge on the Neba, though? That was troubling. And the fact that he hadn't let Belphagor know could only mean he was either being coerced or couldn't afford to blow his cover because something critical was about to go down.

"We found something else." Olivier was bursting with excitement. "While we were huddling in the window well, something hit the cellar window from below. There were bars on it, and it was frosted over, so it was hard to see, but I managed to clear off a little square with my sleeve." He paused, drawing up straight with his chest puffed out. "We found the girls."

The tinny twang of a pie plate hitting the kitchen floor rang out, spiraling rapidly against the tile like a spun coin until a wobble slowed the momentum to a stop.

Anzhela appeared in the doorway, her face white and her chest heaving. "How many?"

"All of 'em, I think." Olivier shrugged. "Couldn't talk to 'em, though. Glass was too thick."

"They're all there? They're okay?"

"I mean, they didn't look happy, but they seemed okay to me."

Belphagor let out a breath of relief. He'd half-expected to discover Kezef had given him only one of several buyers or was making it up entirely.

"We tried to pry the bars off," Danila added. "But the bolts are soldered in place."

Anger flared in Belphagor at the thought of the girls being confined like caged animals in a root cellar. Fine setup that would be if a fire broke out. It was obviously the least of the dangers the girls faced, but focusing on practical concerns helped keep his mind off the real peril.

Although a fire might be exactly what they needed to get them out. Acquiring the Fletchery's "unspoiled goods" had no doubt cost Auria dearly, and he'd want to protect his investment. With Vasily about, an accidental fire wasn't far-fetched. How to get him inside the house at the right time would be the tricky part. Perhaps the only way might be an invite to that despicable party, though he hated the idea of cutting things so close. But the more immediate problem was why Vasily was heading for the Alimielov Bridge and what Belphagor was going to do about it.

He brushed wood dust from his hands with a decisive motion. "I have another job for you boys. And it's very important."

Anzhela cornered him after the boys had sprinted into action. "You knew. You weren't at all surprised to hear the girls were in that house."

"I only learned of it this morning. That's why Vasily's gone to confirm the report."

"What are we waiting for? Let's go get them." Her brow was white and flat with determination.

"We can't simply charge into an angel's villa and demand them." He pressed her forearm in reassurance, but she resisted. "We know where they are now. I'm formulating a plan. As soon as I find out what Vasily's gotten himself into and get him out of it, we'll put it in motion."

Anzhela pulled away, her gaze hard. "Vasily's a big boy. He can take care of himself."

"Anyushka—"

"Don't call me that. You're not family."

That stung. He'd begun to think of them all as family. But perhaps he'd underestimated the trauma she'd been through. Knowing she'd been raised in Masha's brothel, he tended to view her as worldly wise and unflappable. It was the aura she projected as surely as a glamour. She'd escaped the Fletchery without enduring physical harm, settling immediately into her role as the Lost Boys' surrogate mother, their "Wendy," with her usual pragmatism. But Belphagor hadn't considered the emotional and psychological harm.

Tears pooled in her eyes, and Anzhela brushed them away furiously. "It's been months. Heaven knows what they've been through. How can you think of leaving them there another minute?"

"My source says they haven't come to any harm." He didn't add *yet*, but Anzhela winced as if he had. "I won't lie to you. This angel has plans for them that are beyond despicable. But he's patient. He wants to make a spectacle of his cruelty with a carefully curated audience. He's engaged in other business tonight. For the moment, they're safe. And I intend to make sure they stay that way. Have faith in me."

Anzhela's scowl said she had anything but.

# CHAPTER FOURTEEN

The brilliant glow of a pair of Seraphim flying on either side of the Neba heralded the approach of the queen. But the expected carriage didn't arrive. Instead, a chorus of sound greeted Vasily, the incongruously joyous melody of jangling bells.

For an instant, he thought he was back in the world of Man. Belphagor had taken him to Vladimir to hear the ringing of cathedral bells at dawn as a backdrop to his first winged flight. He watched in surprise as an elaborate enclosed sleigh appeared on the ice, gilded and decorated with the two-headed Seraph crest of the House of Arkhangel'sk. Bridle bells on the trio of magnificent Aravothan horses drawing it were the source of the sound.

Yoked with a troika, the horses moved as a unit, the one in the center trotting at a steady clip while the two on the outside ran in a coordinated canter. This arrangement made them much faster than an ordinary team of horses, and the runners on the sleigh flew over the ice.

In the few moments it took to process this, the sleigh had nearly reached the bridge, thwarting Vasily's plan to steer them away from the weakened ice by spooking the horses with a display of his element.

He darted forward, shouting for them to stop, but the driver, of course, was Kazbeel, the demon who'd volunteered for the job. Even if he heard Vasily shouting, he would have no intention of heeding the warning.

With the otherworldly melody of breaking ice, like metal bending and bowing beneath them, time seemed to slow.

The sleigh lurched violently, and the right runner plunged through the ice. Scrambling onto the back of the center horse, Kazbeel cut the traces and urged the team on, fleeing without a backward glance.

The Seraphim, as predicted, were useless, circling overhead like bright beacons. Without pausing to think, Vasily dove into the icy water and pulled at the door of the conveyance, but it wouldn't budge. The terrified faces of Sefira and her companion stared back at him. Foolishly, the companion scrambled toward the other side of the sleigh as if Vasily were a greater danger than drowning. But Sefira, clinging to the ceiling over her head, kicked at the latch. Despite several strong blows, it held fast, and she was half submerged already. The sleigh careened farther into the water, one runner still half on the ice, and the screaming companion's flailing wasn't helping.

Vasily jerked hard on the latch as Sefira continued kicking, fierce determination in her eyes, and the door at last moved on its hinges. Luckily, it opened toward the front, which had hit the water first, allowing Vasily to push the door down and out of the way rather than having to hold it open against the current while he helped the passengers out.

He reached in to take Sefira's hand, but her companion's frightened scrambling dislodged more of the ice, and the sleigh broke free and plunged downward. He dove with it, hanging on to the doorframe, and managed to grab Sefira around her prominent middle and pull her free. As he swam toward the surface, the companion's face, contorted in a muffled scream, was visible through the rear window of the sinking sleigh.

Listless from the cold and her clothes a sodden weight, Sefira had no strength to help as Vasily tried to push her up onto the ice. Certain he was going to lose her, and becoming sluggish himself, he thought he must be imagining things when he heard shouting from the bank. He looked up to see the Lost Boys racing over the ice toward him.

"Another angel!" he gasped. "In the sleigh. Help her, please!"

Tilli and Danila dove into the icy river while the rest took hold of Sefira's arms to slide her from the water. They had her out in an instant, laying her on her back on the solid ice well back from the break. The dark, wet garments starkly outlined the mound of her pregnant belly.

Vasily hauled himself over the edge. "Put your coats down for her. The ice is too cold."

Looking chagrined, the boys scrambled out of their coats, making a bed for her. Vasily managed to lift her up a bit to let them slide the pile beneath her, keeping two to drape over her. She was breathing, but she would still freeze to death if they didn't get her indoors.

As Tilli and Danila reemerged with an unconscious angel between them and climbed out to lay the limp form on the ice, the blinding glare of seraphic fire from the guardians who'd been circling fecklessly overhead appeared on the bank.

"Time to go, boys," Vasily murmured. "Stay on the ice until you're well away." He knew the Seraphim wouldn't come any closer. With the heat they gave off, they could melt the spot.

Sefira moved weakly, pulling at one of the coats as if she wanted it off.

Vasily pried her fingers away. "You have to keep that on, Your Supernal Majesty. You'll freeze."

She shook her head. "Sophia. Cold."

Realizing what she wanted, he wrapped one around the unconscious angel, though he feared it was too late to help her.

Sefira took his hand. "You're very kind," she managed before closing her eyes.

He opened his mouth to reply, but a terrible sound split the air, obliterating all thought. He'd never heard anything so horrible. It was like the sound of a steel post being pounded and dragged over the jagged edge of a metal sheet, but he had the impression it was words from one of the Seraphim.

While his head still throbbed with it, another voice rang out. "Stand down! In the name of the principality of all the Heavens!" Above him on the bridge, an angelic officer on horseback pounded toward the bank. They all looked alike to Vasily, but he was pretty sure this one was Phaleg. Half a dozen soldiers followed him. Sefira was in good hands.

Vasily rose and headed away from the bank, carefully avoiding the weakened ice, and covered his ears against another metallic roar. But in the echo of the horrid noise, a welcome sound reached him.

"*Mal'chik!*"

No word had ever sounded so sweet.

By the time Belphagor got him back to their room, Vasily's teeth were locked together from the cold, and his skin actually felt cool to the touch. Belphagor led him to the bed and sat him down, crouching to unbutton his wet shirt.

"Let's get these clothes off." Belphagor smiled fondly as he worked his way down. "Though I have to say, you look damned hot with wet fabric pasted to your skin." He pressed his hand against Vasily's chest as Vasily peeled the shirt off. "But you're not hot, are you? You're cold. I don't think you've ever felt cold before." Vasily had goose bumps.

"There's a reason firespirits don't like swimming." He unbuttoned his pants and stood to strip them off. "It's not the cold. I can handle cold. Usually don't even feel it." The fact that he hadn't worn a coat when he went out was proof enough of that. "It's being surrounded by all that water. Having that much of our element's opposite on every surface of our skin kind of puts us out. Temporarily."

Vasily stood there in all his glory, and Belphagor reflected that it might be the only time he'd ever seen him naked without a stunning erection. "Then I should warm you up." Belphagor prompted him onto the cot and under the covers and stripped down himself before lighting the brazier. As he moved about the room, he knew Vasily's curiosity was piqued by the unimpeded view of his ink. He didn't offer to satisfy it.

Crawling under the covers in the absence of the firespirit heat was a novel experience. Turned out it was damnably cold in this room in winter. He'd forgotten. He wrapped Vasily in his arms—or as nearly as he could, at any rate—and kissed an icy shoulder.

On any other demon, he supposed it wouldn't be called icy, but on Vasily, it was downright unnerving.

"Are you sure this is temporary? You're not sick or anything?"

"No, I'll be all right." Vasily snuggled closer. "You called me *mal'chik* again."

"I did." Belphagor played with the spikes on Vasily's neck. "Because you're my boy."

Vasily's muscles tensed. "I'm your boy?"

"Were you under the impression you were someone else's boy?"

"No." He growled with irritation. "But you *said*—"

"I said we had to earn back that right. And I said I'd decide when I'd had enough punishment . . . *my boy*." Saying it, even in angelic, made his dick hard.

After a few seconds of quiet, Vasily spoke in his usual rumbly register. "I think I'm warming up."

The news came directly from Phaleg in the morning that the queen had suffered no lasting ill effects from her ordeal in the river, and her pregnancy appeared to be in no danger. He'd taken a chance by meeting Belphagor and Vasily in their room—after slipping into The Brimstone from the back—and out of uniform.

"You saved her life, Vasily." Phaleg was genuinely moved.

Vasily stuffed his hands into his pockets and leaned back against the wall, uncomfortable with praise from an angel—and this angel, in particular. "I did what anyone would do."

Phaleg shook his head gravely. "No. Even the Seraphim balked at jumping into that river. They're being replaced, by the way."

"Replaced?"

Phaleg scrunched up his face with distaste. "The only way to discipline the Seraphim is to return them to the river."

Vasily shuddered, knowing Phaleg didn't mean the Neba. The molten River Pyriphlegethon was their birthplace. And their death place, apparently. "What happened to the driver?"

"He was apprehended trying to sell the horses. He's to be hanged for treason."

Vasily felt sick to his stomach. That might have been him. *Damn*—might still be, if Kazbeel gave him up. "Are they looking for anyone else?"

"No." Phaleg's expression was hard. "I interrogated him myself and gave him the impression that his end might be made more merciful if he gave up his fellow conspirators. He immediately named you and your friend Gaspard but didn't seem to know the names of any of the angels involved. Or perhaps he knew implicating angels would be futile." The hard expression softened as Vasily's grew worried. "Don't fret, Vasily. I'm not going to mention your involvement to anyone. And if your name ever does come up, the queen will attest that you risked your life to save her and her companion. I'll testify to the same. For now, we're keeping that bit out of the official story for your safety. If the angelic conspirators get wind of it, you'll pose a risk to them."

"The companion." Vasily had almost forgotten about her. "How is she?"

"Not well, unfortunately. She survived, but her mind was affected by the deprivation of air."

"I tried to get her out with the queen, but she was afraid of me and wouldn't let me near."

"It's not your fault, Vasily. Don't torture yourself."

"That's *my* job," Belphagor murmured, and then looked chagrined when both Vasily and Phaleg glared at him. "Sorry. No disrespect to the poor woman. Just trying to lighten the mood." Straddling the vanity chair facing the wrong way around, he rested his chin on his arms over the back of it. "So what's to happen with the rest of the conspirators?"

"Gaspard didn't seem happy to be going along with the Virtue's plans." As much as Vasily disliked him, it didn't seem fair that he should hang for it. "None of the demons did. The angels, on the other hand, seemed more than happy to go that far."

"It's the angels I want to pay for their treason. But without proof beyond the word of demons, I'm afraid I haven't much hope of prosecuting any. That's why I'm also withholding Gaspard's name, at least for the time being. I've detained him for questioning, but so far, he's remained mum." Phaleg chewed on his thumbnail. "Since Kazbeel and Gaspard are unable or unwilling to name any angels, the principality believes only demons were behind the attempt on the queen's life."

"I could testify," Vasily offered.

"Testify to what? That a Virtue with an invented name was behind the whole thing? Sorry, I don't mean to be curt, but unless I'm mistaken, you don't have the names of any other angels either. This 'Auria' has been very clever." He glanced at Belphagor. "I'm afraid this worked far better than anything I pushed you to do. The principality feels betrayed by the Fallen. He's given up his plans to sign the decree."

Belphagor sighed. "To be honest, I doubt the decree would change anything. But it would have been a nice gesture." He sat back. "Nevertheless, now the queen is safe, there's a much more pressing concern. It turns out Auria is the one who purchased the girls from the Fletchery last summer."

The shock on Phaleg's face was profound. "A *Virtue*? Are you certain?"

"Positive. The boys spotted them through a window last night when they tailed Vasily to make sure he wasn't in any danger."

Vasily narrowed his eyes at Belphagor. This was the first he'd heard of having been followed.

Belphagor didn't seem to notice Vasily's reaction—or didn't care to acknowledge it. "That's why he went to Auria's house, in fact. He was only aware of the impending attack on the queen because he'd gone to see what he could learn about the girls. Since I presume this Virtue can claim to have legally purchased them as house slaves, I assume there's nothing the law can do, at least without proof of what he means to do with them. If indeed it is against the law."

Phaleg swallowed. "What does he mean to do?"

"According to my source, Auria auctions off the right to abuse them to other angels at a very elite party. The aim is to see how much pain they can endure before they expire."

Phaleg's complexion went from porcelain to green. "You can't be serious."

Vasily folded his arms. "Why, because they're angels?"

The skin tone changed again to a bright blush. Phaleg didn't need to answer. Instead, he addressed Belphagor's earlier statement. "Of course it's against the law. Heaven would no more tolerate such a despicable practice than it would the pandering of children. Whatever their bloodline." He pushed his hair back with a look of frustration. "But proving it, particularly against someone as prestigious as a Virtue . . ." Phaleg glanced at Belphagor. "I presume you have some kind of plan."

Belphagor's dark, determined look was for once absent of pleasure. "I thought I might need one." He swung off the chair and paced. "What we need is to get Vasily inside."

Vasily pushed away from the wall. "Wait a minute."

"You could say you have some urgent information for the Virtue, that you believe the demon who got arrested is going to give him up."

"And then what am I supposed to do? March down into the basement and march back out with the girls?"

The expression on Belphagor's face meant trouble. Not that he wasn't always trouble. "Actually, I thought you might set the place on fire."

"I might *what?*"

"Nothing too drastic. An accidental smoldering of the draperies. Enough that it can't be put out easily and the place will need evacuation. The Virtue is bound to go for his valuables in the cellar first. My source says Auria got them at an unheard of price. We'll get *him* to march straight out onto the street with the girls." Belphagor smiled, presumably at his own cleverness. "At which point, Phaleg shows up to question Auria, saying he's been implicated in the conspiracy against the queen." Phaleg opened his mouth, but Belphagor continued with a wave of his hand. "Whether any formal charge can be made against him is irrelevant. We just need him distracted long enough to get the girls away."

Phaleg was dubious. "What if something goes wrong? The place could go up in flames with the demonesses inside."

"Vasily isn't going to let that happen."

"*Belphagor.*"

The growled address got his attention. Belphagor turned, his lips parted as though he hadn't expected any opposition, and certainly not displeasure.

"I'm not doing it."

"What do you mean, you're not doing it?"

"I mean I don't like it. It's too dangerous. I'm not doing it. I'm not setting anything on fire." Vasily folded his arms as if forming a compact and impenetrable brick wall around himself.

Belphagor frowned. "What happened to trusting me?"

"This has nothing to do with trust. It's a bad idea. I think you're wrong."

The warning spark was back. "So you're refusing to do what I ask."

"I am."

"What if I order you do it?"

Vasily stared him down. It was never a good idea to engage a firespirit in a staring contest. "Seraphim."

Belphagor's eyes widened. He observed Vasily silently for several moments, contemplating something with an enigmatic expression. Then he moved suddenly—too suddenly for Vasily to react—and wrapped a shock of Vasily's locks in his fist. Belphagor pulled him close, head down, like he meant to force him to his knees, but instead brought his head up beneath Vasily's and kissed him with unexpected passion. "*Ya tebya lyublyu,*" he murmured against Vasily's cheek and let him go.

Vasily resisted the urge to put his fingers to his tingling lips. "What was that for?"

"For doing exactly as I asked. For letting me know I'd gone too far."

Phaleg was staring at the two of them as if they'd sprouted wings in the middle of Raqia.

Belphagor's pierced eyebrow twitched. "Something wrong, Phaleg?"

"I— *Nyet, ser.*" Phaleg reddened. "I mean, no." The struggle not to add *sir* in angelic was visible on his face.

Vasily suffered a momentary surge of jealousy, picturing Phaleg on his knees before Belphagor. But his jealousy was pointless. That was over. Belphagor hadn't so much as touched Phaleg since he'd broken things off.

Phaleg cleared his throat. "I don't suppose you have any other ideas?"

Vasily leaned back against the wall with one leg propped behind him. "I have one." He ignored the little *oh, really?* lift of Belphagor's brow. "If anything went wrong in the attempt on the queen, the group was to meet back at Auria's villa this evening after dark to determine their next course of action. What if Phaleg had a few agents of his own infiltrate the meeting?"

Belphagor glanced at Phaleg. "Are there any Powers within the Supernal Army you trust absolutely?"

Phaleg looked unconvinced. "One or two, yes."

"Have them question Gaspard and reveal their supposed support for the cause. Say they've heard whispers of the plan but didn't know whom they could trust among their fellows. They offer to help him escape. Pledge to assist. Ask him to convey their support to the Traditionalists. Vasily can talk to Gaspard once he's been freed and encourage him to recommend your Powers to Auria. Perhaps he's serviced them before at the Horse and can vouch for their Traditionalist sympathies."

Phaleg's slow nod said he was coming around to the plan. "And if Vasily claims to be familiar with them, he can get word to them to attend this vital meeting."

"Precisely. Once inside, they formally charge Auria and the other angels with conspiracy and sedition. Again, the charges may not stick, but it will give us a chance to get the girls to safety. The actual conspirators will resist, but this is where you arrive. Don't tell anyone in advance. No Supernal Army patrol. Not to impugn the honesty of your men, but we don't know who may be in league with the Traditionalists.

"Instead, bring a pair of Ophanim Guard as an escort, claiming there's a report of trouble at the house. With the two Powers inside, that gives you four very formidable agents. Certainly enough to subdue a handful of angels. Meanwhile, I let myself in through an upstairs balcony window, and Vasily will use the opportunity to secure the girls' location and ensure none of Auria's agents manage to spirit them out." Belphagor glanced Vasily's way, his face stern. "Won't you."

"*Da, ser*." He answered in Russian more to get under Phaleg's skin than because he was feeling particularly obedient. But the words always made him want to be in that space with Belphagor, owned and cherished. *His.*

They seemed to have a similar effect on Belphagor. "I think that will do, Phaleg. I'll contact you with the details." The tone was a clear dismissal.

Phaleg bowed and let himself out.

There was no need for Vasily to go in search of Gaspard to set the plan in motion, as Gaspard sought him out at The Brimstone as soon as the Powers had freed him from detainment. Vasily joined him in a private booth after a barmaid came to fetch him.

Gaspard grasped his hands across the table, and Vasily had to work to keep from recoiling in revulsion. "I'm so glad I found you." Gaspard squeezed his fingers. "But I'm not glad I found you *here*. What happened to leaving that odious gamester?"

Vasily managed to free himself as the barmaid arrived with their ale. He spun his glass between his fingers. "I would have, but I didn't have anywhere else to go. After Kazbeel was arrested, I figured I should lie low."

"I suppose that was wise. If you'd been with me, you would have been picked up by the gendarmes. Kazbeel named us both."

"They arrested you? How were you able to secure your release so quickly?"

"Friends in high places." Gaspard smiled as if he'd arranged the escape himself. "Well, new friends, anyway. It seems many in the Supernal Army are eager for change. I was quite persuasive in my arguments and not only managed to convince two of my captors to free me but recruited them to the cause. They'll be attending our meeting this evening."

"That's fortunate. And encouraging news." Vasily buried his face in his mug to avoid breaking into a grin at Gaspard's arrogant stupidity.

"But you need to come away with me at once." Gaspard clutched his sleeve, nearly making Vasily spill the last of his drink. "You aren't safe here. Someone is sure to direct the gendarmes to this establishment when your name and description are given."

Vasily set down the mug and tugged his arm away to wipe his sleeve across his mouth. Gaspard gripped his hand once more, and Vasily suppressed a shudder. "But I'll see you in a few hours, Gaspard. Surely there's time for me to pack my things."

Gaspard tugged on him and got to his feet. "Leave it all. I will give you everything you ever need. I plan to take care of you and cherish you as your shiftless Prince of Tricks never has."

If Vasily protested any further, Gaspard was sure to become suspicious. He nodded and rose. "I don't know how to thank you," he managed in a low rumble that anyone who knew him better would have recognized as utter contempt.

"I'm sure you'll think of something."

On the way out, Vasily managed to free himself from Gaspard's grip by reminding him that others would see. On the pretext of leaving a tip, he murmured a message to the barmaid to let Belphagor know he was going.

By dusk, everything had been arranged. Belphagor had sent word to Phaleg that the gathering was imminent, and Vasily was already en route. But as Belphagor was heading out himself, Tilli arrived with unexpected news from Silk: Anzhela had been missing since the night before.

He frowned as he dragged the boy over to the bar. "What do you mean missing? Why is this the first I'm hearing of it?"

"She went out while Silk was at the club. Told us she was going to visit Koshka. Silk came back around dawn and went to bed while the rest of us were still sleeping. He didn't find this in his room until he woke up." Tilli slid a piece of paper across the bar.

Belphagor perused it and swore aloud. Anzhela had gone to Auria's villa to demand the return of the girls. If she hadn't been harmed, she was no doubt Auria's prisoner, and her presence would have alerted him to the fact that demons were aware of the existence of his girls. And he'd had almost a full day to do something about it. Meanwhile, Vasily might have walked straight into a trap with that creep Gaspard. There was no time to warn Phaleg of this new development.

Belphagor pocketed the note. "Thanks, Tilli. Tell Silk I'm on it."

Anzhela had used a visit to her mother at The Cat as her cover story for the boys. Perhaps an actual trip to the brothel was in order—not to see Koshka, but to enlist some aid.

# CHAPTER
# FIFTEEN

S now was coming down heavily as they crossed the bridge to
the Left Bank, and Vasily wished he had his frock coat, if
only to give him another layer against Gaspard's touch. Seemingly
anxious that Vasily might change his mind and go back to
Belphagor at any moment, Gaspard had hovered close to him all
afternoon as his tailor had fitted Vasily for a new wardrobe.

The few angels braving the weather on the Elysium side gave
him hostile looks and hurried past him as if he were a criminal.
It was a bit insulting. He hadn't picked a pocket in at least three
years.

At Auria's villa, they found the angels in the group already
assembled, including two Powers Vasily hadn't seen before. They
must be Phaleg's men.

"Vasily. So good to see you." Auria's sincerity was almost
believable as he took Vasily's arm and led him to the parlor
as though they were old friends. "We were worried you might
have suffered your compatriot's fate. I understand several young
hooligans happened by at precisely the right moment and rescued
the occupants of the supernal sleigh." Somehow, he'd been privy
to information that Phaleg had insisted wasn't included in the
official story. His smile lost its warmth. "Gaspard tells us you're
closely aligned with such a group."

Vasily glanced at Gaspard, whose usual solicitous expression
was absent. In fact, his gaze slithered away from Vasily's like oil
repelling water.

"It seems an odd coincidence," Auria went on, "that you
should manage to evade capture at the very same moment that a

gang of youths just like those of your acquaintance happen by. In the middle of Elysium."

Auria withdrew his arm and sat in the gilded armchair that was the only other unoccupied seat in the parlor, leaving Vasily standing awkwardly in the entrance with everyone's eyes on him. "One might surmise," he said drily, "that you got cold feet and double-crossed your accomplice."

Vasily cast a glance at the two Powers he assumed were Phaleg's plants but got nothing but grim stares in return.

"No need to confirm it." Auria crossed his legs beneath his Aravothan robe, his arms draped elegantly on the arms of the chair. "I've received independent confirmation. Fortunately for us, your cowardly actions have resulted in a favorable outcome. The principality has withdrawn his pledge to sign the Liberation Decree. While he is still not an ideal ruler and must be closely watched, the urgency to encourage his more competent brother to supplant him has been ameliorated for the time being." The cool smile never left his face. "This society will continue to hold the principality's feet to the fire over the issue of special demon rights and uphold the truth and rightness of angelic supremacy. As you can see, our cause has even grown in support." His eyes pinned Vasily with an inscrutable gaze. "You, however, are an unfortunate problem that must be dealt with."

Gaspard shifted in his seat. "You promised no harm would come to him."

Auria didn't bother to look his way. "It was a mistake to believe demons of any class could be trusted."

Gaspard rose, sputtering with indignation. "What do you mean by making such a gross generalization? I've supported this movement from the start, as have many of my contemporaries, though I see they have not been invited to this meeting." He glanced around the room with a frown. "I'm beginning to think I've been brought here under false pretenses."

"You were brought here," said Auria, "to tie up loose ends."

"Tie them up? Tie them up how?" His voice rose with a pitch of alarm. "I brought my protégé here to answer for himself. Just as you asked."

"Yes, and you brought him here in the first place. A spy bent on foiling our aims." Auria's unnerving gaze fixed on Vasily once more. "Who has said nothing to refute our accusations."

Vasily had remained silent, expecting Phaleg's Powers to make their move. But perhaps they couldn't act until Auria actually confessed to treason. His words so far hadn't implicated him in the conspiracy to murder the queen. Fine. If Auria wanted Vasily to talk, he'd talk.

"I did nothing more than you directed me to," he insisted. "On your orders, I awaited the supernal carriage at the spot where your agents had weakened the ice to ensure it would break through and plunge into the river. How was I to know the queen would come by sleigh instead, making a rescue attempt easier? Or that Kazbeel would be such a poor driver and a coward? He didn't stay to see the job was done, just took off and left me to it. There weren't any hooligans there when the ice cracked. No one saw what happened. They must have come later after I stayed to make sure the sleigh sank."

Auria wasn't taking the bait. "You see, gentlemen? This is what I mean. Demons understand nothing but violence. They've perverted the noble aims of this group. Our loyalty is to Heaven and the House of Arkhangel'sk. A demon's loyalty is only to himself."

Beating around the bush wasn't going to work. Vasily went straight for the jugular. "You're the one who said the queen had to die."

"I?" Auria was unperturbed. "Has anyone here heard me say such a thing?" No one said a word, although the two new Powers were exchanging looks. "It's clear, Gaspard, that you and your 'houseboy' have become a liability. We cannot afford to have our good name tainted by the ravings of radicals."

"Now, see here—"

Gaspard's indignant squeak was cut short when the Power next to him—not one of Phaleg's—rose and belted him in the mouth. Stunned, he fell back into his chair, his lip split down the middle and his long coat spattered with blood.

Auria frowned, drawing his long platinum hair forward over his shoulder. "Not here, Major General. Look, you've gotten blood on my carpet."

The Power glared back at the Virtue. "Exactly what do you want us to do with them, then?"

Auria looked Vasily over. "Take them to the cellar. We can dispose of them later. Perhaps one of my guests at tomorrow's affair would be interested in breaking this one. I hear he actually enjoys it."

Vasily snarled as the major general came toward him with the other Power to attempt to subdue him. "*Idi na khui.*"

"Is that some peasant curse?" Auria smiled. "Luckily, I don't believe in elemental magic."

"Well, you'll believe in this." Vasily's eyes flared as he flung the two away and lunged toward Auria. He managed to grab him around the throat, letting the Virtue feel his heat before the Powers dragged him off.

Auria clutched his reddened skin as he rose from the chair. "Get him out of here!" His voice, for once, was charged with emotion.

Gaspard, in the grip of another angel, snorted. "Did I forget to tell you about his fire? He's rather famous for it."

Auria threw Gaspard a scathing look, though it lacked the authenticity of a firespirit's. "I want them both out of my parlor this instant. Filthy mongrels."

Vasily could have easily tossed the two angels who held him, but if they were dragging him to the cellar, he needed to play along. Gaspard, dazed, stumbled after him in the grip of his captor.

The cellar door was to the side of a grand kitchen that could easily have housed several families. He made a mental calculation of the distance from the cellar door to the front entrance as they took him down the stairs.

But what met him at the bottom wasn't the girls. Instead, a solitary demoness looked up from where she knelt with her arms bound behind her. The swollen black eye threw him, but only for a moment.

"*Anzhela?*"

"I screwed up."

One of the Powers grabbed hold of his wrists to bind him. Vasily submitted without protest, but Gaspard sniveled and begged for mercy. Vasily rolled his eyes, wishing he'd shut up.

Satisfied that their captives were bound tightly enough, the angels left them. Vasily immediately concentrated his element into his hands and burned through the ropes.

"What are you doing here?" He moved quickly to release Anzhela. "Where are the girls?"

"The angels moved them. Somewhere upstairs." When the charred rope dropped away, she brought her arms from behind her back and rubbed her wrists with stiff motions. "I thought I could get them out." Her last word ended on a wince as Vasily examined her eye. "I paid a demon to pretend to be a messenger delivering me as a gift from an anonymous admirer. I even came with a card: 'To complete your set.'"

"You wrote a card to go with your own delivery?"

"I know. It was a stupid idea. But I couldn't leave the girls here another night. And the angel bought it. For a minute, anyway. I made my move too soon. He tried to examine me like I was livestock, and I pulled my knife on him." She gestured to her eye. "He moves fast and hits hard for a fancy, pampered shit."

Vasily shook his head. "He could have killed you. Belphagor has a plan to get the girls out. Gone a little haywire at the moment, of course, but we'll find them. Don't worry. This is a momentary setback."

"What in Heaven's name is going on?" Gaspard's sharp interruption, probably meant to convey defensive anger, merely sounded panicked. "Who is this? What plan? What girls?"

Vasily turned on him with a growl. "The young girls your upstanding Virtue bought from the Fletchery to have beaten for sport. I came here to find them."

Gaspard gaped at him. "Preposterous. And what do you mean, you came to find them? *I'm* the one who brought you, to . . ." He trailed off.

"To what, Gaspard?" Vasily let him see the fire in his eyes. "To turn me in for deceiving you? What did you think the angels would do, scold me? Maybe give me a thrashing to teach me a lesson?"

Gaspard shrank from him, apparently unable to respond to such plain truth.

Vasily shook his head. "You're an idiot." He helped Anzhela to her feet. "Come on. Belphagor should be letting himself in on the second floor right about now. We'll meet him upstairs while Auria's busy congratulating himself in the parlor. The three of us will find the girls."

"You can't leave me down here," Gaspard protested as they headed for the stairs. "You do, and I'll shout and give you away."

Vasily glanced around and found a pile of cleaning rags. "You're right. We can't have that."

Gaspard took a nervous step back and let out a strangled yelp as Vasily stuffed his mouth. Anzhela offered her hair ribbon to tie it in place, but before Vasily had secured it, the door at the top of the stairs swung open with a bang.

Auria glared down at him furiously. "You think you can tangle with me, demon? I will be the next Sar of the Virtuous Court of the Elohim!" His eyes sparkled with menace when Vasily didn't show the appropriate level of awe. "Bringing loyalist Powers to my home and trying to entrap me was a foolish move."

Auria stepped aside, and behind him, the major general and the brigadier shoved Phaleg's Powers down the stairs. The angels tumbled to the ground, blood dripping from their slit throats. The light from above illuminated their vacant eyes.

"You've brought about the deaths of two of the Host." Auria regarded him coolly. "I shall see that you hang for it."

Gaspard made an incoherent sound of fear, spitting the rag from his mouth. "I had nothing to do with this. I am loyal to the cause!"

Auria sneered. "You're a demon. An abomination."

"And what are you?" Vasily moved toward the stairs, a harsh growl thick in his throat. "You're nothing but a flaccid angel who can't get it up without inflicting pain on someone weaker than yourself. I had no idea impotence was a virtue."

His face white with fury, Auria took a step down, hands convulsing at his sides.

A distant bell sounded, someone calling at the front entrance of the house.

He motioned brusquely to one of the Powers. "Secure those two, and this time use something sturdier. Chain them to the posts. And Major General?"

The Power turned back at the bottom of the stairs.

"Break the merchant's neck."

It took Gaspard a moment to register that this instruction was about him. His horrified protest was cut short with a snap of the Power's broad hands against his spine before he dropped to the ground.

"It's not going to work," Natalya hissed at Belphagor from the bushes where they hid. "He's never going to let in a demoness whore."

"You're the one who insisted Tabris be allowed to make the attempt," Belphagor hissed back. "Now you're getting cold feet?"

"Not cold feet. Just bitterly resigned to plan B." She glared at him, brushing away a strand of raven hair. "*B.*"

Belphagor's smile was smug. "There's a reason my best plans start with *B.* I never come to the table expecting A to work. It's basic wingcasting strategy."

"You're impossible."

"So I've been told."

Light flooded the entry as the door opened, illuminating Tabris's torn bodice and bleeding lip.

Belphagor shook his head. "I can't believe you punched her."

"I didn't punch her, you bastard. She grabbed my hand and struck herself. Now be quiet so we can hear."

There wasn't much chance of missing it. Tabris had begun to wail at an alarming pitch. "He won't take no for an answer, sir! Please! Don't let him beat me again!"

Belphagor had been adamantly opposed to bringing Tabris in on this, but he had to admit, she was doing an outstanding job. He'd only intended to get Natalya's help as she was far more adept at spells than he.

Natalya had been instrumental in helping shut down the trade in underage demons on the Celestial Silk Road. But Tabris had overheard Anzhela was in trouble and insisted on being included. Though she'd suffered from mental confusion ever since the Ophanim had tortured her during the Duke Elyon affair, it was evidently one of her good days. She was quite lucid, and she was furious that Belphagor was treating her as if she were feebleminded.

"This is a proper angelic home," the servant announced with disdain. "You are not in Raqia." He tried to close the door, but Tabris launched herself at him, sobbing.

Belphagor watched with admiration. "She might actually do it." If Tabris managed to get inside, the charm tucked into her bosom would activate Natalya's spell. Natalya would be able to constrain the inhabitants of the house for long enough to give their friend Polina time to warn Phaleg and get reinforcements, while Belphagor would break in the back way and find Vasily and the girls.

"What the devil's going on out here?" Auria himself appeared in the circle of light from the interior chandelier, like a glowing Heavenly visitation from one of Andrei Rublev's iconic paintings.

"This *person* appears to be confused about her place." The servant held Tabris at arm's length as if she would soil him.

Auria grasped her by the shoulders and shoved her back with unexpected vehemence. "I have had enough of demons!"

"Plan B," muttered Belphagor and charged out onto the path, weaving drunkenly. "There you are, you trollop!" He caught Tabris as she stumbled backward on the snow-dusted steps and whirled her about, dipping his hand into her bosom to snatch the charm while pretending to drunkenly maul her. Her eyes went wide, and he hoped her lucid state held. "Thinks she can cheat me of my facets!"

"Take your bitch and go," Auria snapped. "I don't care what she's done, and I don't care what you do to her. I want you all off my lawn and back across the river where you belong."

Any hope that Auria's supposed virtuosity would prompt him to protect a young woman from being assaulted on his doorstep was dashed. Belphagor pretended to slap the side of Tabris's head and pushed her back along the path with a murmured "Run" before turning and charging up the steps like an angry drunk.

Auria stepped easily out of his way as Belphagor's swing went wide. "Leave at once, you foul cur, or I'll have you in the stocks in Palace Square."

Belphagor almost laughed at the affected threat. Who talked like that? And who used the stocks anymore? The Virtuous Princedom of Aravoth must be charming. "You, sir, are a scoundrel. I challenge you to a duel." He threw off his coat, belched loudly, and dropped his pants.

Auria jumped back in disgust as Belphagor's piss spattered his slippers. "Major General," he bellowed. "Your assistance!"

In an instant, Belphagor was inside. On his face, with his dick on the cold tile, and his back and shoulders being savagely beaten, but inside nonetheless. And the charm was in his pocket. If Natalya's spell held, no one was leaving this house until Phaleg arrived to take Auria into custody.

Chains were considerably more difficult for Vasily to warm his way out of. He'd burn himself—and Anzhela on the other side of the post—long before the links came close to giving. He had to come up with something else.

"I'm sorry." Anzhela's tone was defeated. "This is my fault."

"Your fault? Don't be ridiculous. It's the damned angel's fault."

"But he wouldn't have been onto you if I hadn't shown up here. You'd be smuggling the girls over the garden wall right now. I should have listened to Belphagor."

"First of all, nobody listens to Belphagor. Including him. Every plan he has, he comes up with on the fly. That's his skill.

And if he listened to somebody else for a change, his plans might go a little more smoothly. Second, that fool Gaspard is the reason Auria was onto me. Nothing to do with you at all."

Anzhela was quiet for a moment before trying again. "Well, you wouldn't have to worry about getting me out if I hadn't gotten myself in here."

"That's true."

She craned her neck to stare at him, looking shocked.

Vasily laughed over his shoulder. "Have to give you something to beat yourself up over. You seem to be enjoying it."

Anzhela sighed and sat back. "Thanks. I appreciate it." At least she sounded less dejected.

The pressure of her shoulder against his gave him an idea. "Come on, let's stand up together. I think I can do something with this post."

They pushed against each other awkwardly to get to their feet, Vasily keeping his knees bent to avoid yanking her arms up at an unnatural angle. He felt behind him to see if he could get both hands around the wood.

"Ball up your hands, and try to keep them away from mine," he advised. "This is going to get a little uncomfortable." He concentrated the heat into his fingertips, keeping as much away from his wrists as he could so the chain wouldn't get unreasonably hot. The smell of wood charring began to permeate the air.

"Ow. What are you doing?"

"Don't touch the post. I'm burning my way through it."

"I'm not touching the post. The chain is hot. *Damn it.*"

"I think I've weakened it enough. Bend with me, and we'll get the chain around the charred part and pull in opposite directions. Ready?"

"Are you going to pull the ceiling down on us?"

"No. One, two, *three.*" They jerked away from each other, but there wasn't enough room between them to exert much force.

"What about sideways?" Anzhela suggested.

"Good thinking. We'll do a hard lunge on three. To the right."

"My right or your right?"

"Yours, I guess."

"Are you left-handed?"

"No."

Anzhela sighed. "To *your* right. One. Two. Three." They lunged and were rewarded with a splintering sound as the charred section of the post cracked.

Vasily took a deep breath. "One more ought to do it."

"You're going to have to do it alone. I think I sprained my wrist."

"Shit. Sorry. Hang on." He grasped the post and gave it a burst of heat as he lunged, and the two of them tumbled onto their sides as the smoldering wood snapped in two. The loop of chain that had been around it left enough slack for them to wriggle out. Vasily helped Anzhela to her feet, and they headed up the stairs, but the cracking post had apparently drawn the attention of the angels. When they reached the top, the door opened, and the Powers were there to greet them.

The major general grabbed Anzhela around the waist and hauled her into the kitchen. "You're going upstairs with the other little sluts."

"And you—" the brigadier grabbed Vasily by the collar "—have proved to be too much trouble." He raised a short, curved blade, bringing it down toward Vasily's throat. Vasily managed to wrench himself from his grasp and dodge the swing, but he lost his footing and tumbled backward down the stairs, bashing his head against the stone floor. Dazed for a moment, he braced for the Power to come after him, but the angel stared past him. A smoky scent had begun filling the air, and it wasn't Vasily. In the corner, the pile of rags was going up in flames. A charred bit of the post had landed in them.

All around the cellar, heavy fabric draped the walls, probably to dampen sound. The blaze was moving fast.

"Fucking hell." Vasily scrambled for the stairs, but the Power backed out and slammed the door, shoving a bolt home on the other side as he yelled for Auria.

Vasily charged up after him and rammed his shoulder against the door, but without solid footing to brace against, he couldn't build up enough momentum to break through. Thick smoke billowed up around him, and he coughed into his sleeve. Even a firespirit couldn't breathe without oxygen.

"*Grebanyy angel*!" Vasily swore, his throat raw with smoke, and pounded on the door, throwing his weight repeatedly against the wood. Auria had to know the place was burning. He was leaving Vasily down here to die.

Belphagor smelled the smoke before the Power running in from the kitchen began to yell. Falling for his feigned drunken blackout, they'd bound his wrists and left him lying on the floor of the foyer where he'd landed. All he could see were feet.

"The whole cellar's going up! The damned demon set the place on fire!"

Auria's white robes swirled across the floor. "Well, put it out, damn you! What are you waiting for?"

"It's too far gone already. We have to get out of here."

"Upstairs," Auria shouted at the servants running for the door. "Get my trinkets. Quickly." He and his Powers tried to move past Belphagor but stopped in their tracks. "What in Heaven's name is happening?"

Natalya's spell was holding them in place.

Belphagor raised his head. "Untie me, and I can get you out of the house."

"What are you talking about?" Auria must have signaled to the Powers, as they stepped in and dragged Belphagor onto his feet. Auria held a silk scarf to his face, trying to screen out the smoke seeping through the cracks around the door in the kitchen. "You have something to do with this? Out with it! Now!"

"As I said, untie me, and I'll get you out."

Coughing harshly behind his scarf, Auria nodded. "Do it."

One of the Powers obliged.

"This is some peasant trick. Some kind of mesmerism." The words were punctuated with more wretched coughing as Auria's face reddened. "I suppose you want a ransom. Be quick about it, cretin, or you'll burn with us."

Wrists freed, Belphagor buttoned his pants with one hand while he closed his fingers around the charm with the other. The moment he touched it, he discovered the fault in plan B. The charm had been calibrated to Tabris's touch. Without her, the only way the spell could be broken once the charm had crossed the threshold was for the author of the spell to speak the release.

Behind him, the servants were hurrying down from the second floor, and with them, the Virtue's "trinkets"—Anzhela among them. Belphagor's eyes were starting to water.

"Hurry up, demon!" Auria's hacking had become violent, as if the smoke were much thicker. Perhaps Virtuous throats were more delicate than other celestials'. "What are you waiting for? What do you want?"

"I want my boy."

"Who the damned hell is your boy?"

"He's in the cellar," said Anzhela. At the same moment, the bell rang out overhead. *Phaleg. Thank Heaven.* Natalya's spell dissolved. Evidently, she'd stuck around.

Propelled forward as he realized he could move of his own volition, Auria shoved Belphagor aside and threw open the door.

"Your Virtuous Serenity." Phaleg bowed. "In the name of His Supernal Majesty the Principality of the Firmament of Shehaqim and All the Heavens, I hereby arrest you for treason and conspiracy to assassinate the queen."

Auria lunged into the fresh air. "Play your little game. No one will speak against me."

Belphagor grabbed Anzhela. "Where's the cellar? Quickly!"

Vasily had inhaled too much smoke to shout again. He'd never expected his own element to be the thing to take him down. At his final, feeble attempt to shoulder the door, the wood gave unexpectedly. He stumbled out and barreled into someone on the other side, falling on top of him. His eyes were burning, and he couldn't see who it was.

"*Mal'chik.*"

"Beli!" Vasily squeezed him tight.

"Get the fuck off me, boy. You're crushing my organs."

Vasily rolled to the side, and Belphagor pulled him to his feet, stumbling with him through the house and out into the brisk, winter air.

"Anzhela. The girls," Vasily managed.

"They're safe. The fire flushed Auria out with his most valuable property, right into the arms of the Ophanim and a full platoon of the Supernal Army." Belphagor grinned in the light of the blazing house behind them. "I see you recognized the brilliance of my original plan after all."

# CHAPTER SIXTEEN

The flat was filled to capacity, but Silk couldn't complain. Draped in oversized coats and blankets, the rescued girls had huddled silently together at first, no doubt overwhelmed by their change of fortune. But as they warmed up by the fire and listened to the boys' tales of adventure in the world of Man, they seemed to shed the last months like a bad dream.

The adults—Silk had to laugh, thinking he qualified—had all congregated in the kitchen with Anzhela. Belphagor and Vasily shared a cigar at the window—opened a crack at Anzhela's insistence to keep the apartment from "smelling like the gaming room at The Brimstone"—while Natalya examined Anzhela's black eye. Tabris hovered nearby, sporting a conspicuous bruise of her own.

Natalya glared when Silk noticed it. "I did *not* punch her."

Silk's eyes widened. "Why would you have?"

"I did it," said Tabris with a shy grin. "Nat was supposed to make it look as though I'd been roughed up, and she wouldn't, so I caught her off guard and swung her hand myself."

Silk laughed. Tabris was an odd one, but it was understandable given what she'd gone through after her sister's death. He knew she'd also gotten her start in the Fletchery.

"You shouldn't have put yourself in danger," Anzhela scolded, brushing off Natalya's fussing.

Tabris clucked her tongue. "You're one to talk. When Beatrix told us what you'd gone and done." She shook her head, as if she'd finished her sentence.

Silk glanced about. "Who's Beatrix?"

"Don't ask." Belphagor blew cigar smoke out the side of his mouth while Vasily snorted. Except for that one gruff noise, he'd been conspicuously quiet in the presence of the girls from The Cat. Silk was sure there was a story there, but he figured he'd get it out of him later.

Tabris's eyes clouded, and her cheeks went pink. "Did I make a mistake?"

Natalya squeezed her hand. "Not at all, Tabi. B's only being modest."

Polina rose and put her arm around Tabris's shoulders. "Come on. Let's help the girls get settled."

Natalya watched them go. "She's been better lately, but it comes and goes. Thank goodness she doesn't know what that damned Virtue meant to do with the girls."

Anzhela, perfectly stoic since her arrival and in recounting her ordeal, burst into tears.

"Oh, sweetie." Natalya gathered her into her arms. "It's okay. You're safe. They're all safe."

Silk got how it was for her. She hadn't been the "matron" of the girls' dorm, as he'd been to the boys', but as the oldest, she'd felt an intense responsibility for them. Though she hadn't talked about it much, he could tell she harbored guilt for having been spared their fate and not being able to protect them. The things Anzhela spoke the least about were those she felt most deeply.

"It's silly, I know." Anzhela tried to laugh. "But they wouldn't be safe if you all hadn't helped Belphagor after I nearly ruined everything."

"You didn't ruin anything," Belphagor assured her.

Anzhela's laughter took on a slight pitch of hysteria.

"You merely added an interesting layer of challenge." He set his cigar between his teeth with a grin when she smiled despite herself.

"All right. Enough of this." Anzhela dried her eyes on her sleeve. "Nat, help me gather some blankets and pillows."

Watching from the kitchen doorway as Anzhela turned the parlor into what Belphagor called a "slumber party," complete with whispering and giggling, Silk glanced at Vasily. "If I'd known sleeping together in a big pile on the floor was a thing in the world of Man, I might have stayed." He winked provocatively. "Maybe we should make it a thing here. A cozy pile of you, me, Belphagor, and—" He broke off in shock at what he'd been about to say. "The three of us," he finished.

"You could give him another chance," Belphagor suggested.

Silk blinked. "Who?" Vasily's snort wrecked his composure. He folded his arms and glared. "Shut up, Ruby."

"*Bozhe moi*, you're ridiculous." Vasily took the cigar from Belphagor for a puff but coughed violently, his lungs apparently still full of smoke. "Why don't you just admit you want him? Put him over your knee and get all your pouting out of your system with a good spanking. Works for Belphagor."

"Pouting?" Belphagor paused with the cigar at his lips. "I most certainly have never pouted in my life." When both Silk and Vasily responded with the same incredulous laugh, Belphagor's dark eyes narrowed. "I'll put you both over my damned knee— show *you* pouting." Vasily laughed again, and Belphagor pointed the cigar at him as though he were skewering him to the wall with it. "Later, *mal'chik*. I promise there will be consequences."

Vasily's skin flushed in that adorable way of his that mixed embarrassment with both defiance and arousal. It was something to watch the two of them. Their relationship seemed so easy. They could read each other without words, and the trust between them skewered Silk's heart with envy.

Why couldn't Phaleg have trusted him? And why couldn't Silk get the damned angel out of his head? He could have anyone he wanted among the deviant set in Raqia. Any number of sexy demons vied for his attention nightly at the Stone Horse. But all he could think of was Phaleg's complete surrender and vulnerability. Phaleg naked on his knees, wide ice-blue eyes gazing up with an intoxicating blend of fear and shame and desire, waiting to see what Silk could make him do next. Silk ground his teeth and forced himself to think of something else.

In the morning, however, there was no avoiding him.

Phaleg had arranged for the girls to take posts among the Winter Palace staff. He arrived with the news after breakfast. The queen was feeling generous toward demonkind after her ordeal, and having heard what the young demonesses had been through, she'd insisted on taking them under her wing.

While Anzhela said tearful good-byes and made sure the girls were well bundled against the cold, Phaleg stood inside the door, shoulders stiff and hands clasped behind his back, his eyes on nothing.

Silk had come out of his room to show Phaleg he didn't care one way or the other about his presence. The fact that he was wrapped in a glorious red dressing gown in his namesake fabric embroidered with a deep-scarlet curled droplet motif and lined with matching dyed Aravothan wool had nothing to do with the damned angel. It happened to be the warmest thing he owned.

"Have some tea." He'd been trying for a casual tone of disinterest and instead sounded like he was giving Phaleg orders.

Phaleg jumped and came forward with a nod as though relieved to have a command to obey. Silk stepped into the kitchen and poured him a cup.

Phaleg sipped it where he stood while Silk stared at him and said nothing to ease the awkwardness of the situation. He knew Phaleg preferred cream and sugar. He didn't offer it.

After a moment, Phaleg set the cup in its saucer and cleared his throat. "Thank you. This hits the spot. It's chilly this morning."

"Isn't it."

Phaleg stared down at his tea. "Silk." He stopped, sounding as if he had nothing else to say, but then took a deep breath. "I know you don't want my apology—"

"Of course I want your fucking apology." Silk stifled the urge to knock the cup and saucer right out of his pale, shaking hand. "I want you groveling on your knees, admitting you're an anti-demonic, privileged little asshole and begging me to forgive you."

Phaleg blushed and made a jerky, conflicted movement as though he might drop to the floor and do it.

"Not literally, damn it." Silk ran both hands over his scalp, smoothing hair that didn't need smoothing. "Oh hell."

Phaleg set the tea aside. "I *am* sorry. I betrayed your trust, and there's no excuse. I couldn't have been more wrong. About everything." There was certainly no doubting his sincerity. But Silk couldn't decide if sincerity mattered. "I wish I could take it back, erase it all with some kind of demon magic from the market and make it so I never hurt you. And that you didn't hate me."

"What do you care if I hate you? I'm a demon. It's a wonder I can bathe and dress myself, or walk about Raqia without succumbing to the urge to charge across the Palace Bridge and eat an angelic baby."

Phaleg's eyes bulged in their sockets. He opened his mouth and closed it, trying again to say something after clearing his throat and finally emitting a high-pitched squeak of uncontrollable laughter. He covered his mouth, obviously mortified.

Silk looked down at his crossed arms to keep from smiling. Why the hell did he want to smile? Why did he want to close the space between them, take Phaleg's hand from his mouth, and replace it with his lips?

The thought of Phaleg spying on him while sharing his bed stifled the urge. "There's no magic that can restore trust, Phaleg. You didn't trust me to simply ask me about the rumors or tell me what was going on."

"I know, and I—"

Silk raised his hand in a gesture that silenced him. "And I don't know if I can trust *you*. You're not a demon. We live on opposite sides of the same river, but we're from two entirely different worlds. Your loyalties will always lie with the Host, which is as it should be. But I don't know what future there is in our association if I will always be second to the entire angelic race."

Phaleg's expression was stunned, as if Silk had slapped him. "That's not how it is— It doesn't have to be. It's not how *we* have to be."

"Doesn't it? What happens when the next accusation comes? Or the next group of demons poses a threat to the principality because they demand freedom?"

Phaleg blinked. "The counsel I gave the principality was wrong. And my methods were wrong. But I realize those are just words. How can I show you that you can trust me? Tell me how to make amends."

Silk shook his head. "I'm afraid you're going to have to figure that out for yourself."

Silk's words repeated in Phaleg's head as the carriage conveyed them to the capital. He wasn't a demon and didn't belong in Silk's world. No matter how intense their intimacy—no matter the connection he felt when he surrendered himself to Silk—he could never really understand what it was to be a demon. He could never be anything other than an angel. And he wasn't likely to experience such a connection again. With anyone.

But dwelling on what he couldn't have was self-indulgent. He had his duties, and the repercussions of the failed conspiracy against the queen still had to be dealt with.

A grueling meeting with the principality and his advisors over the problem of the Virtue Sabrael—who had protected his identity by calling himself Auria in all his illicit dealings—went on until well after midnight. Helison had reluctantly come to believe in Sabrael's guilt given Kazbeel's testimony. But the word of a demon was worth nothing in court.

There were difficult waters to navigate when it came to relations with the Princedom of Aravoth. A nation ruled by a council of Sars—Aravothan princes—rather than a sovereign principality, they had long resented being subject to the Firmament. To accuse one of their own of actually committing a crime—and such a crime—might create a diplomatic incident.

Sabrael had said nothing to to implicate himself in the attack on the queen, and no angel would speak against him. With the Powers Phaleg had planted in his group now dead, there were no angelic witnesses to the conspiracy—and Sabrael had pinned the deaths on the demon Gaspard. The bodies were burned beyond recognition, and any forensic examination to determine the cause of death would be conducted by the Virtues themselves. Pursuing such an investigation would be fruitless. The only thing they might have on Sabrael was his questionable treatment of lawfully purchased slaves. But Phaleg couldn't prove that either.

At length, the principality's advisors convinced Helison that it would be a great insult to place the value of a few demon girls above the unimpeachable virtue . . . of a Virtue. Instead of facing prosecution, Sabrael was to be quietly invited to leave Elysium and never return to the Firmament.

For that, Phaleg was certain, the Virtue would make him pay.

# CHAPTER SEVENTEEN

Belphagor sat atop Vasily's ass with the blanket around his shoulders. Even with a firespirit in his bed, it was too damned cold in here. He leaned toward his boy and kissed the back of his warm neck.

"*Mal'chik.*"

Vasily stirred slightly but didn't wake.

Belphagor kissed him again. "*Mal'chik.*" Still nothing. Belphagor had fucked him senseless, after all, following several hours of sweet discipline. The poor boy was probably exhausted. "*Mal'chik. Mal'chik. Mal'chik. Mal'chik.*" He punctuated each sensuous murmur with a kiss, and at last Vasily opened his eyes. Or at least the one Belphagor could see.

"What are you doing?" The sexy growl had its morning roughness, as reliable as Vasily's morning erections.

"I'm waking you up, *mal'chik.*" Kiss. "*Moi mal'chik. Mal'chik moi. Milyy mal'chik . Lyubimyy mal'chik.*" Kiss. Kiss. Kiss. Kiss.

"Have you lost your mind?"

"Yes, *mal'chik.* Utterly."

Vasily twitched beneath him. "Why do you keep saying my nickname?"

"Because I can. Because it's yours. Because you're mine. I missed you being my boy."

"I was always your boy. You just wouldn't say it because you're a sadistic bastard."

Belphagor had felt Vasily's buttocks clenching beneath him as he spoke the endearment in Russian. It obviously affected him more than he was letting on.

Vasily yawned, feigning indifference. "Why did you wake me up, anyway? It's still dark out."

"It's after nine o'clock. Winter, remember?"

Vasily propped himself on his elbows. "How could I forget? You keep trying to steal my heat."

Belphagor grinned. "I wanted to go to the market." He loosened the drawstring on his pajama bottoms. "But now I want to fuck you again." He rocked against the small of Vasily's back while he slid a hand beneath his warmth toward the enthusiastic hard-on Vasily was trying to hide.

"*Fuck.*" It was somewhere between a hiss and a groan.

"Exactly." He proceeded to steal some of Vasily's heat right from the source.

When they emerged from their room in search of breakfast, there was no word yet from Phaleg. Belphagor had hoped to hear that Auria had been charged with treason, though he had little hope of actual justice being served.

They headed over to the flat to see if there was news about the girls, stopping in at the butcher's on the way. But as they neared the apartment, Belphagor drew up short. Phaleg, dressed in civilian clothing, stood waiting outside the bakery on the ground floor.

At their approach, he slipped the woolen cap off his head, his curls flattened by it. "Belphagor. Vasily." Phaleg nodded to them both. "I stopped at The Brimstone, and the bartender said you'd just gone out. I assumed you were heading here and thought I might overtake you, but I must have gone a different way."

Vasily held up the packet of meat. "Stopped for bacon."

Phaleg's expression had Belphagor worried. "Is something wrong?" He clutched Phaleg's arm. "It's not the girls?"

"No, nothing like that. They're very well, apprenticed to the supernal seamstress." Phaleg twisted the cap in his hands. "Could I speak with you privately?"

"Of course." Belphagor looked to Vasily. "Why don't you go on up? We'll join you shortly."

Vasily eyed Phaleg with his usual mistrust, but a glance at the paler-than-usual face seemed to make him think better of objecting. With a nod, he headed upstairs.

Phaleg turned back to Belphagor. "I've lost my commission."

Belphagor blinked. "You've what?"

"The principality had no choice. In seeking prosecution against the Virtue Sabrael—Auria—I opened myself up to the scrutiny of the Virtuous Council. They uncovered my association with known demonic agitators—" Phaleg avoided his eyes "—and managed to secure the secret testimony of a former Stone Horse patron. Apparently, the fellow had an attack of conscience and confessed his aberrant behaviors to one of his superiors. He described one of my engagements with Silk."

"*Phaleg.*" Belphagor touched his arm.

"But that's not the worst of it. The principality has offered me a chance to redeem myself if I name Silk in the conspiracy against the queen. To claim I was using him to uncover it. Sabrael put the idea in his head. After the accusations I made against him, 'maligning' his character, he convinced the principality that I must have had an agenda in doing so, deflecting blame to protect my—my lover."

Phaleg took a breath as if the word had winded him. "I refused. There's no evidence against Silk. Even Vasily, whom they managed to actually involve in the conspiracy, cannot be linked to it without an angel's testimony. The whole thing was absurd. But somehow, Sabrael learned how important Silk is to me, and he wanted to twist the screws. My refusal cost me my position. And earned me a dishonorable discharge from the Supernal Army."

"I'm so sorry."

Phaleg exhaled and stared at his feet. "It's all right. I think I'm all right. I mean, I'm not, but I'm somewhat relieved. The constant lying and vigilance against saying the wrong thing—I hadn't realized how heavily it weighed upon me." He glanced up at last. "But I think I'm going to need your help."

"Anything." Belphagor slipped his hand down to Phaleg's and gave it a reassuring squeeze. "Name it."

"My family has disowned me, which means I've been stripped of my noble rank as well, leaving me without protection. The principality's hands are tied. Though he has no wish to prosecute me, technically I've committed a crime against Heaven. Sabrael and his comrades have vowed to make an example of me." Phaleg took a breath. "There's a bounty on my head. I have to fall."

"You intend to live in the world of Man?" Belphagor couldn't imagine Phaleg there. He was utterly unprepared for life in the terrestrial sphere. Any angel would be. "Are you sure that's the right idea? Couldn't you stay here with Silk? I realize you two haven't yet patched things up, but I feel confident in saying—"

"I can't live in Raqia." Phaleg reddened. "I don't mean that to sound— It's not as if I think I'm superior to the Fallen."

Belphagor let go of his hand. "But of course you do. You are. You're Host. Why should you have to lower yourself?"

"That isn't it. You're not listening to me. Sabrael has employed the Seraphim. I can't simply slip away and hide among the Fallen. He'll destroy me and anyone associated with me. I can't bring that down on you. And I most certainly cannot bring it upon Silk."

The unarguable truth of this sank in. Belphagor tried for a moment to imagine an angel living among the Fallen without repercussions from both sides. The prospect was untenable, even without the price on Phaleg's head. "Damn."

"Help me." Phaleg's eyes searched his. "*Pozhaluista*."

Belphagor gathered Phaleg into his arms. This wasn't going to be an easy one. "Of course, sweet boy. I'm sorry."

"*Spasibo, ser*." Phaleg's voice shook. "And if you could keep this between us, I'd be grateful."

Belphagor cupped Phaleg's chin. "Silk deserves to know."

"He's made his feelings clear. I've written a letter for you to give to him once I'm safely away." Tears glittered in Phaleg's eyes as he took an envelope from his pocket, Silk's name written on it in a flowing, graceful hand.

Belphagor stared as Phaleg placed it in his palm. "Do you think that's wise?"

Phaleg laughed bitterly. "I don't think I've made a single decision that would qualify as 'wise' since the night I met you. But it is the *right* thing. That much I can do."

With a sigh, Belphagor put the letter into his vest pocket. "You'd best go on ahead, then. I'll meet you at The Brimstone within the hour. Ask for Oza at the alley door and tell him I've sent you to fetch my 'lucky ace.' He'll let you into my room. If there's anything you want to take, have it with you then. We won't be stopping anywhere on the way."

"So it's now? We'll leave straightaway?"

"It wouldn't be wise to linger if what you say of Sabrael's intentions are true."

As Phaleg nodded and turned to go, Belphagor paused on the stairs. He felt certain Silk would have forgiven Phaleg in time, but a fall to the world of Man might separate them forever. And both of them were likely to regret how they'd parted. "You're sure you don't want to see Silk before you leave?"

Phaleg answered without looking back. "If I see him, I don't think I'll be able to."

Belphagor was lying for Phaleg. Silk might have spent his youth as an indolent prat at the Fletchery, but he wasn't an idiot. He'd seen Phaleg from the window. Asshole hadn't bothered to come up. Apparently, he wasn't as contrite as he'd painted himself.

Before the smarmy, self-satisfied prick slipped on his coat and claimed he was heading out on an errand, Belphagor had murmured to Vasily in the kitchen that he should keep Silk occupied.

The worst liar in the Heavens, Vasily could only keep his head down over his plate of pie while Silk glared at him across the table.

"I don't need you to coddle me." Silk folded his arms, watching Vasily make himself sick on the dessert in trying to avoid speaking. "I know when I've been given the brush-off."

Vasily paused with a forkful of pastry in his mouth and swallowed. "The brush-off? By Belphagor? He's running an errand for— I mean, an errand."

"For fuck's sake, Ruby. Not Belphagor. I saw Phaleg on the street. I know the 'errand' is for him. He told me he wanted a chance to make amends, but he's obviously had second thoughts and doesn't have the decency to say so to my face. And now he's meeting privately with Belphagor. Without you, I might add. Aren't you bothered?"

"I'm sure it's nothing to be concerned about."

"Stop making excuses for him. Just go. I don't want you here."

Vasily set down his fork and stared at the plate for a moment before letting out a steamy growl. He took a crumpled paper sleeve from the pocket of his jeans. "I'm supposed to hold on to this until I leave. So if you want me to go, I guess you should have it now."

Silk stared at the folded envelope. His eyes prickled at the sight of the scrolling characters. The privileged little bastard hadn't bothered to consider whether Silk could read them. Block letters were one thing, but he was hopeless with angelic script.

"Read it to me."

Vasily gave him a worried glance before unfolding the envelope and taking out the letter. "'*Dorogoi* Silk.'" He paused. "That means 'dear.'"

"I fucking know what it means. I live in Raqia, don't I?" *Shit.* He was already crying. Why the hell did Phaleg have to use peasant tongue?

Vasily's gruff voice rumbled on. "'I know I have already done far more than you can forgive. This transgression will be one more.'" Vasily blushed impressively as he glanced up. "This gets kind of personal."

"*Read* it." Silk swatted at his leaking eyes. "Damn it, Ruby, please just read it. I never learned to read script."

Vasily cleared his throat in a rather futile gesture before he continued. "'If I could, I would offer myself up for a lifetime of penance, submit myself to your will, and kneel at your feet naked and downcast, ready to atone in whatever manner you command.

If you bid me to take the lash in the midst of the Demon Market, mocked by passersby, I would do it gratefully. If you cast me out into the bitter Elysium winter and bid me crawl naked across the frozen Neba, I would take my punishment without complaint, knowing that it gave you pleasure.'" Vasily took a deep breath before plowing on. "'If you ordered me to grovel at the feet of strangers and beg to be violated for your amusement, I would count myself one of the luckiest angels in the Heavens to be so used by you.

"'But I cannot do any of those things, because fate is unkind. It breaks my heart and hurts my soul to imagine never again feeling the silk of your skin, bearing the sting of your crop, or swallowing your cock until I am aching. But worse is the idea that you might think me a coward who can neither face up to his mistakes nor risk losing his status and privilege among the Host. Nothing could be further from the truth. I have asked Belphagor not to tell you until he—'" Vasily stopped reading abruptly, his eyes sparking with outrage as they coursed over the words. "What the *fuck?*"

"What?" Silk's stomach clenched, and his chest felt tight. "What, Ruby? Damn it!"

"'Until he returns from the world of Man'!" Vasily shook the paper in his fist. "That fucking bastard. He's falling with your angel."

"He's what?" Silk grabbed the paper and stared uselessly at the scrolls and swirls. "Ruby!" He shoved it back at him, and Vasily continued.

"'I have asked Belphagor not to tell you until he *returns from the world of Man* that I have lost my commission and my noble rank. I must flee Heaven with a price on my head. For me to remain in the celestial sphere would bring danger to everyone close to me—but especially to you. So I have chosen exile, and I will fall. But I will cherish the memory of every stripe you gave me, every sneer as you took delight in my debasement, every moment we have spent together, for the rest of my days.'" Vasily stopped again and folded the paper with angry jerks. "Fuck that shit, Silk. He can damned well tell you the rest in person."

"In person?" Silk shivered—in part, at the images Phaleg's words had conjured up—and hugged his arms.

"I assume you want to have it out with him?"

Silk considered, his mouth slowly turning up at one corner at the thought of exactly how he might *have it out*.

"Thought so. We're going to the world of Man."

# CHAPTER EIGHTEEN

Belphagor worried he might have done the wrong thing after all in agreeing to help Phaleg fall. The Trans-Siberian Railway proved almost too much for him. Demons seemed to take the differences in the worlds in stride after their initial amazement, but for an angel who'd been told all his life that the world of Man was either a figment of the Fallen's imagination or a bottomless pit full of torment and depravity, it was little wonder Phaleg spent much of the journey vomiting into the small metal toilet.

It couldn't have helped that he was missing Silk and that he faced an uncertain future in a world where not one of its inhabitants was truly his kind. The Grigori might be the pure angelic descendants of the race of Powers, but they had considered themselves demons since the first fall—as had Heaven.

Belphagor finally managed to calm Phaleg's distress by ordering him to kneel on the floor of the compartment. He slid to the ground so swiftly that his relief was palpable, as if it had been agony to stand on his own two feet—which he would have to, soon, of course, in a way he had never in his life.

"You're going to be all right." Belphagor stroked Phaleg's curls as he leaned against his knee, though he wasn't sure Phaleg was going to be any such thing. "I'm not going to leave you here on your own. My friend Dmitri will help you get acclimated. That's what he does. This network has been in place for a long time, for occasions such as this. Don't fret, sweet boy."

When they reached St. Petersburg, however, Dmitri wasn't as welcoming as he'd hoped.

"Why the fuck would I want an angel in my house?"

Belphagor shushed him, though he was speaking Russian and Phaleg couldn't possibly understand. He led Dmitri farther into the living room, leaving Phaleg to wait in the kitchen where Lev was preparing tea. "He's fallen. Little 'F', but fallen all the same. Heaven considers him no better than you or me."

"I highly doubt he shares Heaven's opinion."

"He's a good man." Belphagor's tone was clipped, but it softened as he added, "And a good boy."

"*Bozhe moi.*" Dmitri shook his head with dawning understanding. "This is the angel you told me about. The one you trained. You expect *me* to take care of one of your lovesick boys."

"He's not lovesick for me. Not anymore. It's Silk he fell in love with."

Dmitri's eyebrows rose. "Silk? Vasily's little twink morsel?" He glanced down the hallway toward the kitchen. "But Silk didn't love him back."

"I can't say for certain, but I'd lay odds at the wingcasting table that he does. But Phaleg didn't want to endanger him. He knew trying to stay with Silk in Raqia would put us all in danger."

Dmitri nodded and sighed. "And I suppose he doesn't speak a word of Russian."

"He can say *yes, sir; no, sir; please;* and *thank you.*" Belphagor smirked at Dmitri's exasperated eye roll. "Look, I'm sorry to dump him on you like this. I didn't really have a choice. He couldn't stay in Heaven. But you'll be well compensated, I promise."

The Grigori's dusty blue eyes seemed to darken. "Now you insult me. I have never taken money for giving someone sanctuary, and I don't intend to start now. He'll have bed and board here like anyone else. But I *will* expect him to learn the language and earn his keep as soon as possible." He scratched his trim beard. "Things in St. Petersburg are a bit volatile right now with different factions fighting amongst themselves for power. They say a new constitution is in the works. But I imagine I can find him something outside the city. Lev and I will have to move anyway."

"Sorry. I know I've compromised you one time too many."

Dmitri smiled reluctantly. "You do tend to put a demon in more compromising positions than anyone I've ever known."

Phaleg lay staring at the ceiling in the little guest bedroom after spending a mostly sleepless night. Every word of his letter to Silk repeated in his head like an accusation, while the memory of their last night together tormented him. He couldn't stop thinking about what Belphagor had shared with him on the trip—how Silk had been sold out of Heaven when the Fletchery was shut down, and Belphagor had found him being abused by the worst dregs of human society, drugged into compliance.

It must have been what Silk had been unable to tell him the night he'd recoiled from Phaleg's desire. The bad memories that had haunted him. And Phaleg had been so focused on his own pleasure that it had never occurred to him what Silk might have suffered until he'd pushed him to the breaking point. It was a wonder Silk hadn't tossed him out on his ass there and then.

The strangeness of this place hadn't helped matters. The deep, mournful hoot that called out periodically he recognized as the sound of the train that had brought them from the frozen lake country at the foot of the Hell Staircase that had seemed to descend from Belphagor's Brimstone room.

There were other sounds: the odd hum of the ubiquitous machines in the building that no one else at dinner had seemed to notice and the occasional roar of the larger, moving machines outside in the distance. It all served to make this world seem more like his childhood conception of the mythical demonic hell than anything he'd ever encountered. The prospect of remaining here for the rest of his days—where no one knew him and where he was certain never to connect with anyone else as he had with Silk—made the odd meal he'd eaten sit in his belly like a stone.

Lev, at least, seemed kind. A little like Silk in his mannerisms and physicality—though he was taller and looked more like an angel than a demon—he was easy to be around, and he'd made an extra effort to make Phaleg feel welcome. He'd even offered to show him around St. Petersburg the next day, which Belphagor promised Phaleg would find remarkable in its resemblance to Elysium. That, at least, might give him some comfort.

A knock on the front door of the apartment startled him out of his reverie. It was still dark, but like the Firmament, this place was situated in a part of the world where the winter days were short, and he suspected it was late morning. He couldn't make out the voices in the foyer, but the distinct bass rumble could only be Vasily. What in Heaven—*Earth*—was he doing here? Phaleg had hoped Vasily would comfort Silk in his absence, though it had pricked him with miserable jealousy to think that comfort might be physical.

He rose and pulled on his pants—the rough, stiff "jeans" Belphagor had bought him at one of the stops along the train's path—and remembered to stick his feet into his cozy house shoes. The earthly custom Anzhela had implemented at the apartment in Raqia reminded him of Silk, who had a pair of *tapochki* to match every elegant outfit he owned. How was it possible everything reminded him of Silk in this completely alien world? How was he going to live in this place if he couldn't put him from his mind?

When Phaleg opened the door and stepped out into the hallway, his heart nearly stopped. Not only was Vasily here, but Silk himself stood in the foyer.

"Silk?" Breathless, he could barely form the word.

Silk turned toward his voice nonetheless, eyes fixed on Phaleg without giving away any emotion. But his words did. "You complete and utter ass."

Before Phaleg could respond, Silk crossed the hall, spun him about, and pushed him back into the guest room, pulling the door shut behind him.

Silk held up the letter Phaleg had left him and shook it in his fist. "What the hell is this?"

"I don't—"

You think you can get rid of me with a letter? A *letter*?"

"Get rid of you? We weren't exactly—"

"You said you wanted to make amends."

Phaleg's face warmed. "Of course I do. But circumstances changed. Swiftly. It was too dangerous for me to stay."

"Too dangerous for you to walk up a flight of stairs and tell me to my face?"

Phaleg felt his blush deepen. "No, that was— Well, *that* was cowardice, to be honest. But the fall—it was something I had to do. Seeing you would have made me lose my nerve. And I needed all my nerve to do it. Besides, you weren't exactly happy to see me the last time we spoke. I thought we were over." Heat crept up his face once more. Maybe he was still misunderstanding. "Are we . . . not over?"

Silk's eyes narrowed. "You think I'd come all the way here just to tell you to fuck off?"

"I mean . . . maybe?"

The glare deepened, and Silk stared at Phaleg a moment longer as if trying to decide whether to smack him or kiss him. Then he did both.

Phaleg wrapped his arms around Silk as he relished the kiss, cheek smarting and eyes watering. The latter he tried to pretend was from the sting of the slap, without conviction. There was nothing in any world that felt so good against his body and his lips as Silk.

When Silk finally pulled away, he regarded Phaleg with a smirk. "You're not wrong. I would do that. But, as it happens, I think I must have forgiven you. Not that I won't still expect your penance. What was it you said?" He glanced down at the crumpled letter in his hand. "Something about having you violated by strangers?"

Phaleg's skin tingled with the thrill of fear and arousal. But he was still uncertain where things stood. He wasn't sure he could stand to be Silk's once more only to lose him again. "How long can you stay?"

"*Bozhe moi*, but you can be thick." Silk rolled his eyes. "I'm staying here with you."

"But I thought . . ." Phaleg faltered. He wasn't supposed to know about what had happened to Silk. Belphagor had told him in confidence.

"You thought what? I swear, you won't be able to sit for days if you don't spit it out this instant."

"I—" Phaleg blushed as his ass warmed at the thought of Silk making good on his threat. "I thought you hated it here. Because of your last trip." Now he was blushing with discomfort.

Silk slipped his hands into his pockets. "Belphagor told you what the drovers did to me. Where he found me."

"Not in any detail, but yes. He said Vasily offered to stay with you, but you refused because you couldn't bear it here after what you went through."

Silk exhaled through his nose with obvious irritation. "I don't know which one of you is more of an idiot. I turned down Vasily's proposal because I wasn't in love with him. Yes, I have some unpleasant associations with this place—as I have in Raqia—but I'm not incapable of appreciating what the world of Man has to offer. Would I rather be home, watching over the Lost Boys? Running the Stone Horse? Of course. But not without you."

The reality of what Silk was saying finally made its way through his embarrassment, guilt, and regret, and the effect was so profound, his legs nearly gave out beneath him. "You're staying with me. You'll be with me. Always."

Silk's lips turned up in a devilish half-smile. "Just try and get away from me. Dirty angelwhore."

Lying together later, with Silk spooning against him, felt comfortable and right, the silence between them natural, and Phaleg had nearly drifted off to sleep when Silk spoke softly into the pillow. "You asked me before if someone hurt me."

Phaleg, now wide awake, nodded against Silk's shoulder.

"I'm the one who hurt someone. I'd made myself forget it until that night you asked me." Silk's voice was small and tight.

Phaleg waited, almost holding his breath in the silence that followed, afraid to spook him.

After several moments, Silk spoke again, his voice detached. "I had a master before the Fletchery. I'd come to his house as a chimney sweep, but when he saw me, he said I was too lovely to be covered in soot, and he made me his 'special valet.' He's the one who— He said he loved me and that he couldn't control himself around my beauty. I believed him, and so I . . . I let him have me. When he tired of me, he sold me to the Fletchery, misrepresenting me as still unspoiled."

Phaleg had never considered how the construct of purity, invented by the Host, demeaned and objectified those it purported to protect. It reduced the assault of a child to nothing more than the significance of a tin of food with the lid opened. Once sampled, it became tainted, to be tossed out. *Spoiled.* The word filled him with rage, but he managed to stay silent, giving Silk room to tell his story without judgment, though he ached for the child Silk had been. He'd done the math. Silk couldn't have been much more than Ruslan's age at the time.

Silk took a deep breath as if to prepare for what was coming next. "Shortly after I came to the Fletchery, I caught Kezef's eye."

Phaleg's jaw clenched. Belphagor had told him about Kezef when they'd been forced to include him in their plans to take down the traffickers. He'd given Vasily a savage beating while Vasily was glamoured as a youth and had nearly beaten Silk to death for defending him.

"He put a 'hold' on my fletching," Silk continued, "which meant no one else could have me. He was allowed to do what he liked with me and to keep me at the Fletchery indefinitely, so long as I remained 'chaste.'

"But he said he knew I'd been done before. He wasn't interested in my chastity. He wanted to train me as a submissive." Silk shivered, and Phaleg stroked his arms. "Everything I do to you. Things I will *never* do to you. He taught me." When he spoke again, his voice was so quiet Phaleg had to strain to hear it. "He caught me once kissing a boy I was sweet on. Kezef said he knew my secret desires. He purchased my friend and caned him in front of me until he was unconscious. And then he told me to take what I wanted. But I didn't want that. I didn't." His breathing had become rapid and shallow as he choked the words out. "He caned him again. Lying there. Still. He said he wouldn't stop unless I—" Silk began to tremble, tears sliding over his cheeks into the pillows, and Phaleg held him tight. "I couldn't. I just couldn't. Kezef kept growling into my ear. *You know you want to. Let's see what your former master taught you. Fuck him, boy. I want to see you fuck him.*"

Phaleg flinched at the words and the change in Silk's voice as he repeated them. It was as if the sadistic demon were there with them in the room.

"When I wouldn't, Kezef held my hand around the cane and beat him again until he was bloody. He wouldn't stop. I don't know if I killed him. I don't know. But there was so much blood."

"Oh, Silk." Phaleg couldn't keep the exclamation in.

Silk went limp in his arms, as if the words had exhausted him. "He left me alone after that. Mostly. Though he maintained his reservation, to make sure I'd never be sold. To make sure I couldn't get away from him. I suppose I could have run away, but I stayed to keep him from the other boys. They needed someone to see that they were treated fairly. They needed someone to show them kindness." Silk drew in a shaking breath. "So that's it. Now you know what I am. If you want me to leave—"

"What you are?" Phaleg hugged him tightly. "You're a demon who had his childhood stolen. A beautiful, sensitive demon, despite what was done to you."

Silk turned his head. "Done to *me*? Were you not listening?"

"Yes, I was listening. And I'm sorry, so sorry, sweetheart, for what he did to you. For what *he* did to that boy, making you feel responsible for it. For everything."

For a moment, Phaleg was afraid he'd said something wrong, until Silk broke the silence.

"You called me 'sweetheart.'"

Phaleg felt the blood rush all the way up to his ears. "I'm sorry. I don't know why I—"

"I liked it." Silk stroked his arm. "It was nice."

"I didn't think you liked nice."

"Don't let it go to your head." His tone was once more the amused bon vivant as he rolled onto his back and drew the coverlet up over them both.

Phaleg tucked the fabric around Silk, his hand discovering the sticky evidence of the morning's activities. "We've ruined their coverlet."

Silk laughed, a soft giggle that verged on hysteria, as if the release of everything he'd been holding in had left him slightly giddy. "Your aim is fantastic. I love you." They both tensed as if they'd been hit with a static shock. Silk bit his lip. "I really just said that, didn't I? I've never said it before. To anyone."

Phaleg tried to breathe normally. "I won't hold you to it."

Silk pulled away and sat up, throwing off the covers, his eyes flashing. "Hold me to it?" He slapped at Phaleg's chest with both hands in a furious tattoo. "You asshole. You damned well better love me back."

Phaleg was so surprised by this uncharacteristic reaction that he actually laughed. Shocked tears spilled over Silk's cheeks, and he tried to extricate himself from Phaleg's grip, but Phaleg tightened his hold. "Don't be daft, milord." Heat rose up his face once more. "Of course I love you back."

Silk shoved the tears off his cheeks with the heels of his hands. "*Slava Bogu.*" He kissed Phaleg softly. "If there's a God somewhere in an alternate Heaven, that was a thank-you to him. Just in case."

Phaleg gave him a slightly chagrined smile. "And if there's a Hell, I'm fairly certain I'll be going there. With bells on."

Their absence had obviously been conspicuous, but the demons were nice enough not to mention it when Silk and Phaleg finally emerged. Silk insisted on holding Phaleg's hand as they joined the others in the parlor, his grip tightening relentlessly when Phaleg attempted to pull away.

The Power—*Grigori*, Phaleg amended mentally; he could see the earthspirit ruggedness, though Dmitri seemed less imposing than his celestial counterparts—regarded Silk thoughtfully. "Will you be needing sanctuary also?"

"I will." Silk glanced at Belphagor. "I'm afraid you're going to have to manage the Stone Horse on your own. I left Khai in charge, but I didn't tell him I wasn't coming back. He's also staying with Anzhela and the boys for a few days. I thought maybe you and Ruby might move in, finally get rid of that tawdry room at The Brimstone, until I saw the reason you keep that room. Your little 'ace in the hole' smuggler's portal."

Belphagor smiled. "Indeed. It's not the only reason, but it is chief among them. Don't worry about it. I'll figure something out. I only wish I'd thought of *this* solution before I left." He indicated Silk's hand around Phaleg's. "I'm afraid I may have been projecting a bit, hearkening back to my own first fall." Vasily's gaze narrowed on him intently, but Belphagor somehow managed to ignore the heat of it. "Suffice it to say, the world of Man took a while to grow on me."

"The reason I ask," Dmitri continued, with the sort of authoritative impatience that typified Powers in the celestial sphere as well, "is that I'm afraid I don't have any good prospects for you here in Russia."

Phaleg was startled by this pronouncement. "Forgive me, but when we spoke yesterday, you didn't seem to have any reservations."

Dmitri nodded. "My reservations are new. It's the combination of you and Silk together that presents a problem." He glanced at his partner beside him. "Lev and I have had a hard enough time trying not to attract attention, and we were born here. On your own, Phaleg, I've no doubt your experiences in angelic culture would have served you well enough. But together—and particularly together with Silk—you'd have targets on your backs. No offense, Silk, but the way you are . . . It's likely to get you and your angel killed."

Phaleg expected Silk to lose his temper, but it was Vasily who jumped to his feet. "Wait a damned minute. You're going to blame Silk for the hatred of some irrational humans?"

"I'm not blaming him. I'm telling him plainly that he stands out. And what you do not want to do here is stand out when you're in love with a member of your own sex."

"I can't go back." Phaleg clutched Silk's hand more tightly as if he could keep Silk from deciding to return without him if he gripped it hard enough. "It's impossible."

Dmitri nodded. "I understand that. What I'm recommending is not for you to go back to Heaven but for the two of you to leave Russia altogether. There are other nations where you'll find more welcoming communities. Or at least communities that will treat you with indifference. I have contacts across the globe, and I've already made some calls. I'd recommend the Netherlands or England. Perhaps the USA."

Phaleg stared hopelessly at the sounds of these utterly foreign princedoms. The prospect of living here in a land where the culture seemed in some ways familiar to what he'd known had been unsettling enough with its strange language and stranger contraptions. But if he couldn't stay here— Phaleg was floundering in a sea whose depth and breadth he couldn't fathom, his hand in Silk's numb as if he'd already lost touch with him. Perhaps he was spiraling away on his own into the Outer Darkness, and Silk was an illusion.

"We'll go wherever you think is best." Silk's voice grounded him once more. "You've rightly surmised that I'm a leopard who cannot change his spots, so I'll have to trust your judgment. We'll need language lessons, of course, and a primer in the culture."

"Of course." Dmitri nodded. "All will be arranged."

"There's one other thing I'd like to arrange." Silk gave Phaleg a sidelong glance. "I have it on good authority that the New Year marks your birthday."

Phaleg's eyes widened. "How did you know that?"

Silk's smile was secretive. "I have my sources." He turned to Belphagor on his other side. "Since I assume you and Vasily will be leaving shortly for Heaven, and Phaleg and I will be off to our new destination soon after, I think I should give Phaleg his present early."

The gleam in Belphagor's eyes as his gaze fell on Phaleg spelled trouble. "Marvelous. Looks like *Ded Moroz* is bringing all of us an early present."

Phaleg was banished to the bedroom while Silk discussed the particulars with Belphagor. His skin tingled all over as he imagined what Silk might have in mind for him that would put that look in Belphagor's eyes. Some show they wished to put on for the rest, no doubt, judging by his comment. Phaleg was mortified and thrilled at the thought of being ordered about naked in front of everyone.

Silk opened the door, face serious. It wasn't the mood Phaleg expected. He rose from his seat on the edge of the bed.

"Tell me you understand the importance of your word and that you will use it if your comfort level is exceeded."

Phaleg's heartbeat sped up. "Of course I will."

"And when I explain how this is going to go, you'll tell me right now if you need to use it and preempt everything. You won't allow me to start something you don't think you can handle because you want to please me. This is for *you*."

"Yes, milord. I promise."

Silk took a step toward him. "I love it when you call me that. But not this time. This time we will be strangers."

Phaleg swallowed. "Strangers?"

"Strangers—demons—who've spotted you on the wrong side of town. An angel. Alone. With no one to heed your cries for help."

Phaleg nearly tripped against the bed as he took an involuntary step back. His fingers convulsed on the edge of the coverlet. It was the fantasy he'd harbored all his life. His secret shame. And Silk was going to give it to him.

Silk's stare was uncompromising. "Do you want it? Yes or no."

Phaleg's limbs were trembling violently. He lowered his eyes. "I do. Yes."

Silk closed the space between them, and Phaleg moaned against his kiss as Silk's arms enveloped him. When Silk stepped back, he placed something small and cool into Phaleg's hand. Phaleg uncurled his fingers and glanced down. A little copper ball rolled against his palm, emitting the cheerful tinkling of a delicate bell.

He cocked his head at Silk. "What is this?"

"This is your word. You will hold it tightly in your fist no matter what's being done to you. If you need us to stop, if you've changed your mind at any time, you release your grip and let it fall."

Phaleg shivered at the words *being done to you.* "Why wouldn't I *say* my safeword?"

Silk's smile seemed a bit pitying. "You presume your mouth will not be occupied." The shivering intensified. "I won't be angry or disappointed in you if you use it. No one will. And afterward, I'll take care of you. I'll still love you. This is a game. A very serious one but a game. It isn't us. Do you understand?"

Phaleg didn't trust himself to speak. He nodded and made a wheezing sound as he breathed in too quickly.

Silk searched his eyes, and Phaleg closed them again. "Tell me what you're thinking."

"I'm afraid," he gasped. He couldn't seem to get air.

Silk's hand stroked his temple. "Do you want to be?"

Phaleg leaned into Silk's hand and nodded. "Yes."

"Good." Silk drew him close with his hands on either side of Phaleg's head and kissed his brow lightly. "I love you. Stay here."

Phaleg collapsed onto the bed when Silk had gone. "Heaven help me." But he was beyond Heaven. Beyond help.

He had no idea how long it had been since Silk left him and no idea what anyone was doing outside his door. Whatever it was, they were doing it quietly. The grim afternoon light had faded. He left the light off. It occurred to him then he ought to have used the water closet. But the door was opening.

In the dim glow from the hallway, a figure stood staring at him, dressed in dark clothes he didn't recognize and wearing a woolen knit cap that came down over his entire face, with small cutouts for the eyes and mouth. Phaleg couldn't tell who it was.

"Well, look what I found in here." The rough voice didn't illuminate. All Phaleg could be sure of was that it wasn't Vasily. His heart began to pound painfully in his chest, and his fingers tightened around the copper ball.

A taller figure came up beside him. "*Bozhe moi*, a fucking angel." The earthly accent had to be Dmitri's. Or Lev's. "What do you think you're doing here? This is demon territory." The demon—Phaleg had given up trying to identify him—moved with unexpected swiftness and grabbed him by the hair, yanking him off the bed. "I asked you a question."

"I—I don't know."

"Well, you're about to find out what happens to angels who wander where they don't belong." The demon thrust him toward the door, and Phaleg fell against the other blocking it. This one grabbed Phaleg between the legs without ceremony—and without gentleness—and Phaleg groaned.

"Oh, he wants to find out." The demon yanked open Phaleg's jeans and exposed him. Phaleg hadn't realized he was almost hard. The demon said something in Russian, and the other answered him in the same language, prompting both to laugh. The shorter one grabbed Phaleg's semi-erect cock and fondled it roughly until his arousal was unambiguous. The demon growled close to his ear. "You like demon dick, boy? Is that it?" Was this Belphagor? The demon's chuckle sent a chill down his spine. "You're about to get more than you can handle."

The two of them took Phaleg by the arms and dragged him into the hallway. All the lights were out. They pushed him toward what must be the parlor door. He stumbled through but didn't recognize the room. Dark cloth covered everything, and a dimly lit oil lamp threw strange shadows. Several figures rose at once, seemingly appearing from the furnishings, all clad like the first two. Phaleg's mouth went dry. He was no longer sure how many there were. He recognized none.

Before he could acclimate to the uneven light, they descended on him and pushed him to the ground, yanking at his clothes and stripping him. Phaleg struggled helplessly. It was freezing in the room. He couldn't remember his word. He couldn't remember his fucking word.

The ball was cold in his hand. "Heaven help me," he whispered and clutched it tighter.

The demons laughed, and one of them knelt on his shoulders and unbuckled with unhurried motions while the others egged him on and mocked Phaleg in the language he couldn't understand. Tears spilled from the corners of his eyes as his mouth was forced open by a pair of gloved hands he couldn't place with their owner. His fingers loosened around the ball.

The demon on his chest lowered his head to Phaleg's and whispered at his ear. "Do you want this, angelwhore?" *Silk.* Sweet Heaven. It was Silk.

Phaleg closed his eyes and steadied his breathing. When he opened his eyes once more, he looked into Silk's above him. They were plainly his. How could Phaleg not have noticed? No one but Silk had such beautiful eyes. He nodded. Despite the gloved fingers holding his jaw, the nod was clear. Silk nodded in reply before his eyes hardened, and he pushed himself roughly into Phaleg's mouth.

"Eat cock," Silk growled. "Show us all how much you love it. Choke on it until it spits down your throat." The rough words coming from Silk, knowing he was safe with Silk, made him shiver with arousal despite the way he was being used. He could barely call this cocksucking. He was helpless, and Silk was practically suffocating him, kneeling over his head and grinding into his mouth. When Silk came loudly, pressing into him, Phaleg nearly choked, but he managed to swallow the sweet demon seed. As usual, Silk pulled out before he'd finished to make sure some dribbled down Phaleg's chin.

The demons laughed, moving back for a moment to have an animated conversation in Russian while Phaleg lay naked on the floor with his prick at attention. One of them spat into his glove and shoved his hand between Phaleg's legs without preamble, smearing the spittle on his asshole. He gasped as a gloved finger played at his opening and then thrust in. The others didn't seem to be paying attention, engaged in some kind of argument. Demons were holding each of his limbs. He couldn't pull away. The finger pumped him vigorously, making him moan, and the demon grinned inside his hood.

Someone tossed a coin onto his stomach, and Phaleg jumped at the cold, making his ass clench around the demon's finger. The demon shoved another finger inside him while the arguing grew more heated. The coin was picked up and tossed onto him again while two of the demons shouted something. It was a contest, he realized, to decide whose turn it was next. But the demon who'd ignored the contest had three fingers in him now, leering down at him and flicking his erection.

Phaleg twisted his body uselessly, groaning, and the demons holding his legs took the opportunity to yank him forward, mounting him deeper on the ruthless fingers. The demon barked an order to someone, and a cold, slick liquid squirted beneath Phaleg's balls and dripped down. The demon pulled back his hand and scooped up the liquid, thrusting in this time with four fingers tented together. Before Phaleg could draw enough breath to cry out, the thumb was tucked inside the cup of the demon's hand, and it was all going in.

The demon made a lewd gesture with his tongue, rolling his wrist inside Phaleg. *Belphagor.*

"Fuck," Phaleg gasped without meaning to, followed by a long groan as Belphagor penetrated him deeper.

"*Bozhe moi,*" someone whispered. "Hold me, Ruby." Silk had slipped out of character, apparently overcome by the sight of Phaleg with Belphagor's entire fist up his ass.

There was no time to enjoy that moment as a sudden rapid thrust caused him to groan and clench up painfully. He'd lost his erection. Belphagor had coached Phaleg the first time he'd been penetrated—by a stone phallus almost as thick as the demon's wrist—on how to relax his muscles to accept what he was taking. And again when he'd taken his first cock: Vasily's. Phaleg put the lessons into practice now, breathing out slowly and pushing himself back against the invading fist.

"That's it, fancy boy. Take it all." Belphagor's knuckles twisted inside him. "This is what you deserve. So high and mighty. *Heavenly Host.* You're nothing but a sniveling little bitch." He fucked Phaleg steadily with his fist until Phaleg let out an involuntary wail. "Somebody shut him up. And turn him. I want his ass in the air."

They flipped him bodily, Belphagor managing to keep fist-fucking him the whole while. On his hands and knees, Phaleg instinctively tried to pull away, but the demon in front of him stopped him with a hand around his throat and silenced the desperate noise he was making with a mouthful of cock. He swallowed it so he wouldn't gag, groaning and wailing around the cock pumping his throat while Belphagor's fist pumped him without mercy. The little ball tinkled in his hand. He'd almost forgotten he was holding it, but he stilled it with a convulsive squeeze.

They'd pushed him into an awkward position, two demons holding his arms out to the sides and his face pressed into the groin of the one kneeling at his mouth, while his legs were spread wide and his ass was lifted. Belphagor had Phaleg's cock in his other fist, masturbating him back to a helpless erection.

The demons were talking and laughing again, passing around a bottle of alcohol, not caring if it spilled on him, cold and stinging where it dripped into his ass. He was an object, like the bottle. Like the coin they were flipping to establish the order they'd have him in.

Phaleg cried out around the thrusting cock as Belphagor pulled out without trying to go easy on him. Another demon lined up behind him, and his ankles were held firmly in place. A thick demon cock burrowed into the opening Belphagor's fist had vacated. The warmth was extraordinary. It could only be Vasily. Phaleg tried to brace himself, but there really was no doing anything the way they had him. All he could do was submit to the cock driving into him in that angry, excited way Vasily had.

Belphagor's hand still dragged on him. He whimpered into the shaved groin as he realized he was going to come and there was nothing he could do about it. Belphagor and Silk had trained him not to do so without permission, but this was the opposite—his body's responses completely at the demons' mercy. He was grunting like an animal—impossible not to do with a cock like Vasily's pounding him and another deep in his throat—and Belphagor was working him expertly. His climax seized him, and he jerked violently, making incoherent noises that would have sounded like an animal's even if his throat weren't full of cock.

The demons cheered as it burst out of him, milked into some kind of glass by Belphagor's hand. Behind him, Vasily fucked him harder, hips slamming into him, making him jolt, and then let out a telltale roar as he gripped Phaleg's hips for one final thrust and shot deep inside him. The heat made it impossible not to feel where it went. Demons were groping at him, slapping his ass as Vasily pulled out, squeezing his cock and driving shock waves through him.

"Who's next?" He was pretty sure the raucous shout was Belphagor's.

"Look at him go to town on that dick."

"Hold him still, I'm going to shoot."

Phaleg stiffened for the expected pulse of semen into his throat, moaning helplessly as someone else mounted him. There was no time to wonder whose cock was driving relentlessly into him as he struggled to swallow what the demon was giving him.

"Fill him up. He's sucking the whole thing down."

"Hurry up. I get his mouth next."

Phaleg lost track of what was happening to him. He heard Silk's anxious voice a few times at his ear.

"Do you want it to stop, love?"

Nodding and shaking his head at once, he babbled something with "please" in it, to the demons' amusement.

"You remember your word?"

His head cleared for a moment. Silk was trying to remind him, to be sure he'd use it if he truly wanted it to stop.

"Yes, milord." He wasn't supposed to say that. "Sorry, milord." He showed him the ball in his hand and squeezed it tight again.

"That's my angelwhore."

The demon who'd finished in him had been wearing some kind of prophylactic sheath, and the come was dripping out of it into the glass with his own in it.

Someone yanked him by the hair, forcing him up off the blanket and onto his knees. The demon crouched in front of him, about to fuck him in the mouth, but paused to look into his eyes. "He wants it. He knows he deserves it. Don't you, boy?"

Phaleg focused on Belphagor's voice and nodded up at him, feeling the heat in his face as he admitted it.

"Hold your mouth open."

Phaleg obeyed, and Belphagor entered him forcefully. Another demon held him up while Belphagor had his way, making comments and jokes about the way he sucked. Phaleg's mouth hurt from being stretched.

"I'm going to come down your throat," Belphagor promised and made good on it. "That's it. Drink it down like the filthy angel slut you are, being fucked in an alley in the Devil's Doorstep with everyone watching." Belphagor had the glass that had been passed around, and he raised it and dribbled the thick, cooling fluid over Phaleg's face as he finished in him. "That's what you are. A jizz-holder." Belphagor pulled out and put himself away. "Can't get enough. Luckily, we've been selling turns on you to the rest of the crowd."

Phaleg began to weep, forgetting this wasn't real, thinking for a moment that a horde of demons was waiting to have him, and the ball he'd forgotten he was holding dropped out of his hand and rolled along the wood floor with an incongruously cheerful sound. Silk swept in and pushed Belphagor out of the way, pulling off his woolen hood. Phaleg collapsed sobbing in his arms.

"Hush. It's all right, angelwhore. I'm here. I love you." Silk rocked him, and his voice turned furious as he rounded on Belphagor. "You took it too far. You always have to take everything too far."

"No." Belphagor ran his hand through the sweaty spikes of his hair as he unmasked himself. "He needed that. He needed to feel despair." Belphagor crouched in front of them, his hand gentle on Phaleg's dirty face. "Didn't you, sweet boy?"

Phaleg tried to nod, but the tenderness in Belphagor's voice made him cry harder.

"Let him cry. He needs the release."

No longer in their disguises, Dmitri quietly gathered up the dirty blanket, and Lev laid down a soft, clean one, along with pillows. Silk prompted Phaleg into the center. They were all gathering around him in a protective pile on the blanket, like puppies in a litter trying to snuggle close, stroking him and kissing the top of his head.

Lev washed his face with a warm cloth, and Silk held him and let him cry while Belphagor told him what a good boy he was. Even Vasily curled around him tenderly, warming him with his firespirit heat. He'd feared they'd think little of him afterward for submitting so fully, that they'd consider him weak, but they were cherishing him like he'd done something beautiful and brave. He'd never felt so safe and loved.

Phaleg had imagined this scenario a hundred different ways in the privacy of his wanton fantasies—though he'd never expected it to actually happen—but he'd never imagined afterward.

He was so crazy in love with Silk right now, he couldn't fathom how he could ever express it. A week ago, he'd thought his life was over, that he and Silk were over. Only this morning, he'd still believed nothing lay ahead of him but the few dozen years of a human lifespan in the drudgery of terrestrial exile before he died alone among strangers. Now he had a future with a demon who knew him more intimately than any angel ever could have, who knew his darkest needs and desires and wasn't afraid to give him what he ached for. And who cherished him for it. He had a future of infinite possibilities with the demon he loved.

He wasn't sure when he'd stopped crying, but Silk had let go of him and was crawling down the blanket, his soft mouth flitting over Phaleg's skin. Phaleg sighed, so relaxed he couldn't have stopped Silk if he'd wanted to, when that softness closed over his cock, making him hard immediately, though he'd have sworn he had nothing left in him. This time, they all took turns worshiping his cock, two demons at his sides sucking his nipples till they were tight and hard as facets. It was Vasily who made him come, with that crazy heat of his, while Silk kissed him and moaned in unison with his pleasure.

He fell asleep in Silk's arms and woke sometime later to find they were alone, a pile of blankets on top of them.

Silk must have sensed him waking, arms tightening around him. "Hey. Are you okay?"

Phaleg nodded. "How could I not be, waking up in your arms?"

"I mean it. I need to know if you're all right. The game got pretty intense."

Phaleg rolled onto his shoulder and played with Silk's glossy hair. "I mean it too. I'm very okay. That was . . . It was crazy. Wonderful. Awful. Thank you." He smiled shyly. "Milord."

Silk grinned. "I can't believe I get to keep you. It's like getting a pony for a Solstice present."

"I can't believe you're comparing me to a pony."

"Come on, Pony." Silk threw off the blankets, and the cold rushed in like a harsh slap. "You need a bath. You're caked with demon come."

Phaleg let Silk prod him to his feet and hustle him to the washroom, not at all against the idea of a bath. The water came out of the faucet already heated from a boiler somewhere below; he'd taken a shower yesterday, but the prospect of a bath in that warm water was like Heaven itself.

He slipped into the water closet next door while Silk ran the bath, finally able to relieve his bladder, amazed at the little button that plunged it all away as if into some mysterious other dimension and replaced it with a bowl of clean water. Phaleg giggled to himself at the idea of a dimension full of piss and soil. Thank Heaven he hadn't had to fall there. But these little conveniences, he could get used to them. Maybe the world of Man wasn't going to be so bad.

In the bath, he sat in front with Silk's soft legs around him and let Silk pamper him while they soaked, lathering him with sweet-smelling soap. He was sore and bruised in a lovely way, like he'd ridden a rather violent horse but had an exhilarating ride. Silk nibbled at his ear and drew Phaleg's head back to kiss him, bubbles trapped between them.

Draping his arm around Silk's neck, Phaleg gazed up at him. "I love you."

"I love you too." Silk kissed him again. "Pony."

# CHAPTER NINETEEN

Lev was up before the rest of them, making a grand breakfast of *blinchiki* and sausage. They all tiptoed around Phaleg a bit when he and Silk emerged. Vasily realized this must have been how Dmitri and Lev had felt after the four of them first played together. He'd done nothing to ease their discomfort, acting like a jealous ass. But Phaleg merely blushed prettily and couldn't stop smiling. Seemed he was just fine.

While they relaxed with tea, Phaleg even managed to make a joke about Belphagor's fist *almost* making room for Vasily. When everyone agreed that getting fucked by him was a dubious if delightful prospect, Vasily was sure the color in his face must rival Phaleg's blush.

"Vasily was my introduction to that particular delight." Phaleg grinned over the rim of his cup. "For months afterward, I thought every demon in Raqia must be hiding a monstrous weapon in his pants."

"*Bozhe moi.*" Vasily drank his tea, trying to ignore the ribbing, but they were all enjoying themselves too much. "Shut up," he growled at last. "Or I'll fuck you *all* in the ass."

"Oh, Ruby." Silk rested his elbows on the table and his chin in his hands with a dreamy sigh after the laughter died down. "I'm going to miss you."

After breakfast, Belphagor suggested a walk in the park. Silk thought it sounded a bit dull, but if it prolonged their leave-taking, he was all for it. The "park" turned out to be a magical place where the palaces of the long-dead tsars who'd once ruled this world still stood, museums to their former glory.

It was a rare sunny day, the snow that had been falling since Silk and Vasily themselves had fallen now coating everything like glittering facet chips. Above the white-on-dark lines of the wintering trees, golden domes and spires rose against a fierce blue winter sky, the paler blue of the grand Ekaterina Palace a stunning complement to it.

Silk glanced at Phaleg beside him and let out an involuntary gasp. It was the blue of his angel's eyes.

Phaleg squeezed his hand through their gloves. "What's wrong?"

"Nothing." Silk looked away, inexplicably shy. "You're breathtaking," he murmured after a moment.

"*Bozhe moi,*" growled Vasily, passing them. "Get a room."

Silk grinned, hooking his arm in Phaleg's, a bit giddy at the realization that he alone among the Fallen had an angel all his own.

In the quiet of the snow-blanketed park, a soft thump sounded beside him. Vasily stopped in his tracks, shoulders hunched, while a snowball crumbled into the back of his collar. Belphagor's laughter rang out from several feet behind them, and Vasily turned, his eyes smoldering.

"Snow bees." The words wheezed out of Belphagor through his laughter, and he ran for it as Vasily tore after him like an angry bull. He managed to evade him for a few yards before the larger demon tackled him, and they rolled together down the slope of a snow bank, coming to a stop on the powder-covered ice of a frozen brook.

In front of Silk, Dmitri shook his head. "Vasily's liable to melt that beneath them if Belphagor's not careful."

"You should probably be worrying about what's melting on you," said Lev beside him, and Dmitri turned to get a face full of snow.

Silk grabbed Phaleg's arm. "We'd better make a break for it. Looks like this could get ugly."

The two of them dashed away through a corridor of overhanging branches while the laughter and shouting continued, coming to a breathless stop on the top of a wooden footbridge over one of the frozen canals. Nestled in the trees across from them, a charming little outbuilding in faded celestine-blue paint, its gabled roof capped with snow, broke the monotony of white.

Phaleg leaned back, resting his elbows against the rails of the bridge, eyes twinkling as Silk settled beside him. He looked strangely right in this setting in his heavy, peasant coat and utilitarian blue canvas pants, yellow curls peeking out from under a dark cap and his cheeks blooming with color in the cold. He looked like a painting.

"Not such a terrible world."

"Could be worse," Silk agreed happily. No one seemed to be about in this wooded corner of the park. He leaned in, figuring it was safe to steal a kiss, and grunted in surprise at the double thump of a pair of snowballs striking the backs of their heads in unison.

Phaleg laughed and ducked down to scoop a handful of snow from the bridge. "This means war." He grinned at Silk as he joined him in stockpiling ammunition.

It was four against two, but they had the advantage of cover while the others were out in the open, and Silk had an angel from the Armies of Heaven on his side. The odds were decidedly in his favor.

The skirmish in the park was over all too soon, and after a warming pot of tea at the Grigori flat, Belphagor and Vasily were saying their good-byes. Vasily picked Silk up and held him off the ground, making him breathless. There were promises to keep in touch—and Dmitri would have their contact information once he and Phaleg left the Russian princedom—but Silk knew there was a strong probability they'd never see each other again.

"You be good." Vasily set him down, his eyes steamy with moisture, as if his heat evaporated the tears he didn't want to shed.

"Always, my ruby plum." Silk batted his lashes provocatively to keep his own tears at bay.

"And be good to your angel," Belphagor put in with a warning in his voice, stepping up after his private good-bye with Phaleg.

Silk narrowed his eyes. "Don't ruin it, Prince of Tricks. I don't fancy having to duel before we part ways."

Belphagor ruffled Silk's carefully parted hair, and Silk gaped at him in outrage. "You're adorable. I'm going to miss you too."

Raqia seemed quieter to Belphagor, as if Silk had been the leader of a madcap adventure who had drawn all of the Demon District under his spell. Peter Pan had grown up and fallen in love. Khai would take his place as the manager of the Stone Horse and at The Boudoir.

As for the Lost Boys, they were growing up too, but they'd be boys a little while longer. At least they still had Anzhela to keep them in line. Belphagor was glad to learn Silk had said his good-byes to them, though he hadn't told anyone else he was leaving the sphere for good. Only young Ruslan, newly returned from the palace, had missed the opportunity to say good-bye.

In the week they'd been gone, Grand Duke Lebes had left his son in the care of the supernal family and returned to Iriy, too grief-stricken to deal with him. None too fond of demons at present, the principality had turned Ruslan out. While angels had no problem employing demons in a service capacity, a demonic personal companion was apparently too close for angelic comfort.

The irony of the Traditionalists attempting to prevent Sefira from giving Helison an heir was that little Grand Duke Kae was now in the principality's custody, being groomed as the consort of the future queen. To protect his family and circumvent any future attempts to usurp his rule, Helison had issued a supernal decree allowing the firstborn daughter of a principality to inherit her father's rule in the absence of male issue.

Queen Sefira had given birth on the Solstice to yet another daughter. Four girls. It had all been for nothing.

It felt good to be back in their room. Small and humble as it was, this was home. Belphagor undressed at a leisurely pace, knowing Vasily was impatient for some private time as evidenced by the fact that he already lay naked and propped on one elbow on the bed, sporting a healthy erection.

Belphagor unbuttoned his cuffs with his shirt hanging open, letting Vasily get a decent look at the king-of-thieves cross inked on his chest. "You're feeling pretty pleased with yourself, aren't you, boy?"

"Maybe."

"Letting that fat cock give you a fat head."

"I can't help the size of my head."

Belphagor laughed and slipped off the shirt, dropping it on the floor. That one sensuous hip in the air was tantalizing. Looking at it, he could feel the bounce of the tight muscles against his hand, reverberating from a well-placed smack like a precision instrument. He climbed onto the cot and pushed Vasily onto his stomach, straddling him. "I can't tell you how delightful it was to watch that wickedly beautiful cock pounding sweet Phaleg's ass." One hand teased along Vasily's hip where it met the mattress. "You really let him have it."

"So did you." The breathy growl from within the crook of Vasily's arm was deep with arousal.

"True. But then that's kind of my thing." Belphagor licked the warm skin between Vasily's shoulder blades and watched a shiver ripple over his spine. "But you were utterly selfless, giving him what he needed—both the brutality he craved and the tenderness necessary to bring him back from it."

"I learned from the best," Vasily rumbled.

"Ah, sweet boy. Straight to my heart." Belphagor let his breath tickle against the piercings at Vasily's neck. "You've been such a remarkably good boy." He grabbed Vasily's locks without warning and yanked. "Inflated self-conceit notwithstanding."

The surprise maneuver was redirection for loosing himself from his jeans and oiling up without Vasily noticing. He'd gotten pretty good at it over the years. Vasily was still wincing and tugging against his hold, oblivious to the very practical reason Belphagor had for pulling his hair. Having something to hang on to when he drove himself in deep was a bonus.

He demonstrated it now, and Vasily groaned with genuine surprise. Belphagor burrowed in slowly, enjoying the way Vasily moaned and arched to take him deep even as he squirmed with resistance. Watching his cock disappear into Vasily's insulted backside was a singular pleasure that never got old.

He lowered his body onto Vasily's, forcing his hand under the warm hip to take hold of the warmer erection, and twisted Vasily's hair in his other fist to make him look over his shoulder. "Whose is it, *mal'chik?* This pretty prick you buried in an angel's backside?"

"Yours," Vasily groaned, his fiery eyes bright.

"And whose boy are you?"

"*Yours.*"

"Say it." Belphagor thrust hard as the words burst out of Vasily.

"I'm your boy."

"Tell me again." *Thrust.*

"I'm your boy."

"Again."

"*I'm your boy.*" He grunted out the words with each deep penetration.

"More," Belphagor growled at his ear. "Keep up."

Vasily repeated the words while Belphagor fucked him, the rumble of his voice getting deeper and more feral. "I'm your boy. I'm your boy. I'm your boy. *Bozhe moi. Fuck.* I'm your boy!" Muscles rippled along his back as if his wings would tear through right here in Heaven with the force of his orgasm.

Belphagor fucked him harder, his fist pumping him mercilessly. "That's it, boy. Give it all to me. It's mine."

Vasily roared and shook beneath him, thrusting into Belphagor's hand as hot spunk kept streaming out of him, until at last he whimpered, empty, his body limp beneath Belphagor's rapid pounding. "I'm your boy," he moaned weakly into the blanket while Belphagor kept fucking.

"Damned right, you are." Belphagor slowed his motions. "*Moi mal'chik. Lyubimyy mal'chik. Milyy mal'chik.*" He rose onto his knees, withdrawing gently while Vasily moaned with regret. "Roll over, boy. I want to see your face while I come."

Vasily flipped onto his back, clasping his hands behind his head with his ankles crossed in a characteristically unself-conscious gesture, hazel eyes gazing up at Belphagor working himself. "I love you, Beli."

"Damn, I love *you*, you beautiful boy." Belphagor groaned out the words as he came, watching the pearly droplets spill over onto Vasily's abs and chest. He collapsed onto him, kissing Vasily while he thrust his cock against the come he'd spilled on him. He was crazy about this demon. He'd been tamed and enslaved by the wild beauty, and he didn't care. He belonged to his boy as much as Vasily belonged to him. More.

He laughed against Vasily's shoulder when his body had calmed. "Damn. I meant to have you tongue my ass so I could feel that slick heat inside me. You took me by surprise, and I came too soon."

Vasily made a sound in his throat like a contented lion and wrapped his arms around the small of Belphagor's back. "Oh, well. There's always tomorrow."

Explore more of the *Demons of Elysium* series at: riptidepublishing.com/collections/series-demons-of-elysium

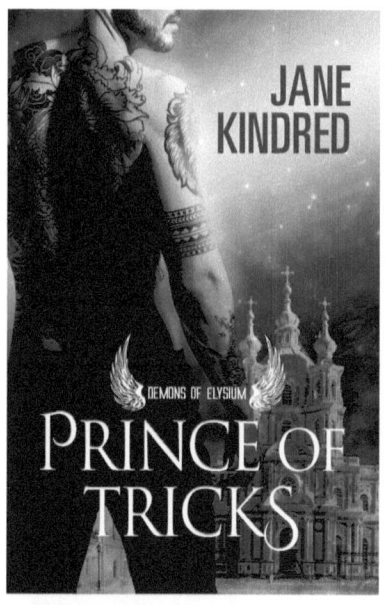

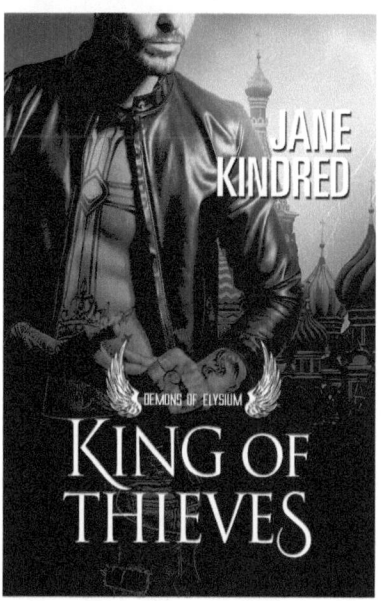

Dear Reader,

Thank you for reading Jane Kindred's *Master of the Game*!

We know your time is precious and you have many, many entertainment options, so it means a lot that you've chosen to spend your time reading. We really hope you enjoyed it.

We'd be honored if you'd consider posting a review—good or bad—on sites like **Amazon, Barnes & Noble, Kobo, Goodreads, Twitter, Facebook, Tumblr,** and your blog or website. We'd also be honored if you told your friends and family about this book. Word of mouth is a book's lifeblood!

For more information on upcoming releases, author interviews, blog tours, contests, giveaways, and more, please sign up for our weekly, spam-free newsletter and visit us around the web:

**Newsletter:** riptidepublishing.com/newsletter
**Twitter:** twitter.com/RiptideBooks
**Facebook:** facebook.com/RiptidePublishing
**Goodreads:** tinyurl.com/RiptideOnGoodreads
**Tumblr:** riptidepublishing.tumblr.com

Thank you so much for Reading the Rainbow!

RiptidePublishing.com

# ALSO BY
# JANE KINDRED

# ABOUT THE AUTHOR

Jane Kindred is the author of the Harlequin Nocturne series Sisters in Sin and the epic fantasy trilogy The House of Arkhangel'sk and its M/M erotic romance prequel series, Demons of Elysium. She spent her formative years in the desert Southwest ruining her eyes reading romance novels in the sun and watching *Star Trek* marathons in the dark. After escaping to San Francisco to write to the sound of foghorns from a slowly sinking Victorian flat, she found she missed the sunlight and the smell of creosote after the rain. She now writes to the sound of desert thunder while her spoiled cat, Sophie, blinks at her from her fancy bed like Baby Yoda having just eaten a Frog Lady's egg.

You can find Jane on Twitter @JaneKindred, on her cleverly named Facebook page, JaneKindred, or via her website, at the unsurprising address of www.janekindred.com.

Jane is represented by Sara Megibow of KT Literary Agency.